THE PLOTTERS

DOCTOR WHO – THE MISSING ADVENTURES

Also available:

GOTH OPERA by Paul Cornell
EVOLUTION by John Peel
VENUSIAN LULLABY by Paul Leonard
THE CRYSTAL BUCEPHALUS by Craig Hinton
STATE OF CHANGE by Christopher Bulis
THE ROMANCE OF CRIME by Gareth Roberts
THE GHOSTS OF N-SPACE by Barry Letts
TIME OF YOUR LIFE by Steve Lyons
DANCING THE CODE by Paul Leonard
THE MENAGERIE by Martin Day
SYSTEM SHOCK by Justin Richards
THE SORCERER'S APPRENTICE by Christopher Bulis
INVASION OF THE CAT-PEOPLE by Gary Russell
MANAGRA by Stephen Marley
MILLENNIAL RITES by Craig Hinton
THE EMPIRE OF GLASS by Andy Lane
LORDS OF THE STORM by David A. McIntee
DOWNTIME by Marc Platt
THE MAN IN THE VELVET MASK by Daniel O'Mahony
THE ENGLISH WAY OF DEATH by Gareth Roberts
THE EYE OF THE GIANT by Christopher Bulis
THE SANDS OF TIME by Justin Richards
KILLING GROUND by Steve Lyons
THE SCALES OF INJUSTICE by Gary Russell
THE SHADOW OF WENG-CHIANG by David A. McIntee
TWILIGHT OF THE GODS by Christopher Bulis
SPEED OF FLIGHT by Paul Leonard

THE PLOTTERS

Gareth Roberts

First published in Great Britain in 1996 by
Doctor Who Books
an imprint of Virgin Publishing Ltd
332 Ladbroke Grove
London W10 5AH

Copyright © Gareth Roberts 1996

The right of Gareth Roberts to be identified as the Author of
this Work has been asserted by him in accordance with the
Copyright, Designs and Patents Act 1988.

'Doctor Who' series copyright © British Broadcasting
Corporation 1996

ISBN 0 426 20488 3

Cover illustration by Alister Pearson
Internal illustrations by Paul Vyse

Typeset by Galleon Typesetting, Ipswich
Printed and bound in Great Britain by
Mackays of Chatham PLC

*All characters in this publication are fictitious and any resemblance
to real persons, living or dead, is purely coincidental.*

This book is sold subject to the condition that it shall
not, by way of trade or otherwise, be lent, resold, hired
out or otherwise circulated without the publisher's prior
written consent in any form of binding or cover other
than that in which it is published and without a similar
condition including this condition being imposed on the
subsequent purchaser.

Contents

Part One – PLOT DEVICES

1. Knavish Tricks 3
2. The Strange Young Men 43
3. The Wisest Fool 63

Part Two – HOLES IN THE PLOT

4. Strangers in the Night 103
5. Hindsight Aforethought 119
6. The Tree 135

Part Three – THE PLOT THICKENS

7. Intrigue Down Below 159
8. Strange Allies 174
9. A Dead Man's Shoes 192

Part Four – EXPLAINING THE PLOT

10. The Grand Behemoth 205
11. Nudging History 230
12. Covering the Cracks 254

Author's Note

A word on historical accuracy. One of the aims of the Missing Adventure books is to re-create some of the character of the television series which inspired them; and where some of my fellow authors have been unstinting in their research, what follows is as faithful a portrait of the final days of Robert Catesby's plot as, for example, Dennis Spooner's TV script *The Romans* was of the burning of Rome.

To any reader interested in the precise factual detail of Fawkes *et al.*, I would recommend they consult *The Gunpowder Plot* by Alan Haynes (Alan Sutton, ISBN 0-7509-0332-5), and steer well clear of *Doctor Who – The Plotters* (Virgin Publishing, ISBN 0-426-20488-3).

G.R.
Cricklewood
June 1996

Part One

Plot Devices

1

Knavish Tricks

The King of England, who was also the King of Scotland, adjusted himself on the cushions piled three-high on his throne, raised a well-kept hand and produced an affected yawn, fanning his fingers in emphasis. All eyes were on him, awaiting his judgement on the latest act.

Before James's mouth had closed the yawn was spreading like a fever around the hall. It first stopped on Hay, his special favourite, who sat at his feet and whose head rested against the royal knee. Its travels then took it across the long line of courtiers and advisers assembled on wooden trestles ringed against the walls, and at last to the mouth of the Lord Chamberlain, who stood flanked by guards at the barred doors that led to the main body of Whitehall Palace. The singers could not have failed to miss this reception. Undaunted, they persevered manfully with their ballad, redoubling their efforts on lute and tabor and crashing with vigour into chorus.

'With a hie and a fie and a merry down-derry, love is lost and crossed 'twixt wife and belly,' they sang, smiles fixed, faces sweat-streaked.

Their exertions were not enough for the King. 'God's wounds, 'tis more of a merry cacophony!' he said loudly. The songmakers stopped dead and the yard resounded with the court's appreciation of their monarch's wit. Spurred on, he added, 'We have no love, neither lost nor crossed, for this gang of' – he searched for a potent epithet – 'gang of iron-ears!' The court roared again. Men closest to the throne laughed politely, men further from it threw their heads back and guffawed until their lungs smarted in the hope that doing so often enough might, one day, move them closer.

The King allowed the corners of his lips to curl up in self-satisfaction. After the day's journey from his hunting lodge in Royston, four hours across Hertfordshire's hard ground and hills in freezing rain, he was glad to be indoors, warmed by the huge crackling fire and sated with roasted meats and spiced puddings. By immersing himself in jollity and sensual delight he hoped to cloud his mind, and so forget the tasks of state set for the coming days. In fact, it was his wish to forget he had come to this polluted, overcrowded, plague-bound city at all. His tactic seemed to be working. Already he was so woozy with wine he could barely recall whatever tedious business had called him to London. And yes, the company was very good. Most of the lords assembled here were agreeable men, and he had taken trouble to prohibit the admittance of anyone irksome. No Catholics, then, as that always led to arguments, and most certainly no Puritans. And it was good to be with Hay once more, after several weeks of separation. He looked down at the dear fellow. Amusing, cultured and bonny enough, with his dainty snub of a nose and the fluffy beard of a boy. The darlingest creature in all London. What more could a king ask for in a companion?

Hay put his goblet down and raised his clipped, cultured voice to take up the King's theme. 'More,' he said, sneering at the singers' faded garments, 'their threads are stitched as unfortunate as their rhymes!' There was a lesser ripple of mirth. While the remark might have been the wittier, it had not been made by the King.

One of the singers stepped forward and bowed low before the throne. 'Your Majesty, if it pleases you, we have prepared another –'

'Another!' The King gasped in mock horror. 'Oh! No, no, we think we have had our fill. Your verse is too rich for our taste, perhaps.'

'Be gone,' Hay said, popping a grape between his thin lips and spitting out the seeds. The singers slung up their instruments, genuflected awkwardly to a further gale of laughter, and departed through the porch leading to the preparation room.

Hay giggled and clapped his hands. 'Such wonderful dross!'

'Aye,' the King agreed. When he spoke to Hay alone his Scottish accent, which he tried to keep subdued when at court to ensure he was understood, often came roaring back. 'Did you ever see the like? Still, we swiftly tire of these vanities.' With a snap of the fingers he summoned a boy to refill his goblet (boy-summoning was a choice pastime of his) and turned his gaze towards the figure at the door. 'Chamberlain, tell, what delight next awaits our scorn? Tonight, in all, we have seen a tableau that wobbled like jelly, a Puncinello who spread misery rather than mirth, and a ballad lacking in tune. What has befallen the entertainers of London? Are these misfits the best she can offer?'

The Chamberlain wrung his hands and shuffled forward. He was a small man, only an inch above five feet, swathed in a voluminous blue robe that seemed almost to swallow his portly frame up in its folds. His feet were concealed under the robe's trailing hem, making the motion of his passage resemble the waddle of a duck. The similarity was reinforced by the nervous darting of his eyes and the continual fluttering of his hands. Patches of pink bloomed on his cheeks, making plump mulberries of them. 'I apologize, Your Majesty. I did not have time to hear the singers for myself.' He looked pleadingly up at the throne and lowered his voice. 'The facilities here at Whitehall are limited. There are no backdrops or traps, and only one small changing-room. We are not equipped to engage proper players, as we would at Hampton.'

Hay made a scoffing noise. 'Room enough for *im*-proper ones, it would appear.'

The King coughed. 'Enough tattle. We would know what is next.'

'Your Majesty.' The Chamberlain quickly consulted a list. 'We have had brought in a Barbary ape for your amusement.'

'An ape?' The King stroked his fully bearded chin and raised an eyebrow. 'This interests us.' Immediately the mood of the court switched to reflect his pronouncement, and there were several fascinated murmurs. 'We have read of apes in bestiaries but have yet to clap our eyes on one.' A thought struck him – his own safety was his prime consideration, hence his thickly padded doublet and the guards posted on both sides of the door – and he leant forward and whispered, 'It is not – wild?'

'Oh no, Your Majesty,' said the Chamberlain. 'Although borne from far shores, the animal is docile as a lambkin.'

'Good. So have it brought in.' The Chamberlain nodded and backed away to his position at the door, signalling through the porch as he did. The King sipped at his replenished goblet and said quietly to Hay, 'The Chamberlain excels himself. I am appalled, yet intrigued.'

'Yes,' said Hay. 'Perhaps you should surprise him more often. These impromptu revels are so bad they are good.'

There was a delay of a few seconds, and sudden quiet as the King craned his neck for a better view of the performance area, which was contained between two buttresses. The Chamberlain was right about the lack of space. With the lords assembled on their trestles and the feasting tables set up there was less than five square feet left for the use of performers. The silence dragged on, broken only by the spitting and rattling of coals on the fire. 'Must an ape take a very age to prepare itself?' the King muttered. 'Has it lines to learn or a character to prepare?'

Then there was movement at the porch, and a man emerged, dressed in a clean set of working man's clothes, a jerkin over a cloth shirt. He was tanned and healthy-looking, and he held a knotted leather belt tight in one fist. After bowing to King and court, he tugged on the belt. 'Your Majesty,' he said, 'in the hope it will please and startle you, I bring the bride of Barbary.' With a scampering movement a hairy figure the size of a dwarf appeared in the doorway, the other end of the belt tied tightly around its waist. There was a gasp of genuine astonishment from the onlookers, and the King, who made it a habit not to appear dazzled by anything, was momentarily aghast. The beast had a hairless, wrinkled face like an old man's, and its eyes were alive with intelligence and curiosity. To emphasize its close conformity to human shape it had been dressed in a bridal gown complete with veil, which was pinned up over its forehead. Its hairy forearms emerged from the gown's sleeves and hung down, trailing the ground. Its tail flicked the flagstones anxiously.

The King drew a breath. 'You, keeper. Does it talk?'

'No, Your Majesty.'

'Then does it fight?' asked Hay.

'It is slow to anger.' The keeper pulled out an apple from a fold in his jerkin and held it up before his charge. Instantly the ape raised its arms and leapt for the apple, which the keeper raised out of reach. The ape's reaction was to gibber like an enraged child, and flare its nostrils anxiously.

The King nodded his approval. 'A true spectacle.' There were nods of agreement around the yard. 'What is the limit of its intelligence?'

'Your Majesty,' replied the keeper. 'I shall cause it to dance.' He started to clap his hands in a staccato rhythm. The ape's attention was caught at once, and it began to flap its long arms.

The King slapped Hay on the shoulder and shrieked with delight. His uproar began its journey around the hall.

Sir Robert Cecil, Lord Salisbury, chief minister and closest adviser to the sovereign, heard the King's high-pitched laughter from the other side of the hall's door, and his pacing back and forth along the arterial corridor became quicker and angrier. The pinched features of his thin, aristocratic face flickered with irritation, and he thwacked a parchment scroll against a black-gloved hand. He had waited outside for an hour, and this fresh wave of glee was an indication that the King had no intention of breaking up his party early.

The thought pushed him to take action. He stormed up to the door, which was guarded on this side by two soldiers with set jaws and drawn swords, and raised his fist to knock.

One of the guards stayed him with a respectful but firm grip of his arm. 'We were instructed not to disturb the King's entertainments, sir. As we have already told you.'

Cecil wrenched his spindly arm free. 'My audience with His Majesty takes precedence,' he said in his deepest, most censorious tones, the voice he had cultivated to counter his lack of stature.

The guard gulped. When the King was away from Whitehall, which was the greatest share of the time, to disobey an order from Cecil would have been unthinkable. 'I'm sorry, sir. But our orders came from the King himself.'

Cecil pondered a second. He knew the guard well from his daily rounds of palace security. 'Your name is Hunt, I am right?'

The guard nodded. He kept his eyes fixed straight ahead.

'Hunt,' Cecil went on, 'you are a fine man and a good lieutenant. You have proved yourself alert and loyal and been rightly rewarded. There is no higher honour at court than to guard the royal personage.' He leant closer, insinuating himself right under the big man's nose. 'But should I have cause I can detail you to cleaning cast offal from the cobbles of Cripplegate with a hair mop. So have that door unbarred!'

The guard's eyes showed his fear. He sighed and nodded, turned about and tapped lightly on the door himself. There was no response. Further screams of hilarity spilled through the boards. Furious, Cecil pushed forward and rapped hard on the wood.

A few moments later he heard the bar being drawn up. The door opened a fraction, and the Chamberlain's chubby head popped around. His eyes rolled heavenward when he saw Cecil. 'Oh, it's you. For a moment I thought the Spanish were at the door. What is the cause of this pounding?'

Cecil held up the scroll. 'I have some business with the King. Urgent business.' He made to move forward.

The Chamberlain stopped him. 'You can't. No, you cannot simply bustle in, unannounced.'

Cecil mustered what remained of his patience. 'Then have me announced.'

The Chamberlain flushed, looking between Cecil, the guards and back over his shoulder into the hall. His fingers wiggled, an outward sign of his inner dilemma. 'I can't. We're in the middle of the Barbary ape. It's been the only hit of the night. You mustn't spoil it.'

Cecil's ire grew. 'The middle of the what?' he said, slowly and dangerously.

'The Barbary ape,' repeated the Chamberlain. Again he put out a hand to Cecil's advancing breast. 'He's hated everything else. It isn't my fault if he turns up and starts demanding entertainment at this late hour. I got the best I could. I mean, I know it's hardly Thomas Decker.' He was now almost hopping up and down in agitation. 'But tell me, what could I do?'

'Out of my way,' Cecil said. He strode through the gap in the door, pushing the Chamberlain aside with his most powerful shove. A second later and he was advancing on the King with barely a glance to spare at the grotesque creature juggling apples at the end of the hall. Passion and purpose consumed him, but his good sense caused him to moderate the force of his entrance by bowing reverentially as he reached the throne. As he crooked himself he briefly caught the mocking eye of the vile young Hay, who was sprawled drunkenly at the King's foot. Cecil shuddered as he thought of the vast sums from the public purse James had thrown away over the last year and a half on the whims of this youth, the most disgusting of his favourites. Every time his eyes met Hay's a look of mutual loathing passed between the two men, and this occasion was no different.

But it was King James who spoke first, cutting through

the silence that had fallen over the yard at this almost unprecedented interruption. 'Salisbury!' he cried, uttering Cecil's title like a bawdy oath. 'We did not request your presence! What is this rudeness?'

'Perhaps he is sore he was not invited,' wheedled Hay. 'After all, there was never such a merrymaker.'

Hay would not have dared to make such a remark outside the King's company. Cecil reminded himself that soon James would tire of the lad and throw him aside like a greased wiping towel as he had all his predecessors. It was a day worth waiting for, so he ignored the barb, reminded himself of his obligation, and said, 'Your Majesty, I regret the suddenness of my entrance. I have come to remind you of my earlier request for an audience.' He lowered his voice. 'You will recall our agreement to meet as soon as you were rested from your journey.'

James groaned and leant forward. 'But I have sent you the speech.' He pointed to Cecil's hand. 'There, see, you hold it. Isn't that enough for today?'

Cecil tapped the scroll slowly and deliberately against his upper leg. 'You have sent it, Your Majesty, yes, and I have read it. And its content is what has sped me here.'

Hay said tartly, 'Oh, can't we go back to the ape, James? This funny little man of yours is not quite so diverting.'

James tapped him lightly on the head. 'Ssh ssh, boy. Cecil, must we discuss state matters here?'

'You have left me little choice.' Cecil looked around the hall, at the courtiers, lords and his fellow ministers, all of whom were sitting with heads lowered in embarrassed silence. 'James, in our summer meetings at Royston we decided on further legislature against the Catholics. The speech makes barely any mention of further stricture, and still papist priests walk your streets spreading the doctrine of revolt.'

The King drained his goblet. 'Oh, dear Cecil. Always banging on about something or other. Can't this wait till the morning?'

Cecil frowned. In his mind's eye he saw Elizabeth,

who had sat on the same throne with upright, unflinching dignity. He decided to make headway by pandering to the King's greatest fear. 'While Catholics roam, your own safety cannot be assured.'

James tutted, apparently nonchalant, although Cecil caught the moment of doubt in his eye. 'They are hardly roaming. And I am protected well enough.' To make his point he patted the padded doublet which ballooned around his already ample girth. 'My wish for this night was to place some variety in my experience. As you see, I am without my blessed Queen or my beloved children. Am I, your sovereign, not to be allowed even an hour's brevity of fun, for this night only, before taking on the onerous burdens of state once more?'

'My actions,' Cecil said levelly, 'are motivated solely by concern for you and for the isles under your reign. We must discuss the Catholic question.'

James snapped, 'Aren't the recusancy fines enough? I tell you, Salisbury, the more the Catholics are stirred, the more likely they are to attempt rebellion. If we let them fade away quietly, as they have been doing, all will be right enough. Let them flee abroad to their foreign seminaries and dream of revolt. It is a fantasy that will never see fruition.' He raised a hand. 'And that is all I will say tonight. Go to your bed, Cecil, and I will see you tomorrow.' He raised his goblet and summoned a serving boy. 'More wine! We shall return to the Barbary ape.'

'Godamercy for that,' said Hay. He sneered up at Cecil, tossing back a tress of his long hair. 'I found the last act so tedious.'

Cecil stormed from the hall without looking back. He was conscious of the Chamberlain fumbling at the doorway, the resumption of laughter among the courtiers, and then he was back out in the corridor, his heart pounding with shattering force, his breath roaring furiously in his ears, his black-gloved hands clenching and unclenching convulsively.

He thundered out of the banqueting hall and crossed the small open yard that linked it to the Stone Gallery, the largest of the buildings that made up the palace. Its three storeys dominated the other structures. At the side door stood a guard carrying his pike in one hand and a lantern in the other. He nodded to Cecil and admitted him. As Cecil passed he snatched the man's lantern without a word.

He passed through the dark and empty corridors, only distantly aware of the paintings and fine furniture, of the thick carpet underfoot, of the shadows thrown by the flambeaus spaced at intervals along the walls. Such luxury was quotidian to him; he had spent all his life in the service of the crown, as had his father. His loyalty, to the King and to the new alliance between England and Scotland, an alliance that he had not only created but cemented with years of delicate negotiation, was unquestionable, unswervable. It outswayed all personal considerations, all immediate concerns. Which was why he had to act as he now did.

He ascended three long flights of stairs, passing the state apartments and the sumptuous guest bedrooms. Finally, he strode through an arch and into a narrow hallway that ran the length of the attic floor. He stopped before a window, unhooked and threw open its steel shutters, admitting a haze of freezing drizzle.

He peered out over the Privy Gardens, his eyes accustoming themselves to the dark and painting in the detail of the gravelled pathways and lawns. Running along the garden's far side was a row of thick, lofty oak trees, cultivated to protect the business of the palace from the eyes of commoners, acting as a double barrier with the high brick wall that divided them from King Street.

It was at a specific point between two of the bare-branched trees that Cecil stared intently, waiting for the signal.

After a peaceful night's sleep, Barbara entered the TARDIS control room to find the Doctor busy at work, hovering over the six-sided console and attending to its varied switches, levers and dials. She stood in the doorway that led from the living quarters and observed the Doctor. His characterful face, with its perky eyes and habitually downturned lips, was uplit by the displays, which gave him an air even more grand and mysterious than usual.

He looked up. 'Ah, Barbara. You're just in time, my dear, I think we are about to materialize. We'll be, er – emerging shortly, as it were.'

'Have you any idea where we'll emerge?'

The Doctor arched a querulous eyebrow. 'Yes, as a matter of fact, I have. The instruments indicate that we are returning to your own planet Earth. And what is more, if our present heading holds true, in the England of the twentieth century.' He lifted his long-haired head up sharply. 'What do you say to that, hmm? You know I don't make rash promises.'

Fortunately for Barbara, Ian had entered in time to catch this latest remark. 'I can think of a couple of other times we've landed back in England in the twentieth century, Doctor,' he said as he slipped himself into his sports jacket. 'Perhaps it's wiser not to raise our hopes.'

The Doctor turned to face him. 'Chesterton, are you capable of making an adequate study of the TARDIS systems?'

Barbara smiled. It was amusing to see the Doctor treating Ian, like herself a schoolteacher, as a wayward pupil of his own. 'No, Doctor,' Ian replied with good humour.

'No. However, fortunately for us all, I am. And my study confirms a return to Earth in your time, young man.' He was still talking as Barbara noticed, with a dread sense of familiarity, the alteration in pitch of the TARDIS's mighty engines that signalled an imminent landing. 'There, you see?' said the Doctor, although this didn't settle anything at all. 'In a matter of moments we'll be able to open the doors. On London itself, I shouldn't wonder.'

Ian grinned. 'I admire your pluck, Doctor,' he said. 'I'll go and fetch Vicki.' He went back through to the living quarters.

'Pluck? What does he mean, pluck?' The Doctor

frowned. Barbara stood by patiently as he flicked up a row of coloured switches, humming and muttering to himself under his breath. What if they were returning to Earth, and to the England of the 1960s? How long would it take to adjust back to the comparatively mundane life she'd lived there, after all of her adventuring? And what were Ian's plans?

She tried to force the questions to the back of her mind as she watched the glowing central column of the console slow to a definite stop.

Cecil stood at the window, cloaked by silence and shadows. The drizzle glistened in pearly drops on the black velvet pelt of his apparel, causing him to resemble nothing quite so much as one of the floating, disembodied heads rumoured to stalk these more remote passages. An hour had passed; an hour in which he had remained stock-still, his eyes alert and never wavering from the same point. Such was the zeal of his vigil, nothing in the vast, well-tended lawns below distracted him, not even the change in the weather as the rain softened into snow. He registered only vaguely the return of several of the Gentlemen Pensioners through the grounds, their faces puffed up and weary, moustaches drooping over yawning mouths; the scurrying, mouselike movements of the bed-makers and gyp women were of no interest; even the noisy departure of the King himself, surrounded by his small army of guards and supported by the Chamberlain on one side and a guard on the other, exercised his mind only to the extent of confirming his earlier unquiet thoughts. It was one of James's worst habits when in town to get loudly drunk and stagger off into the night to some dancing house or tavern, often not returning until the early hours of the following day. The absence of Queen Anne and the children removed the last check on such behaviour. No plans for mutiny crossed Cecil's thoughts, however. James was irritating, certainly. But he was also predictable and, to an extent, malleable. One of Cecil's current aims, one of the reasons he was standing here at the window, was to discover the extent of that malleability.

At last, not long after the King's party had passed through the main gate, the signal came. A bright light, blinking on and off, from the centre of the line of oaks, right at the spot at which he'd been staring. It flashed quickly, three or four times. By then Cecil had picked up his own lantern and was prepared to signal back. He used the flat of his hand to cover the lantern's light, three times, in reply. Then he hurried from the window and tripped quietly and quickly down the flights of narrow, twisting stairs. This brought him directly to a portico leading into the narrow walk bisecting the lawns. Another guard waited there.

'I couldn't sleep, and would take a stroll,' Cecil told him.

'It's like an ice-box out here, sir,' said the guard good-naturedly.

Cecil ignored him and walked on. The air blew chill against his bearded cheeks, snowflakes whirled around him, and he shivered involuntarily as he strode up the path towards the trees, conviction etched in every line of his grave face. The city was sleeping now, and the only sounds were the hoots of owls and the metronomic crunching of his own footfalls over the gravel. When he reached the far side of the garden, where the lawn bordered the trees, he stopped, and stood still as a straw dummy once more, apparently looking into nothing.

There was a rustle in the trees near by. Although Cecil was prepared for the arrival of his colleague, the suddenness of this appearance was disturbing, and somehow unnatural. It was as if the man had spontaneously generated himself from the soil, brought his outline into being beneath the canopy of tangled winter branches. He stood a foot and a half higher than Cecil, and was wiry and poised. That was all that could be discerned, for he was covered both by the darkness and by his long black cloak, and a cowl was thrown far forward over his face. Cecil understood the need for secrecy. Still, he couldn't resist taking an occasional glance into the depths of the hood to catch a glimpse of the features it concealed. What details he had seen over the past year and a half added up to little more than an impression of a cold, hard, well-defined face, mask-like, imperturbable. And was there a curl to the lip and a hook to the nose, indicators of the man's ancestry, or had he imagined that of a Spaniard and let himself see them there? Most likely he would never know. When this operation was over the Spaniard would no doubt melt away as strangely and suddenly as he had appeared.

Cecil gave no conventional greeting. Instead he raised his left arm and dangled it down from the elbow joint, and said distinctly, in a loud whisper, enunciating the three syllables, 'Orange Man.'

The Spaniard raised his right arm and made a circular sign with thumb and forefinger. His hands were unusually smooth and long-fingered. 'Blue Boar,' he replied, in a steely, accented voice.

Cecil made no further preamble. He slipped a sealed, unaddressed letter from a pocket and held it out to the Spaniard. 'The operation will continue as planned,' he whispered. 'All is prepared here. You will take this to Red Bull tomorrow.'

The Spaniard took the letter from Cecil's hand, and instantly it vanished in the depths of his cloak. He inclined his head to indicate his understanding, and turned to go. His gait was unsteady, one foot dragging strangely behind the other.

Cecil swallowed, turned away himself, and started to walk briskly back up the path to the Stone Gallery. As always, the swiftness of these dealings made them seem all the more unreal, as if they occurred in a dreamlike pocket of existence divorced from the business of state and the intrigues of the court. The sensation was confirmed when he turned to look back at the Spaniard and saw only the rattling, clacking branches of the great trees against the sky. In seconds the hooded man had absented himself utterly.

Cecil walked on up the path, soothing himself against

the cold by imagining the hot spirits and freshly starched sheets waiting in his room.

As far as Barbara could tell, the TARDIS had brought itself down safely. The pilot's confidence, however, had taken a knock. He was squinting at the panel that showed the findings of the sensor apparatus and his face gradually lost its hard lines of certainty. 'Yes, well, interesting, yes, very interesting, indeed,' he said, sensing the others hanging on his words. 'The temperature is lower than one might expect . . .'

Ian grinned. 'And don't tell us, the atmosphere's pure nitrogen and we're sinking into a swamp infested with pink octopi.' He mimed groping tentacles with his fingers.

'There's no call for facetiousness. The Ship is quite steady, and the atmospheric composition is, er, all, er . . . it's perfectly acceptable. And it's a well-known fact there are no pink octopi anywhere in all the universes.' He consulted another display. 'The air is fairly fresh, with gases that are signs of nearby animal and human population. It's bitter out there, and we must wrap up warmly.' He nodded to Vicki, who had emerged from the living quarters with her customary brightness. 'Fetch my cloak and scarf, will you, child?'

As she obeyed him, unhooking the garments requested – a patterned scarf and a flowing black opera cloak with antique gold fasteners – from the hatstand, Vicki said, 'Why don't you take a look at the scanner, Doctor?'

'It's a reasonable suggestion,' said Barbara. The Doctor seemed not to have heard, his attention taken up by the console as he pulled on his cloak. 'Doctor?'

'Eh, what? The scanner? Unnecessary.'

'We'd probably see a polar bear up there,' Ian whispered as he passed Barbara her raincoat from the stand.

'Or a woolly mammoth,' she whispered back.

The Doctor had overheard. 'Tch. Well, if we must have this rigmarole.' He reached over to the scanner switch. 'I dare say we're in Dundee, and we shall have to partake of the splendid local . . .'

The words died on his lips as the scanner screen, suspended high on the wall facing them, flared white and then cleared to reveal nothing more impressive than a pile of stones. It consisted of a jumble of oddly assorted, jagged-edged flints. At first Barbara took it for a natural rock formation, such was its roughness and irregular shape, until she saw the way the stones had been chipped at and shaped to form a sturdier structure. There was about it an aura of neglect.

'Dundee?' said Ian, conveying a world of scepticism.

'Somewhere in the Highland region, yes. That's most probably a crofter's cottage.' The Doctor recovered his composure quickly. 'A slight geographical error. It's of no consequence, really no consequence at all.' Now adorned in his full winter coverings, he reached for the big lever that operated the main doors.

Barbara stayed his hand. 'As long as it's only an error of geography.'

The Doctor made a tetchy sound. 'I have brought you only a few hundred miles from home. From here, it will be a matter of ease to return to London.'

'And what if that's a Siberian crofter's cottage? How are we supposed to explain our sudden arrival to the KGB?'

'Will nothing satisfy you?' the Doctor huffed. 'I suggest it will be a deal easier than explaining yourselves to a Menoptera or a Venusian, both of which you have managed quite adequately, under my guidance. Now, really, we must get on, I can't abide all this faffing around.' He operated the door control.

The two doors opened inwards with a jarring electronic whine, and admitted a gust of biting cold air. The Doctor strode through with no apparent qualms, his silver-topped cane swinging at his side, looking for all the world like an Edwardian paterfamilias stepping out into one of the grand streets around Regent's Park. Vicki, now buried in a fur several sizes too big for her, hurried after him. Not for the first time, Barbara reflected on how the girl seemed to cling to the Doctor's side like a mislaid puppy.

Ian turned to her, a gloved hand outstretched. 'Well?'

'Have we any choice?' she said, taking it.

Vicki tucked her mittened hands under her arms and stamped up and down in the snow. She was wearing a pair of plastic open-toed sandals; she supposed they were fashionable, but they were no protection against the cold. 'Brr, it's freezing!' she exclaimed.

'Evidently, child, evidently,' said the Doctor condescendingly. He seemed less affected by the cold than her, and he had stepped behind the Ship to scrutinize the wall they had seen on the scanner. Above the stones the sky was a blinding, uniform white, giving no clue as to their new surroundings. Vicki turned a full circle, repressing a desire to make a snowball. The Ship seemed to have put down at one side of a wide thoroughfare, and a hundred yards opposite was another wall. There was nobody in sight, and Vicki got the impression they had arrived early in the morning. It was difficult to see clearly more than a few feet ahead. She stretched out her arm and her fingers vanished. 'Are you sure this is the 1960s, Doctor?'

'Of course I'm sure,' he replied curtly. He rapped on the door of the TARDIS, the frosted glass windows of which had misted over. 'Come along, no dawdling,' he called in.

'It's just . . .' Vicki shrugged, unable to put her feelings into words. Sometimes she wished she was cleverer. Often her own voice sounded so stupid, especially when she was asking questions. 'Surely there should be some motor traffic?'

The Doctor narrowed his eyes. 'So, you doubt me now, then, do you?'

Vicki swallowed. She felt an enormous debt of gratitude to the Doctor, and didn't want to upset him. 'It isn't like that, it's just . . .' She faltered again. 'It's so quiet.'

The Doctor spread his hands expansively. 'Apply your intelligence to the evidence, as I do.' He gestured about them. 'Just look at all this snow. It's far too deep for people to go motoring through, isn't it? I imagine we'll see a snowplough or some such before long. Or one of those gritting lorries they have.' Again he tutted and hammered on the door of the TARDIS with the silver knob of his cane. 'What are you two getting up to in there?'

Ian and Barbara emerged, shielding their faces against the cold. As soon as they had stepped out of the Ship, its door slammed shut. That sound always unnerved Vicki, as she knew the Doctor possessed the only key.

Ian rubbed his hands together briskly. 'Well, if this is Earth, it looks like we've arrived in time for the January sales.' He looked around keenly. 'Can't see a thing.'

The Doctor gave a pshaw. 'I'll thank you not to be so flippant. I suggest we walk on until we come across some locals, and perhaps you'll believe them.'

Vicki slid her arm around the Doctor's and looked up at him. 'What if there aren't any people? There are no footprints apart from ours.'

It was Barbara who replied. She had wandered over to the wall and was testing its integrity with her fingers. 'The snow's still falling, Vicki,' she said. She tapped the stones. 'And look at this. It's very sturdy, and fairly new. The sort of building made by a community that means to stay put, whatever the weather.'

The Doctor nodded. 'Well done. At last, somebody in this small party of ours, apart from myself, is using their brains.'

Barbara added sourly, 'But not the sort of building I'd expect to see in modern-day Scotland.'

As she was speaking, something ahead caught Vicki's eye. Dimly, through the veil of the snow flurry, she glimpsed movement. It resolved itself into the outline of a small, stooped figure, too distant to be distinct. At least it was humanoid. Gently she tugged at the Doctor's sleeve. 'Doctor, over there. A local.'

'What's that?' He followed her finger and peered at the approaching shape. 'Ah yes, very good. Let's settle this dispute.' He removed his arm from hers and strutted confidently forward to address the stranger.

Vicki moved back to join Ian and Barbara. 'I wonder who it is.' She looked back at the figure, who was becoming clearer. She sensed rather than heard Barbara's defeated groan as the man's clothing revealed itself as a tattered assemblage of leather scraps held together by loose stitching and thongs. A filthy wool hat was jammed so far down on his head that it all but hid his face. What could be seen of his features was a long, straggly beard and coarse, weathered skin. He viewed the Doctor with a bright-eyed curiosity, looking up and down at his fine garments, and they conversed, but the wind was so strong it snatched away the words.

'Well, that's it, then,' said Ian. 'Back to the Ship and pull the handle on the fruit machine again.'

Vicki searched her memory for a possible twig of comfort. 'Could it be a beggar? There were still vagrants in your century, weren't there?'

'Not dressed like that, Vicki,' said Ian. 'But thanks for the thought.'

Vicki smiled sadly and patted Ian on the arm. In truth, she was trying to cover her relief. A part of her desperately wished for Ian and Barbara to find a way back home; another part hoped that they wouldn't. Caught up in her thoughts, she was unaware that Barbara had again broken away and returned to her examination of the wall.

It was Barbara's sudden cry that brought her attention back to the present. 'Ian, Vicki, look over here! The mist's clearing!' There was real excitement in her voice. Vicki and Ian hurried to join her. She was pointing forward, excitement colouring her cheeks red. 'There was a clear patch, I'm sure I could see houses.'

'What kind of houses?' Ian asked anxiously.

Vicki screwed up her eyes. At first she could see nothing but the familiar whiteness. Then, with the rapidity of a desert dawn, a city revealed itself. It was a city of cramped wooden buildings, their awnings and slatted rooftops covered by thick dollops of snow, the streets between paved by cobbles. Vicki's eyes roamed over the scene, trying to take in the details. A wide river divided the dwellings, and the near side was more populous. The spires of Christian churches were spaced along the banks, and there were several tall stone buildings, including one she felt she ought to recognize which was surmounted by four stone turrets and decorated in white edging. Straddling the water was a bridge about fifty feet wide, which supported more wooden dwellings, jammed so tightly together they might have been compressed in an earthquake. At the side of the bridge nearest to them was a tall building decorated in black and white, which appeared somehow incongruous and tacked-on.

Ian was the first to speak. 'Well, he's really gone and done it this time.'

'I don't know,' Barbara said brightly. 'We're only about three hundred and sixty years out. That's quite good for the Doctor, all told.'

Vicki did a quick mental calculation. 'The turn of the seventeenth century. How can you be sure?'

Barbara pointed. 'You see that black and white building, at the edge of London Bridge?' Vicki nodded. 'That's Nonsuch House, erected by decree of Henry the Eighth, and burnt down in the Great Fire of 1666.' She seemed momentarily awestruck. 'I can't believe we're here.' Something caught her eye, and she jumped up and down with glee and caught Ian's hand. 'Ian, I think I could see the Globe Theatre, just for a second, on the far side of the river!'

Vicki, who was starting to feel rather left out, turned at the sound of an authoritative cough. The Doctor was coming back through the snow, his eyes scanning the view of the city, his expression sour. Behind him the man in rags was tramping away, shaking his head in puzzlement. 'When you've finished,' the Doctor said gravely.

'So, Doctor,' said Ian. 'You asked him the time?'

'Yes, yes, and I don't see any need to gloat. With all of time and space to choose from, this was a very near thing.' He coughed again. Vicki had noticed before how he faked symptoms of ill health when bringing bad news or trying to conceal a mistake. 'In point of fact,' he said through splutters, 'it's the winter of 1605.' He gestured to Vicki to come forward and then indicated the TARDIS. 'I suggest we give the Ship's computers time to warm up and then try again. Come along.'

Vicki was prepared to follow, but they were stopped from entering by Barbara, who threw herself in front of the doors of the police box before the Doctor could insert the key. 'Wait a moment, Doctor, please,' she said. 'If this is 1605 . . .' Her eyes sparkled with delight. 'Don't you see what that means?'

'It means, young lady, that we are lost again, and frosting over into the bargain.' He waved her aside. 'Now kindly stand away.'

Barbara didn't budge. 'Doctor, London in the Elizabethan and Jacobean ages has always fascinated me. I can't let the opportunity to see it at first hand pass me by.'

Ian came to her side. He appeared equally eager. 'I can see your point. Doctor, somewhere near by they're performing Shakespeare.' His eyes widened with childish wonder. 'Come to think of it, Shakespeare himself must be down there, right now.'

The Doctor tossed his head back contemptuously. 'Along with the pox, the Black Death, and several thousand plague rats. No, I'm afraid it's out of the question, we must get on.'

Vicki caught Barbara's crushed expression and tugged at the Doctor's arm. 'Surely they can have a look around if they want to? I mean, I know it's cold, but they're young, and . . .' She trailed off at the Doctor's steely glare of reply.

'Oh, I see, I'm old and feeble now, am I?' he said dangerously. 'Because I don't fancy turning into an icicle. Really, what a lot of nonsense.'

'You don't have to come with us,' said Barbara. 'Why not wait in the Ship? We'll be back in a few hours.'

Vicki looked up at the Doctor. He glanced between her and the schoolteachers, as if considering, and then grunted. 'Oh, very well.'

Barbara clapped her hands together exultantly and for a moment Vicki wondered if she was going to kiss the Doctor. 'Thank you.'

The Doctor held up a hand. 'On these two conditions.'

'Yes?' asked Ian.

'One, that you return here before night falls. And two,' he added more forbiddingly, 'that you do not get yourselves involved in intrigue or adventure of any sort whatever, do you hear me? Follow my example and keep yourself to yourself.'

'Of course we will, Doctor,' said Ian flatly. Vicki could tell he was trying to keep his face straight. He turned to Barbara. 'Well, we'd best get cracking, eh?' He took her hand and made to move off.

'Oh, good grief,' the Doctor said under his breath. 'They have no idea, no idea at all.' He said harshly, 'You can't go blundering into seventeenth-century London dressed in plastic mackintoshes. And you'll have no chance of getting into the Globe without the correct coinage, now will you?'

'Have you got suitable clothing, Doctor?' asked Barbara.

He put the key in the lock and opened the door. 'You will make these demands of me. Now, hurry inside, go on.' He held the door open for them and they passed through. 'The sooner you two get away the sooner I can make myself and Vicki a nice hot drink and rest these weary old bones of mine.'

He reached out and chucked Vicki under the chin. As he did, she thought she saw a strange, secretive smile pass briefly over his lips.

The Chamberlain bustled along the palace corridors, the blue hem of his robe trailing behind him like an outgoing tide, his fingers knotting and unknotting, his front teeth worrying his lower lip. He'd compiled a list of specific instructions to the cooks, detailing the King's dietary needs and special preferences, and had it posted on the wall of the huge kitchen. That was as far as his responsibility for catering went. But after the shaky success of last night's revels the delicate strings of his naturally nervous nature were turned to an unbearable tautness, and he had barely slept a wink all night for fretting about the next few days. The opening of parliament was always like this: hasty, with arrangements thrown together and the air full of arguments. He shuddered at the memory of last night's indelicate scene between the King and Cecil. Only in the first days of November could an indiscretion like that have been contemplated. So now he hurried towards the kitchen, having convinced himself he'd forgotten to remind the cooks of James's innate loathing of meringues. He could almost recall noting it on the list, or had he only thought of doing so and forgotten in his haste? He could not settle until he knew, and of course there were a thousand and one other things to organize. The wealth of ceremonial gowns would have to be got cleanly out of storage, first off. Then there were the crown jewels to put in place and keep well guarded, and the seating arrangements for the lords would have to be settled, and the trumpeters were complaining about being given a restricted view, and ... The Chamberlain's head reeled, enough to make him stop at a corner and put his hand to his temple. So much to remember, so many possible hitches!

He was unprepared for the sudden appearance of Cecil, that disagreeable scroll of his still tucked under one velvet-clad arm. The dratted man was a dab hand at popping out of corners like that and giving one a fright. In fact, the Chamberlain often felt as if Cecil was going to arrest him. 'Ah, Chamberlain,' he said, 'you seem out of breath. And so early in the morning.'

The Chamberlain straightened himself. 'Not at all.'

Cecil nodded and stroked his neat little black beard. 'I am glad to hear that. At this delicate time we must all be at our fittest.' Without pausing he switched the subject, which was another of his bad habits. 'I seek the King.'

'I don't think His Majesty would thank you for rousing him,' said the Chamberlain. 'He retired only recently, and then with a sore head.'

'Out all the night? On his first day in London, after complaining of tiredness?'

The Chamberlain spread his hands wide. 'The King has an appetite for pleasure.' He added significantly, 'And none of us can deny him his wants, surely.'

Cecil grunted. 'Where did he lead you?'

'To a dancing house in Clerkenwell,' the Chamberlain replied, attempting to reserve the censure from his tone. 'I was given leave to return here early. I am told that the King and young master Hay remained until the small hours, as is their wont.'

Cecil's response to this information was to sigh, close his eyes briefly, and to tap the scroll against the inside of his arm as he had the previous night. 'A dancing house in Clerkenwell,' he repeated. 'While the hours pass by in which this speech might be corrected.' He caught the Chamberlain's eye. 'You share my concerns on the Catholics, do you not?'

'Theirs is a lesser creed, of course,' said the Chamberlain cautiously. 'But the King believes in this matter, as in many others, that tolerance should be our watchword, and that further measures would be inflammatory.'

'Chamberlain,' Cecil said quietly. 'The question of religious tolerance is nowhere in this debate. Remember, the Papal Bull urged all Catholics to work to overthrow our Protestant government. The Catholics do not even recognize James as king. This is a matter of treason, and traitors must be sought out and punished.'

The Chamberlain didn't want to get involved in this conversation. He knew from experience how Cecil loved to draw people into debate and try to twist their viewpoint. He had no opinion of his own, anyway. It was his simple duty to follow the King in politics as in all (well, nearly all) else. 'We have Catholic lords, do we not, who sit quite happily in Parliament? Tresham, Monteagle. Men who are loyal enough.' He waved a hand awkwardly. 'Now, Salisbury, please allow me to pass, I must see all is well with the cooks. You can settle this concern of yours better with James than with me.'

That said he swept past Cecil as authoritatively as he could.

Cecil's voice floated angrily down the passageway after him. 'Give the papists freedom to associate, and they will associate to kill us all!'

It had occurred to Vicki to wonder why the TARDIS was stacked with clothing from an incredible variety of times and places. She knew better than to ask the Doctor outright; his crabbiness was always aggravated by personal questions. Her own theory was that whoever had owned the Ship in its prime – and the Doctor had hinted it was not strictly his property – had taken such samples aboard as a matter of course, presumably for analysis, just as the first space travellers from Earth had done. Ian and Barbara were inside the wardrobe room now trying things on, and she couldn't help feeling slightly envious.

She entered the control room with a warm drink dialled from the food machine and passed it to the Doctor, who lounged in his wing-backed armchair. 'Ah, bless you, my child,' he said kindly and took a sip. Again Vicki sensed an air of repressed excitement emanating from him. His eyes had twinkled in the same way on the day they'd set off for Rome, and on the day he'd examined the parasitic webs woven by the evil Animus. The prospect of hours spent inside the TARDIS didn't seem worth such anticipation. Instinct warned her not to remark on this. Instead she enquired, 'Ian and Barbara won't really be at risk from disease outside, will they?'

'I don't suppose so, no. They will both have been vaccinated against the more common infections.' He took another sip of his drink. 'Yes, I'm sure they'll be safe, on that score at least. You've had your jabs, haven't you?'

Vicki laughed and settled on the arm of the chair. 'Hardly jabs. I had the full range of vaccinations injected by medical laser when I was five.'

'Of course, of course,' said the Doctor. 'I was forgetting the lead you have over the others, my dear.' He took her hand and squeezed it gently. 'Still, at least you aren't forever clamouring to get back to your own time.'

'There's nothing left there for me now,' Vicki said sadly and truthfully. 'And there's so much to see with you.'

He nodded. 'Exactly, yes, that's the spirit.'

They were interrupted by the return of Ian and Barbara from the wardrobe room. The change in them was startling, especially in Barbara. She was dressed in a light green gown that was fastened tightly around her neck by small brown buttons. It was all the more fetching for its lack of elaboration, and showed off Barbara's figure to its full effect. The impression was set off by her hair. She had washed out the lacquer which normally kept it fixed high, and had pinned it up in a chignon that rested beneath a fetching lace bonnet. Also, she had substituted her normal subtle layer of make-up with a fine dusting of white powder, and added a beauty spot and bright red lipstick.

'Barbara, you look fabulous!' Vicki cried. She got to her feet and circled her friend, taking in every detail of the costume.

'What about me?' asked Ian. He gave a courtly bow. 'Aren't I fabulous too?' He had chosen a distinctive grey doublet with puffed sleeves and a ruff. His grey leggings were a perfect fit, and were tucked into a pair of sturdy leather boots at the knee. Tucked under one arm was a wide-brimmed hat with a peacock's feather on its front.

'Ian, you look like a hero,' Vicki enthused. 'A proper d'Artagnan.'

'Hmm. A proper something else, in my opinion,' said the Doctor, draining his drink and getting to his feet. He pottered over to the console and pulled the door lever. Once again Vicki felt the blast of cold air. This time there was a slight difference. The sun had come out, and a warm beam of its light came through the door and sparkled over the console's metallic instruments.

'Have you got your money sorted out?' Vicki asked.

Ian took out a drawstring purse from a pouch at his belt and weighed it in his hand. 'I should say. This'll see us through comfortably. Quite a magpie, aren't you, Doctor?'

The Doctor ignored the comment. 'Off you go, then.'

He waved them towards the open doors. 'And remember what I said.'

'We'll be back by evening,' said Barbara. She unhooked cloaks for herself and Ian from the hatstand. 'Sure you don't want to come with us, Doctor?'

'I shall spend the day on worthier pursuits. Calculating a formula for returning you home, perhaps.'

Vicki felt an anxious twinge as Ian and Barbara moved off. It always felt wrong to split up. 'Be careful, won't you?' she called.

Ian nodded. 'We'll say hello to Shakespeare for you, shall we, Doctor?'

The Doctor pretended to be absorbed in the TARDIS's workings and didn't look up. 'As you wish. Please hurry, I want those doors closed, the draught is abominable.'

With a final smile to Vicki, Ian followed Barbara through the doors. The Doctor pulled the lever to close them, then unchained his fob watch from his waistcoat. He wound it carefully and examined its face.

'I don't know why they're making such a fuss over Shakespeare,' said Vicki. 'I mean, I know he was good, but he was hardly Lynda LaPlante, was he?'

The Doctor wasn't listening. 'Now, let's see,' he said, and his secretive smile returned. 'It must be just about eight a.m. . . .'

Vicki glanced around the big white room. Barbara had described London so vividly, and it seemed wrong to be missing out on all the wonders of this age. Quelling her disappointment she moved off to the living quarters.

The Doctor's voice halted her. 'Where are you going?'

'Back to my room. To finish the book you lent me, the one about magnetos.'

He looked her right in the eye and gave a chuckle that was full of mischief. 'And why would you want to be poking your nose in a stuffy old book, hmm? When you could experience life for yourself?'

'I didn't want to disturb you, if you're going to be working on that formula.'

The Doctor came forward, still chuckling, and took

her hand. 'Really, I must congratulate myself on that performance, if it passed your alert young eyes.'

Vicki frowned. 'I don't follow.'

In reply the Doctor pointed through the inner door. 'We shall need our cloaks, and something to fit you underneath.'

It took a while for Vicki to puzzle his words out. Her eyes flicked to the doors. 'We're going with Ian and Barbara after all?'

He shook his head. 'Tch, tch. If you have a fault, my girl, it's that you're too trusting.' He held up his watch and sent it spinning before her eyes. 'We'll give them a quarter of an hour to be on their way and set off ourselves.' He radiated an aura of vigour and sprightliness, a marked contrast to the theatrical spluttering of the past hour.

Vicki wasn't sure whether she should feel amused or appalled. 'You rogue. Why didn't you want to go with them?'

'You heard. The Globe Theatre, Nonsuch House. Behaving like two twentieth-century tourists, indeed. This way, we shall be able to conduct our investigations unencumbered by vulgar sightseeing.'

'Investigations into what?'

'You'll see, my dear, you'll see.' He led her towards the wardrobe. 'Now, I wonder what we have in here for you.'

Vicki's confusion had been replaced by a sense of guilt. 'But Ian and Barbara will be coming back later, won't they?'

The Doctor sniffed. 'Oh, we shall have returned long before them. They needn't know a thing, need they? It can be our little secret.' He tapped her on the shoulder and walked away, laughing to himself. Sometimes he could appear quite mad.

Vicki followed him through into the wardrobe room.

It was a measure of their considerably broadened horizons that Ian and Barbara were able to pass into the central

thoroughfares of London without stopping to marvel at
the spectacle of living history. The snowy track gave way
to a steep decline, which took them down through the
city wall into the narrow streets. The weather was
improving, the sky had cleared to a joyous blue, and as
morning rolled on more doors opened, more people
emerged, and soon they found themselves surrounded by
a fair-sized crowd. Some were armed with shovels,
working industriously on the snow piled up against the
wooden walls of the buildings, and on every other corner
it seemed somebody had lit a small fire. As they walked,
Barbara and Ian listened to the chatter of the streets and
looked up at the cramped, ill-assorted houses with their
frail-looking windows, sloping eaves and criss-crossed
black and white beams.

As they passed into another street, Ian leant closer to
her and said, 'I'm trying to work out where we are.' He
pointed left. 'The Tower's over there, I caught a glimpse
of it, a few miles away. And there's the river, ahead of us.'
Barbara followed the direction indicated and saw the
river, which could be glimpsed in the gaps between the
streets that sloped down to the embankment. Although
the grassy banks were frosted over, its central course was
flowing freely. 'This must be near enough Aldgate. We
put down in what'll be the East End one day.'

Barbara nodded. 'So if we keep going along here we
can cross London Bridge and get to the Globe well in
time for the afternoon's performance.'

She couldn't help her excitement at the prospect spilling
over into her voice, and Ian smiled. 'This is your
dream come true, isn't it?'

Barbara gestured around them. 'Just look at these
people. You can sense their strong spirit, their sense of
community. There are many bad things here, I know, but
you can see the threads of our way of life, of our
civilization.'

She noticed that as they walked on down this long
street, the crowd around them seemed to be thickening,
and there was a corresponding increase in noise, with

shouts and cries coming from not too far away.

Ian shot her a troubled glance. 'Sounds like something's going on up there.' Barbara peered past him. The activity was centred on the street corner, where a small mob, most of them men, were gathered in a rough ring. Those at the back were craning their necks to get a look at whatever was in the middle, and some of these were standing on wooden crates for a better view. The overall impression reminded Barbara of the street entertainers of her own day, although the audience here were much more enthusiastic, shouting encouragement and clapping frantically. She moved closer, intrigued.

Ian followed. 'I suppose it could be someone in the stocks. Or have I got my history wrong again?'

Barbara didn't answer. She joined the ring of men, wrinkled her nose at the odour that was coming off them, and pushed in as far as she was able, straining her neck. She felt Ian's hand clamp tightly about her arm, and for once was glad of his protective instincts. They moved as one, jostled forward against the knees and elbows of the crowd.

Above their heads came an animal cry, something between a roar of rage and a rattle of anguish. At the sound the crowd reared up, some gasping, some laughing. Barbara glanced back at Ian, whose face was pinched tight with pity. A foot or so taller than her, he could see what was happening, and it was not pleasant. She turned back to face the spectacle and raised herself on tiptoe. And, for a moment, she saw.

At the centre of the ring, with his back to a tall building, was a man in rough clothing and heavy leather mittens. His hands were outstretched, and held taut between them was a cruel whip, with a wooden handle around which was tied a knotted clump of thick birch twigs. Whip and gloves alike were spattered with blood. The man's face was disfigured, and made worse by his lack of expression. Passing around the mob were two more men with blank thuggish features. They carried collecting bowls, demanding payment and roughing up anyone who refused to contribute. At the side of the first man was a cabinet which had been unloaded from a nearby cart, and inside, its four limbs tightly chained to make it upright, was a brown bear, pathetically thin, its fur worn away in patches, its snout scarred and its upper lip all but bitten away. All eyes in the crowd were upon it. It waved its forepaws in a futile fashion, and Barbara winced at the sight of the bleeding sores where the cuffs of the chains had dug deepest. The nearest men of the mob were reacting to what they took as a challenge, and were pelting it with dirty snowballs. The bear threw back its head and whined in pure anguish.

A wave of revulsion passed through Barbara. Unconsciously she pushed herself back through the mob, disgusted by their raucous shouts and taunts. She and Ian popped back out into the street and nearly lost their balance on the slippery cobbles.

'What was that you were saying about civilization?' asked Ian.

Barbara smoothed her clothing down and shuddered. 'I don't see how people can be so wicked. So primitive.'

'Ever been to a bullfight?' Ian managed a weak smile and took her hand. 'We'd better move on. Remember what the Doctor said.'

Barbara nodded and followed him, but she couldn't help but glance back for a final look at the show. 'It seems so unfair.'

'I know, but there's nothing we can do, is there?' He was looking about, trying to navigate and see them safely through the massing crowd, which was gaining more members, pressing into them with no regard for personal space. A man walked right into them, without even looking, pushing Ian aside with a swing of his arm. 'I think we'd better get under cover,' said Ian. He grabbed Barbara's hand tight and pushed on through the crowd.

Vicki stepped out of the TARDIS for the second time. The change in the weather was apparent. The day had turned bright and clear, the mist had dispersed, and the view of the city was distinct and sharp-edged. The surrounding snowbound fields about its perimeters had a crunchy beauty. She quelled an inner desire to whoop, and settled instead for study of some of the larger landmarks. This time she recognized the Tower of London right away, and not too far down the river to its right was the bridge Barbara had remarked on earlier. The only other building that could compare was far to the left side of the city, a magnificent white-fronted stone block flanked by extensive grounds and a cluster of lesser redbrick outhouses.

She turned as the Doctor emerged from the police box. Beneath his cloak he wore his own Edwardian outfit, which Vicki didn't dare point out was as anachronistic as any plastic mac. He had dressed her in a pair of comfortable, stretchy woollen leggings, a rather fine slashed doublet, and a smaller cloak.

Having made certain the door of his craft was secure he came across to examine her. 'Yes, yes, suits you very well.'

'Do I have to be a boy again?'

'Much the safest option.' He took her arm and guided her along the road towards London. The wall died away as they walked down the slight slope, replaced by a border of bare elm trees and untended patches of bracken which delineated the highway from the fields beyond. There were now some people about, and they passed a horse-drawn cart laden with wine barrels and a number of workers with tools slung over their shoulders. 'You shall be my ward,' the Doctor went on. 'A young girl accompanying a gentleman of my years and position might give rise to unhealthy speculation.'

'Who from? You still haven't told me where we're going.'

His eyes roved the vista of the city. Irritated with himself he fumbled for the spectacles he kept in a waistcoat pocket, rested them on his nose and tried again. 'Now, where . . . ?' He tapped his finger against his lips, then settled on something and pointed it out.

'Do you see that large stone building, on the left of the city?'

'Yes, I noticed it earlier. It's rather grand.'

'It's supposed to be. It's Whitehall Palace, quite probably home at this time of year to King James himself, and thus the supreme centre of political activity.'

She looked at him suspiciously. 'You told Ian and Barbara not to get themselves involved, and here we are going off to meet the King.'

The Doctor snorted and tucked his spectacles away. 'For purely scientific reasons. Yes, an academic study into what's going on in that palace is long overdue.'

'Academic study?'

'Yes, my dear. Surely you know to what I refer?'

Vicki grimaced. 'Sorry. All this is ancient history to me.'

'Well, we shall have to improve your mind, and bring you up to date.' He nodded once more to the distant palace. 'In there, the Holy Bible is being translated into the definitive version that will serve the Christian faith for the next few centuries.'

Vicki felt stupid again. 'The King James Bible. Yes, I know about that.'

'Good, good. Fascinating work, at a fascinating point of history. And well worth a closer look, wouldn't you say?'

'I suppose.' Vicki felt deflated. She might have guessed the Doctor would be interested in something musty and erudite. Although he had what might be called a talent for adventuring, he could often be inspired when confronted by some abstract, intellectual challenge. 'We won't be going into the centre, then. Pity. I was looking forward to Trafalgar Square.'

The Doctor looked down at her, appalled. 'Trafalgar Square? Child, what are you talking about?'

'It was one of the great landmarks of old London, I thought,' she protested. 'With the column, and the pigeons. Ian told me he'd seen it.'

'Dear dear dear,' said the Doctor. 'I shall really have to

take you in hand. Pigeons, indeed. This is 1605. The battle of Trafalgar won't be fought for another two hundred years.'

Vicki's confusion increased. 'I didn't know there'd been a battle in Trafalgar Square. Who won?'

But the Doctor shook his head firmly, showing he was unprepared to carry on this conversation, and they went on.

The inn consisted of a large, rectangular serving area with a ceiling so low that both Barbara and Ian were forced to lower their heads as they entered. It reeked of beer and sweat. Their first impression was not of discomfort, however, because the room was served by a warm log fire, and the wooden walls contrasted with the whiteness outside, making the inn appear cosy and welcoming. The rough, flagstoned floor was scattered with straw and sawdust. The bar was lined with kegs and wooden taps, the wall behind decorated with a huge old wooden wheel, the chairs and tables arranged regularly against the walls. It was a scene that would remain almost unaltered for centuries, and the continuity made Barbara smile as she slipped off her gloves. 'Almost like home,' she whispered to Ian.

He returned the smile, and looked through the nearest window. The street was now thronging with noisy, excited people. News of the bear-baiting had spread, and they had found it impossible to move against the crush in any direction. Ian's squared shoulders had propelled them over to the door of the inn, which stood on a corner. It possessed a hanging sign, but the name had faded long before. 'We'll wait here until the excitement dies down,' said Ian, moving to warm his hands on the fire. 'And take a draught of the local ale while we're about it, eh? Their opening hours must be a bit freer than ours.'

Barbara looked around. Initially the place had seemed deserted. There was nobody behind the bar, although a pervading smell of cooking meat wafted from beyond a wooden serving hatch. Now she saw they were not alone. Seated in one of the darker recesses of the long room were two men dressed in simple sacking tunics and shining leather aprons. She nudged Ian and pointed them out.

Ian nodded to them. 'Good day to you.'

The shorter of the men raised his beer mug. 'And a ha-ha to you, good sir.' He belched and his companion laughed. Barbara studied them more closely. The smaller man was stocky and broad-shouldered, and his swarthy face might have been attractive had it not been for the pockmarks that peppered it. He was sprawled in his chair, the arm not attached to the beer mug hanging behind him at an awkward angle. She had seen the surly disregard in his eyes in hundreds of schoolboys during her career. It denoted a wilful character absolutely determined to go its own way. His colleague was much thinner and taller, a beanpole of a man whose long arms and legs were barely covered by his garments. He was sallow and his hair hung plastered in greasy bangs against his white forehead. His greeting consisted only of a nod of the head.

The shorter man went on, in a broad cockney accent, 'Not drawn by the bear show, then?'

Barbara replied, 'No. I don't find it very entertaining.'

The man slammed his mug on the table with good humour, sending splashes of foam over the rim. 'There, my good Hodge, what did I say to you when these two gentlefolk strolled in? They are a godly pair like us, with refined tastes like us.' His words were underscored with a hint of mockery, although his tone was not unpleasant. 'And as fine a gallant gentleman and his wife were never seen before in Lark Street.'

Barbara was unsure how to take this remark, and smiled pleasantly. She gestured to the bar. 'Is anybody serving here?'

The man laughed and nudged his companion in the ribs. 'Ay! And 'twas the same question that came to my mind when I first saw yourself, good mistress.' He chuckled throatily and winked at Ian.

Barbara was reminded of her university days studying

the Jacobean comedies, of forever having to check the meaning of long-lost innuendoes in the footnotes. Essentially, the seventeenth century was the golden age of the dirty joke. She let the moment pass and although she wasn't sure if she'd been insulted or flattered or both gave the polite smile she felt the situation required. 'We're seeking refreshment,' she said. 'Where is the landlord?'

'Landlord, is it?' He took a long gulp from his mug. 'As sure as my name's honest John Firking of the gentle craft, there's no lord in these premises, nor even a lady.' He dissolved into laughter once more.

Ian exchanged a raised eyebrow with Barbara. Evidently deciding to make the best of things, he extended a hand. 'I am Ian Chesterton. This lady is . . .' He faltered a second. 'My wife, Barbara.' He gave Barbara an apologetic shrug. She could see the logic in his lie, and found she didn't mind at all.

'Oh ay?' Firking frowned. 'And what's your trade?'

'We are schoolmasters,' Ian said patiently. 'At a school in Shoreditch.' There was an awkward silence. 'And what is your trade?'

Firking and Hodge both looked confused. 'Ay, we have told you that.' Firking tapped the apron at the swelling of his beer-gut. 'We are true gentlemen of the gentle craft.'

Realization came to Barbara. 'Cobblers.'

Ian stared at her. 'Don't upset them,' he whispered.

She sighed and gestured to the two men. 'Shoemakers.'

'The wife catches on well,' said Firking. He smote himself on the chest rather grandly and declaimed, 'John Firking of the last house in Tower Street, and this is poor Ralph Hodge of the same.' He winked at Barbara. 'He may look lame, good wife, but if you let him he's as fine a workman as any on a prick and an awl!' At this both shoemakers roared with laughter.

'We could do with a phrasebook,' Ian whispered.

'I'd rather have a drink,' she replied.

As if on cue the door next to the serving hatch was flung open violently, and an extraordinary figure stormed through. For a moment it was difficult to tell if the newcomer was male or female. It was definitely large and broad in the beam, and a filthy cloth garment was wrapped around and around it like a bandage right up to its stub of a neck. Its hair was close-cropped in curls with patches of baldness, and beneath its heavy black eyebrows was the red face of a devil, with a huge ugly nose at the junction of a mass of quivering, broken-veined jowls. The eyes were black, the expression stormy. It was a face that could not be imagined at rest. Surely, thought Barbara, it had always been so tightly scrunched.

When it spoke, the voice seemed to originate from two places at once, from the gaping black-tongued mouth and from somewhere deep down in the chest. 'Where's that scheming little Sybil?' it thundered, and Barbara decided this was a woman. 'I'll chase her from here up to Doctor's Commons when she shows herself! Marry gup, sure I'll have her hide for pastry!' She slammed a bunched fist down on the bar. 'It has struck past-half nine. Where is the girl?'

Hodge spoke for the first time. 'Don't you fret, Mother Bunch. I'd wager saucy Syb has done a good night's work for some young fellow!'

'I'll box her ears purple,' the landlady fumed. She seemed to notice Ian and Barbara for the first time, and as she viewed them her face tightened up even further. 'And who are these in their finery?'

Ian tried his best to look diplomatic. 'We've dropped by to sample your ale.'

'They're schoolmasters, Mother,' called Firking. 'Man and wife, of Shoreditch.'

'Are you now?' Mother Bunch continued to stare at them suspiciously as her thick arms worked automatically, pouring out a jug of ale from one of the kegs. 'And what brings you out here, then? Is there no school today?'

Barbara worded her reply carefully. 'We have been given leave to study, at the theatre.'

'The theatre?' She put the full jug down on the bar together with two big mugs. 'What's to study there? Half the while it's nothing but clapdoodle.' Fortunately she didn't seem remotely interested in either of them, and she turned back to the serving room. 'When that bear packs off in its cart there'll be a crowd of 'prentices baying for pies in here, and I'll have none baked to give them if that girl doesn't show her freckled face. She keeps bad time.' She pointed to Firking. 'You, shoemaker, if she pops her head around that door you warn her I'll have at her with a wanion, see if I won't.' With that she stormed back out to the servery.

Hodge and Firking laughed heartily after her departure. 'Poor Sybil,' said Hodge. 'Old Mother Bunch is as sour as verjuice.'

Firking broke through his giggles and managed to say, 'If Sybil delays any further, her employment will go the way of her maidenhead!'

Barbara and Ian chose this moment to take their jug of ale and sit as comfortably as they could and as far away as was polite from the shoemakers. Ian poured out the ale into a mug, and raised it to his nose. He inhaled and pulled a sour face. 'Strong stuff. There's salt on the head, perhaps it settles the flavour.'

Barbara was lost in thought. 'That woman thinks of the theatre as we might think of television.'

Ian risked a taste of the beer. 'Actually this isn't all that bad.'

Barbara sighed. 'If only the Doctor wasn't in such a tearing hurry and we could stay here a few more days. There's so much to see.'

'Yes. I've been thinking about that, you know. Doesn't it strike you as odd, Barbara, the old boy giving us the push and locking himself away in the Ship like that? I've never known him to pass a chance to nose about before.'

Barbara poured herself some of the ale. 'He's an unpredictable man.'

'Maybe.' She watched his fingers, which he was unconsciously drumming at the edge of the table. 'I wonder if perhaps he just wanted us out of his way.'

'Then why not send Vicki with us?'

Ian raised an eyebrow. 'Vicki's a lot less trouble for him than you or me, and he likes to have somebody to sound off to.'

Barbara didn't like his disapproving tone. 'I like Vicki,' she said.

'So do I. That's not what I meant.'

'Then what did you mean?'

'Think about it. He's got some plan of his own, I reckon, something dangerous or silly he knows Vicki wouldn't object to.'

'You're frightening me.' Barbara took a sip of the beer and winced; it was pungent, salty, and there were particles of foreign matter in the foam. 'I'm sure you're just imagin–'

She broke off at the sound of a sharp scrape from near by. It was an innocent enough sound in itself. She was startled because she had believed they were alone in this area of the inn. Both her and Ian's heads whipped round to the source of the noise.

It came from a darkened corner a few feet away.

Barbara whispered, 'I didn't know there was anybody over there.'

'Neither did I,' Ian replied.

In the shadows they could just discern a figure. A tall man dressed in a black robe, with a cowl thrown far forward concealing his features, was seated at a small table. Before him was a jug of ale, and a mug was clasped in one of his thin, long-fingered hands. His presence was altogether sinister, and Barbara suppressed a shudder at the thought that he had most probably overheard every word of their muttered conversation. He had none of the cheeriness of Hodge or Firking, and made no move to register their presence or greet them.

'I don't like the look of him,' Ian said, lowering his voice another notch. 'Could he be a monk or something?'

'In an alehouse?' Barbara shook her head. 'Anyway, it's none of our business. We should keep our noses out.' She took another swig from her mug and tried to put the doubts Ian had raised to the back of her mind.

But as she turned her back to the hooded, immobile stranger in the alcove, she couldn't suppress a shiver.

2

The Strange Young Men

The Doctor had guided Vicki without erring through the city wall, and navigated with suspicious ease the zigzag of cluttered streets leading to the palace. Her feet, nipped by the sandals, ached abominably, and the exposed toes had turned blue with cold. Twice the Doctor had offered the protection of his cloak, thicker than hers, and twice she refused. In it he appeared entirely congruous, and it was amusing to see him returning the neighbourly nods of other elderly men.

All the same, as they entered the final strait, a wide, magnificent roadway with the looming palace visible several hundred yards ahead at the very end, she was beginning to cross the line from awe into indifference and exhaustion.

To make her point she sat on a tree stump at the roadside and nursed one of her feet. 'Can we just stop a moment?' she pleaded, turning her most winning expression to the Doctor.

'Stop?' The Doctor stood over her sternly. 'What is the matter now?'

'These shoes are killing me.' To emphasize her words she removed her sandal and wiggled her sore toes up at him.

'Hmm,' said the Doctor, examining them. 'Do you know, these may come in rather useful.'

'My toes?' Vicki pulled them back and restrapped the sandal.

The Doctor looked around. His face lit up when he saw a covered market, jammed together not far along the way. He clapped his hands together sharply, making a sound like a pistol shot. 'Ideal, yes. I think I should find a farrier in there.'

'A farrier? What do we need a farrier for?'

'What else but for a horse? Now you sit there, and rest those feet of yours, and don't talk to any strangers. I shall return shortly.' With a nod he disappeared into the crowd clustered around the market.

Vicki watched him go with misgivings. She had a feeling her intelligence was being undervalued.

The Doctor returned a few minutes later. He was leading a very weary-looking horse on tattered reins. Its eyes were mournful and heavy-lidded and signalled tiredness with life. Vicki felt a twinge of emotion. Why, an inner voice asked, was she moved so much more easily by cuddly animals than humans? She reached up to stroke it. It snorted resentfully. 'Oh, you poor thing,' she said, patting its moist nose, from which issued huffs of cold air. 'I shan't be cruel to you.' She turned to the Doctor and lowered her voice. 'Somebody saw you coming. How much did you pay for this old nag?'

'There's no need for whispers, child, the beast can't understand you,' the Doctor said patiently. He gestured to the worn saddle on the horse's back. 'Now, up you get.'

Vicki gulped. 'I couldn't put even my weight on his back. He's so thin and bony he'd shatter.'

'He'll be fine to the end of the drive,' said the Doctor. 'You're a wisp of a thing. And the King's stables will be the best place for him, with plenty of the finest oats and hay. So you'll be doing him a favour, won't you? Now up, up.' He registered her nervousness. 'You have ridden a horse before?'

Vicki twisted her hands. 'Well, I had a pony, once, when I was younger. He was called Saracen, and I . . .' Seeing the irritability growing in the Doctor's eyes she added, 'I'll give it a go.' She put her throbbing right foot in the stirrup, steadied herself, and brought herself up and around, landing with a little bump on the saddle. To her surprise she was comfortable, and the horse didn't seem to mind too much either. She smiled and patted his side. 'Good boy, Charger.'

The Doctor looked up disapprovingly. ' "Charger"?'

'We don't want to hurt his feelings,' she replied.

The Doctor sighed. He tugged on the reins and made an extraordinary clicking noise at the back of his throat. It didn't sound the sort of noise a human ought to be capable of making, but then the Doctor, as he was fond of reminding his companions, was not human. Immediately the horse responded, and followed him with fatigued willingness as he set off down the road at a measured pace. 'I am not a half-wit. Do you imagine I purchased Char– this mangy creature for no good reason?'

Vicki relaxed. The gentle up-and-down movement of the horse was soothing. 'I think he's on his last legs.'

'Precisely,' said the Doctor. 'So when we arrive at the palace, it will appear as if we have travelled several hundred miles on him rather than several hundred feet, now won't it?'

'Is that important then?'

'For pilgrims,' replied the Doctor, with the smuggest gleam in his eye, 'I should say it's vital.'

The rumble of the crowd was fast escalating into a tumult. Men were packed so densely in the street that the windows on either side of the inn's door were blacked out, which left only a couple of flickering candles to illuminate the long, low room and its five disparate occupants. Mother Bunch had retreated to her kitchen, and curses and oaths of all possible origins and interpretations could be heard coming from behind the servery door as she laboured on alone with her stews and pies. Ian and Barbara sat quietly in their corner, taking an occasional sip from their mugs. They remained very much aware of the presence of the hooded figure. He hadn't moved from his place in the shadows. The shoemakers continued their drunken conversation, Firking breaking away from his mate now and then to comment either on Barbara's loveliness – comments which she acknowledged with a gritted grin, to Ian's amusement – or on the riotous nature of the men pressing against the walls.

'And all for a brutish bear,' Firking said, smacking his lips. 'Now, had that been a hanging I might understand it.'

Hodge raised a finger. 'And we cannot hear the clock striking. But I reckon it's gone half ten now, and the master'll be wanting us back to work.'

Firking snarled. 'Who needs the ring of a bell with you around? Follow this idea, good Hodge.' His tone was conspiratorial but he was performing to all. 'The crowd was so stirred up and crammed tight as sardines that we could neither hear the chimes that pealed an end to our Friday half-holiday, nor push our way through back to Tower Street.'

Hodge shook his head ruefully. 'It's a fine story. But it won't stop the master raging at us.'

'A story?' Firking winked. 'True in all but the small details. It suits as well.' He raised his mug to Ian and Barbara. 'What say you good folk?'

Barbara shrugged and smiled politely. 'Well, if you can't get back to work, your master can't hold you responsible.' She pointed to the windows. 'When will the crowd clear, do you think?'

'They'll tire of the tragical beast soon enough,' replied Firking. 'That, or it'll tire of its work and expire. You'll get to the Globe in time.'

Barbara nodded her thanks and turned back to Ian. 'I should hate to waste the day cooped up here.'

'I've been thinking,' said Ian. He pointed over her shoulder. 'Look, there's a back way out.' Barbara followed his finger and saw a heavily bolted door in the shadows at the end of the bar furthest from the main entrance. Presumably it led to a back alley. 'We could persuade the old woman to let us through.'

A particularly obscene oath came from the kitchen. Barbara pulled a sour face. 'I'm sure your charm will have her eating out of your hand.'

Ian smiled. 'Perhaps not.'

The moment was broken by a sound from the fifth occupant of the room. He stood, his chair leg scraping against the wooden floorboards, and tossed a handful of change on the table. His cowl still thrown fully forward over his face, he walked towards the main door.

Ian said in a friendly manner, 'I don't think you'll get very far in that lot.'

The cowled man ignored him. Barbara expected that his figure would become more distinct as he stepped into the light, but his features remained hidden and the black robe covered his entire body. For a second, as he passed one of the candles, what lay beneath his cowl was picked out vaguely. She caught a glimpse of an oddly shaped nose and a curled lip, but her attention was more taken by his shuffling gait. It looked almost as if he walked on three legs; every other step he took was accentuated by a dull thudding sound, the sound of some heavy object striking the floor. In spite of this handicap he moved swiftly and was out of the door in moments.

Firking shouted after him, 'And good luck to you in the mob, sir!' He smiled conspiratorially to Hodge. 'Like as not, the pockets in that robe will be empty by now. It'll be a thieves' delight out there.'

Ian was opening his mouth to speak when the door was flung open again. A petite figure dressed in a dirty white linen dress bustled in, fanning her face with exaggerated daintiness. Her garment was bunched in tight against her waist, accentuating her trim bust and slender figure, and padded out to a wide diameter about her legs, where it trailed across the floor and was sooty and black. Her reddish curls were pinned up tight beneath a frilly cap, and her young and rather pretty freckled face was dabbed with rouge over a layer of white powder. She looked exhausted and terrified, and her lively sea-green eyes shot in every direction at once as she tumbled down the steps into the inn proper. 'Oh, monstrous!' she said in a squeak that was half-voice, half-giggle, and delivered at a speed that defied the listener to keep up. 'By my troth, I come from Cornhill as fast as I could, scudding apace, and it must be gone an hour I've been pushing against that riot! I sweated purple against the varlets, ooh, with their hands and elbows and knees jutting right into me.' Her tone of saucy innocence amused Barbara, and she shared a raised eyebrow with Ian.

Firking and Hodge chuckled. 'You should be used to a man's outgoing before now, Sybil,' said Firking with a seedy, deep-throated laugh.

Sybil pushed his shoulder playfully. 'You tickle it, i'faith, Firk.' She looked fearfully over at the kitchen door. 'Oh, Mother Marge will have my guts for goose giblets.'

'It's a wonder you didn't hear her cries over the bear's roaring,' put in Hodge.

The kitchen door slammed open with a crash that made Barbara jump. Mother Bunch, her fists like giant hams, stood in the frame. Her face was dripping with sweat from her stoves. 'Syb-whore!' she growled. She pounded around the bar and loomed over the serving-girl. 'While you, little mammet, have been lying idle in your bed, I've had this tavern to run!' She raised one fist as if to strike.

Sybil recoiled from the imagined blow and skipped lightly away from her mistress. 'I was up with the cock, by my troth,' she protested, taking refuge behind the giggling shoemakers. 'It's that crowd that's held me back, it stretches half as far as the Exchange!' She dodged a second swipe, and scuttled to take protection beside Ian and Barbara. 'As true as God's in heaven!'

Mother Bunch pointed to the kitchen. 'You get yourself through there, cheeky strumpet, and set to scrubbing! There's stews to be warmed and meat to be cut! For think of the riot to come when the bear is done and those mad Mesopotamians roll in to find nothing but last night's chitterlings on my tables!' She reached out, grabbed Sybil by the scruff of the neck, and marched her through the kitchen door. Sybil's skirt was hitched up as she was thrown through. Barbara was amused to see her footwear consisted of a pair of scuffed black boots, a far cry from the elegant, heeled court shoes she had selected from the Doctor's wardrobe room.

Firking sat back, rocking on his chair's back legs. Barbara quelled an almost instinctive reaction to order him to stop. 'Why, I've never seen the Mother so riled! She looked like a musty ale bottle gone to scalding! And poor Syb white with fright!' He slapped his thigh and called, 'You won't see a scene acted well as that in any theatre!'

Barbara gave another of her polite smiles and turned back to Ian. But his attention seemed to be elsewhere. He was holding a rectangular piece of white paper in his hands. 'Look at this.'

'What is it?'

He pointed to the foot of the table. 'I just saw it there, on the floor.' He turned it over. 'It's sealed. I think it's an envelope.'

'It wasn't there a moment ago.'

Ian considered. 'The man in the cloak. He must have dropped it on his way out, and we didn't notice because of that fight.' He looked over at the door and the blacked-out windows, the continuing hubbub. 'Too late to follow him now and give it back. Probably best to leave it where we found it, eh?' He moved to throw it down.

Barbara stopped him. 'Unless he meant us to have it,' she whispered, taking care not to arouse the suspicions of the shoemakers.

'Don't be silly,' said Ian. 'How could he?'

'Why not open it and find out?'

'It's not addressed to us.'

'It's not addressed to anybody.' She took it from him and examined it closely. 'It can't do any harm. If the Doctor was here, he'd open it.'

Ian frowned. 'Oh, and he's a model of good conduct.'

'Conduct.' Barbara chuckled. 'That's a word I haven't heard for a while. I'd give the Doctor a B+.'

'He has a lively curiosity but must learn to be more disciplined if he wants to get on in the universe,' said Ian playfully.

The shoemakers were beginning to show an interest in

their mutterings, so Barbara hid the letter beneath the table and gently unsealed it with a fingernail. Revealed were a few lines of tightly scrawled but immaculately neat writing in black ink. It was not easy to read in the faint yellowish illumination of the inn, and her initial impression was not formed by the sense of the text but its arrangement.

The sheet was unlined, but the words were spaced with military precision and each line was exactly the same length. The lower loops were trim and unemphasized, the dot over each i aligned exactly. There was something powerfully formal about it and Barbara imagined its author as a highly placed official or a stiff-backed general putting troops into position. The image was shaken when she started to read. 'It's not English.'

Ian leant over the table. 'What then?'

Barbara handed it over. 'Well, it looks like French, but it doesn't make any sense.'

'The French language of this time would be very different to the French we know.'

'Not that different.' She gestured to the shoemakers. 'We can understand their English, just about.' She tapped the letter and gestured for him to hand it back. 'But there's no grammatical sense to that.' She pondered over it once more.

Scarlet – Orly, Seine re dire ne c'est – Qui ne guerre, sous p'eycque tes notte re. Maine wausch aux Fulles – Orange

'Some of those words don't seem right at all,' she surmised. 'Orly and the Seine are French enough, but surely *notte* is Italian? And *wausch*?'

'German?' Ian took a second turn with the note. 'Or code? The Doctor could work it out, I'm sure. We did promise not to involve ourselves. And it definitely wasn't left for us, was it?'

Barbara was immersed in her thoughts. 'But doesn't it intrigue you?' Absent-mindedly she took a lengthy swig from her beer mug; she didn't even notice the strength of the barley flavour. 'And who is Scarlet?'

'Too early for the Pimpernel.' Ian tucked the letter away in a pouch at his belt. 'I wish that crowd would break up. I don't like sitting around in here.' His eyes roved suspiciously over the windows, past the shoemakers and across to the kitchen door, behind which the storm of Mother Bunch's anger still raged. 'There's something I don't like about this place, and that letter's put the tin hat on it.'

Barbara had to agree. Whereas at first the inn had been welcoming it now appeared boxlike and confining, and the cries of the crowd outside increased the claustrophobic sensation. She longed to open a window and take in clean air.

Suddenly, with a crash that seemed for a moment that it would tear the tavern's door off its hinges, two young men were thrown in with all the force of corks popping from champagne bottles. The pressure of the crowd had left them sweating and dishevelled their clothing, and yet they retained an air of dignity and refinement that was in marked contrast to the shoemakers, who greeted their entrance with dark murmurs and mumblings.

'How now, who are these lovelies?' Firking said darkly.

The taller of the new entrants fixed him with a sneer. 'And who are these,' he snapped back, in nasal tones that suggested an acute awareness of his own stature and social standing, 'that seem to have taken soil in this place, so much that they are barely seen out of it?'

His friend frowned. 'Don't aggravate them, Rob. They're small fry, not worth your effort.' To Barbara's surprise he had a soft Yorkshire accent, and she found herself captivated. He was tall and solidly framed, and his good looks shone from behind the customary beard of the period. His hair was ginger, with flecks of grey premature in a man in his early thirties. When he moved it was with a slight inclination to defer to his colleague, as if he was following on, awaiting orders. His dense, powerful musculature suggested regular training.

His superior's body was taller and less muscular. He had a blunt nose too big for his face, and wore a long dark cloak that did not conceal fully the bright red doublet beneath. The colour was an unusual choice for a man, but somehow it reinforced his air of energy, lending him an angry, explosive quality. It was as if he was on fire. After dusting himself down, his first action was to sweep the full length of the tavern, swiftly, with his cool blue eyes. To a person less sensitive than Barbara to the workings of the human face this might have appeared to be simply a natural expression of curiosity. She saw it for what it was; he was looking for someone, and he was extremely anxious.

Without saying another word, the two newcomers arranged themselves before the bar.

Firking couldn't resist making another dig. 'Haven't you finer places to quaff than Old Mother Bunch's inn? I mean to say, you high-thinking papists won't want to mingle with the lowly-lived.'

The taller man turned his head and spat, 'Why don't you just go away and cobble something, coxcomb?'

Firking growled. 'Be careful what you say. Prince am I none, yet I am princely born.' He slapped himself on the legs. 'These are St Hugh's bones, and I am a fine journeyman of the gentle craft!'

'A prince, eh?' The red-doubleted man gave a mock bow. 'Oh, then I stand corrected, and do most humbly beg your pardon, your cobbling majesty.'

The effect of this on Firking was not pleasant to see. He made to stand up and clenched his fists. Hodge put out a bony hand to restrain him. At the same time, in response to the unspoken challenge, the tall newcomer stepped forward and swept aside his cloak to reveal a sword at his waist and the full splendour of his red outfit. Mimicking Hodge, his friend laid a hand on his shoulder and pulled him gently back. 'Be wise,' he whispered. 'It is a folly to fall for these annoyances.' His voice was even-toned and reasonable, matching his handsome face. The moment passed. Firking sat, the man in red let his cloak fall and stepped back. They locked eyes for a second more, then turned their backs on each other contemptuously.

Ian leant over the table and said *sotto voce*, 'I think we can guess who that note was meant for. Papists, he said. Er . . .' He looked rather shamefaced. 'I get a bit confused with the Tudors and all that.'

Barbara frowned. 'Stuarts, actually. Just. I thought every English schoolboy knew his kings and queens.'

'And every schoolgirl her periodic table?' Ian teased. 'King James was a Protestant, wasn't he?'

'He is a Protestant,' Barbara corrected. 'At this point, the Catholics aren't popular. But they're tolerated a lot more than they were. There are no burnings or martyrs under James's rule. He realized that to govern well it made sense to unify people rather than drive them apart.'

Ian's hand reached for the pouch at his waist. He took out the letter. 'Should we pass it on?'

'Is that wise?' Barbara looked between the newcomers and the shoemakers. Firking's drunken babble, which had formed a constant background noise since their entry, had suddenly snapped off, and both he and Hodge were staring at the newcomers with barely concealed suspicion.

'The fact is,' said Ian, 'if we don't, we'll have interfered more than if we do. It could lead to something serious if the message, whatever it is, doesn't get through.'

'We can't even be certain it's for them,' Barbara said. 'France is a Catholic country, but even so . . .' She laid a hand on his arm in caution. 'Let's wait and see what happens.'

Charger had made a gallant attempt to live up to his new name, perhaps taking his inspiration from the Doctor, who had carefully arranged his features to suggest a stoic, apostolic character, and deliberately dirtied the trailing hem of his robe in a puddle to complete the contrivance. Looking at him now Vicki might have believed him to be a priest or a missionary, such was the zeal in his eyes.

The huge black wrought-iron gates of the main entrance to the palace were now right in front of them. She was surprised at the apparent lack of security. Only ten guardsmen were stationed at the gate, all in a line with pikes held still in perfect alignment with their noses, like the chorus of a comic opera. The gates were standing open to allow the admittance and egress of a small amount of traffic; carts drawn by horses disgorged lords, some in ceremonial gowns, who were permitted access with nods of recognition from the leader of the guards. Vicki supposed the more mundane entrants, those bringing in food or fresh laundry, were admitted at the compound's rear. It was typical of the Doctor to take the more dangerous path.

He clicked his teeth as they came up to the line of guards, and Charger stopped instantly, throwing her forward slightly. She waited to see what would happen. Through the open gateway she could see the palace's grounds. The snow had either melted or been shovelled away, and the gravel pathway leading up to the vast palace was bordered by lawns that shimmered in the noon sun.

The main building of the palace was even grander on close inspection. It dominated the others with its three storeys, an outer expression of the British state's confidence in its own godliness and right to govern. It seemed impossible that anyone could simply walk in there unexpected.

But it looked as if the Doctor was going to give it his best shot. He strolled imperiously over to the leader of the guardsmen, who had viewed his approach at first with anxiety and then with some amusement.

Each waited for the other to speak. The Doctor clasped his lapels and threw back his head. The guardsman raised his pike slightly in a meaningfully obscene gesture and made a circling movement with his index finger.

The Doctor pretended not to notice. 'Well?' he snapped.

The guard reached out and pushed him none too gently in the chest. 'Get gone, old mumbler. The King will see none with the evil, and his touch cannot cure it, that is now well known.' Again he made the circling gesture. 'Now, get gone, I say.'

The Doctor pulled an outraged face and pulled himself up to his full height. 'Sir, you are mistaken. My ward here' – he gestured to Vicki – 'and I have no taint of disease on our brows, as you may observe. Further, we have no desire to be touched by the King.' He paused, as if he had made himself clear, and to Vicki it appeared that he was crackling with authority and strength of character. The guardsman kept his face still, working out on which side to come down. The Doctor continued, 'Surely we're expected? The journey has been most trying to a man of my age and delicacy.' He waved at the guardsman to stand aside. 'Now, put that silly stick of yours down and show us through, would you?'

'It's a pike,' said the guard.

'Pike, stick, don't quibble.'

'Journey from where?' the guardsman asked cautiously.

'York, of course.' The Doctor sighed. He winced and rubbed his shoulder. 'Two weeks in this atrocious weather has dried me out until I can't bear to move another inch.' He fixed the guard with his most baleful stare. 'Will you stand aside, sir, or must I take a note of your name to pass to the King? He would not be best pleased to hear of this obstruction.'

For the first time the guardsman flinched. He stood back from the Doctor. 'His Majesty commands your presence?'

The Doctor waved a hand as if he were a king himself. 'In a manner of speaking.' He lowered his voice and his eyes significantly. 'On the translation, you know. The Scriptures.'

The guardsman's Adam's apple bobbed. 'There has been no notice posted, and as you have no escort, I assumed –'

'You assumed I had the scrofula,' the Doctor completed for him, not unkindly. 'Tell me, can you see the signs in myself or in young Victor here? Are we not, as you might say, spotless?'

'Yes, sir.' The guardsman signalled to his fellows and they raised their pikes stiffly in salute to the Doctor and Vicki. 'As I have said, no notice was posted,' he babbled. 'If there had been, then I would surely not have thought to –'

'Oh, please be quiet, my good fellow. It's a simple error to make and you are forgiven. Remember, "Man looketh on the outward appearance, but the Lord looketh on the heart." Now, if you wish to restore my favour, send word ahead of our arrival, and have a berth made ready for this fatigued animal.' The Doctor clicked his teeth and Charger came back to what passed for life. He seemed to know which direction to take, and Vicki found herself being carried right through the gateway.

He sidled alongside her as they passed under the arch. 'Very impressive,' she whispered. 'But what happens when the King finds out?'

'Ah, they won't trouble him with such trivia. We shall pop in, observe the translation, and be out in a trice.'

Vicki watched as one of the guardsmen rushed by, tugging his forelock to them as he went, racing to the palace to announce their arrival. It was difficult to share the Doctor's confidence. 'You're enjoying it.'

'Enjoying what?'

'Lording it over these people.'

The Doctor shrugged. 'It's a question of expedience.' But he couldn't catch her eye.

The bear-baiting was coming to an end at last, and the door of Mother Bunch's tavern was flung open to admit the first of the men to break from the crowd. Mother Bunch and Sybil took turns to serve. A couple of other maids had slouched in to help them. The food consisted mainly of thick beef stews ladled into dirty pottery bowls and pies with crusty pastry sides that were eagerly snapped up by the dispersing revellers. The air started to fill with noise, and some of the better-dressed men began to puff on long slender wooden tobacco pipes. Someone picked up a stringed instrument and started to strum. Where before the inn had seemed boxed in and oppressive it now took on an easy conviviality. Hodge and Firking had been joined by a couple of friends, distracting their attention from the two Catholics, who remained anxious and watchful. They were sitting in the same corner chosen earlier by the hooded man.

Barbara peered through the door. The street beyond was almost clear; distantly she saw the bear-baiter and his men hauling the bear's container on to the back of their cart using oiled ropes fastened around the runners of a pulley mechanism. 'We could probably slip out now,' she told Ian. 'It's only noon. We've still plenty of time.'

Ian shuffled uneasily. 'And what about the note?'

Barbara considered. 'I know. Just drop it where you found it, back on the floor. Nobody will see you.'

Ian gestured with his shoulder to the watchful Catholics. 'They'd be bound to see me.' He shook his head. 'I should never have picked it up.'

'And I should never have opened it,' said Barbara.

'A pie for the fine husband and his schoolmarm?' A sibilant voice cut across the exchange, startling Barbara. The girl Sybil had appeared at their side and was swiping up their empty flagons. 'Oh, monstrous, you have a mighty thirst,' she went on, nudging Ian playfully. 'Shall I fill you up again, sir?' She winked at Barbara. 'It'll give him the vim to dance the shaking of the sheets right proper tonight.'

'No, thank you,' Ian said stiffly. 'I'd like to pay, actually.' He reached for the drawstring purse tucked into his belt, and slipped one of the large silver coins into her hand. 'There you go.' Noting her puzzled expression he added, 'Keep the change, eh?' and made to stand up, putting out a hand to Barbara.

His move was noted by Firking, who said in a loud, drunken voice, 'Ah, see how the best of companies depart when there's a Catholic stench in the air.' There was a general murmur from the men grouped around the shoemakers' table, and a correspondent darkening in the inn's mood. The stringed instrument fell silent. 'They fly out of doors to take fresher breaths from the gutters.'

Barbara turned to see how the Catholics would react. The red-doubleted man was already on his feet, and though he said nothing, his hand had fallen significantly to the hilt of his sword. His colleague was staring into space with a resigned expression, his muscles tensed, shoulders squared. With an unpleasant jolt she realized that she and Ian were caught directly between the two factions, with the threat of violence growing by the moment.

Firking spoke again. 'What say you, Ian Chesterton, you, a gentleman? Should fellows of the English Church, respectful of the Crown, allow these churls to flout their graces in our rooms?'

Remembering Barbara's account of King James, Ian attempted to take a middle course. 'My wife and I have to leave now. We don't have time for argument.'

'See, he is a gent and a polite one, and would not be drawn,' said Firking. He raised his voice and stood up, thumping down his mug of ale. 'But I and my mates have no such handicap, and would make our feelings known with our fists!' There was a coarse cry from the rabble, several of whom, inspired no doubt by Firking's laddish good looks and confidence, slammed their drinks down in sympathy. Hodge was among them, although his watery eyes expressed misgiving.

The man in red responded by throwing open his cloak and drawing his sword. 'You are dawdling fools, and your English Church lets you dawdle still more. An English Church, marry, with a Scotch king at its head! The country goes to ruin and your eyes are closed to it!' Barbara noted the wince that crossed the face of his companion.

She and Ian were still caught in the middle of the dispute, with both parties – the two Catholics and the great mass of Protestants now hulking with fists raised – moving closer. Ian's hand rested protectively on her shoulder, and she could sense him preparing to spring into action if needed.

What she did not expect was the suddenness and the ferocity with which the drunken Protestants, enraged by the words of their opponent, swept forward.

Three things happened in quick succession. Ian was knocked away from her by the mob; she was thrown backwards by a carelessly aimed blow from the Protestant side; and her waist was encircled by a strong arm that lifted her off her feet and away. She screamed and kicked to no avail.

'Hold, raw pups!' the voice of the man in red bawled. He raised the sharpened point of his sword to her throat.

'Ian —' she heard herself gasp.

'Look how he uses a woman as his shield!' one of the Protestants shouted.

Barbara had a second of clarity, perhaps a final attempt by her fading senses to overcome the attack, and then her vision faded abruptly. The ceiling's wooden planks gravitated towards her and the raised voices all around swelled into a single great rushing roar. Her stomach heaved and with a dizzying spin her sense of up and down receded, as if she had been flipped like a tiddlywink, leaving her limp as a rag doll. A pain jabbed like a hot nail at the base of her skull. It was only now she realized that she had been struck on the head by the man in red at the same moment he'd grabbed her. She felt herself being pulled back, her heels scraping the flagstones, but the sense of what was happening was lost in a tide of greyness that pulled her inexorably into herself and blotted out the world.

Her last impression was that a woman was screaming uncontrollably.

Sybil let out a piercing scream as the Yorkshireman, his sword drawn in sympathy with his master's, loomed towards her. 'Open that door!' he ordered gruffly, pointing to the back exit from the inn.

Ian was stunned by the sudden turnaround of events. He stood paralysed by indecision, with Barbara only a few feet away from him, her unconscious form draped in the arms of the man in red, whose sword still rested at her throat. He weighed his options. If he leapt forward, no matter how quickly, Barbara was doomed. The look in her captor's eyes was goading and fanatical, as if something had ignited deep inside him. In contrast his mate, the Yorkshireman, retained his air of considered deliberation. He was evidently accustomed to such situations.

Ian did the only thing he could. 'Let her go!' he snarled. Behind him the crowd of shoemakers, similarly immobilized by concern for Barbara, growled and shook their fists in support.

'Rob!' shouted the Yorkshireman, who had succeeded in coaxing Sybil, using the point of his sword, to pull back the bolts on the back door. 'We must away!'

The man in red sneered again at the crowd. 'You will fall to Rome soon enough, and you'll be glad of it! Your Scotch king will crawl to kiss the devil's toes!' Under cover of these words, which he enunciated in a way that Ian thought demented, he bundled Barbara over his shoulder and was through the door after his mate in moments. It slammed shut after him.

The inn erupted with a fearful roar. With Ian at its head the mob surged forth. He wrenched open the door and emerged into a stinking back alley, narrow and composed of not much more than two overflowing gutters and several piles of decomposing meat, the offcuts of Mother Bunch's cookery.

Ian caught a glimpse of the man in red turning a corner, moving at alarming speed, and ran after him. But he was not familiar with navigating such hazardous surroundings. He had not gone three paces before he skidded on a patch of a slippery substance and fell painfully on his back.

By the time he had righted himself the man in red had fled, and Firking and the others stood massed in the doorway with sullen expressions. Ian realized they were being reprimanded by Mother Bunch, who had appeared from her kitchen wiping her hands on her apron. 'You boys create another fuss like that and I'll put a bar on you, and you'll have to seek some other ordinary in which to make fists!'

Everybody's eyes were on Firking, the ringleader. 'Ah, Marge, that redsocks has a temper that takes to flame over naught!' There was a mutter of agreement. 'He flares up as if lightning-struck!'

'Then piss out his fire and douse him down!' cried Mother Bunch. 'Don't throw coals on!' There were hoots of bawdy laughter. To Ian's horror, the crowd started to move back into the tavern.

Ian staggered over. 'Please,' he said, catching Firking's sleeve, 'you have to help me.'

Firking shrugged him off. Incredibly he was smiling. 'Ah, the lady will be fine, they will have tossed her down near by. They are dogs but not murderers.'

Ian was revolted by their casual acceptance of this violence. He pulled himself together sharply and ran down the alley, alone and friendless in a world that had appeared so welcoming minutes before.

Barbara felt as if a massive bruise had been clamped on to her head like a hat. Pain obscured all other impressions, although she was dimly conscious of being thrown down roughly. And then there were two voices.

'Rob, you must put a lid on your temper.' The Yorkshireman. 'It is not worth risking all your work on such knaves.'

His associate replied hotly, 'That work is put at risk anyhow. Can you not see? Where was the Spaniard? And who were these in his place, this one and the man?' He made an extraordinary noise, suggestive of a state exactly between frustration and fear. 'So close to the outcome. Only three more nights. The appearance of these strangers is not good.'

'You fear treachery?'

'I fear they are agents of an enemy.'

Barbara tried to open her eyes. She wanted more than anything to be left alone, to rest and recover. The world spun about her. Her captors' faces were punctured and distorted, as if seen underwater. She had to explain that she posed no threat to their plan, whatever that might be.

She tried to speak. Her thoughts were muddy, unconnected, unconsidered. Every couple of seconds the pain surged. 'I . . . we didn't mean to look . . . at the note . . .' she blurted up at them. 'We wanted to . . . pass it to you . . .'

She heard the man in red gasp. 'The note! She has the Spaniard's note! The final instruction!' He grabbed and shook her, but her awareness was diminishing and she felt no discomfort. 'Where is it? You have seen it?' He shook her more roughly and shouted, 'Where is it?'

Barbara was too dazed to reply.

The last thing she heard before she blacked out was the man in red. He said, 'The operation is threatened. We shall return to the house, taking her along. The horses are tethered along this way. She will ride with you.'

He paused. As if from an infinite distance Barbara heard him say, 'And when we arrive there, I will force her to speak all she knows.'

3

The Wisest Fool

For the umpteenth time in an indecently long and indecently uneventful life, Haldann wheeled the step ladder into position, took a firm hold on the guide rail, and climbed up shakily. His wizened index finger trailed along the chubby spines of the volumes on the top shelf, most of which had lain undisturbed for a century or more. As he strained his rheumy eyes at the worn gilt lettering of their titles he took lungfuls of the musty air, imbibing deep draughts of frayed vellum and yellowing parchment. Surely there was no fragrance sweeter than the wafts of antiquity's wisdom! And made especially dulcet in the present circumstance, when he was about to deliver the killing blow to his opponent's thesis!

His eyes alighted at last on the volume he sought, the writings of Tertullian, and he strained to pull it out. It moved a fraction and dislodged a swirl of dust-motes that shot right up his nostrils and tickled the bridge of his nose. 'Pah,' he said, 'I will not let this defeat me. There were days I was up and down this ladder ninety times or more.' With renewed vigour he returned to his labours. He hooked his fingers around the top and bottom of Tertullian and grunted with strain. The muscles in his upper arm sang with pain.

He heard light, padding footsteps enter the classical annex and looked down to see Otley, his fat face made even uglier by his most sentacious smile, his hands folded in the long sleeves of his robe in an infuriatingly superior and monkish way. Haldann had lived with that face for as long as he could recall. It always shocked him to see how withered and jaded it had become. Naturally, this was not out of any concern for Otley, who was a specious idiot, but because it reminded him that he was seven years older and thus seven years more stooped and decrepit.

'Trouble with weighty Tertullian, I see,' Otley observed. 'His contentions are too heavy and verbose even for you.'

Haldann snorted and, spurred on, redoubled his efforts. 'At least,' he said, '*I* do not cling like a mewling infant to the skirts of a flighty girlish mind such as Nestorius's!' He was rather pleased with this rejoinder, and his self-satisfaction must have increased his energies, because with a shocking suddenness and a horrifying crack, like the pit of hell opening, Tertullian burst forth from its housing and he found himself toppling backwards. Only by whirling one arm in the air was he able to recover his equilibrium. Swiftly he gathered his dignity and descended, the book held against his side, resting on his bony hip. 'Now, let us see how he put the case for materialism.' He swept past Otley in a fluid movement that was an attempt at high-handedness and emerged into the central workroom. Unlike the annexes, which admitted daylight through narrow, grey-mullioned windows, the workroom was considered sacred and was illuminated only by two unornamented candelabra suspended from the vaulted ceiling. Along its middle was the table where the two scholars quarrelled, bickered and occasionally worked; around the three walls facing the heavy oaken door was a continuous stand laden with all manner of texts, abstruse and famed, indispensable or apocryphal, thrown open in the course of research (or, more usually, argument). Haldann added to their number, depositing Tertullian with a thump and throwing open its cover. He turned the pages with a pair of pincers cleansed by a candleflame, so as not to damage the precious contents.

'You waste time,' Otley pointed out as he followed. 'Nestorius has it right. It was not the God but the man Mary carried in her womb. Therefore she has no claim, despite the mystery of the Incarnation, to the title of Mother of God.'

The implacable conceit behind his pronouncement sent Haldann's heart pumping. His eyes scoured the pages top to bottom and up again, pages he'd last seen as an acolyte of thirteen. He was sure what he wanted was on the right-hand page, about a third of the way down. He was right. Strange, the operations of the memory. He couldn't recall a thing that had happened yesterday. 'Here we are, o mighty Analytic,' he said, tapping with the pincers the page on which his response was written as if to prove its strength. ' "Anything which lacks a body does not exist",' he quoted freely, displaying his power of instant translation from the Latin, ' "therefore everything which exists has a body of its own." It follows that the existent body of Christ was incarnated in the womb of Mary, and that she is the Mother of God. Dispute that!' He wagged a finger aggressively at Otley to reinforce his point. Sadly the finger wobbled about, which hadn't been the intention at all.

Otley puffed out his cheeks. 'The dogmatic doctrines of a niggardly old abstinent with nothing more to occupy himself than mealy-mouthed abstracts.'

Haldann flushed. 'Never in this world! How dare you insult me!'

'Oh, pay heed.' Otley gestured to the open volume. 'I mean Tertullian.' He smirked. 'Although it is not an inaccurate description of yourself.'

Haldann put his hands on his hips and let out a peal of mocking laughter. He knew how this particular affectation drove Otley wild with anger. 'Ah, another similarity between you and the lazy-minded schismatic Nestorius! You can show not one quotable aphorism between you.'

Otley made a big show of turning back to the work table. 'On, on, on you drone, Haldann. I wonder if you realize how ineffably otiose you and your arguments are.'

Haldann threw up his hands. 'Ah,' he cried, 'how entirely like *you*, Otley, to turn away with the airs of a grandee when you know yourself to be defeated. But I won't rise to your pettiness, oh no.' His opponent turned through a copy of the Vulgate and compared it to his most recent scribblings. Haldann fumed. He knew he was right; yet again he had been made to feel he was wrong. 'Well, I shall follow your lead and return to the job in hand,' he said sniffily, moving to Otley's side, 'knowing myself to have been correct, and taking quiet satisfaction.' He took a few deep breaths to calm himself down, and reached for his quill and notepaper.

There were a few moments of silence, which Haldann used to think up ways to start another argument.

Then there was a knock at the door. Haldann did not look up. He cast a surreptitious sideways glance and saw that neither had his companion. There was another knock.

'Shouldn't you answer that?' Otley said.

'You're nearer the door.'

'But you are not halfway through a sentence.' Otley scratched the nib of his quill noisily to reinforce his point.

Haldann sighed. 'Well, if needs must.' He put his notes down and walked to the door, mouthing 'schismatic' silently over Otley's shoulder and poking his tongue out.

He flung open the door with a haughty 'Yes?', expecting to be faced by some minor official with a trifling request. He liked to appear daunting to menials. He was confronted instead by two unfamiliar figures. The first was a fellow in his sixties, with a spritely quality not wholly concealed by his grave expression and the hands knitted in a prelate-like way before his cloak. There was an intelligence in his deep brown eyes, but it was of the active, experienced kind, undulled by the wearisome formulae and repetitions of academia's groves. He looked the outdoor type, self-educated, and he wore his silver hair conspicuously long. Haldann immediately felt rather envious of the man and wondered if he had been so straight-backed at that age. The second figure was a slender fair-haired boy in a jerkin and one of those ridiculous felt hats favoured by the young. As Haldann got older he found it harder and harder to discriminate individual characteristics from the great mass of youthful people, and barely took the trouble to examine the smooth faces of messenger boys or guards. He turned his attention back to the man. 'Yes, what do you want?'

The man offered a personable smile. 'Oh dear, there *has* been a grave breakdown of communication,' he told his boy. To Haldann he said, 'A courier was sent on three days since to notify you of my visit. He has turned out to be quite unreliable, and no doubt has squandered the ten portuguese I handed him on sweetmeats and strumpets, leaving me to announce my own coming.'

'Indeed?' Haldann peered at him, unsure if he was somebody important or not. 'And may I know the details of this coming? Your name and business?' He added quickly, 'Our work here is vital and requires intense labour of the mind. Any distraction or disturbance is as anathema to us.'

The stranger nodded. 'Quite. It is definitely not my intent to disrupt your labours merely to inspect your progress and take the good news back to my superiors.'

Haldann's heart sank. 'Oh, another priest.' He felt justified in taking a grander tone. 'Priests, priests, priests, this city is black with them. We are plagued with advisers and set upon by observers, so much that we are too often diverted and delayed from our *principia*.' He pulled himself upright. 'Let it be known that we have all books in hand, that progress is good, and that such visits as yours act only to cramp our patience and put off the day when the printers can make up their plates. Good day to you.' With a curt nod he made to close the door.

The stranger said patiently, 'You misunderstand, sir. I am a Doctor of Divinity, from York Minster, sent by the Bishop himself. My intention is to consult the King's wonderful library, and to converse with you on matters of theological import regarding the translation.'

At the word 'Bishop' Haldann had perked up and pulled the door open. It wouldn't do to alienate the Church's higher echelons, no matter how many infernal envoys they dispatched. This one was the third in as many months. Everybody wanted a hand in or a dedication or a mention in the acknowledgements. 'Doctor of Divinity, you say?' he said pleasantly. 'From York?' He regarded the boy. 'And this?'

'My ward, Victor,' said the Doctor with a casual motion of the hand. 'A most devoted acolyte.' He gestured over Haldann's shoulder. 'I would be honoured to step in and look through the products of your exertion. "By their fruits ye shall know them", and all that.'

Haldann shuffled. If they'd had warning they could have tidied the place up a bit. As it was, there were volumes of philosophy scattered all around. He stepped back and waved the Doctor through. 'As you wish.'

Otley looked up as they entered and nodded. 'Good day, Doctor. You studied at York Minster, you say?'

'That is correct.' He peered at Otley. 'Forgive me, have we met?'

They shook hands. 'I think not. I am Doctor Roger Otley, this is Doctor Henry Haldann.' Haldann flinched at Otley's superciliousness in introducing himself first, and cursed him inwardly for appearing so smooth and unflustered.

'Doctors three, eh?' said the newcomer. He walked over quickly to the nearest open book on the stand, the Tertullian, and nodded. 'Hmm, yes, interesting stuff.'

'But hardly relevant, you would agree,' said Otley. 'During a moment away from our work – an occasional short divergence, we find, helps clear cobwebs and stills the soul – Haldann and I were discussing the question of the triple hypostasis.'

'Ah, yes, that old chestnut,' the Doctor said cheerily. For a moment it appeared he was about to say something. There was an uncomfortable silence.

Haldann decided to break it. It was time they had a third opinion to prove him right. 'Where do you stand, Doctor, on the material nature of the body of the Christ? Can the Virgin claim the title Mother of God?'

'Or is such an insistence an exemplar of quibbling casuistry?' Otley added.

The Doctor rubbed the fingers of one hand together in apparent concentration. 'I think,' he said at last, wording his reply carefully as he looked from one to the other, 'there are convincing arguments to be aired by both sides.'

If there was anything Haldann and Otley could agree upon it was a hatred of equivocation. Haldann was first to speak. 'We are talking on a topic clear as glass, and one in which there can hardly be shades of meaning. Either the Redeemer had a body which belonged to Him or He was entirely spirit in human form and did not.'

'It behoves us to agree to differ in such cases. And really it is not my duty to discuss these points.' Quickly the Doctor moved back to the central table. 'Now, this is what I really came for.' He cast his eyes over the translations. 'May I?'

Haldann waved a hand. 'By all means.' As he took his seat at the table he whispered to Otley, 'I never knew a Fellow at any college that could resist a tussle over the hypostasis.'

Otley whispered back, 'Prevarication, the curse of the modern age. The triumph of evangelical passions over rational analyses. All this... *praying*. See where it ends.' He nodded to the Doctor, who was poring over the pages produced lately, nodding, and pointing out passages to his ward. 'Such enthusiasm is unseemly. Let this Doctor go by, I say.'

'But for today, at least, we are lumbered with him,' Haldann said bitterly. He'd been looking forward to a pleasant afternoon of disputes, and now he was to have to make at least a show of working. Most unsettling. He sat down at his desk, dipped his quill into his inkpot, and reached for some scrolls.

It was raining when Ian returned to Lark Street. A wet wind blew dirty droplets in his face. The changing weather made no discernible alteration in the Londoners, except that they turned up the wide brims of their hats. Illogically, and in spite of the agonies of heart and mind that were churning his insides, Ian found himself wishing for an umbrella, and wondering at the reaction if he were suddenly to produce one. Going into the past was similar to being caught in a power cut; one was always reaching for a light-switch or some other invention that wasn't there.

He stopped outside Mother Bunch's tavern and watched the rain skittering down the slanted roof. He pushed the wooden door open with the flat of one hand and passed through the large vestibule area, where men hooked up their hats and coats, and into the tavern. His eyes turned automatically to the table where he and Barbara had sat. It was now occupied by a small band of men who were laughing and playing cards, and who were not at all disturbed by his entrance. The tavern had regained its rowdiness. It was as if nothing had happened. Ian saw that many of the men wore shields and swords at their waist, and concluded that Barbara's kidnap was not, in these parts, such an extraordinary event. He forced down a reflex impulse to call for police help, and shouldered his way through the crowd to the bar.

Mother Bunch was at work. She filled three mugs in quick succession from the barrel, each crowned with a frothing head, and slammed them down on the bar, which was already sopping with overflowed beer. Her customer dropped coinage into her hand, which she dropped into a pouch in her apron, and then she was off up the bar again, slapping one of her serving girls on the bottom as she passed. 'Landlady!' Ian called. She did not react.

One of the men at Ian's side jabbed him with a bony elbow. 'Wait your turn, sirrah!'

Ian took one of the large gold coins from his drawstring purse and held it over the heads of the other drinkers. 'Landlady!' he said again, forthrightly. Experience gained on his travels told him that only two things were universally respected: money and superior status. He had one, and it would be easy enough to fake the other. The Doctor did it all the time. He reached forward and chinked the coin on the bartop loudly. 'Landlady!' This time there was an immediate effect. Those around him stepped away, and Mother Bunch caught his eye and moved back along the bar. Her face remained tight and red but there was a gleam of suspicion in her tiny black eyes.

She stopped before him. 'And why have you turned about?' she asked. She rested her elbows on the bar and brought her hideous face on a level with him. This was the closest Ian had got to her and he had to fight down his reaction to the stench of the woman. She smelt of rotten potatoes and offal and the dregs of beer bottles. Unsurprising, as these were her business. 'Where's your lady?'

'They took her along with them,' he replied. He played with the coin meaningfully. 'Those Catholics. I need information if I'm to get her back, and I'm prepared to pay.'

Mother Bunch knotted her eyebrows. 'What sort of information?'

Ian thought a moment. 'Well, if they drink here regularly, you must know their names or where they reside?'

'It doesn't do me well to talk freely of my customers,' she replied. 'What I might hear or what I might not is no business of anyone else's. Catholic, Protestant, their money's the same when it reaches my purse. I'm here to cook brewis and serve ale.' She made to move away.

Ian grabbed her arm. 'It's important.' She flinched, and for a moment Ian feared she was going to strike him. 'I have to find my wife. You saw those men, they were –' he struggled to find a correct-sounding word '– villains, cut-throats. She is in danger.'

'Then you go and find the city guard or a watchman,' she spat. 'I'll tell you nothing.'

That's just what I mustn't do, thought Ian. The more people who got involved, the more difficult questions would be asked. 'I can't do that,' he said.

'Ay, much! Then I'll have none of you. I cannot be bought, for what I'd win from you I'd lose in custom.' She pointed to her ears. 'These are clammed up and will stay so, and such is the fame of my house.' She strutted away and there was a loud cheer and sporadic applause for her stance from the men around Ian.

He pulled himself back through the drinkers, conscious of the suspicion and aggression in their eyes. If he'd been able to get Mother Bunch alone she wouldn't have been so unforthcoming, he felt certain. By blundering in and fluffing his chance he'd closed a vital link to Barbara's safe return. He walked briskly to the door, holding himself up proudly in an attempt to deter any would-be attackers.

There was a soft tap on his shoulder. He turned and saw, standing in one of the dark and partitioned alcoves, the serving girl Sybil. She put a finger to her lips and beckoned him over. He looked cautiously around. The inn seemed to have returned to normal and attention had slipped from him, so he slid quickly into the alcove and on to one of the stools. This time he was glad of the corner's darkness. 'Yes, what do you want?'

'Oh, good master,' Sybil whispered. She sat down next to him and patted him on the shoulder, while her other hand fiddled with the lace frills of her dress. 'I saw the abduction with my own eyes, and terrible it was. But did the rascals not set her free when they were away into the street? That is the usual way with these hostage-takings that complete many a fight in this wicked town.'

'No,' said Ian. 'They carried her away. I couldn't find them.'

Sybil shivered. Her words came gushing out, obscuring their sense. 'Oh, it is too awful, by my troth. And Mother Bunch will not say what she might know of 'em? It is always this way with her. I sometimes think if I was cut down here before her very eyes she would plead ignorance before a magistrate. The lady has no guiding morals. Oh, I should upbraid myself, for she is no lady, she chides and chaffs at me like I was a slave.'

Ian raised a hand. 'Please. I have to hurry. Can you tell me anything?' He discounted an impulse to reach for his purse. The people here had a kind of pride, and it was best not offended.

'Marry gup,' said Sybil. Ian had no idea what that meant, but it was said with the same inflection as a modern-day 'well'. 'I have been wracking at my brains.

Sure, I have seen those men drinking here before, and that Robert in all his papish finery and careless of who he offends with his bombast. The other man, much the quieter, I have heard him call John or Johnson.'

Ian leant forward urgently. 'But do you know where they live, or what their business might be?'

Sybil considered a moment, her freckled face screwed up tight in concentration. 'Not in the slightest.' Her face fell. 'Just that they are varmints, and loud-talking ones. Oh, I hope your wife has not come to harm!'

'Listen, Sybil. There's something else I need your help with. Just before you arrived this morning, there was another man in here with us.'

Sybil looked puzzled, then her face cleared. 'Ah, you mean the lusty Firking. He is harmless enough for all his tease and talk.'

'No, besides him and his mate.' Ian pointed. 'He was sitting there, dressed in a black cloak, with the hood thrown forward to hide his face. I think he might have had something to do with the Catholics.'

Sybil clicked her fingers. 'Ah, and does he walk very strange?'

'That's him,' said Ian. 'You know him?'

'By sight only. He is in here sometimes, always by himself, and sitting in shadows. But I have heard him speak, and I'd say he was foreign. I can almost hear the voice.' She frowned. 'This near to the ports we are often host to butter-box Danes; but let that pass, he is not one of them.'

Ian remembered the letter. 'Could he be French?'

'Oh no, sir. We have entertained many a Frenchman here. Although he only spoke to ask for ale, and very quietly, I have always had him down as a Spaniard.' She shrugged. 'But that is all. Why did you think him connected with the others?'

Ian thought it wisest not to mention the letter. 'Just a suspicion.'

They were interrupted by a bawdy laugh. Ian looked up to see Firking, whose arm was now wrapped around Hodge's neck. He was using his friend's thin frame as a leaning-post. 'How now, Sybil, at your work already, and this good man has only just lost his wife!'

'You are a proper saucebox,' Sybil scolded him. She gestured to Ian. 'Can't you see he is sore at the loss? Those Catholic dogs have carried her away.'

Firking's expression changed instantly and he tried to pull himself upright. 'They have not set her free?' Ian shook his head bitterly. 'A plague on them,' spat Firking. 'What say,' he addressed Hodge, 'we whistle up all the journeymen of the gentle craft and have at them to defend the lady Barbara's honour?'

'No, thanks all the same,' Ian said hastily. He stood up. 'I think I'd better be on my way.' He smiled at Sybil. 'Thank you.'

'You're going to rouse the militia?' she asked excitedly.

Ian decided to be honest. 'I don't think so. I have a friend I must call on, and he'll know what's to be done.'

She reached out and squeezed his arm. 'Well, take care, you and your friend. Men like Robert and Johnson are dangerous.' There was a thoughtful look in her eyes, for which Ian felt suddenly grateful. 'Now,' she said, picking up the mugs from the table, 'I must set to work or face more wrath from the Mother.' She smirked at Firking. 'I cannot make my holidays stretch like yours, for she watches over me constantly. I thank heaven that we shut up in the afternoon, or my legs would be worn to stumps.'

'Yes, and we've tarried here long,' said Hodge. 'Our master will shout furious at our return, blast him.' He secured his grip on Firking and they lurched away.

Ian gave a final nod of thanks to Sybil and made for the door. The shoemakers were waiting on the threshold. 'Listen,' said Firking, slapping a hand on his shoulder. 'And this is not the wagging tongue of a drunk, this is a pledge made in the name of St Hugh. I like you, sirrah, and feel for you in this hour, and if you have needs of any material kind, present yourself at the door of the last in Tower Street. You'll be well greeted by as merry a company as you can find.' He belched.

'I'll bear that in mind.' Ian waved farewell to Hodge, who was smiling at him with an insipid expression on his thin face, and left the inn.

Vicki sat on one of the library's uncomfortable wooden benches and rubbed at her cramped legs. While the Doctor hummed and muttered over the manuscripts, she had been detailed to put the books back in order on the shelves. Initially the task was bearable, but by her fourth journey from stands to annex and up the steps her arms were beginning to ache from hefting and hoisting, and she started to feel as if she was being punished by the translators, and by the Doctor as well, simply for being young. Over her shoulder she could see the Doctor peering at more pages of manuscript through his spectacles and muttering to himself. She suppressed a strong urge to walk over and kick him in the shin. Instead she rolled her shoulderblades back and forth to ease the muscular tension. Facing her was one of the window-slits, and at this angle she saw the sky, which was already beginning to darken and fill with clouds, although it was only about half-past three. It was time they returned to the Ship.

There was another dispute brewing between the old men. Otley was holding a freshly inked page in his hand and shaking his head. 'Oh goodness, no. What does this mean?' He tsked. 'Such an elementary error.'

Haldann made a show of ignoring him. The Doctor, acting out of politeness, asked, 'What do you have there?'

Otley shook his head more forcefully. 'Oh dear, this will have to be completely rewritten.'

Haldann looked up at last. 'That's the page of Jeremiah I did last week, is it not? There is nothing wrong in that. And I do wish you wouldn't check my work. I don't go around checking yours.'

'Nothing wrong, he says. It is as well that I check.' Otley handed the page to the Doctor. 'Read, Doctor.'

The Doctor scanned the page quickly. 'Well, really, I can't see anything especially glaring...' His attempt to remain even-handed amused Vicki. It was fun to see him being bullied for a change.

Otley snatched the sheet back and ran his finger along the lines of text. 'And what of this, in chapter eight verse twenty-two? "Is there no treacle in Gilead?" '

Haldann blinked. 'It is the correct word, translated from the original tongue. I consulted all dictionaries rigorously, as always.'

'It is balm, not treacle!' Otley thundered. ' "Is there no balm in Gilead?" '

'Oh yes,' said Haldann. His face brightened, he looked a little less certain of himself, and Vicki felt just a smidgen's sympathy. 'I must have been distracted.' He nodded. 'Yes, it must have been when that Chamberlain popped round . . .'

'The Chamberlain hasn't been in for months,' snapped Otley. He took his own quill pen and scribbled out the mistake. 'It is your aged mind wandering.'

Haldann flushed and pulled himself as upright as was possible. His mouth opened and closed soundlessly for a few moments.

Characteristically, it was the Doctor who intervened, raising his hands and adopting his most kindly expression. 'Gentlemen, gentlemen, please,' he said. 'There is hardly need for opprobrium over this treacle – er, trifle. I am very impressed with your progress. Why, if you've reached Jeremiah, there is much cause to rejoice. Only another few books to go before the New Testament, and from there it'll be plain sailing. Good news for me to take to the Bishop, eh?'

His words dispersed the tension between Haldann and Otley, and yet strangely they seemed to bring into being another kind of anxiety. The old men exchanged a meaningful glance and then looked away. Then Haldann spoke. 'Ah. We'd rather you didn't tell the Bishop that, actually, Doctor.'

The Doctor frowned. 'Aren't you proud?'

'Yes, yes,' Haldann burbled. 'It's just that . . . well, our process of translation has not been entirely . . .' He waved a hand, searching for the right words. 'Entirely . . .'

'What he means to say,' said Otley, 'is that we aren't doing it strictly in order.'

Vicki couldn't keep quiet any longer. 'You mean you're skipping bits?'

Such was the tone of injured innocence in her voice that the old men could not bring themselves to order silence. 'I suppose,' said Haldann, 'you could phrase it so.'

The Doctor was turning over the pages collected in a volume at the end of the table. 'I see, your work so far.' He picked a few pages at random and gave one of his chirpy high-pitched chuckles. 'The burning bush, the writing on the wall, Sodom and Gomorrah. All the more colourful sections.'

Haldann sniffed. 'Well, would you like to be stuck on the begats for week after week?'

'You'll have to do it eventually,' said Vicki.

Otley looked down rather sadly. 'Eventually is a word that has no real meaning when you reach our time of life.'

'You're going to die and then leave some other poor soul to finish off the boring sections?'

Otley frowned at her. 'Only the young have the naïvety to sound so righteous.'

Haldann rolled his eyes heavenward. 'I don't know about that.'

Their debate was interrupted by three raps, sharp and insistent, on the library's door. Instantly, as if following a long-established ritual, the translators shuffled back to their table and put their heads down. There were another three raps.

'Pardon me,' said the Doctor, 'but there appears to be someone at the door.'

Haldann kept his eyes on the page before him. 'Another interruption, at a most crucial stage. No wonder mistakes — very slight mistakes — are made.'

'You had better answer it,' Otley said smoothly.

'I answered it last time.'

'You're nearer the door.'

'You were nearer the door last time, and I still had to open it.'

'Yes, but I was working, wasn't I?'

'As I am working now!' Haldann looked fit to explode.

Vicki had had enough. 'Oh, for heaven's sake,' she said. Nimbly she darted around the table and pulled the door open.

The man on the threshold was of such a singular and striking appearance that she stepped back inadvertently. He was in his fifties, she guessed, only a fraction taller than herself, and he wore a neatly tailored black velvet garment, with a modestly sized ruff of white lace about the neck. He looked undernourished. There were traces of grey in his hair, which was pushed back over a high forehead. Like nearly every man she had seen today he had a beard, in his case a pointed goatee. His eyes were heavy-lidded and burnt with fierce intelligence and a kind of restrained anger. That was why she had flinched; his expression was so stormy she'd half expected him to strike her. His bearing suggested formidable character.

Immediately Haldann and Otley assumed obsequious faces, put down their pens as quickly as they had picked them up and bowed to the newcomer. The Doctor followed their example. Instinctively Vicki curtsied. She realized her mistake halfway through the action and converted it into an odd, knees-bent bow.

'Haldann, Otley,' the man grunted. His voice fit his face. It was gravelly and masculine, and cut through the time-locked atmosphere of the library like a rapier. Here, thought Vicki, was a representative of the physical side of human endeavour.

'Cecil,' the two old men intoned as one, and raised their heads.

'And you,' said the newcomer, 'will be the Doctor of Divinity?'

The Doctor nodded graciously. 'Yes, sir. This young fellow is my ward, Victor.' Vicki inclined her head once more, but decided not to smile. The sweep of the newcomer's eyes over her was oppressive.

'So I have heard,' he said. 'From the guards at the gate. Rooms are being prepared for you in the Stone Gallery.' Without pausing or altering his tone he put out a hand and said, 'Your paper of authorization.'

Vicki looked at the Doctor and prayed he could come up with a ready, and convincing, solution. This Cecil had such force of personality she couldn't see him falling for one of the Doctor's bluffs, which relied for their effect on the victim's fear of authority.

The Doctor's hands were plucking uneasily at his cloak. 'I have no such paper.'

'What?' Cecil said quietly and dangerously. 'You do not travel with the Bishop's sanction?'

The Doctor's nostrils flared. Vicki could almost see the lightbulb blinking on above his head. 'What I mean to say is that the paper was taken from me on my journey by a band of miscreants. They assaulted me and made off with it. After making sure that I was unharmed, Victor pursued them and found it thrown into a stream, in tatters.' To add veracity to the tale Vicki nodded. 'They also took my purse and other effects.'

'And this assault occurred . . . ?' demanded Cecil.

The Doctor floundered for a moment. 'Near Coventry, sir. We made the rest of the journey in the pilgrim's tradition, through the generosity of almshouses and monasteries.'

'I see.' His eyes flicked between Vicki and the Doctor. 'You have no letter of authorization, and we have had no word of your arrival.'

The Doctor threw up his hands. 'Another mishap. I fear the man was a drunkard, and squandered his wages and sold on his horse. It is a disgrace.'

'What is his name?'

Again the Doctor looked nonplussed. 'Sorry?'

'His name. You must know it.'

'Lacy,' the Doctor said.

There was a long pause. Vicki held her breath. Cecil's expression was unchanging as he regarded them. Then he sprang to life. 'Very well,' he said. 'Your rooms are now prepared, and I have assigned you a servant each. I request only one thing from you.' His tone made it clear this was more in the way of being a demand. 'This is the most important time in the political calendar. There is much business of state to attend to. Your arrival has already caused me to be distracted from this. In your stay here I want there to be no more such incidents.'

The Doctor nodded. 'I assure you we will be no further trouble.'

Cecil returned the nod and made to leave. 'You will dine with us tonight.'

Vicki's spirits sank. 'But we can't possibly –'

He fixed her with a terrible stare that silenced her straight away. If this was how boys were treated in this age, she thought, what must life for a girl be like?

'What Victor means to say,' said the Doctor, 'is that we are too humble to dine at the King's table.' He waved the objection aside. 'Of course he is quite wrong. As His Majesty's guests we will be honoured.'

'As His Majesty's guests,' said Cecil emphatically, 'you are obliged.' He swept out. The door slammed shut behind him like an exclamation mark.

Vicki breathed a sigh of relief. 'That was a close one,' she whispered. 'Do you think he believed you?'

The Doctor tapped his chin with a finger. 'If he hadn't we'd have been thrown on to the street by now.'

'Which wouldn't be such a bad thing. It's getting dark outside.'

'So it is.'

'We can't abandon Ian and Barbara,' Vicki hissed.

'It's hardly that,' said the Doctor. 'Besides, now we've been spotted we can't leave right away. It would draw all kinds of suspicion. No, I'm afraid we must remain for the time being.' Catching Vicki's accusing eye he added, 'Chesterfield and Barbara can look after themselves, they're very resourceful.'

'The TARDIS is locked up,' said Vicki.

'They have money, they'll find rooms somewhere,' he said briskly. 'That reminds me, we must examine these quarters that have been prepared for us.' He turned to the door. 'The Stone Gallery, that will be the large building that overlooks the Privy Garden . . .'

Vicki laid a hand on his arm. 'You promised them.'

He shook her off. 'I did no such thing. They promised me, if you recall.' He turned to the two old men and raised his voice. 'Thank you once more, gentlemen, for your hospitality. We will retire now.'

Otley looked up briefly. 'We will meet again tonight.'

'You're attending the banquet as well?'

'Of course,' said Haldann. He frowned. 'You will be back in tomorrow, though, won't you? That boy of yours is very helpful.'

Vicki fumed. 'You don't have to talk about me as if I wasn't here, you know.'

Haldann tsked. 'The manners of the modern young.' He shook his head and made a show of returning to his work.

The Doctor held the door open for Vicki. 'Now, come along.'

'It's not fair on Ian and Barbara,' she protested again. 'What is anything's happened to them?'

'Come along,' the Doctor repeated, as if she hadn't spoken at all.

Awareness returned to Barbara in the shape of a black cloud seen distantly. It started to throb in time with her heartbeat as it drew closer. Eventually it moved inside her and became a throbbing bruise above her left eye. An inner voice warned her not to move her head or open her eyes.

She was lying on her side, her knees drawn up in the foetal position. Unbidden, the events of her capture flashed up in her mind. She saw the face of the Yorkshireman, the concern on Ian's face, the sudden pain on her brow. It felt like waking from a nightmare. Except that the images were genuine recollections. She shuddered.

Gently, without thinking, she collated the information her senses provided. The floor of the place was uneven, with a gravelly texture. A draught was biting at the exposed skin of her hands and face, and there were muffled voices coming from a nearby room. She wiggled fingers and toes without difficulty. Then she steeled herself and prepared to raise a hand to her wound. She felt drained of energy, as if her living skin had been stretched over a lifeless skeleton. The simple action was going to take tremendous effort. She moved her hand, and was conscious immediately of restraint. A second attempt confirmed her fears. She had been bound with a thick coil of rope. The realization brought forth a wave of panic, and before she could stop herself she had opened her eyes and rolled over.

The pain was immediate and horrible, as if a wire had been inserted in the top of her head. She let out a stifled cry and screwed her eyes shut tight again. In the second they were open, she'd seen nothing in the darkness but a low ceiling, only three or four feet above her, with a sole wooden beam. There had also been a powerful sensation of being underground.

She choked back a scream and forced herself to remain calm. The aftershock of the movement reverberated around her skull, and she countered it by taking long deep breaths. She thought of Ian. Faith in him was the only thing that had sustained her through previous crises.

And just as this strategy appeared to be taking some effect, as her stomach unknotted and the pain in her head decreased to its previous insistent throb, she heard two things that reversed its advances.

At her side there was an insistent rustling sound, followed in quick succession by the pattering and scampering of many pairs of tiny rodent feet, overlaid by an insistent squeaking. At the same moment there came voices from nearby. She struggled to make sense of the words, to link the audible syllables. One of the voices, the louder, she recognized as belonging to the man in red from the inn. It followed that the other was his quieter companion, the Yorkshireman.

'I tell you,' said the first voice, 'there is no space left for debate.' Barbara detected signs of good breeding in the man's well-modulated, almost accentless vowels. 'It is a regrettable decision but I have made it. We cannot keep her here, we cannot set her loose!'

'Then what can we do?' asked the Yorkshireman.

There was a pause. Then the first man said, 'You know the answer.'

The sumptuousness of her surroundings was almost enough to dispel Vicki's troubled thoughts. Her room was adjacent to the Doctor's in the palace's guest quarters on the second level. It contained one brocaded chair, a large teak dresser, a mirror and a portrait hung in a golden frame. The fastidiousness of these arrangements put her in mind of a hotel. The elaborate gilt carvings that adorned each corner, the gaunt face of the portrait's subject, the coldness that even the crackling logs in the hearth could not overcome; Vicki felt as if she might as well try to be comfortable in the library. Still, the huge comfy bed with its massive pillows and quilted counterpane was a relief after the aches of the day. She took her sandals off and flexed her feet, then sank back with a half smile on her face. Was the Doctor right? Ian and Barbara could look after themselves, and they had the advantage of being without the Doctor and his snooping nose. She banished the doubts and concentrated on enjoying herself. She was certainly looking forward to the banquet. She pictured venison, roasted pig, syllabubs . . .

Without even intending to, she was sleeping. The flat wooden bed was a change from the moulded couch in the room she shared with Barbara aboard the TARDIS, and as a result the quality of her sleep was altered. She drifted dreamlessly, feeling that the bed was pulling her down, embracing her in its folds, soothing her aching arms and lifting her worries from her shoulders.

A shadow fell across her sleeping form, its outline defined in the light thrown from the torch bracketed on the facing wall.

Cecil narrowed his eyes. The boy looked to be between thirteen and fifteen, yet there was not a trace of beard on his skin. He looked closer to confirm his suspicions. This boy's hips were widening, and there was a tender delicacy to his upturned nose and pert lips.

Taking care not to wake his guest, Cecil turned and stalked out, his face darkening, his mind racing. The arrival of this bizarre couple, only three days before the conclusion of the operation, could not be coincidence.

The Doctor reclined in a chair in his own room, his fingers curled around a wineglass. Idly he swirled the liquid around at the bottom, congratulating himself. This excursion was turning out quite satisfactorily, particularly without those schoolteacher people to distract him.

There was a timid knock at the door. The Doctor pursed his lips. 'Hmm. Not Vicki, she'd simply barge right in. And not that Cecil, either. Some minor official, then.' He raised his voice. 'Come in, come in.'

A short rotund fellow in a trailing blue gown admitted himself. He greeted the Doctor with a nod and a weak smile. As an experiment, the Doctor did not rise. The entrant did not take umbrage at this. He said nervously, 'Good evening, Doctor. I trust you are settled here?'

'It is adequate,' the Doctor replied. He took a further sip of the wine. 'This is a cheeky little malmsey. The King has a magnificent cellar.' There was a silence in which both men refused to catch the other's eye. The Doctor found that the man's nervousness was unsettling him. 'Well,' he said at length, 'be about your business then.'

The short man spluttered. 'I am the Lord Chamberlain.'

The Doctor nearly shot out of his chair. 'Why didn't you say so? Do forgive me.' He set the glass down and bowed with all the reverence he could muster.

The Chamberlain twisted his fingers. 'Sir Robert Cecil has entrusted me with your comfort, Doctor. If I seem shaky, it's just that your arrival has thrown me out a bit. I had the table for tonight's banquet all sorted, and now with two more mouths to feed, and two more spaces to be found . . .' He completed the sentence with a vague hand gesture. The Doctor found his constant gesticulations irritating, and quelled a desire to reach out and slap him. 'I came in to see if you minded sitting with the translators. They're to the left of the King at the main table. I've had to shift a couple of ladies to the vestibule, but they shouldn't mind. And the King won't, I'm sure. His interests in Divinity and Theology are much greater than his interest in female company.'

'Certainly, these arrangements suit me,' said the Doctor. 'The King's table, yes.' He considered. 'Tell me, will Salisbury be joining us?'

The Chamberlain nodded. 'Cecil? Oh yes.' He lowered his voice. 'Although, I ought to warn you, I suppose . . .' He trailed off.

'Warn me?'

The Chamberlain hesitated. 'This is a most delicate moment, and voices have been raised.'

'I see.' The Doctor raised an eyebrow. 'Between the King and Cecil?'

'I shouldn't really discuss it.' The Chamberlain leant closer. 'Between you and me and the gatepost, there may be angry scenes, as there were last night. Do not be surprised. It is most unfortunate.' He started to withdraw with a bustling movement and an apologetic expression. As he neared the door he backed straight into Vicki, who was entering with a fresh twinkle in her eye. 'Oh, I'm so sorry,' he muttered, and blundered out.

Vicki watched him go with amusement. 'Who's that?'

The Doctor laughed. 'The Lord Chamberlain himself, would you believe. The poor fellow has been completely cowed.'

'Well, if that bloke in black's his boss, I'm not surprised.' Vicki shuddered. 'He was a right creep.'

The Doctor raised an admonishing finger. 'That creep is none other than Sir Robert Cecil.'

Vicki pulled an apologetic face. 'Never heard of him.'

'You should have. Cecil was – is – one of the greatest statesmen this country has ever produced. A diplomat of unparalleled ability, like his father. He served in

85

Elizabeth's court, and was responsible for ensuring the smooth succession of James to the throne. It was a time of potential turmoil. But with James's intelligence and Cecil's wits they succeeded in bringing order and maintaining peace.' He shrugged. 'For most of the time, anyway.'

Vicki frowned. 'Hang on. One thing I do remember about James. He was a fool, wasn't he? They called him the wisest fool in Christendom, full of book learning but impractical.'

' "They" being those who came after him, with all the righteous certainty of hindsight. No, my child, this king was far from foolish, as you will shortly see.' He opened the door and they passed into the corridor that led to the palace's central staircase. 'That is the advantage afforded us by our travels, my dear. An opportunity to make up our own minds.'

With a heartfelt sigh James slammed the wooden door of the yard behind him. The noise served a triple purpose: to announce his entrance, to silence the guests, and to express his exasperation. It hardly seemed a day since the last banquet. With a jolt he remembered that it *was* only a day since the last banquet. Hadn't he been supposed to do something important today? In fact, wasn't this banquet connected with that important thing? It must have slipped his mind. Couldn't be so important, then.

He cast his mind back over his day. He'd woken late in the afternoon with a splitting headache. His physician came up with a fizzing tonic that had little effect, so he went to find Hay, but the lad wouldn't answer his knock. Robbed of sympathetic company, James returned to his rooms and read a few chapters of one of his own books to pass a couple of hours, all the time pretending he couldn't hear Cecil's insistent pleas for an audience. He was keeping the important thing, whatever it was, locked in a vault right at the back of his mind.

After acknowledging the salutations of his guests, James paced across the yard to take his place at the centre table.

Hay was waiting, and patted the seat of the throne in a welcoming way. The boy looked slightly queasy and pale, and his pretty green eyes were bloodshot. As James took his position he leant over and said quietly, 'Heavens, Bob, you're white as chalk. How much of that whippincrust did you put down last night? I mean, you kept popping to the privy.'

Hay grinned. 'Only half as much as you.' He patted the King on the knee. 'I bet you don't recall dancing the "shaking of the sheets".'

James gulped. 'In public? I'm not even sure I know the moves when I'm sober.'

'You were much admired.'

James searched his memory. 'Oh dear. You know, I can't even remember coming back here. Everything after about two is sort of hazy. But I can remember the music, yes. Great minstrels. And when they mixed that one in at just after one I went crazy. It makes a most welcome change, to be out of the sight of my beloved queen.' He slapped himself heartily on the thigh and flexed his arm muscles. 'I suppose I might as well write today off. I knew I couldn't get anything done, I've felt quite ill.' He poked Hay in the ribs. 'I knocked on your door this afternoon, but you would not open up.'

Hay shrugged. 'I knocked on yours this morning, and neither would you.'

'Point scored,' James said pleasantly. He turned his attention for the first time to the dishes set before him. An equitable selection. All his favourite meats present: duck, boar and rabbit, cut up in manageable chunks as befitted his delicate palate, each animal slightly undercooked so as not to trouble his delicate teeth. As a special token of London's esteem for him, a whole haggis had been laid out on a silver platter, surrounded by a ring of seven sauce boats. Quickly, so as to conceal his interest, he cast his eyes across the food on the outlying trestles. Everybody else's were smaller and more hastily prepared, which suited him well. He was constantly searching for these little reminders of his specialness. He remembered his father warning him that the first sign of serious levels of unrest in one's subjects was everybody's dinner looking the same. Poor Dad. Blown to bits at Bannockburn. 'Well,' he told Hay, 'I suppose I'd better go through the motions.'

He signalled for a serving boy to tuck a napkin into his collar, and raised his goblet. Instantly, the muttered conversation of the yard fell silent, and all eyes turned to him. 'Good gentlemen,' he said as loudly as his sore throat allowed, 'it gives us great pleasure to welcome you, our most loyal and exalted subjects, to this banquet in honour of the forthcoming...' He licked his lips and concentrated. What was the big, important tedious thing he had deliberately forgotten? 'In honour of the forthcoming...' Again he stalled. 'What is it?' he whispered to Hay urgently.

'The State Opening of Parliament,' said a loud, masculine voice from his right.

'The State Opening of Parliament,' James said hastily, with a nod to Cecil. Of course, all that fuss about his speech. It had taken him a whole afternoon to write that, an afternoon he could have spent hunting and exercising his sinews, and all Cecil could do was complain. He raised his goblet to the company again. 'So. Welcome, one and all, and let us now begin our feast.'

With relief he signalled for the plate of duck to be brought before him. He kept his eyes well away from Cecil's, which were boring into him with a drill-like intensity.

Vicki observed these proceedings with amusement. She sat at the Doctor's side, a few places to the King's left, and opposite Haldann and Otley. As the King gave the command to begin, she raised an eyebrow at the Doctor and said, 'How very unregal.' Immediately he shushed her.

'I wouldn't advise mocking the King,' he whispered. 'Your head looks very pretty on your shoulders. A basket wouldn't suit it half as well. Now then.' He reached for a plate of pheasant garnished with parsley, raised a gigantic serrated knife, and started to slice. The meat was succulent and its aroma wafted under Vicki's nose. She remembered she hadn't eaten for hours. The Doctor carved at the bird like an expert, working carefully around the bone, and he presented her with a slice of the breast with a muttered, 'Ladies first. Unofficially.'

'Thank you.' Vicki looked around. The other diners were tucking in with gusto. The custom seemed to be to hold a napkin in one hand, and alternate between meat and drink with the other. She picked up the towel folded at her place and spread it over her lap. Despite her hunger she quailed at the size of the portion. 'I'm not sure if my stomach's up to this.'

'There'll be another three courses, and to refuse any of the food would be seen as treason.'

'Oh, great. How educational.' Vicki sighed and tore off a piece of the bird with her fingers. 'I'll be too nervous to eat.' She watched the Doctor carving a slice of pheasant for himself. 'Where did you learn to do that?'

'In the kitchens of the Tetrach of Phibbli. Although the bird life on Phibbli is very different to Earth's. Their sparrows are the size of a house. Principle's the same. The trick is to strike below the wing joint.' He popped a shred in his mouth and chewed. 'Excellent, excellent.' A courtier from further down the table nodded to him and they both raised their free hands with thumb and finger pressed together in an appreciative gesture. The gesture was taken up around the table and Haldann and Otley joined in, smiling obsequiously and making appreciative noises. The King looked over and smiled.

'Crawlers,' Vicki said, although she had to admit the bird's texture was mouthwateringly tender and full of flavour. As she ate she looked closer at the King. He was a remarkable figure. He was of average height, and his body bulged around the hips and shoulders, an effect enhanced by the padded doublet and hose he wore, which were silver in colour and studded with an elaborate pattern of jewels. Above his high, upturned collar his face was whitish and his beard full. Overall, it seemed to Vicki that in spite of his dress and the grovelling that went on around him, he didn't look like an all-powerful sovereign. She might have believed him to be a kindly uncle with a streak of mischief, suddenly thrown into a position of power, if it hadn't been for the evident tension in the yard at his presence. She turned her attention to Cecil, who sat close at the King's right side. His dark eyes were level and alert, and he made the act of eating with his hands seem dignified. She recalled the Doctor's earlier portrait of the man. Here, she felt sure, was the source of true power in Britain, the fever in the political blood that had unionized two nations with a history of conflict. In his company anyone would feel jittery; she thought of the Lord Chamberlain with a smile.

'Boy,' a voice called. 'Boy!' It took Vicki a moment to realize that it was addressing her. She snapped out of her reflections and saw Haldann putting out a hand. 'Pass the sauce boat,' he said imperiously. As she complied, Vicki saw that the aged librarian had already finished his first chicken leg. Otley was chomping at a slice of duck with quiet enthusiasm.

Haldann proceeded to smother his companion's food with sauce. 'There,' he said spitefully.

Otley spluttered and looked up in outrage. 'Why have you done that?'

Haldann blinked innocently. 'Done what?'

'Drowned my meat so!'

'Oh, I didn't think you would care,' said Haldann. 'After all, the duck, lacking life, has no material existence. According to your precious Nestorius, it is not there, and you are not eating it.'

'The duck was hardly a vehicle for the holy spirit,' grumbled Otley.

'Irrelevant,' said Haldann. Otley scowled and reached past him for another dish.

Vicki sighed, and said quietly, 'Two grown men, great men, squabbling like spoilt children.'

The Doctor nodded. 'Spoilt is precisely what they are. Them and everyone else in this room, most of all the King and his friend there.'

Vicki turned for a closer look at the young man. Not long ago he must have been a ravishing beauty. Now he had an incipient beard and his cheeks and nose were dotted with premature liver spots. His manner was preening and unpleasant, and he took deliberate and evident pleasure in the King's company. 'Hmm. I don't like the look of him. What's his job, then?'

The Doctor looked uncomfortable. 'Ah, hmm. Well, I don't think he has an official position . . .'

Vicki twigged. 'But the King's married, isn't he?'

'In a level two society that can count for very little.' The Doctor seemed rather flustered and embarrassed, and quickly changed the subject. 'My point is that you shouldn't expect perfection from the privileged.' He caught the King's eye and raised his goblet with a smile that was out of place on his normally stern features. 'Do as I do, child,' he muttered to Vicki. She lifted her own goblet and smiled at the King.

'Hello, down there,' the King called.

'Hello, up there,' Vicki called back, realizing as she did that she had committed a terrible error. The yard fell suddenly silent. The Doctor took a sharp intake of breath. The King fixed Vicki with a penetrating stare, and he seemed to lose all of his silliness.

After a moment the Doctor stammered, 'Ah, Your Majesty, I – I must apologize for my ward, he is – er, unused to your exalted, er . . .'

The King waved a forgiving hand. 'Not at all, not at all.' He peered at the Doctor, then turned his gaze again on Vicki. His eyes travelled up and down the length of her body. She had an uncomfortable feeling that he was mentally undressing her. 'You would be the Doctor of Divinity, out of York,' he said at length.

'Er, yes, Your Majesty,' said the Doctor. 'This is my ward, Victor.'

'A comely lad,' the King said, stretching out each syllable suggestively. 'Fair of hair and with such splendidly plump and rosy cheeks. A model of health, and with a lively wit to him. "Hello up there," indeed.' The yard echoed the King's appreciation with an automatic and artificial ripple of laughter.

Vicki felt she ought to say something. 'Thank you,' she said. The Doctor nudged her in the ribs. 'Your Majesty,' she added quickly.

The King leered. 'Victor, you would like to play me at loggets tomorrow?'

Vicki felt the situation slipping away from her. 'Well, of course, I'd love to – I mean, that would be nice, but – well, I have to help the Doctor with his researches . . .'

'Oh,' the Doctor said loudly. 'How devoted the boy is to me. Of course, yes, I shall be glad to place him in your care, Your Majesty. A few hours of playful loggets will do him a power of good after our long journey.'

'Indeed,' Hay put in. 'Loggets are good for a youthful soul.' There was another mumble of agreement. In spite of her misgivings, Vicki noticed that Cecil did not join in this time. She recalled the Chamberlain's earlier words of warning.

As if on cue, Cecil pushed his chair with a scrape and got to his feet. 'Your Majesty,' he said, with an undisguised glance of contempt at Vicki that froze her blood, 'I would respectfully remind you that your commitments to the state are such that further time away cannot be spared.' He blinked rapidly, as if forcing down a wave of anger. 'We have yet to discuss the speech.'

'You will not raise your voice in this chamber again, Cecil,' James said pettishly. 'Remember. I am King. And who appointed me so?'

Cecil cast his eyes down. 'Almighty God,' he said sullenly. Vicki remembered the Doctor's earlier words, of how Cecil had worked to bring James to the English throne, and could understand his bitterness.

'Exactly. And by divine providence, you are at my side.' He struck a fist down on the table. 'If the Lord wants me to dance, I shall dance, if He directs me to play loggets, loggets I shall play! I listen to Him before you. Do you presume to exalt yourself above the highest?'

Cecil took a rolled-up scroll from a fold in his robes. 'I

act as I have always done, out of my love for you and for this nation. The Catholics –'

'The Catholics nothing,' James said fiercely. Vicki was impressed by his sudden gravity. She cast a sideways glance at the Doctor, and found him following the exchange keenly, his eyes darting between the two men as if he were following a tennis match. 'Cecil, my tactics I have made plain, and my successes are palpable. We have peace with the Spanish, peace with the French, peace with the Dutch, and peace in the country. Let there be no return to burnings and persecutions. These bring forth only martyrs, and thus further disharmony. Moderation,' he said sagely, 'moderation is the key to good politics. You will hear that in my speech the night of the fifth, which you have in your hand, and of which not one word, you hear, Cecil, not a letter will I suffer to be altered.'

There was a long silence. The two men held each other's gaze. Finally Cecil said, 'And while you play at loggets, James, what if the papists should be plotting some disruption, at this most vital and vulnerable time of our calendar?'

James rolled his eyes. 'You are the greatest disruptor, Cecil. I'll tell you, if anyone, Catholic, Puritan, or even one of my closest advisers –' he emphasized the warning '– whoever, tries to interrupt this parliament's opening, there'll be fireworks. I would advise such a person to back down and trust in my divine right. Any other course might be regarded as blasphemy.'

Cecil nodded and sat down. The court returned to its food in embarrassed silence. There was something in the quietened atmosphere that reminded Vicki of children after a particularly stern ticking-off. She found she was missing democracy, for all its contradictions.

The Doctor was muttering something under his breath. It was an especially irritating habit. She listened closely. 'Fireworks,' he was saying, 'fireworks, indeed, if only he knew!'

'What are you mumbling about, Doctor?'

'Nothing, my child, nothing.' He looked up and she saw that his eyes were wettening with stifled laughter. His face reddened as he forced his reaction down. 'Oh, dear, yes, yes, fireworks . . .'

Vicki returned her attention to the meal, and tried to ignore a worry that nagged at her like an aching tooth. Was the Doctor still holding something back?

In her makeshift prison Barbara lost any sense of passing time. The daylight faded, and the only thing she could see, a beam in the low ceiling, faded gradually into blackness. The scurrying of the rats was insistent. Time and again she clenched her stomach and increased her fortitude, promised herself she would not become tearful or hysterical. Holding to that was made more difficult when one of the rats brushed against her side and used its forepaws to hook itself on to the fabric of her dress. Sobbing with fear, she rolled herself over and over on the hard, uneven floor, her face pressing against the filth and gravel. The violence of her action startled the rat, who must have presumed her to be dead, and it squeaked and hurried off. The feel of its four tiny feet as they padded across her front gave her shudders that took a few minutes to subside. The rat would return soon, once it had reasoned that she was helpless, and might bring its fellows. She imagined their slinky, odorous pelts slithering over her, their sharp teeth gnawing at her flesh, pictured them pouring in a wave through the cellar's crevices and descending on her.

There was no point in trying to escape. Only the hope of rescue sustained her. Ian must have found the Doctor by now. Also, she reasoned that she was too important to her captors to abandon. In a strange way, they feared her. When they returned, if they gave her the chance to speak, would her plea of innocence be accepted? The thoughts turned continuously through her mind as she lay in the darkness, her head turned to a wall.

She was unsure how many hours had passed when she heard footsteps descending a flight of stairs. Instantly she was alert. She pushed herself backwards in a wormlike motion, inching herself into position with her back vertical against the wall facing where the door had to be, in the direction of the sounds. She heard the voices of the two men, as before, but this time they were moving unmistakably towards her, descending a flight of steps, their swords jingling, the boards creaking under their heavy tread.

She swallowed and took a deep breath. Their steps came closer. Their voices sounded clearly.

The second man, the one she had heard called Johnson, was talking. 'Catesby, I say now as I said before, this woman is an innocent.'

'There are always innocents in war,' Catesby grumbled. 'When men struggle for power, losses are expected. And when needs must that power shall be taken, savageness has its useful moment. If we set her free, this house and our work will be common knowledge in every pothouse in Old Street by the night.' She heard the rattle of keys under his words; then, frighteningly close, the turning of the key in the lock. All the time, the name Catesby was battering at her brain. At the first mention of it her heart had started to pound. She sought desperately for its association, knowing she had heard the name before. Tantalizingly it remained out of reach.

Johnson spoke. 'Rob, I do not say "set her free". You must grasp that on the night of the fifth all London will see the shape of the future. Her knowledge will not make her special then. She will be one among the million. If we keep her here she'll not talk until the talk means nothing.'

The cellar door was flung open, and Barbara almost cried out at the harshness of the lantern light it admitted. After hours of deprivation the sensory input was almost overwhelming. In the same fraction of a second she saw her hideously blackened dress, the crumbling walls of the cellar, and the lantern that swung from a long pole carried by Catesby. He had thrown off his cloak, revealing the bright red garments beneath. The lamplight played about his lean aristocratic features, the long triangles of shadow under his cheekbones and the string of drool glistening in the hairs of his neat, pointed beard. There was a frightening certainty in his eyes, a crazed conviction Barbara had seen before in the faces of madmen. In contrast the outline of Johnson, who stood behind him, was made saintly. It was only now that Barbara realized how serious the knock-out blow to her head had been. Both men appeared to her as if on the other side of a frosted glass panel. She was concussed.

Catesby angled the pole downwards and the lantern slid off the end. He caught it and passed it back to Johnson. Then he advanced on Barbara, moving into the gloom with an air of repressed exultation. Johnson held the lamp higher, dazzling her for a second. It reflected off the pole in Catesby's hand as he drew it back. With a jolt of terror, she realized the pole was a sword.

Barbara threw back her head and made the only noise she could, a gagged scream. She squirmed from side to side, frantically, her terror giving her strength.

Johnson moved forward. 'Catesby, this is not right. This was never part of the plot. To kill a tied woman in the dark when she is no threat to you?' He drew his own sword and brought it down over the end of Catesby's in one fluid movement. There was a harsh percussion as steel met steel. 'Touch a hair of her head and I'll be away, and who'll set your barrels alight then?'

Catesby fixed him with a furious stare, and for a moment Barbara thought he would run Johnson through where he stood. Then, with a snarl, he pulled his sword back and sheathed it. He took a last look at Barbara. 'You have a protector, lady,' he told her, his voice contemptuous. 'A man who will gladly strike tinder under any man when he is paid, but behaves like a knight of old otherwise.' He lurched away, calling behind him, 'We will keep her here, then, tied.'

Johnson knelt down and reached for Barbara's gag. 'Don't worry,' he said, 'you need only be kept here three more days, and Rob will not trouble you again, I promise. He is full of hate, and sometimes it blinds him.' Barbara felt the gag being pulled from her mouth. She longed to sit up properly and take in deep lungfuls of air, but the pressure on her skull from the bruise was increasing and effort was impossible. 'Come Wednesday morning the whole Christian world will know what you know.'

The moment before exhaustion triumphed, Barbara's brain made the connection. Another time and place whirled into her mind's eye. Hampstead High School for girls, class 5G. The summer of 1952. Desks spaced at intervals of four feet, dust motes caught in the strips of light cast by the gymnasium's high windows. The second History O-level paper, piece of cake. There were five questions, and the rubric asked the candidate to choose two.

2. *'The Gunpowder Plot altered the relationship between Catholics and Protestants in Britain for ever.' Discuss this statement paying particular regard to a) the planning of the plot and b) the way in which it was subsequently portrayed by the Protestant hierarchy.*

Catesby, London, the winter of 1605. Johnson. The alias used by . . .

'You're Guy Fawkes,' she heard herself say just before she was consumed by blackness.

The track leading east was difficult to follow in the dark. The lights of London acted as Ian's guide only for a while. Street lighting was non-existent, and most people had sensibly retired indoors. In this age it was still possible to see the stars, and as he trudged up the road Ian stopped more than once to look up and wonder which of them he had visited.

He saw the beginnings of the rough stone wall on the other side of the road, and doubled his speed, breaking into a jog. The Doctor's claim that the stones belonged to the side of a crofter's cottage seemed to have happened a million years, rather than just a few hours, ago.

He ran on into the dark, his thoughts focused on Barbara. The Doctor had a way with people, and might be able to coax information from Mother Bunch. Barbara's kidnapper had been a very distinctive figure, easy to locate. And Barbara was still alive. He would not allow himself to think otherwise.

The fading indentation in what was left of the snow brought him up short. It was about four foot square, and the object that had made it had been positioned a short distance from the stone wall.

A familiar sinking sensation weighed down on him. He tasted the beginnings of despair. The TARDIS had gone.

'I hardly think I'm going to faint with surprise this time,' he said.

The assignation took place in the usual spot, at the usual hour. The Thursday night meeting was always followed by a report on Friday night. Cecil waited for the signal and descended, crossed the garden, pushed his way through the dry leafless branches, his feet crunching over fallen twigs, until the Spaniard's outline was picked out in the light of the moon. The tall hooded figure turned slowly at the sounds of his approach. More curious than ever, Cecil gazed into the ring of rough sackcloth that concealed the Spaniard's face, searching for the curled lip and hooked nose. But a large oak behind the Spaniard gave him a partial covering of shadow, and the crisscrossed pattern made it more difficult than before to pinpoint any distinct features in the dark maw of the covering.

They exchanged passwords. Immediately afterwards Cecil asked, 'The letter. It was passed on?'

For the first time since Cecil had made his acquaintance the Spaniard did not reply with an immediate nod. Instead he drew himself up awkwardly inside his cloak and grunted. 'There was a problem.' He spoke gutturally, each word spaced out.

A sharp fear stabbed at Cecil. He forced himself to remain calm. 'What problem?'

'Catesby was very late,' said the Spaniard. Cecil noted the precision of his speech. Although his voice was strongly accented he had no difficulty with English grammar. 'I waited for hours. Then came strangers. A man and a woman, in fine clothes. They were not in place, at the inn. The man, I thought, was one of the Catesby's associates. I am not familiar with all of their faces.'

Cecil swallowed. 'You mean to say that you – passed on the letter, to this stranger?'

The Spaniard inclined his head. 'But I was wrong. Later I saw Catesby and Fawkes enter the tavern.'

'God forbid,' Cecil whispered, his mind racing. 'I chose the code specifically for its crudeness. A stranger could unpick its meaning with ease.' He cursed. 'I have planned the operation to the minutest detail. Discovery must come at the last possible moment. If things move too quickly, if these strangers act on suspicion of the note, the plot will lose its impact. My ultimate aim will be impossible to enforce.' He looked up through the branches at the stars and contemplated the day's events. Another fear jabbed at him as his reasoning ticked over, matching fact to fact. 'Wait. These strangers. A man and a woman, you say? Describe them.'

'He is tall, young and strong. She is the same age, dark-haired and beautiful.'

Cecil nodded. 'A young man. Good. And the woman full grown?' The Spaniard assented, and Cecil let out a sigh of relief. 'That is well. There are strangers in the court today, impostors in fine clothes. I do not care for their sudden arrival. The man claims to be a Doctor of Divinity, his companion claims to be a boy. The King has been gulled, but I do not believe either story.'

The Spaniard raised one of his long-fingered hands. 'Wait. A doctor, you say? The couple at the inn spoke of a doctor, and of travelling by ship.'

There was a long silence while Cecil digested the information, broken only by the whistle of the wind and the plangent hoot of an owl. 'As I suspected,' he said when the matters were settled in his mind. 'The doctor and his ward are spies come from Holland. One of Catesby's men has opened his pocket and spoken. The Dutch have some inkling of the operation, and have sent spies here to investigate us. They mean to destroy the Crown.' He smacked his fist into his palm. 'Already they know of the rendezvous point. The entire operation is threatened.' He rubbed his bearded chin thoughtfully. 'What became of the couple at the inn?'

'I do not know,' said the Spaniard. 'But I can find them again, I am certain, and deal with them. But tonight . . .' He pointed through the trees and said slowly, 'This doctor. He and his ward now reside at the palace, you say?'

'Yes,' said Cecil. 'They arrived this afternoon, saying they were out of York.'

'But they have no papers, no status?'

Cecil turned to look more closely at the Spaniard. Instinctively the other man drew back. 'Why do you ask?'

'They will not be missed, then,' said the Spaniard. 'Except by their Dutch paymasters. What if they should . . . leave in the night?'

Cecil nodded. 'An excellent idea. You will attend to it?'

'With pleasure.' The Spaniard fumbled beneath his cloak and to Cecil's astonishment there was suddenly a gleaming dagger clutched in his hand. Carved into the hilt was a silver ornamentation that the moonlight lent a horrid delicacy: a rectangle. 'Holland shall lose her emissaries,' the Spaniard said, enthusiasm colouring his normally flat delivery. 'I shall slit their throats from right to left as they sleep.'

Part Two

Holes in the Plot

4

Strangers in the Night

Vicki was trying to convince herself that by the standards of the day her room, to which she had retired, was luxurious and that she had no right to complain, when a fierce moaning wind sprang up. It rustled through the trees outside, rattled the fixtures and whipped up fistfuls of leaves against the windows. Vicki felt the weather was bringing a warning. She shuddered.

Under her pillow she found a long silk nightgown. Quickly she changed into it and then, after locking the door and sliding the bolt across, she climbed into the bed and drew the counterpane up to her chin. She felt wonderfully warm and soothed for a few seconds, but the weariness of the afternoon had gone, and her mind was spinning on several different levels. Primarily, her thoughts concerned the Doctor. She recalled his excitement in the TARDIS and his amusement at the King's remarks at the banqueting table, and frowned. He had seemed almost manic. In comparison his interest in the translation work was mild. Could there be yet another reason for their expedition, a second deception? She racked her brain for an answer. London, King James, 1605...

The silence of her thoughts was broken into by a sound, gone so quickly it was unidentifiable. She sat up in bed, clutching the sheets tight to her chest instinctively. Every place made noises in the night, and this was probably the seventeenth-century equivalent of active plumbing. She waited a few moments more before settling down again, chest heaving, heart pumping.

The noise came again, more clearly. A hesitant scraping

sound, something hard glancing repeatedly across stone. It was coming from outside. Vicki gathered her wits, threw back her sheets and lifted the candle in its holder from her bedside. She tiptoed over to the door. The scraping continued, gentle but insistent, as if the scraper, whoever he was, intended to accomplish his task, whatever it was, both quietly and quickly. She blotted out the moaning wind and heard only the scraping, overlaid by the resounding rhythm of her own pulses. As she neared the door she realized that the sound was coming from an angle, from the left, towards the Doctor's room. Somebody was trying to break in there.

With all the courage she could muster, she reached out and gently worked at sliding back the bolt of her own door. She had no wish to draw the interloper's attention. Carefully she moved the bolt a fraction at a time until it was clear of the bracket. Then, with the candle held behind her, she turned the key in the lock and prepared to leap out and confront the scraper.

Then there was another noise, this time from the right, and the person making it had no desire to conceal his purpose or his identity. 'Ay, with a hie and a fie and a merry down-derry,' he sang. 'Love is lost and . . . och, I lose the words . . .' The tone was jaunty and the melody tilted by alcohol, but there was no mistaking the Scots brogue of the King. As he drew nearer the scraping stopped, and when she emerged into the hallway, Vicki caught an impression of somebody scurrying from the Doctor's door. It was as dark in the hall as it had been in her room, and the movement was so quick she couldn't tell whether she'd seen it or heard it.

Her attention was drawn away by the King, who lurched towards her with a golden goblet still clutched in his hand. His ruff was loosened slightly, and in spite of the gloom she could see his nose had turned red.

She bowed. 'Your Majesty,' she said, at the same time stepping back and moving to close her door.

He moved with surprising agility and stuck a slippered foot in the door to prevent her slamming it. 'What ho!

Naughty naughty, young Victor. His Majesty desires a word or two with you.' He came closer, licking his lips. 'And he would remind you that to deny His Highness his wants is treason.'

Vicki's prim upbringing had not prepared her for this eventuality. She smiled politely, tried to make it appear that she thought his words a joke, and made another attempt to withdraw.

The King barred her way a second time. 'Dear dear, such insolence,' he said playfully, 'I should have you thrown in the Tower!'

Vicki said the first thing that came into her head. 'If it's the Doctor you want he's the next door along.'

James hooted with laughter. 'Want the Doctor? Zounds, I should hope not! No doubt that wrinkled forehead conceals much wisdom, but he is many years out of his prime, a . . .' He struggled to find words. 'A winter apple. Whereas you, dear Victor smooth-of-cheek, are a peach in spring's initial bloom.' He stepped forward, and to avoid him Vicki had to duck under his arm in a pirouetting motion. Unfortunately this cut her off from her room, and she was forced to back away down the hall. James made a springing movement, imitating a leaping tiger. 'Won't you stay still for me, peach? Remember, fair fruits that are not eaten in their prime will rot and wither off the vine.'

'I'm afraid I don't fancy being peeled,' said Vicki. She dodged his grasp. 'I just want to go to sleep.'

'Well, then!' he said happily, as if he was settling a dispute between children. 'So do I. You want to go to sleep, I want to go to sleep. We can both go to sleep together!'

'Oh dear,' said Vicki.

The King shook his head. 'How now, Ganymede!' He leapt forward, took her hand and planted a slobbering kiss on the fingers. 'You can't know if you don't like a thing until you've tried it. Dip a little toe in the water and who knows, you might soon be swimming like a duck. I promise if you let the King have his way you will get a lovely surprise!'

'Not half as lovely as the surprise you'd get,' said Vicki. She pulled her hand free and trotted away down the corridor, cursing her bad luck.

James came hurrying after her.

A moment later, the door of the Doctor's room opened a fraction. The Doctor poked his head out through the gap and squinted into the dark, his head turning in sharp, precise movements like that of a bird in search of worms. 'Winter apple? Tsk. In my day I was considered quite a looker.' He tapped an index finger against his chin and muttered, 'Still, this is fascinating. All quite fascinating.'

Vicki skipped through the passages, her bare feet making almost no noise on the stones. She sighted sanctuary and increased her speed. At the end of the corridor, where the hallway met a flight of descending steps, was a stone arch with enough room for concealment. She pressed herself into it and blew out her candle. Her journey had disoriented her; she was fairly sure she'd turned a couple of corners, which meant that she was now on the side of the Gallery facing away from London. From the glimpse she'd got before blowing out her light, these quarters seemed better appointed. An awful chill ran through her at the realization that she might very well have been letting James chase her to his own room.

Light came from near by, and there were padding, uncertain footfalls on the flagstones. 'Victor, Victor,' James's voice called playfully. 'Where are you hidden?' Huddled in the arch's overhang she held her breath and waited for him to pass. Her shoulders were pulled right back and the discomfort was intolerable. 'Like with a canny fox in a briar bush, the King shall beat you out!' Vicki was grateful that his tone remained jocular. The smell of alcohol came closer. She closed her eyes tight shut as he brushed by, the edge of his ruff's wide disc inches from her face. 'Not this night, then, shall I be the victor of dear Victor!' She held in a sigh of relief as he walked on into the dark. 'Ah, James, you're not as spritely as once you were, but your wit remains untouched,' he said sadly.

Vicki was preparing to move her aching shoulders from the arch and slip back to her room when there was a loud crash from the darkness ahead. The King swore. 'God's teeth, and people will leave suits of armour round every corner . . .' Then his tone altered, his voice rising a notch in pitch. 'Wait a — what's that? Who goes there? Victor, is that you?' In the pitch blackness Vicki's senses somehow detected another presence. She caught her breath. Was it possible that the shadowy scraper had run the other way around the building and crashed into the King? James's voice came again. 'Wait — I — who is this, I —' He sounded truly terrified.

Then another voice was raised in reply, equally nervous and at first unintelligibly squeaky. 'Oh heavens,' it said. Vicki recognized the speaker as Hay. 'Oh, James, you gave me such a shock in the dark.' He sounded gently chiding, and Vicki marvelled yet again that someone of his status could talk in that way to the King.

'Bob,' the King sighed. 'Why are you out of your room?'

'I — I heard movement,' Hay replied after a moment's pause. 'And you know how I sleep so lightly. I ventured out to tell whatever fellow was abroad to get to bed, and brushed against a ghastly figure in the dark.'

'Ay, watch your tongue, that ghastly figure was me,' James said.

'No, no,' said Hay. 'I know the feel of you, James, and this was a minute before you arrived. It was a phantom, I swear it.' Vicki heard him swallow exaggeratedly. 'Perhaps — perhaps your own dear mother, her head tucked 'neath her arm. Did you not see it or hear it?'

'Dung-for-brains,' said James. 'How can you bump into a wraith? Your ghoul was young Victor, the only soul living or dead that's haunting these passageways. He'll be away back to his precious bed, more's the pity.' Vicki heard a slap. 'You retire to yours now, and I will see you in the morning, Cecil permitting.'

107

'Of course, James, I shall go now, as bidden.' Vicki heard Hay move off. There was an anxious moment of silence. Although her shoulders were aching for release there was a good chance the King was only a few feet away and ready to pounce.

There came a long, drawn-out sigh, and James walked on. 'Ah, Victor, what hunting,' he said, 'not for a hart or a deer, but for *a* heart and *a* dear.' His voice was swallowed up by a bend in the passageway.

Vicki waited a full minute, then uncorked herself from the corner and rotated her shoulders in their sockets. As she trailed carefully back the way she had come, hands outstretched to feel for the corners that would act as a guide to her room, the significance of what she'd overheard dawned. If the figure at the Doctor's door hadn't been of her own imagining it was possibly still intent on its purpose. The Doctor was in danger.

A sudden self-possession came over her spirit. She increased her speed and fairly tore around the second corner back into the London-facing hallway. Halfway along was the Doctor's room. The door was open and a faint light spilled from inside. Vicki halted, and listened intently. A muffled noise was coming from within, a vague coughing or spluttering. There was a tinkle of breaking glass and a stifled exclamation.

Without stopping to think Vicki ran into the room, and was pulled up short by the candlelit scene within. The Doctor, dressed in a long nightshirt and matching cap, was stretched out diagonally across the bed, locked in combat with a tall man who was wrapped completely in a voluminous black cloak. The assailant had pinned the Doctor to the bed with one hand around the neck, and had raised a long-bladed and murderously sharp dagger in the other. Both the Doctor's hands were wrapped around the man's wrist, and every so often he brought up the entire middle section of his body in an attempt to throw off his attacker. She noted the broken crystal tumbler lying at the side of the bed.

Then, to her astonishment, the struggle reversed itself.

The Doctor gave another of those snake-like thrusts of his lower body, and suddenly the hooded man bounced back, losing his grip on the knife and rolling off the bed. The knife fell to the floor with a metallic clatter. Both Vicki and the recovering attacker moved to swipe it up. Vicki was a second too late, but in the instant before the hooded man picked it up she registered the design inscribed on its silver hilt – a rectangle. A moment later it was gone. A moment after that its owner had vanished too with a slam of the door. Vicki ran after him, but there was no sign of him on either side of the hallway, not even the sound of receding footsteps.

Her attention returned to the Doctor, who was sitting up on the bed and rubbing his throat gently. 'Goodness me, goodness me,' he said, taking deep breaths.

Vicki hurried to sit beside him. She laid a reassuring hand on his shoulder. 'Are you all right?' She knew at once this was the wrong thing to say.

He turned his fiercest stare on her, the one he normally reserved for an enemy, and bellowed, 'Does it appear so? And what on earth were you up to whilst I was being strangled?'

Vicki felt stung by his words. 'I did my best.'

The Doctor averted his gaze from her accusing eyes. 'I suppose so. And yes, he was a very tricky opponent. A trained fighter, I have no doubt. Very strong arms.'

'Did you get a look at him? I couldn't see his face.'

The Doctor sat up a little more. 'Do you know, I didn't, no, I didn't. How curious.'

'But he was staring right down at you.'

'Quite. But the hood was flung right over his face, concealing him totally. I caught just a glimpse of his features. A hooked nose, I think. Mediterranean, perhaps?' He waved an arm dismissively. 'What does the pedigree of an assassin matter?'

'What exactly happened?' asked Vicki.

The Doctor made his fingers into a neat steeple just beneath his chin, a sign Vicki recognized as an aid to concentration. He tapped his index fingers together rapidly. 'Hmm. Well, you see, I heard a peculiar noise coming from outside, a sort of scraping. It was the hooded man sawing away at the bolt of my door with some sort of file.'

'I heard it too,' enthused Vicki. 'I went out for a look, and then the King came along. In the mood for love.'

'Yes, yes, I overheard your altercation. I think your presence frightened the intruder away.'

'I caught a glimpse of him scampering off.' Vicki felt a flash of temper as a thought struck her. 'You heard the King lusting after me? Then why didn't you come out to help?'

'What could I have done?'

'You could have fought him off, as you are supposed to be my protector or what-have-you.'

'I was lying in wait,' the Doctor answered levelly. 'I knew my uninvited guest was bound to return, so I decided to make things easier for him and unbolted the door. Then I lay down on the bed, crossed my arms over my chest to simulate a state of repose and shut my eyes. Sure enough, only a few minutes later he returned. My intention was to snap my eyes open and confront him. But he moved too fast and struck like a viper. In an instant that knife of his was at my throat, and I was at his mercy.'

'And there I was blundering about with the King on my tail. I could have smacked into the assassin at any moment, like Hay did.'

'Hay?'

Vicki proceeded to relate to the Doctor the conversation she'd overheard between the King and Hay in the opposite-facing hallway. As was her habit she recounted the events concisely, left nothing out and added nothing. When she had finished the Doctor nodded sagely and said, 'I see. The fellow must have fled that way after you disturbed him and knocked into Hay, then doubled back in the darkness. Which suggests a degree of familiarity with the layout.'

Vicki shook her head. 'I would have seen him, then,

wouldn't I? I know it was dark, but I could make out Hay and the King all right without the candle. I would have seen him.'

'Not necessarily. He obviously slipped past Hay and went the other way, making a complete circuit of this storey of the building, and ending up back at my door.'

Vicki shuddered. 'I don't get it. Why should anybody want to kill you? I mean, you've only just arrived here.'

'Precisely, child. It's fascinating, isn't it? I wonder whose pay the fellow was in?' He shook his head decisively. 'We shall have to find out, won't we?'

'I thought the idea was not to get involved.'

He nodded. 'But it's out of our hands now, isn't it? Somebody else has involved us.' Again Vicki noted his excitement at the prospect of adventure. 'Whoever our enemy might be, and whatever his motives, he is unlikely to try again tonight. He knows we're expecting him. So why don't you pop along to your room and get some sleep, eh?'

Vicki stood up. 'I hope you're right. I'll put a chair against my door in any case, to stop the King getting in.'

James nodded wearily to the two young guards posted at the door of his chambers and staggered inside. Normally he might have lingered for a while on the threshold and made banter with them, but the vision named Victor had driven any lesser creatures from consideration, and the only other thing his befuddled mind could visualize at the moment was his big comfortable bed. He tottered over to the massive four-poster and let himself topple into its soft folds face first. Distantly he was aware that the pillowcases needed changing.

He struggled to recall why Cecil was in such a pig of a mood. Was it the Spanish? No, sorted that out. The French, then? No, seen them off. Puritans? A pain, but no. Couldn't remember, so probably it wasn't very important. He let his mind wander back to Victor, and the best way to proceed. What did boys like? Exercise, and plenty of it. Keep the limbs supple. Of course, the very thing. He'd get the Chamberlain to organize a hunt tomorrow. One couldn't get enough hunting.

There was a knock at the inner door, and one of the guards poked his head through. 'Your Majesty?'

'Be away, I've a sore head.'

'Lord Salisbury to see you, Your Majesty.'

James snorted and rolled over. 'At this late hour? I wish you were jesting, but of course nobody dares to tease me. Tell him to –' He stopped and considered. Perhaps if he sorted all the trouble out now, Cecil would stop pestering him, and he could go about his fun tomorrow without doomy works of state lowering like black clouds. 'Oh, better send him in.'

Cecil entered presently, gave a perfunctory bow, and said, 'I am here, Your Majesty.'

'I can see that,' James snapped. 'What's your issue?'

Cecil offered up a perplexed expression. 'We spoke at dinner. You said I was to come here tonight to discuss the speech.'

James couldn't recall saying any such thing. There again, most of the evening's activities were obscured by the cloudy pall of the wine imbibed, and he might well have made the invitation to shut Cecil up. Going back on his word would make him look silly, which would never do. 'Ah yes, the speech.' He patted the pouch at his waist and found it empty. 'Oh dear, I must have set the blessed thing down somewhere. Fiddle. Ah well, you'll have to come back in the morning when I've had time to lay my hands upon it.'

Cecil produced the scroll from under his arm. 'I have it here, Your Majesty. You left it, accidentally I'm sure, in the banqueting hall.'

James blinked. 'Did I? Where?'

'Jammed down the side of your throne.'

James snapped his fingers. 'Of course. The things I've lost down there, you'd be surprised.' He smiled. 'Well, if the matter's settled, I'll bid you goodnight.'

Cecil advanced menacingly towards the bed. 'Far from settled, Your Majesty. There are points that require urgent atten–'

James growled. 'Tomorrow evening, Cecil, not before. I have business in the day. Again, goodnight.'

'What business is this?' Although Cecil kept his tone respectful at all times, James could not fail to notice the sardonic note he placed on 'business'.

'I will charge the Chamberlain to get up a hunting party,' said James. 'There is good game to be had in the fields of SoHo, or perhaps on the Shoot-Up Hill.' He lay back on his pillow and gazed at the beams supporting the ceiling, warming to his theme. 'I shall take the boy Victor along with me, for a lad's place is in the open air, tasting the giddy thrills of nature, and not with crooked old men and their libraries.'

Cecil grimaced. 'I fear then that you shall be disappointed.'

James propped himself up slightly and puffed out his chest. It was hard to look dignified when you were lying down. 'I will allow only so much opposition, Cecil.'

'I mean not to cross you, only to warn you that the boy Victor and his mentor have both gone.'

James's heart thumped. 'Gone? Gone where? And by whose leave?'

'I know not the details, only that their rooms are empty.' He tapped the scroll against his thigh. The relish behind his delivery was evident. 'My feeling is that they have slipped out for good. These overly religious men are of a type, and feel that pleasure and reward are not for them.'

'They were not comfortable?' asked James. 'Why, I saw Victor only half an hour ago. You are certain he and the Doctor are away, and have not simply wandered off?'

'Their rooms are empty, the beds not slept in. And they are not in the grounds.'

James felt crushed. 'By now they will be fleeing London, too late for me to send a notice for their capture. My poor Victor is for ever lost to me.' A wetness formed in his eyes. 'Victor, who conquered my soul with his fair cheeks. Ah, it's like I have swallowed a stone.'

Cecil grunted. 'Perhaps now we can discuss the speech.'

James pointed to the door with a quivering hand. 'Out, Cecil! A bringer of bad tidings is never welcome. Out, I say!'

Cecil bowed hurriedly and departed. 'On the morrow, then.'

As soon as he heard the outer door slammed shut, James fell back on the bed and wrung out a few more tears. Then he slipped into embittered dreams about deceitful boys and spoilsport courtiers.

Ian went eastwards, taking care to keep the river within eyeshot to act as his navigator. His progress was slow. The full weight of his dilemma had descended on him like a back-breaking weight across the shoulders, and he trudged through the slushy, darkened streets, his cloak not affording him adequate protection from the biting night wind. The city was surprisingly quiet. The only people abroad were the vagrants huddled in the gutters or in shop windows and the night-time activities common to all cities. On his journey he'd seen some especially harrowing sights. There were prostitutes at work in the shadows, and a line of sleeping women in the filthiest rags imaginable sat up against a wall with only a line of rope tied at chest level to prevent them toppling into the gutter. Occasionally a trooper with a pike and a silver helmet strolled by, and Ian ducked into cover. As he walked on a mental picture of the site where the TARDIS had stood flashed before him, time and again. There had been many, many prints crossing around and about it, impressions of human feet and horses' hooves that faded as he watched, and it was impossible to work out which way the Ship had been taken or by whom. It was heavier than it appeared, heavier than a genuine police box, and would have taken strength and a certain degree of determination to shift. This gave him a crumb of hope. The thieves were certain to have been observed loading it away, and it followed there were likely to be any number of useful witnesses. He immediately discounted the possibility that the Doctor and Vicki had simply cleared off into space and time, even by accident. It was too dreadful to be true. The Doctor could be forgetful and cantankerous but such a deed was beyond him. Besides, he was notoriously careless with the Ship. Ian had lost count of the occasions on which it had been stolen or interfered with. 'Now,' he whispered to himself as, in the bluish light of dawn he turned into the long street leading to the Tower, 'if only we could immobilize the TARDIS, so that nobody or nothing could carry it off. And make sure the four of us stuck together . . .' He shook his head and in spite of the grim circumstances managed a tight grin.

'The sign of the last in Tower Street.' He surveyed the comparatively smart stone buildings on either side of the uneven cobbles. This seemed to be an area used mainly by tradesmen. At the end of the street, as Firking had said, was the house of the shoemakers, a fattish stone block with two rows of windows, a thatched roof and black timber as shoring. Over the wide entranceway was a banner that displayed the guild's sign, a clog and a set of tools, and proclaimed the name of the business's owner. In the poor light Ian could not make this out. Boldly, he passed beneath the arched entrance and entered the central yard, which consisted of a square of about fifty feet that was open to the elements, surrounded on three sides by a thatched awning that permitted access to the rooms on the building's ground floor. As he walked in, Ian was overwhelmed by a smell that reminded him of leather upholstery. Arranged in rows around the sides of the yard were wooden worktables. He supposed that these were moved out into the centre when weather permitted. It was an ordered, cleanly scene and an oddly reassuring one in contrast to the waste and dirt of the streets. This was where apprentices were raised, sheltered and given a trade.

A peal of bells floated over the rooftops, and he counted the hours struck. It was six o'clock, and already there were sounds of movement from the quarters on the ground floor. He tried to make himself look as unthreatening as possible and climbed the steps to the black-painted wooden door on the far side of the yard. He was readying his knuckles to knock when, with a sharp creak, the door opened from inside, and two men bundled out carrying mops and buckets. It took Ian a second to recognize their oddly contrasting figures, they looked so downcast and dispirited. 'Firking,' he whispered, waving a hand in welcome. 'Hodge!'

They looked up, and Ian saw that Firking's eyes, previously so lively, were ringed red from lack of sleep. Hodge looked more dazed than ever. 'Ah, the schoolmaster,' Firking said slowly, looking him over. 'And what are you calling for?' He set down his mop and proffered a hand. 'Perhaps you have found your lady and are seeking to reward those who stopped to help you?'

Ian shook the hand firmly, trying not to think about what Firking might have wiped with it. 'I'm afraid not. I came because you two are my only allies in London, and if your offer still stands . . .' He shrugged and gave them his most honest, pleading expression.

Firking scratched his chin. 'Offer? What offer was that?'

Hodge answered. 'You said we'd do our best by him for the honour of St Hugh. Are you too soused to remember?'

Firking swelled up with some of his lost energy. ''Course I remember it,' he said. He poked Ian in the chest. 'Yes, as these good hands of mine are the hands of a fine journeyman, I'll give you succour and meat if it's mine to give.' He handed Ian his mop and smiled. 'As it is now, though, this is all I have in my power to bestow.'

Ian looked the mop up and down. 'Er, thank you.'

Hodge laughed. 'Did you think we were two early stirrers by nature? No, the job of cleaning the channels outside, so the stench does not offend the noses of our fine neighbours, was given us by our master, because of our tarrying at Mother Bunch's yesterday. We weren't back until four, and he gave us bedlam. Would have sent us packing off, too, if it hadn't been for the fact we're such able craftsmen.' As he spoke he clapped Ian on the shoulder and guided him out of the yard and back into the street. He pointed to the gutters, which were clogged with detritus. 'We'll pour the water, eh, and you can mop up.'

Ian stifled a rush of anger. He was tempted to throw the mop down and storm away, but he needed their friendship to get anywhere. Rushing blindly into action wouldn't help Barbara or bring back the TARDIS. So instead he smiled and set to, dipping the mop into the water in the bucket, which was none too clean to begin with, and pushing at the stinking garbage. At the sight, Firking and Hodge broke into fresh fits.

'Ah, behold the fine young gentleman,' said Firking, jabbing Hodge in the side with his elbow. 'He must be anxious enough to win our friendship, to take up the maid's mop. But I won't question his eagerness, not if it means I can rest till seven this fine Sunday.'

Ian grinned. 'Is this some sort of a joke?'

Firking took the mop from him. 'You are the strangest fellow I've come across.' He signalled to Hodge, who proceeded to lift the bucket and slosh the gutter with water. 'Your bird, I mean to say your lady, has flown. Why call on us? The militia will help you, and be only too glad for the excuse to take action against those red-frocked Catholics. We are honest men, but poor and not much older than apprentices. What can we do for you?'

Ian sighed. 'It's a very complicated story,' he said. 'Before I begin, I need your assurance. You will help me, advise me?'

'You already have our word,' Firking replied. 'And a shoemaker's word is –'

'All right, all right.' Ian held up a hand. 'I must also swear you to secrecy.'

Hodge nodded. 'Ay. You have that too. Start your story. We like a good tale.'

Ian took a deep breath. 'I am one of a small party of travellers. Aside from myself and Barbara there is an old man and a younger woman. It would take too long to explain how we came together. All I can say is that we arrived in London yesterday morning.'

Firking stopped his mopping. 'Hold about. The school in Shoreditch, what of that?'

Ian thought hard. 'It's true, in a way. Barbara and I both — used to teach there. Anyway, we brought something along with us. A tall blue wooden box that contains all our property. I was going back to it last night after we met for the second time, but I found that it had gone, and so had the other members of our party. I want you to help me find it, and them.'

He went on, trying to win them over as best he could, talking for his life. Without assistance from the locals, he knew he might never see Barbara or the others again.

5

Hindsight Aforethought

Barbara heard the bolt on the cellar door being drawn back. The sharp rattle of metal sliding against metal brought her back to full consciousness in an instant, and she wriggled her back against the facing wall. What if this was Catesby, taking a moment away to ignore Fawkes's pleadings and kill her? The memory of his long sword made her shiver.

The lantern light spilled over the newcomer's face and she gave an involuntary sigh of relief. It was Fawkes, his bright blue eyes full of puzzlement, and he was carrying a silver dish in one hand and a cup in the other. Briefly, his fate flashed through Barbara's mind. He would die in agony, hung, drawn and quartered after weeks of torture, his head set on a spike above London Bridge. She shuddered.

He set the dish down on the floor. The meal consisted of a piece of crusty brown bread and a sliver of fish. Barbara had never been more grateful at the sight of food. She caught Fawkes's gaze and shrugged urgently, at the same time making an angry sound at the back of her throat. He smiled and knelt down, applying his thick masculine fingers to the knots around her wrists. In seconds they were free, and the relief made her want to sob. She stretched her arms to their fullest extent. One thought dominated all others, including the temptation of the food.

'Please,' she said, her voice cracked and an octave lower than usual, 'please don't tie me up again.'

Fawkes reached out and steadied her. 'Don't worry, lady, I'll protect you. No innocent, and certainly no woman, shall die by my hand.'

His words, enunciated in his Yorkshire accent, were assuring, and the movement of his fingers through her hair soothing. After hours of deprivation and terror the simple human contact had a staggering impact, and Barbara reached out for him, desperate to express her gratitude. 'Thank you,' she murmured. 'I'm so very grateful. I really thought he was going to kill me.'

'He would have,' Fawkes said gruffly. 'Death's his stock-in-trade.' There was a repressed bitterness behind the words, and when Barbara raised her head she saw that Fawkes wore a troubled expression. He raised the silver dish and gestured to the food. 'Now eat. In the chaos that's to come you'll need a full belly.'

Barbara took a bite of the bread, which Fawkes helped her to swallow by bringing the cup of water to her lips. 'Listen,' she said as she chewed, 'you must set me free. I don't know anything of what you're doing, I promise I won't tell anyone.'

'Yet you know me by sight.' He looked thoughtful. 'I have thought hard, and I am mighty certain our trails have never before crossed. I am sure I would remember a woman like you. Explain that, will you?'

It took Barbara a second to compose herself. 'I can't,' she said. 'I can't tell you.'

'At least tell me your name.'

'Barbara Wright.'

'A Wright? There is one of your family in Catesby's band. You are not his sister?'

Barbara wondered for a second whether to risk saying yes, but shook her head.

Fawkes nodded. 'You do well not to lie, Barbara. But I am intrigued. What caused you to stray into Mother Bunch's at the exact same hour as ourselves? And the fellow you were with, who is he?'

Again Barbara shook her head. 'I can't tell you.'

Fawkes grimaced and prodded her urgently. 'Catesby has marked you and the man as the King's spies, somehow made aware of one of our meeting places. He suspects treachery, and would set to torturing you if I had not threatened to desert him. I argued against him, for if the King or his lackeys knew what we were about we'd have been arrested before now. I said you must be innocents, and the letter got left to you because of our lateness in the crowd. Our contact was mistaken and passed it to you.'

'That's true,' Barbara said emphatically. 'We went into the tavern because the crowd outside was blocking the street. The man in the cloak dropped the letter, and we read it, but we had no idea what it meant.'

'And yet,' he said, 'you know my name and will not say how.' He pointed upwards. 'Catesby is a man of small patience.' His tone was suddenly more threatening.

Barbara struggled to reply. 'Well, perhaps I – I heard your name. In the tavern, or perhaps when you were arguing.'

'I haven't used that name in open for years, and with good reason. I am wanted for all kinds of things.' He poked her in the ribs. 'I have spared your life, but I cannot guarantee it. Soon, Catesby will set to with his screws and branding irons until you speak sense, and my pleas will be as nothing.' He came closer and took her hand. 'He has much time on his hands at present. All is prepared, you see, and we have only to wait two days for the finish.' He smirked, and a gleam of childish excitement came into his eyes. 'And you cannot know the magnitude of the change we'll wreak with it. It will mark a great turning point for the nation, and cannot be endangered.' He squeezed her fingers with his own, and his breath drifted over her face. Barbara flinched instinctively, but to her surprise his breath was clean and mint-fragranced. 'So,' he finished gently, 'fair lady, you must speak or you will die. Quickly by my sword, or slowly that you may while away Catesby's hours.'

Barbara let her head fall back against the wall. She willed Ian to appear in the doorway, to knock out Fawkes and carry her away. Or the Doctor, who could work one of his confidence tricks. Even the sight of Vicki would have lifted her spirits.

But the doorway remained obstinately empty.

She took a deep breath. 'Before I speak,' she said slowly, choosing her words with care, 'you must promise to believe me, and not to pass on a word of what I tell you.'

He nodded enthusiastically. 'I swear. So tell me about yourself.'

'Not to begin with,' said Barbara. She recalled the Doctor's strict code against intervention in history, and sent a mental apology in his direction. Realistically, she had no other way out. 'First of all, Guy, I'm going to talk about you.'

The morning found Vicki walking wistfully along the levelly raked gravel pathways of the Privy Garden, which had a kind of wintry artistry about it, and ruminating over the direction the Doctor's latest adventure was taking. When she reached the centre of the garden she turned a full circle on her heels, taking in the magnificence of the Stone Gallery, the chapel's lofty spire and the line of bare trees. She supposed she ought to feel awed. 'All this,' she muttered to herself, 'and I'd give anything to be back in the TARDIS.'

'There you are.' She jumped at the sound of the Doctor's voice.

Playfully she struck him on the shoulder. 'You frightened me half to death, creeping up like that.'

The Doctor chuckled. 'What it is to advance silently. Don't tell me, you thought I was our hooded foe from last night?' They started to walk on along the pathway, away from the Stone Gallery towards the trees, and he put a protective arm around her shoulders.

'Him or the King. I don't know which one to be more frightened of.' The Doctor opened his mouth to speak, and Vicki felt brave enough, for once, to interrupt him. 'And don't lecture me, please, about allowing the King his privileges. Even if I would I couldn't, if you see what I mean.'

'Hmm,' mused the Doctor. 'Rather a fix you've got yourself into, isn't it?'

Vicki fumed. 'It was hardly my idea to dress as a boy.'

'No, I suppose not.' The Doctor sighed heavily, blowing puffs of cold air from his nostrils. 'I suggest you play along as far as safety allows, but take care not to be left alone in his company. You offer a challenge. He's had his own way for far too long, and this must be a new situation for him.' He waved a hand airily. 'Still, as part of the general political perspective the King's tastes are quite irrelevant.'

'Not from where I'm standing,' Vicki mumbled. 'And I still can't see what's stopping us from going back to the TARDIS.' Her eyes flicked down automatically to where the oddly shaped key to the time craft's door hung on the end of the blue ribbon fastened around the Doctor's neck.

'We've discussed this,' the Doctor said. 'There is still much I have to see here.' He used his arm to guide her towards a section of the garden that was walled off. It looked too small to be classified an arbour, and from the strands of variously coloured ivies that festooned it, Vicki guessed it to be an ornamental feature of some sort. It was accessed by a tall wooden door dotted with metal studs which was swung half open. 'We shall have a little talk through here, in private.'

Vicki was suspicious. 'You seem to know where you're going.'

The Doctor gave an infuriatingly mysterious grin. 'These garden walks are rather splendid, aren't they? Who do you think had a hand in their design?'

Vicki was never sure if the Doctor's historical name-dropping was a joke or not, so she changed the subject. 'You're going back to the library, then,' she said. 'Leaving me to play loggets with the King. What is loggets anyway?'

The Doctor guided her through the door. 'It's a throwing game, rather similar to darts.'

'What's darts?'

'Oh dear, oh dear, you really have a lot to learn. I must remember to –' He was cut short by a noise coming from inside the walled area. Vicki looked around. The wall contained several bare-branched plant species, a small frozen pond and wooden benches, and a figure it took her a few moments to realize was the King. He was curled up at the end of one of the benches, dabbing his eyes with a puce-coloured handkerchief. Seated alongside him was Hay, who occasionally reached out a silk-shirted arm to give him a reassuring pat on the knee. Standing behind them was one of the palace guards, who typically displayed no reaction to the King's emotional state.

The Doctor and Vicki crept closer. The King was saying, 'I don't know why I came back here, Bob, truly I don't. The way I've been treated by Cecil. If he'd spoken to my father like that his eyes would have gone to the ravens by now. And I had the day all planned, loggets followed by a spot of hunting, because how else am I to keep trim, but the Doctor and Victor are away, Cecil says. It's all so trying to the nerves.'

Hay said, 'Don't take on, James. You've been a king since 'sixty-seven. What does Cecil know, after all?' Vicki reflected that if offered the choice she would have gladly taken Cecil over James as leader. Hay went on, 'Although it does seem odd, the old doctor clearing out so swiftly. Maybe Cecil was mistaken.'

'Indeed,' the Doctor boomed suddenly, making his second spectacular materialization of the morning. He bowed, and Vicki followed suit. 'I would not, Your Majesty, spurn your overflowing hospitality. We have been most generously received.'

The King immediately sprang from the bench and came forward. Such was the top-heavy nature of his outfit that he almost overbalanced. Hay and the guard leapt to his side and held him upright. 'The Lord be praised!' he said. 'Ah, it does me much good to see you here!' It was clear he was not referring to the Doctor. He beamed at Vicki, who looked down shyly. 'Did I ever see your like? I had thought my fancy had added to your glory, but you are as good in the flesh! A stripling, a mere younker, but see the wonted blushing of the lad, ah!' He clapped his hands together. 'Ah, a heart that's without craft sends two blushing roses to the face!'

Vicki wasn't sure how to respond. In the end, feeling she ought to say something, she managed, 'Thank you, Your Majesty.'

Hay smiled snidely. 'You may be at peace now, James, made happy by the sight of this perfection.'

James missed the envious undertone of the observation. 'Ay. I am surfeit with an excess of jollity. Ah, dear Victor, you are returned to me, and to have you back when I'd reckoned you lost only enhances the fecundity you stir in my breast.'

The Doctor coughed. 'Your Majesty, I would chance to make an enquiry. Why did you think we had gone? We spent the night in uneventful rest in your excellent rooms.' Vicki opened her mouth to protest. The Doctor trod on her toe, hard, and continued, 'What business could call us away from your presence, besides?'

'Ah,' said James, 'it is an error made by one of my men, good old Doctor.' He shared a smirk with Hay. 'A man that prides himself on details. Truth told, it is good to have a reason to upbraid him.'

The Doctor, Vicki noticed, was again exhibiting the signs of his concealed interest. She recognized the quickening of his jittering fingers, the slight flaring of his nostrils, the sudden gravity in his deep gravy-brown eyes. 'Would this man you speak of,' he said with feigned casualness, 'be Sir Robert Cecil?'

'Oh yes,' said Hay. 'Cecil, Lord Salisbury, that is kept here year after year like an old ornament in want of dusting.'

James held up a hand. 'Now, Bob, you know Cecil, like his father, is a fine statesman. A bore, perhaps, but none the less a diplomat for it. Anywise, I have no desire to speak of Cecil and his crazes.' He pointed straight at Vicki. 'I've a mind to hunt today, Victor, and you will join me.'

'Er, I've never been hunting before. And I – I thought we were going to play loggets.'

James chuckled. 'We have all our lives to play loggets, but you see how I am stiff at the joints. Hunting keeps me fit, and the King of our twin realm must be fit.' He turned to the attendant guard. 'Send a message on to SoHo. They are to break out the hounds.' He rubbed his hands together. 'Halloo, halloo!'

The Doctor nodded. 'Quite, quite.' Vicki shot him a pleading look. 'But, I fear, Your Majesty, Victor's feet are not yet rested well enough from our journey.'

Catching on, Vicki added, 'The Doctor's right, Your Majesty. I would love to come, honestly, but look.' She slipped off her sandals, and wiggled her toes, which were still red and sore. 'I'd only slow you down.'

James put a hand to his mouth. 'God amercy, such dainty piglets! Nay, rest you shall, Victor, and I'll go about the hunt another day. The fox can wait to die, can't he?'

'Er,' said Vicki, 'don't let me put you off, I mean, I wouldn't want to spoil your fun.' Noting his excessive interest in her feet, she slipped her sandals back on.

'Nothing's spoilt,' said James. He smiled lewdly at her. 'Some pleasures are all the sweeter for being delayed.' He turned to Hay. 'Come, Bob, we must travail indoors. I am without a cloak, and this wind is biting.' Hay and the guard obeyed him and moved to leave the little yard. James lingered a while. 'Doctor, you shall continue your work on the translations. Victor, I think it wise you shall be kitted out in new raiment. Go to the Chamberlain and convey my wish.' He waved regally – '*Au revoir*, then' – and departed.

Alone with the Doctor again, Vicki slumped on to the bench and stared dispiritedly into the frozen pond. 'That was close.'

The Doctor hunched forward, his fingers toying absently with the TARDIS key. 'Sir Robert Cecil, eh?'

'What about him?' asked Vicki. 'He's a bit grim, but he seems the sanest one of the lot. Why didn't you mention what happened last night?'

'Weren't you paying attention, child? Cecil told the King – last night – that we had gone. What does that suggest?'

'Sorry. I suppose I'm a bit dim. Cecil was the man in the cloak, then.'

'Hardly,' the Doctor snorted. 'He is little taller than yourself and walks quite normally. The hooded man was a tall fellow, and moved with a curious shambling gait. They are not the same man, but it is evident that Cecil knew of the attack. That suggests it was he who sent the assassin. He is a renowned spymaster, with agents reporting to him from most European countries, so he can contact such a person at a moment's notice.'

Vicki decided it was time to confront him. 'There's something going on here, Doctor, that you know about. Not just that Bible business. What is it?'

The Doctor stood up, his face turned away from her. 'Nothing for you to worry about at the moment, my dear,' he said patronizingly. 'Now come along, we must return to the library.'

Vicki followed him, muttering rebelliously.

As the bells tolled seven, the doors on either side of the courtyard opened and shoemakers tumbled out from a noisy breakfast, to take up their tools from the racks and set to work. To Ian's eyes the tools looked much alike, but each man was particular about claiming his own set, and the handles and carrying cases were distinctive and personalized. The benches were brought out and arranged in rows.

He was standing with his two companions just inside the entranceway. At the conclusion of his story, Firking and Hodge had both gone quiet, had demanded to be given time to confer, and had slunk off into a dark corner. Ian had told them the truth, broadly speaking. He'd made one large omission – the TARDIS – and added an equally proportioned embellishment – a hint that he and his friends were working on important business for the King, hence their wish not to draw attention to themselves. This had definitely impressed the two shoemakers, who had drawn back a little from Ian with new respect in their eyes. Hodge had immediately taken back the mop and bucket. Ian reasoned that fear of the Crown was so great that nobody would dare lie that they were in its employ.

At last Hodge and Firking stepped back. Firking made an elaborate salute to Ian. 'Sir, you have all the support we can muster.' He snorted. 'But there lies your problem. We are good men, and the best workers in all London, but what use are our qualities to you?'

Hodge took up the theme. 'He's right, Ian. We can cut you a pair of vampres second to none in the land, but shoes cannot lead you where your Barbara has trod.'

Ian smiled and placed a firm hand on each man's shoulder. He thought of how the Doctor would speak in such a situation. 'My friends, I have not lived in London for many years. My travels in the King's service have taken me to places so distant they seemed to me like other worlds. But if I've learnt one thing in my wanderings, it's that good honest companions are as hard to find and as valuable as gold.'

Hodge nodded. 'Wise words, but I ask again, what can we humble shoemakers do for you?'

'You can give me shelter, and advice on how to make my search. And there's something else I want you to see.' He reached inside the pouch at his waist and drew out the little white envelope. 'This was dropped in the tavern by the Spaniard. It's the only clue I've got, and I can't make head nor tail of it.'

Firking took the note and puzzled over it. 'Ah, it's too bad for you, Ian, but I can't properly read. These words are too long for me.'

Hodge took it from him and screwed up his eyes. 'It looks to be in French.'

'French?' Firking stiffened. 'A Frogs' plot, do you think? With Robert Redsocks at the centre of it?' He smiled at Ian. 'I tell you, sir, if there's Frogs involved, you may count on all the journeymen here gathered to rush to your aid, and more besides.' He spat on the cobbles. 'The Frenchies have lamed many good London men with their infernal warrings. And now they make truck with

Spaniards, our second greatest enemies, a scourge of pirates.'

If Barbara was here, thought Ian, she'd probably have plenty to say on the topic. 'Does it make any sense to you, Hodge?'

Hodge shook his head and passed the note back. He scratched the side of his cheek slowly. 'I have picked up a smattering of the language, as written and spoken. I am not slow to learn a new tongue. And the words on that note don't seem French to me, but all jumbled up and meaning nothing. It must, I reckon, be a cipher used by Catholic traitors.'

Ian folded the note and returned it to his pocket. 'You're probably right. The trouble is finding the key to the code. It might at least give us an idea of their location.'

Hodge nudged him. 'We must get to work, see.' He picked up the mop.

Firking nodded and threw the bucket of dirty water into the street. 'Ian, if you'd come in with us we'll talk more and plan a way to free your Barbara. We'll set our heads proper to that note and see if we can't puzzle it out.'

Ian looked down at his clothes. 'Won't I seem rather – well, out of place?'

'Ah, we'll find you an apron, there's always some to spare.' Firking clapped his arm around Ian's shoulder. 'And the master takes little notice in the doings of the yard, for all his bombast. He won't see one more workman. And you can share my tools.' He struck his chest in a heroic gesture. 'It's a hard world, but we shall not let you go by if we can help you.'

As an aristocrat, Robert Catesby was not a man suited to a life of hiding. He sat in one of the upper rooms of the big house in Princes Street, his hands stretched out on the table before him. He examined them: hands that were reaching out to change the world, to restore the Church to its rightful allegiances. In just two days he would be able to walk freely throughout the land.

It was strange. He had anticipated the final hours on many occasions over the years spent in preparation, years of struggle to raise the money and gather men he could trust, and had imagined himself as fired by excitement and emotion. Instead he felt sombre, reserved. His thoughts turned to the past, as they often did in his quieter moments, and underlying the mental pictures he saw was a question he was beginning to ask himself more and more often.

The plot had been born in inauspicious circumstances, the child of a drunken night in the Mermaid tavern in the March of 1600. He had been drinking with a small circle of his Catholic friends, inspired by a trip to the theatre and Shakespeare's *Richard II*. Also present in the large, crowded room had been the Catholic Earl of Essex, and a fierce debate between him and a wealthy Protestant had started up, leading to tempers fraying on both sides. Fired up by a prodigious quantity of ale, Robert had followed the mob assembled by Essex. They poured out into the streets at midnight and set upon a feeble skirmish with the watch. The events of that night came back to him in a blur; he'd been so full of beer he'd cared not a jot for his own life, and staggered blindly onwards, swinging his rapier aimlessly. The consequence had been imprisonment and a demand from the privy council that he take the oath of allegiance to Queen Elizabeth. Flatly he had refused. Execution would have been inevitable, if Elizabeth herself had not intervened to commute the sentence. To his surprise, he was released, and his punishment altered to a crippling fine, which necessitated the selling of his family home at Chastleton. In a way this was crueller than death. As he watched the furniture and all the goods of his family auctioned, and saw the bitter tears of his mother as she was led from the rooms the Catesbys had inhabited for generations, a new and deadly purpose had consumed him. Where others had fallen, he would succeed. Where others had scaled down their designs, he would engender the biggest possible scheme. Where other men of Catholic faith scurried from bolthole to bolthole, he would walk proudly in the streets to tell the world that the new order of his creation was coming.

These memories made his heart beat faster, and the fatigue that had dulled his brain vanished. Again he experienced a twinge of anxiety towards the woman stowed away in the coal bunker. Realistically, she could bring no harm down on the plot. As Fawkes had protested, she was an innocent and knew nothing. She could not escape from their close watch on her, and in a couple of days she could be set free. These considerations aside, Catesby found her presence alarming. The involvement of the Spaniard was a secret he had kept to himself and Fawkes. None of the other plotters were aware of his existence, but this woman knew, and she had seen the note.

Yes, he thought, as he stood from the table and walked with purposeful strides for the stairs leading down to the bunker, he would feel much happier if she was dead. He would have to reason Fawkes out of his stubbornness, even if that meant arranging an unfortunate accident. It would be easy. He would send Fawkes on some errand, and while he was absent, slit her throat. On Fawkes's return he would say that she'd been attempting escape.

Barbara shuddered at the haunted expression on the face of Guy Fawkes. She had just recounted to him in as much detail as she could recall his life history up to the present moment. 'You were a soldier in the Spanish service, and then a wandering mercenary. Your practical skills are renowned, which is why you were asked to join the plot by Catesby, to help with mining the tunnel into the parliament buildings from the house he'd rented. He sent one of the other men, I forget his name, to France to talk with you.' She paused and licked her lips. 'You agreed to return, and you rented a house near Parliament. The other conspirators are scattered across London.'

Fawkes raised a hand. 'Stop there, Barbara. That is this house.' He remained in front of her in a kneeling position. 'This is uncommon sorcery.'

'I'm not a sorcerer. I'm from a time that's hundreds of years to come, from the twentieth century.' She tried to impress her conviction in her words. 'I swear that's the truth.'

Fawkes drew a loop in the air. 'But time advances over us,' he said haltingly, his mind wrestling with the alien concepts. 'We can't advance through it.'

'I know. Don't ask me how it's possible. Only the old man I told you about, the Doctor, understands the workings of our Ship.' She felt she ought to steer the conversation back to her immediate concerns. 'But you must see, that's how I knew your name. To me, the plot happened hundreds of years ago, but your name, and Catesby's, live on in our history.' As she spoke she felt a powerful unease, as if she was doing something irresponsible. 'And I've no intention of interfering. If you set me free you'll never see or hear of me again.'

Fawkes rubbed his brow. 'My head . . .' He closed his eyes. 'My head is spinning with this. I don't possess belief in witches or demons, Barbara. I've journeyed through most of the nations known to mankind and seen many things of the queerest sort, but none of them I couldn't explain with recourse to nature. Once, in Spain, I saw a great flying ball of gas, glowing green above the heads of my battalion. The rest of the company shrieked and fled, but I stayed, as I knew it was only a queer lightning you get near marshground. And anyone that I've met who's claimed to have the sight has been nothing but a charlatan. But this . . .' He shook his head again. 'Another thing I've learnt is how to recognize truth in a woman's eyes. I've been deceived by them enough times. And your eyes are clear, you are speaking the truth. So you must be mad. Yet you aren't that, I'm certain.' He let his head drop. 'I am so confused over this. But your story's so strange I can't see how anyone could invent it, or why. It screams away all sense.'

Barbara was impressed by his sensitivity. Gently she placed a hand on his arm. 'But you can see that I'm no possible harm to you?'

He hesitated. 'Wait. You have told me about myself, many things. I might just believe you had found that out, if you were a spy. Now, if you know of our work here, tell me what it's about, in detail.'

Barbara bit her lip. 'I shouldn't.'

Fawkes raised an eyebrow. 'For your freedom?'

Barbara forced herself to stay calm. It was going to be hard work justifying this to the Doctor. 'You are plotting to blow up the Houses of Parliament on the night of the State Opening, November the fifth. Originally you planned to tunnel through from this house, but the wall was too thick, so you rented space . . .'

'. . . in a cellar beneath the Lords itself. You are storing about forty barrels of gunpowder there, which you intend to light using a line of touchwood.'

Barbara's words echoed out on to the stairwell as Catesby descended, sword drawn.

Fawkes came closer to Barbara, his face inches from hers. 'And then?'

Barbara swallowed. His warm, bearded cheek was almost near enough to press against her own. 'Then, after the explosion, Catesby intends to place Princess Elizabeth on the throne and dismantle the Protestant Church.'

Fawkes reached up and stroked her hair gently. 'You know,' he whispered, 'what only we who've sworn the oath of secrecy should know.' He smiled pleasantly. Barbara felt her body responding to his nearness. As a seduction this was so confident it was refreshing. 'It's weird and sudden, but the detail is such that I believe you, Barbara.'

Barbara thought back to the night she and Ian had stumbled inside the TARDIS. It had taken her only a few minutes to accept the truth of the situation, as there had been no other explanation. Perhaps it was the same now for Fawkes. 'Then will you let me go?' she asked.

He cupped her chin in his hand. 'Are all the women of the twentieth century as beautiful as you?' he asked.

'And the women of the heavenly spheres, how are they?'

Before Barbara could answer there was a crash as the door was thrown violently open. Catesby stood framed in the doorway, his dagger drawn. 'Twentieth century!' he snorted, advancing angrily. 'You have been too long without a woman, Fawkes. You should seek the mutton that hangs around the dock of Billingsgate of a night.'

Fawkes sprang up. 'Rob, you must listen to her.'

'I have listened.' Catesby lunged savagely forward, and pulled Barbara up by the hair. She screamed as he twisted one of her arms behind her back and brought the blade of his knife to rest on her throat. She felt his hot breath on the back of her neck. 'And I have heard more that disturbs me. Nobody but you and I, Fawkes, knows what she has said, not even the Spaniard is aware of these details. It is devilry, dark magic of the most evil kind, and a witch should not be allowed to live!'

6

The Tree

'Stand still, boy, stand still!' the Chamberlain shrieked, his cheeks pinkening. 'Do you want to be stuck full of spines like a porcupine?'

Vicki snapped back, 'I've been standing still for over an hour.' This was the truth. The tailors worked at an agonizingly careful pace, directing her to hold various unlikely attitudes while they jotted down intricate measurements in a little leather-bound book. As a boy she was afforded no maiden's privileges and the taking of the inside leg measurement had been excessively familiar. For once she was glad of her stringy figure. 'Have they nearly finished?'

'Patience, boy,' sighed the Chamberlain. 'You must cultivate a longer span of attention.' His fingers were drumming against his chest, Vicki noticed, to make it plain that there was something much bigger and more important that he should be worrying about. As if in confirmation of her thoughts he mumbled, 'This fitting is a gross inconvenience.'

'Oh yes,' said Vicki. 'The Opening of Parliament. But if it happens every year, you must have it down pat, surely?'

The Chamberlain threw up his pudgy hands. 'Oh, hark, the voice of youth!' he cried. He stepped closer. 'Victor, bid *in statu pupillari* farewell. On Friday the King will sit in session with both houses. The full realm of our nation's government, all in the one place. It is a nightmare, a thick-coming fancy that drives all else from my mind. And I am responsible for its smooth running. Every lord must sit in the correct seat, every commoner in the correct row. Certain people mustn't be placed alongside certain other people. Some must have a better view of the King than others, but it must be kept from them that the King doesn't want to see them. All trumpets must be polished, all pennants laundered. Everybody, from the most elderly peer to the lowest errand boy, must display the correct attire and give the correct responses. And that's only the ceremony itself. They must all be got in and out swiftly and safely.'

Vicki was amused. 'Don't worry. Has anything gone wrong before?'

'Not visibly, I don't suppose. And James is more forgiving, I suppose you might say less noticing, of errors than Elizabeth, God rest her soul.' He managed a conspiratorial grin. 'We all used to have to kneel in her company, you know, to make our reports, and it always took a very age for things to be settled. Usually by warlike means. James won't have any of that. His is a more open character, and favours speed of action rather than ponderous detail.'

'I'm sure everything will be fine,' said Vicki. She remembered the Doctor's interest in Cecil and asked innocently, 'You don't look after the security side of things, though, do you? That must be more worrying for whoever's job it is.'

The Chamberlain blew out his cheeks. 'Ah, you mean Cecil. No, no, he'll have Parliament sealed tight as the skin on a drum. And I've never known him to fret. It was the same with his father. Never panicked. If something bothered him he would turn red and furious. Really I don't know how the King lets him get away with it. Any other person raging like that would have his head on the block in minutes.'

'Because the King realizes how much he needs Cecil,' said Vicki.

The Chamberlain fixed her with a reproving glare, ending their moment of intimacy. He lowered his voice. 'A shrewd commentary, Victor, but it will do you no favours to bandy such opinions, I warn you.' Quickly, he turned his attention to the tailors. 'You men, how goes your work on the suit? You have taken an awfully long time on it.'

One of the tailors stood up and tugged his forelock. 'Well advanced, sir. We have only to take out the pins and measure the feet.'

The other added, 'The boy has a fine, slender figure. We thought a raiment of indigo hue, with wide gaskins and buttoned-up netherstocks, a cambric shirt and feather collar.' As he spoke he pointed to various parts of Vicki's body. 'He shall make the King a friend sweet as sugar-candied figs.'

The first tailor said to Vicki, 'Now, stick out your foot, boy, and let's have your shoe.' She did as instructed, and her heart leapt for a moment at the realization that she was still wearing her plastic sandals. The tailor blinked in surprise as he slipped one off. 'A dainty heel, and the oddest shoe I've ever seen. Look at this.' He passed it to his colleague.

'Oh, yes,' the other tailor said, turning the sandal over and over in his hands. 'Too pliant to be a clog, yet clearly not leather.' He addressed Vicki. 'Where came you by these?'

Vicki thought desperately. 'In a market, along the pilgrims' road.'

'Really.' The tailor tucked both shoes under his arm. 'As long as it fits, there is an end to it, for another, finer pair will be made from the same.' He nodded to the Chamberlain. 'We will hurry to it now.'

The Chamberlain opened the door and shooed them out. 'Yes, there you go.' He called after them, 'Remember, you are to make haste, the command to make this outfit comes direct from the King.'

As soon as they were gone, Vicki slumped into a chair and stretched her aching arms and legs. 'Oh, what I'd give for a hot bath,' she said.

The Chamberlain frowned. 'A bath? You are well scrubbed as it is.' He clapped his hands importantly. 'Now, up tails all. You must return to your Doctor and his books, and I must attend to my real duties.' He put a hand to his head. 'I can't wait for it to all be over for another year. The date of November the fifth hangs over my head like the sword of Damocles.'

Vicki sprang to her feet, an ice-cold sensation chilling her marrow. She felt dizzy. 'November the fifth?'

The Chamberlain looked back at her oddly. 'Why, yes, child, that is the night of Parliament's opening, this coming Tuesday night.'

The truth dawned on Vicki like bright sunlight breaking through a gap in a cloud. She clapped a hand to her mouth to stop her girlish excitement bursting out. Snatches of rhyme passed through her head. *Remember, remember, the fifth of November.* 'I don't believe it,' she whispered. '1605 . . .'

The Chamberlain looked bemused. 'As today is November the third, it follows surely that Tuesday shall be November the fifth.'

'Yes, of course,' said Vicki. 'I should have realized.'

'Quite.' He clapped his hands again. 'Now, about your work. The King awaits you for loggets, if you recall.' He waddled out of the fitting room.

Vicki, now alone, slumped absently back down in the chair. 'Gunpowder, treason and plot,' she whispered. The words dissolved her glee and her mind was suddenly refulgent with her discovery's implications. Thoughts connected with other thoughts. And their central axis was the Doctor.

To Barbara it seemed to happen in a single moment. Fawkes smacked Catesby on the back of the head with shattering force; Catesby fell with a startled expression; and then Fawkes grabbed her hand and was pulling her out of the cellar.

She forced Fawkes to stop on the stairs. 'Thank you,' she said, unable to think of anything better to say.

Fawkes grimaced at his fallen comrade. 'He'll wake in a while. And so you have to be gone.' He dragged her away. 'My word is all I have, and I gave it to you. I hope I was right in that.'

Barbara allowed herself to be rushed up the steps. She

felt an overwhelming gratitude to Fawkes.

And then, with a horrible jolt, she remembered how he was going to die.

The Doctor was halfway up the step-ladder in the library. Haldann had asked him to bring down a volume of Origen – an argument about the application of Platonic principles to Christian orthodoxy was hatching – and his eyes scanned the spines keenly for the name of the Alexandrian. He was not aided by the dust of the ages which flew up his nostrils whenever one of the texts was disturbed, and which eventually gave him a sneezing fit. 'Oh dear, oh dear,' he said, pulling out a handkerchief and dabbing at his streaming eyes, 'this is the sort of experience that makes one nostalgic for computers.' He blew his nose and looked up at the books again. 'Origen, Origen . . .' he muttered. 'What he has to do with the translation, I'm sure I have no idea.'

'The pre-existence of souls,' said a voice from below. The Doctor looked down to see Haldann at the foot of the ladder, excitement etched deep in his every wrinkle. 'Otley and I were disputing this over breakfast. Origenism, you see, purports that the soul pre-exists the body.'

'I am aware of that,' lied the Doctor.

'Now, if the Trinity is immortal and everlasting, which of course it is, there is an Origenic twist to the question of the body of Christ in the womb of Mary, is there not? At least that is my opinion, which Otley dismisses as unchristian and essentially Platonic. And yes, Origenism was condemned at one of those councils the Vatican was always calling in the sixth century, but there again, that was a millennium past, and with the Vatican's pronouncements more than slightly in doubt, I would –'

There was a noise from the library's central chamber, and the Doctor put up a hand to shush Haldann. The trip of a pair of determined footsteps wafted over the high bookcases, and was accompanied by Cecil's voice: 'Otley.'

There was a pause before Otley replied, 'It is courteous to knock for admittance. Now I have faltered, and lost my place.'

'You have lost nothing.' Cecil's tone was more clipped and brutal than ever. 'I have come to tell you, you should not expect the old Doctor today. He and his boy have fled. Back away to York, if it was true they came thence.'

The Doctor bristled and his hands flew instinctively to his lapels, as they always did in moments when he needed to think quickly. Haldann opened his mouth to shout something but the Doctor indicated silence by putting a finger to his lips. They heard Otley say, with an emphasis oiled in sarcasm, 'Cecil, you present an interesting third case in my philosophical wrangle with Haldann. The soul has flown, you say, but I know the body remains.'

'Explain yourself,' said Cecil.

The Doctor took his cue and emerged, taking care to present his most supercilious smile to his enemy. 'Good morning, Sir Robert,' he said evenly.

Cecil's eyes flashed dangerously, and for a second the Doctor wondered if he would lose his reserve. He raised his black-gloved hand as if to deliver a blow. A second later he was back in control. 'Doctor,' he said.

'Yes?' The Doctor threw back his head.

'I – I was told that you had left us.'

'Really?' The Doctor sniffed imperiously, and inclined his head a fraction, just enough to let Cecil worry about how much he knew. 'And who told you this tale? As you can see I am very much present, in body as well as in soul.'

'An attendant,' said Cecil. 'I will have him reprimanded.'

'Please do.' The Doctor, feeling he had the upper hand, could not resist the opportunity to increase his advantage. 'It is a very bad thing, surely, for such manifestly false messages to go winging like wild birds about the palace, especially at this most crucial point in the state's calendar.' He took one of his hands from his lapel and used it to make a grand sweeping gesture. 'Heaven knows what –' he paused and narrowed his eyes '– calamities such errors could bring.'

There was a palpable air of tension in the library. It was broken by Haldann, who said, 'If there has to be a confrontation, might it be done more quietly, and in a more apposite place?'

Otley nodded. 'This is hardly the arena most suited to harsh words and rancour.'

Cecil indicated the door. 'Doctor, would you care to continue our discussion elsewhere?'

'Frankly, no,' said the Doctor. 'I'd rather turn my back on a – well, on an Indian cobra.' A tactic was forming in his mind, one of the sudden inspirations that made his life what it was. 'Will you excuse me, I have business in the classical annex. The ordering in the Alexandrian section is quite gone to plot – I mean to say, pot.' Feeling rather puffed up and pleased with himself for that one he strode away around the corner.

Rising to the bait, Cecil pounded into the annex after him. In a whisper he said, 'Do not try my patience further, Doctor. What was it you said?'

The Doctor made a show of looking over the books on the lower shelves. 'Eh, what's that? Oh, it's only that there needs to be a simpler method of classification.' He chuckled. 'Especially ironic that the Alexandrian scholars should find themselves so jumbled, eh?' Still giggling he went up the ladder.

Cecil gripped one of the rungs and whispered, 'I heard you say – that word.'

'And which particular word was that?' the Doctor said casually.

Cecil came closer, pressing his skinny body against the side of the ladder. 'I have seen through you. There is no messenger out of York named Lacy, and never was. Your Victor is the comeliest girl that ever passed herself away as a boy, a pretty trick to win the King's sympathy. Your identity is bogus, your mission a falsity.'

Without looking down the Doctor said. 'Have me arrested, then. Nothing could be simpler for you.'

Cecil snarled. 'Who are you? Why do you interfere, who sent you?'

'Nobody sends me anywhere, my dear fellow,' said the Doctor. 'And I make it a rule not to interfere. As I say, if you suspect me, report me to the King, throw me into prison. I imagine there would be considerable inquiry into my purposes, but that need not worry you. After all, you've nothing to hide, have you?' For the first time he looked back over his shoulder.

Cecil quivered with rage, the dust motes stirred up by the Doctor's riffling through the books swirling around him like an agitated halo. 'I need utter only one word, one word and you can be removed from this place and flogged until your flesh burns. And then you'll be glad to speak sense. In fact you'll be begging to tell me.'

The Doctor made a scoffing noise. 'Do it, then. Right away. Give your order.' He angled his face right down to a level with Cecil's. 'But you can't. Evidently not, old chap. Quite evidently not.'

Cecil held his stare for a second longer. Then he kicked the ladder so hard it wobbled, and stormed away. The Doctor heard the library's door slam shut after him and stepped down from the ladder. Mentally he congratulated himself on his performance.

Haldann's head popped around the corner. He appeared rather excited. 'Great heaven, what did you say to him? You'd think the Pope himself was in the room.'

The Doctor shrugged. 'I only reminded him to concern himself with the King's business. Now, then.' He returned his attention to the shelving. 'I'm afraid I can't see your Origen anywhere.'

Haldann shook his head sadly. 'Well, that's to be expected. We haven't had him out for a good many years.'

Otley's voice floated over. 'Henry, your desk is ice-cold from want of work.'

Haldann sighed. 'He's got me on the Lamentations,' he told the Doctor. 'Only because he knows how I detest them. Ah well.' He gathered up the trailing ends of his gown with his knobbled hands and walked away.

Alone again, the Doctor let his façade drop. If anyone

unfamiliar with him had been left in the annex to observe this they would have marvelled at the change in his expression, and might have believed a demon had taken possession of him. His eyes sparkled with fiendish delight, his brow furrowed, and he stroked his chin with increasing rapidity. 'Fascinating, how Cecil reacted. It confirms my suspicions. He is involved in the conspiracy, engineering the plot to advance his punitive measures against the Catholics! Hmm, hmm! Catesby, Fawkes and the rest are pawns in his game, if they but knew it! And two days from now he'll have them discovered and pretend to be surprised at it all! You have to admire the sheer gall and cunning of the man!' He broke into a fit of manic giggles. 'Yes, yes, what a character.'

His deliberations were interrupted by another commotion from the main workroom. In short succession there came the slamming open of the door, muffled outbursts and exclamations from the two scholars, and the sudden appearance of Vicki's slight figure around the corner. Her features were pinched, her expression accusatory, and the Doctor could not help but feel a stab of guilt at his own behaviour. Her first words increased this uncomfortable feeling. 'Doctor, you tricked me.'

He shushed her and beckoned her forward. 'Step through into the annex, my dear, you know we mustn't be overheard.'

'I don't care!' she said hotly. 'It was bad enough when I thought it was only Ian and Barbara you were deceiving, but why did you have to lie to me?' She sniffled and wiped her nose with the back of her hand. 'Haven't I always tried to do what you wanted? No matter how dangerous? I thought that you liked me, that you trusted me.' Her voice was breaking. 'I thought we were friends.'

The Doctor couldn't bring himself to look her in the eye. 'My dear, whatever's the matter? Explain yourself.'

Vicki had the presence of mind to lower her voice. 'That creepy Chamberlain says we're coming up to November the fifth. I may not be much of a historian, but I know what that signifies. And you knew all along, from when you spoke to that man on the road yesterday morning. You packed Ian and Barbara off, and you only dragged me along because you thought I was too stupid to guess what you were up to.'

'Oh dear, dear, dear.' The Doctor resisted her version of these events; accurate as it was, it neglected several of the more important factors influencing his actions. He took her hand. 'Not at all, not at all.' Another lie, but two wrongs, he had found, often did make a right. 'I didn't want to alarm you, did I?'

'Well, then you've made a pretty bad job of it,' she said. Her tone remained bitter, but the physical contact had mollified her. She squeezed his hand. Her eyes suddenly seemed very big and sad.

'That's not entirely fair,' said the Doctor. 'I wasn't to know we'd be so warmly welcomed. And Barbara, I'm sure, would understand. What's going on about us is crucial to the course of British history. If we keep our eyes and ears open, we may uncover things that throw a new light on the Plot. Don't you think that's worth a white lie?'

'Worth being killed? What's to stop Cecil having another go?'

The Doctor hesitated about this. 'Cecil is totally hamstrung, my dear. He can't risk imprisoning us because we know too much about his scheme, and we might talk and expose him.'

'But you wouldn't, would you?'

The Doctor tapped her on the nose. 'No, of course I wouldn't. History must be allowed to run on its correct course, with as little interference from us as possible. But he doesn't know that, does he? As for the King, his fondness for you makes him a very good ally.'

'Until he gets his hands on me.' She sighed and came closer, wrapping her arms around the Doctor's waist and giving him a hug. 'I'm sorry. I don't want to fall out with you, I know you always act for the best. I only hope the others are all right. Couldn't I go and find them?'

The Doctor let her head fall on his shoulder and patted

it gently. 'There there, child. I've known Barbara and young Chesterton for quite a while, and they've come through many challenges. They're a very resourceful pair. No, neither of us must leave the palace. Cecil has guards posted all around and we'd be sure to be seen. And away from the King's eyes we'd be in far greater danger. No, we must stay here until the discovery of the Plot, and then slip out in all the confusion.'

Vicki managed a tearful smile. 'I suppose you're right,' she said. 'I was wrong to shout. It's important to explore the places we land in, and to find out all we can about them.'

The Doctor felt stirred by her words. 'Yes, I couldn't phrase it better myself. An enquiring mind is a healthy mind, yes, that I strongly believe.' He smiled down at her. 'Now, you run along before they get you to start hoisting books again. You'll be late for loggets if you don't hurry.'

Vicki wiped her eyes a final time. 'Thank you, Doctor. For everything. You're right, as usual.' She gave him a wave and walked away, calmer now, her arms folded across her chest.

The Doctor breathed a sigh of relief, and reprimanded himself inwardly for deceiving her. 'Hmm,' he mused. 'I think I handled that rather well.' He rubbed his hands together vigorously and started to search the shelves for Origen again.

The King was definitely making an effort. He stood in a paved yard off the palace's main buildings, crunching on a French apple, with his speech held out in his other hand. The problem he had learning things was exacerbated by the brilliance of the composition, which constantly distracted him. Here a nail-on-the-head simile, there a stunningly accurate metaphor. It was no great wonder the Lord had chosen his soul to inhabit the body of a king. He had brought peace to these lands in the face of plentiful obstacles, always by divining a middle way, always following a path of compromise. In only two years as leader of the new union, he had, together with Cecil, arranged a peace with all Britain's neighbours, including Spain, a feat none of his predecessors had attempted, or even dreamt possible. He had drawn Parliament and the people closer together, and employed his own bounteous intelligence to rule wisely. It followed that he was allowed an afternoon's loggets.

He looked up from the speech at the sound of approaching footsteps. His nose wrinkled at the sight of Hay, who was skipping lightly over the flagstones in that emasculated way of his. Initially, James had found it endearing; to his eyes it now appeared effete. He contrasted Hay's mincing step unfavourably with the swinging masculine strides of young Victor. Still, his arrival was an excuse to tuck away the scroll. 'Ah, Bob,' he said, nodding to Hay. 'I was expecting the Doctor's ward. Have you seen him?'

Hay smirked. 'I have not been looking out for him.'

'No,' said James. 'Your eyes are turned customarily upwards along with your nose.' He experienced a sudden desire to be rid of Hay, to send him off, not only out of the palace but out of his life. That was the trouble, he decided, with choosing such companions as grow old and grotesque. Hay was nearing his twentieth year and his attributes were wearing thin. 'Well, I suppose we may need a third for loggets,' he said out loud.

'Ah,' said Hay, with irritating self-importance and improper familiarity. 'That concerns what I am calling to tell you. I have to visit my tailors by Doctor's Commons, who are having my suit for Tuesday made ready. There is some trouble with a wrongly taken fitting that I must settle, and I would go to them now in order to save time. You understand?'

James considered this veiled invitation. A few days ago he would have forgotten his loggets and ridden to town with Hay, simply for the lark of it, and for the pleasure of the lad's company. Now, it was as if a curtain had been lifted from Hay, revealing an ugliness and presumption that were not anywhere in the fresh face of Victor. 'I think I will remain here,' James said frostily.

Hay nodded. 'As you wish.' He turned to depart.

'One moment.' James raised a hand formally, as he did when requesting silence from an earl. 'Bob, this suit of yours, who have you charged to make it?'

'The Cavendishes,' Hay answered.

'Ah. And at what cost to yourself?'

Hay blinked, taken by surprise. 'At none to myself, James. I assumed that the privy purse would cover the reckoning.'

'Do not assume such things,' James said. He had no intention of withdrawing this privilege from Hay as yet, but it would do the fellow – and yes, he was now a fellow rather than a boy – good to remember that favours were not automatically bestowed. He waved a hand. 'Go now.'

'Very well.' Hay, visibly cowed, turned to leave the courtyard.

'Oh,' the King called after him. 'If you should encounter Victor, direct him to me forthwith.'

After Hay had gone he tittered at his own spite, and unrolled his speech once again. Quickly he traced his finger down the closely spaced lines of his handwriting until he found the correct section. 'Ah yes,' he told himself. 'This will be easy enough to lodge in my memory. It is a very masterwork of wit.'

The TARDIS key burnt in Vicki's clenched fist. This was her first direct act of disobedience against the Doctor, and her heart hammered against her ribcage in rhythm with her breathing, which now came in short audible gasps like a suction pump's. She walked through the gardens, acknowledging the nods of the equerries and courtiers she passed.

She was so preoccupied that as she turned a corner she almost slammed straight into a lithe figure coming the other way. It was Hay. She smiled politely. 'Good afternoon.'

His superior sneer made her flinch. 'Good afternoon. You seem in an awful hurry.'

'Yes, I've finished my fitting, and I was looking for the stables.'

Hay threw her a quizzical glance, his hand resting on his hip. 'What of the loggets game? The King awaits you.'

Vicki thought hard. 'It's just I haven't seen my horse since yesterday, and I wanted to see if he was better. The ride from York was exhausting for him.'

'How sweet,' said Hay. The hand that rested on his hip moved with a strange and significant suddenness; absently, as if its movement had no connection with the rest of his body. It scuttled sideways like a spider, towards something tucked into Hay's belt, a shiny silver object. 'Devotion to a favourite beast is an admirably boyish quality.'

Vicki sensed a hidden menace in his words, and found herself backing away from him instinctively. Could Hay's jealousy for James's attentions lead him to attack her? 'So, if you could direct me to the stables . . .'

Hay stalked closer. 'You're going in the wrong direction, my dear,' he purred, his fingers curling around the silver object. Vicki had an awful suspicion it might be a knife. 'Quite the wrong way. This path leads only to the gate on to King Street. You weren't thinking of running away, were you?'

Vicki felt the prickles of a hedge behind her back. She had been backed into a corner. 'Please,' she whispered. 'Please, I don't mean you any harm.'

There was a sound of crunching on the gravel, approaching quickly. Hay muttered a curse and stepped back, his hand slipping from the object at his waist. A moment later a man in the robes of a lord came around the corner with a guard at his heels. He nodded to them both, and Vicki found herself nodding back. Then, without waiting to consider her actions, she slipped behind the old man and his entourage, taking care to stay only a few paces in their wake. She thanked heaven for their interruption. Hay had intended, she felt sure, to kill her in order to reclaim the King's favour. Another sickeningly primitive act, another reason to be leaving.

She snatched a quick glance over her shoulder, but Hay had already melted away back down the path.

* * *

The Doctor had thanked Haldann and Otley for allowing him to help on their morning's work – they had merely muttered darkly in return – and set off through the palace's passageways to locate Vicki. The two scholars had given him cause to reflect on his own great age. It was important in life, he reflected, to cultivate the company of the young.

He turned a corner and saw from the corner of his eye a guard armed with a pike stepping from the shadows behind him. He wheeled around. 'Is it necessary to follow my every footstep?'

The guard looked down shamefacedly, stung by the authority in the Doctor's voice. 'I was instructed to attend to you by Lord Salisbury, sir, at all times.'

The Doctor groaned. 'Oh, dear, dear, can't the man get anything right?' he said, just loud enough for the guard to hear.

'What's that, sir?' asked the guard.

The Doctor affected a stoop, and hobbled right up to the man. 'It is a delicate matter . . . I should better explain. I suffer from a disorder of the bowel, you see, brought on by the advance of the years, Anno Domini and all that –' he broke off in a fit of splutters and coughs '– oh, excuse me, and I may have, er –' he lowered his voice to a whisper '– rather sudden need of a chamber pot, you understand?'

The guard nodded vigorously. 'Yes, I see, sir.' He was trying desperately, the Doctor could see, not to laugh.

'I asked Sir Robert if he could provide me with an attendant to wait on me with a pot at all times, as my ward is indisposed,' the Doctor went on, giving a good impersonation of one of Haldann's watery senile smiles. 'I think perhaps he misunderstood my message.' He simulated an internal pain and put a hand to his chest. 'Oh dear, I believe something is on the move now. You couldn't fetch me a pot, could you?'

The guard backed away. 'Yes, right away, sir. Just you stay right there on this spot and I'll return soon.' He hurried away, his mail clinking.

As soon as he had gone, the Doctor threw back his head and chuckled. 'Yes, yes, age has its advantages,' he said, hurrying away down the corridors in the opposite direction to the guard. 'Foolish fellow. Now, then, to find young Vicki.' He tapped himself on the chest in a reflex action, and immediately he sensed something wrong: a slight rearrangement of the static accoutrements of his outfit. His fob watch was in its place in his waistcoat, his spectacles nestled in their little compartment. But something was missing. 'The key,' he muttered. He hurried into a shadowy recess between two buttresses and examined himself. 'It couldn't have fallen off, the ribbon is strong, and I would have heard it. And I'm positive I had it when I spoke to Cecil, so . . .' He snapped bolt upright and his nostrils flared. 'Of course. Vicki.' There was a sense of sadness behind his aggressive delivery. 'Silly child. I must find her, before she brings disaster on us all.' He experienced a wave of worry. Away from him, and knowing what she did of the Gunpowder Plot, the girl was a dangerous liability. He tapped his chin. 'Now then, she must be heading for the main gate, through which we entered . . .'

He gathered his wits and hurried along the passageways, heading in the direction that would lead him to the privy gardens.

Familiar voices from ahead brought him up short, and sent him scurrying for cover behind a suit of armour at the base of a flight of steps. One of the voices was Cecil's, and he was saying, 'It is a simple thing, hardly the burden you suggest.'

'Well, it's never been necessary before,' came the reply. The Doctor recognized the owner of the second voice as the Lord Chamberlain. 'Now, will you please let me get on with my important business. I've just been to the launderers, and they're not halfway through drying the pennants, hopeless. You cannot throw new duties on me now, Cecil, not at this late stage of the preparations. If you want to search, search yourself, you have guards enough.'

Cecil sighed. 'But as I have said, it is a petty thing, not worthy of my attention.' The Doctor, his fears for Vicki temporarily forgotten, strained his ears to catch the rest. 'The discrepancy in the rents has only just now caught my eye. I'm sure it's nothing, as I say. It will take you only moments to look.'

The Chamberlain emitted a heartfelt groan. 'Oh, go on, then. Lay another distraction on the pile that quivers like a tower of books upon my head.'

Cecil said smoothly, 'It will extend your tour of inspection by only a moment.' The Doctor heard a rustling of papers and peered around the suit of armour as far as he dared for a better view of the two men. As fortune would have it, and by one of the curious coincidences the Doctor had more than his fair share of on his travels, they had chosen to stop only a few feet from him. Cecil was handing the Chamberlain a couple of folded sheets of paper. 'There, you see,' he said, tapping a gloved finger at a particular point. 'This small area here, the former kitchen beneath the chamber, was rented as a coal store by a man called Bright until last March. He died, and his widow passed it over to a man called –' he paused significantly '– Percy.'

The Chamberlain's brow twitched. 'Percy? You mean Thomas Percy?'

Cecil nodded. 'The same.'

The Chamberlain sighed. 'Then what is the problem? Percy is always in and out of the court, as a gentleman pensioner he has free access, and a house in a street near Parliament. Why should he not have a coal store near by?' He shook his head. 'Really, Cecil, you *will* see menace everywhere.' He passed the papers back.

'Percy is also a Catholic,' said Cecil smoothly. 'And the cellar lies directly beneath the House of Lords, where, as I have no need to remind you, the State Opening is due to take place.'

'Percy has a measure of eccentricity, as have all his family,' the Chamberlain said patiently. 'But can you seriously believe he intends harm to the King? What do you imagine he has stored in his cellar but coal?' He gave a mocking laugh. 'A stock of gunpowder, I suppose, right under Parliament itself? To be let off under the King, and blow us all to blazes? How is Percy supposed to have brought it in, pray tell? It is unlike you, Cecil, to be so very silly.'

Cecil tucked the rental papers under one arm. 'I consider myself prudent.'

The Chamberlain laughed again. 'If it will please you, then, Cecil. It will make me a relaxing detour on the inspection. I shall share a moment's mirth with Percy and perhaps I shall borrow a lump of coal off him.' He swept away, his laughter resounding around the high ceilings of the palace passageways. 'Ha ha, a powder plot, bang bang!'

The Doctor watched as Cecil stood silently, his face composed for a moment with white light from one of the tall windows lending him an unsuitably saintish gravity. What conflicts and fears must be raging in that mind, he wondered; and what devious skill the man had, the skill of a master chess player, to position his pieces so expertly as to lead his enemies, unsuspecting, right into his trap. In this light, the attempt Cecil had arranged on his life was unsurprising, as any random element was unacceptable. The Doctor longed to know more. By what agency had Cecil manipulated the plotters without arousing their suspicions? How had he covered his own involvement? His curiosity nagged away at him like an unscratchable itch. He simply had to know. It was his defining characteristic, the thing that made him the Doctor, the impulse that had driven him centuries ago from his own planet and people.

Cecil pulled himself up and walked away. The Doctor waited a few seconds and stepped tentatively out from his hiding-place, trying to decide which way to go. To follow Cecil's or Vicki's trail?

Vicki was crouched in the scant cover afforded her by the overhanging branches of an oak, one of a row that lined the long gravelled approach to the main gate. She had watched from her position as the old lord and his retinue had passed through ahead of her, nodding to the guards on both sides of the gate as it was swung up and then lowered. The faces of the guards were impassive, but they were implicitly prepared for action, and any hope of slipping through such a large body of men – there were five on either side – was crushed. She pondered an attempt to work a Doctor-style trick on them and decided finally that her youth forbade it. The guards would simply not take her seriously. Moreover, she was certain Cecil would have sent them orders not to allow her or the Doctor to pass, and the walls she had glimpsed through the trees were high and unscalable. Besides, she was terrified of heights.

A rush of hot, frustrated tears threatened to overwhelm her. She felt like a helpless child. The Doctor was right, as usual, and now she would have to trail back to him in disgrace and face his anger. Grimly, pushing back her tears forcefully by swallowing several times, she stood up and prepared to turn back. She hoped desperately that she wouldn't meet that vile Hay.

Something brushed through the undergrowth, only a few feet away.

At first she took it for an animal. The sound had been furtive, the snap of a dry twig, the rustle and crackle of autumn leaves. She turned around, expecting to see a squirrel.

Instead, through a gap in the bare twisted branches of the trees that lined the palace's far wall, she caught a second's glimpse of a shuffling figure. It seemed shapeless and black, and it moved away making hardly a sound. Even in a moment's sight of it, she saw that its gait was shambling and uneven. With a shock, she realized this was the hooded assassin she had seen in the Doctor's room.

Without stopping to consider her actions she hurried after it, taking no care to conceal the sounds of her own pursuit as she crashed through the almost disintegrated mass of fallen yellow leaves. Uppermost in her mind was a confused desire to help the Doctor, to atone for her deceit.

The assassin came into view again. He was loping frantically towards a huge old oak tree, which was at least ten or eleven feet in circumference, and grew against the brickwork of the palace's perimeter wall. It afforded him no protection, there was no gap or hidden door in the wall, yet he was making for the tree with the desperation one might reserve for a portcullis that was crashing down. Vicki tore after him, now only seconds behind. Panting, she rounded the side of the tree, expecting to face the assassin. In daylight his hood would be no protection for his identity. A small voice inside her warned that she was hardly equipped for the imminent confrontation.

But the figure had vanished.

Not trusting her own senses, Vicki made a circuit of the tree. The assassin was nowhere to be seen, and he could not have got away without her seeing or at least hearing him.

She made a second, slower, inspection of the tree, her suspicion mounting. She remembered her first step inside the TARDIS, the utter incomprehensibility of its vast interior behind its boxlike façade. This gave her the same feeling. She reached out and stroked the gnarled bark, which in one place had curved itself into a curiously regular design similar to a doorknob. She blinked and looked again. The knob looked entirely natural, and was set deep in the wood. She reached out and, more by instinct than with any real intent, pressed it hard.

With a clunk of some hidden contrivance, the side of the tree swung inward, to reveal a roughly semicircular space just large enough to admit one person at a squeeze. Cautiously Vicki peered inside. There was nothing beyond but darkness and a musty, metallic odour. Distantly she thought she could hear a steady drip of water on stone.

Her concern to repair her relationship with the Doctor pushing her on, she extended one leg through the door, and keeping the other firmly on the outside, manoeuvred herself halfway through. She was reminded of childhood games of hide-and-seek, of pushing her way into an old cupboard or forgotten larder. Illogically she found herself wishing for an electric torch.

Suddenly her right foot, the one that was inside the hollowed-out tree, slid on something horribly greasy and she fell forward, her hand scrabbling for a hold that wasn't there. She was pulled completely inside in her attempt to restore her balance, fell in a flurry of arms and legs and bowled over onto a narrow flight of descending stone steps. The door swung shut with a resounding clunk of its hidden mechanism, cutting off the faint light from outside; somewhere high above her a mechanism squeaked, as a wheel might when a rope winds on a pulley.

Terrified, Vicki tried to pull herself up. The top steps were coated in a thick slime of some sort. It felt mossy and stank of untended drains, and it was only by keeping the palms of both hands stretched on either side of the hollowed trunk was she able, at last, to stand.

The blackness was total. She fumbled for the door and found nothing. 'Come on, come on,' she whispered. 'There must be an opening mechanism.' Her fingers scrabbled desperately all over the smooth-faced surface, but there were no indentations or grooves. An awful, animal panic was building in her chest and she stifled a scream. She had a terror of confinement. In fact, she thought gloomily, she had a terror of just about everything.

It didn't take her very long to realize that she had no choice but to go down and follow the assassin into the dripping depths. Carefully she put out a foot and tested the first of the slimy steps. Keeping her hands on the walls of the circular chamber she went down a step at a time, forcing her breathing to return to a regular pattern. She descended slowly, conscious that the steps were twisting to the right, taking her down on a spiral path. The slime was less sticky as she went on and she increased her pace.

She told herself firmly that the tunnel had to lead somewhere, and a little of her spirit returned.

And then she walked straight into the assassin, who was waiting on the steps. A hand clamped over her mouth, and there was just time to register the pain of the sharp blow to her forehead before another kind of darkness descended.

Part Three

The Plot Thickens

7

Intrigue Down Below

Regularly Firking looked across at Ian, his gateway to renown and heroism, who sat hunched in a dark corner of the yard, his head bowed over his scrap of paper. He had been turning it over and over wistfully all day, staring with such ferocious vigour at its meaningless lines that by rights he should have worn it out. Would that it were a doting letter from his lady-love and not a grim barrier to their ardour.

Hodge broke into these romantic daydreams. 'Here is an end to my day's toil,' he said proudly, holding up a new pair of lady's boots. A typical piece of Hodge's work, they were in all particulars stitched and seamed with painstaking precision. At such bold, creative moments Firking always felt mildly envious of Hodge, whose hands could turn themselves to the manufacture of such dainty products. His own skill lay in the cutting of strips from sheets of hide, keeping waste to the minimum, together with an occasional spot of darning and minor patch repairs. He had neither the craftsman's instincts nor the delicacy required of a true shoemaker. He was in it for the brotherly feeling, really.

Hodge set the boots down and made a show of dusting his hands. 'Gramercy, I'm now fit to rest, for sure.'

Firking picked up one of the boots. He said teasingly, 'It's a fine job you've done here, Ralph. You must have a stool, and a bucket in which to soothe your own poor feet, which must be weak for want of sitting. And a pie to recover your strength, and broth to revive your brain.'

'Ah,' Hodge sighed lustily, 'and I would find a can of ale, and all, to wash them down, and tickle my loins, i'faith.'

A stentorian bellow cut across their conversation. 'Ah, if you would, I would send you to trip out of my workshop!' Firking looked up to see their master, red-faced as usual, bearing towards them across the yard. 'Sops and dolts that laze find no favour in the market, here or elsewhere!'

Hurriedly Firking returned to work. 'As I am hard in my graft your words are not false,' he said ingratiatingly.

The master stopped in front of Hodge and picked up the new pair of boots. 'If you are so eager with your fingerings as these would give evidence, have at a new task, and a most pressing and important one.' His tone was more serious than usual, an indication that he did not exaggerate. Curious, Firking strained his ears to hear the details, brushing the hair back from his ears. The master had another item of footwear in his hand which he now passed to Hodge. 'A commission from the King's tailors. Against Wednesday for Parliament's opening, we are to make up a right splendid pair of boy's shoes, taking the measurements from this sandal.'

Hodge turned the sandal over in his hands. 'Strange. Not like any I've seen before. Too cold to be leather yet bends in my hand.'

The master waved a disparaging hand. 'From abroad, I'd say. A most queer article, and thus doubly worthy of replacement.' He clapped Hodge across the shoulders. 'You must set to and make a fresh pair in all parts like it, and with haste. There will be a good few cans of ale in it if you fulfil the commission.'

Hodge's eyes gleamed. 'Ah, master, a good bargain, and you have my word on this side of it.'

'Then set to, good gentleman, set to!' With a final smile of encouragement the master walked away.

'Well, you are in favour,' Firking said. 'A job from the King is the final seal on your career. You'll be master of this yard one day.' Under cover of this flattery, he grabbed the sandal and studied its odd substance. 'Ah, where would the boy have come by this?'

He had forgotten Ian, who came forward suddenly

from his corner, his eyes widening. 'I think I know,' he said quietly. A smile wrote itself over his face as he came closer. 'It's Vicki's shoe. That clinches it.'

'Clinches what?' Firking was bewildered.

'She must be with the King,' Ian said, muttering under his breath like a moonstruck beggar. 'And that means the Doctor will be there, too. The conniving old trout.' He shook his head with a kind of good-humoured resignation. 'He'll have carted the TARDIS away with him, of course.'

'Your talking is as scrambled as that French note of yours,' Firking said. 'TARDIS?'

Ian beamed at them. 'I've solved one of my problems. The old man I told you about, he must be with the King. This sandal belongs to him.' He spoke slowly, as if addressing an idiot.

Hodge cottoned on. 'Ah, then you can join him at the Whitehall Palace, and enlist the aid of James in the hunt for Barbara.'

Firking nodded. 'With the help of the King's guards you'll soon have her winkled out and back in your loving arms.'

Ian's good mood seemed to pale slightly at these encouraging words. He stared at the sandal. 'I'm not sure. The Doctor may not appreciate me barging in. It could be dangerous.'

Firking snorted. 'Even for the lady's sake!'

But Hodge was nodding. 'I see it. You are in the secret employ of the King, and must watch your step, taking care not to reveal yourself in the open. For then your face would become known wide and far and your worth as an agent lost.'

'You're right,' said Ian. 'I'm still on my own. But I do know that the Doctor's safe.' He sighed. 'And in pretty good digs, as usual.'

'Good digs, what is that?' asked Firking. 'You talk an amount of guff, friend.'

Ian grinned and backed away to his corner.

* * *

Catesby, who was a pounder by inclination, pounded down the streets heading eastward, his eyes alert for any sign of Fawkes or the woman Barbara. His head was growing more thick and muzzy. Tinnitus clamoured persistently in his left ear. He knew he presented a strange sight to the passers-by in his dishevelled red garments and shabby hat.

The Bible, to him, was something one believed in implicitly. He had never questioned its messages, or the miracles performed in its pages, and the tales of demonic possessions and the like, were all very well in a context removed in time and place. But in the modern world, even at a moment of such import, they were not expected. The powers of the devil woman were terrifying. Then, Catesby saw himself as God's agent on Earth; so where was the surprise, asked the part of his brain given over to wild fears, perhaps encouraged by the blow to his head, in the devil's dispatch of opposing players? Fawkes had fallen, and the plot was endangered. Evil had the upper hand, and the Devil was toying with him, challenging him, leaving him hope of success. That, Catesby hoped fervently, would be evil's downfall, for he could still slay the woman and bring Fawkes back in line. He had two days.

Occupied as he was by this frenetic inner deliberation Catesby's watchfulness and instinct for security were blunted, and he was slower than he might normally have been in picking up the fact he was being followed. A tickling sensation, a feeling of being under scrutiny, had been nagging at him since he had shut his door in Princes Street, and it gradually came to prominence as he neared Lark Street. He stopped dead and was aware of someone behind him also grinding to a halt. He turned about and saw only the milling throng of the city, and walked on. Seconds later the same sensation returned. The trick was employed a second and then a third time, and it was on this turn he caught a glimpse of muddied white skirts being pulled into a narrow alley. Enraged, he stalked over and rounded the corner.

A slight figure waited there, her head pressed tight against the alley's wall. She backed away, and he reached out, clamped her jaw in his hand and pulled her to him. He whispered, 'You're looking out for somebody, are you?'

She struggled in his grip. 'Oh, unhand me, sir, else I'll let out a most chilling scream and bring the watch running!'

'In these streets? Screams are heard every minute, a familiarity, and none are stirred.' He regarded her coolly. A spirited child, eighteen or so by his reckoning, wisps of red hair escaping from the frilly cap of the serving maid. He realized he had seen her before. 'You are one of Mother Bunch's girls?'

'That's right,' she said, still struggling. For such a dainty creature her arms were unusually powerful, and he had some difficulty restraining her. He supposed that a pretty girl working at an inn would need to be able to protect herself. 'And you, varmint, are Red Rob, that took away the lady from the tavern yesterday. I have been charged to look out for you, and now, on my way to work and as luck has it, I see you sneaking along.' She stuck out her chin. 'Where is the lady?'

Catesby chuckled. 'A lady? I know of none.'

The girl stopped struggling and caught her breath. 'You are a Catholic dog and a liar. You have cut her throat and I know it, I see it in your eyes!'

'Believe what you will, but trip on.' He released her, confident she posed little threat. 'Bother me no more. Go on, vanish.'

She wiped a line of dribble from her mouth with a lace cuff and sneered. 'I could call the watch and have them set on you,' she said.

Catesby pulled himself up and laughed heartily. 'A drab like you? Skip by, mutton-doings, you think the watch would take your word against mine? And do you even know my name, I wonder? Robert is a commonplace title among gentlemen.'

She shot him a venomous look. 'There's evil in your doings. I know you have killed the lady, that you have some works afoot, and it is a calamitous thing.' She pushed past him roughly and ran away up the street towards the tavern, her boots making a harsh percussion over the cobbles as she fled, near to tears.

Catesby watched her go with a grin. The babblings of such a person would make no impress on a watchman.

Vicki's first thoughts, as the well-furnished room swam into place around her, were that she had somehow been taken back to her room in the palace. Then she began to notice the differences between it and this high-ceilinged, mahogany-panelled den. If this was a cell – and the first thing she did after getting up from the large bed was to try the tall metal door to confirm that supposition – it was an uncommonly luxurious one. There was no window, and illumination came from two huge black candles fixed to a wall. A carpet, dull green in colour, covered the floor. Other furniture included a large writing desk, its drawers secured, and a couple of padded chairs with striped cushions and gold-scrolled adornments.

It was only then she realized that her clothes had been changed. She now wore a simple, fresh white linen dress that covered her arms and legs. A moment later a second shock hit her with the impact of a sluice of freezing water, dispelling in an instant the vestiges of grogginess.

The TARDIS key was nowhere on her person.

Fawkes had dragged Barbara through the streets to an inn some distance from Princes Street, and booked them a room on its top floor. As the door closed behind them, Barbara swallowed and steeled herself. She longed to fall on the bed and let it soothe her aches. But she had work to do, for the sake of history.

'Guy, you must go back.' She wrung her hands and covered a yawn. 'You can't abandon the plot for my sake.'

He smiled and sank on to the bed. 'I don't intend to. But I will see you returned to your friends.'

'No.' She sat down and fought back a desire just to

collapse. 'It's important, you must leave me and get back to . . .'

Her head spun. The pillow rushed up to her face and a second later she was asleep.

The weather had forced James inside. He lounged in one of the many thrones in one of the many royal apartments, the speech unrolled and unregarded on his knee. Craftily, he had chosen one of the less frequented chambers in the hope it would put Cecil off his trail, and left instructions with a guard at the loggets board to send Victor on when he finally arrived. The silence gave him the time to consider fresh strategies. There had to be a way to make the boy weaken. It had always been so easy before. He was the King and everybody else was a subject and had to obey him, whatever the command. Perhaps, he pondered, it was Victor's stubbornness and potentially suicidal refusal of privilege that made this hunt the best yet.

To his ineffable dismay there were three sudden, sharp raps on the door. 'Oh, hell take the man,' he grunted. To the guard on the door he whispered, 'Don't admit him. We shall pretend we aren't here.'

The guard shrugged. 'My mate is on duty on the other side of the door, Your Majesty. Lord Salisbury will know you tarry in these rooms.'

James cursed. 'Then have Salisbury sent in. Honestly, I'm beginning to regret bestowing that title. The little chap now sees himself as a mighty cathedral. I should have made him Reading or something.' Hurriedly he picked up the speech and assumed a studious expression.

Cecil was admitted. James heard the tidy click of his heels. 'Your Majesty.'

Without looking up James said, 'Don't even think of saying that word, Cecil.'

'I beg Your Majesty's pardon?'

'The C word.'

There was a long and uncomfortable silence. James fancied he could hear Cecil stewing like beef in a pot. At last he said, 'Your Maj–'

James cut across him. 'Observe, I am learning my speech, and I would not be disturbed.' He looked up for the first time and had to hide his pleasure at Cecil's red face. 'Is there any pressing business?'

Cecil clenched his fists. 'James, in all urgency, I must speak with you –'

The door opened once again and the outer guard poked his head through. 'The old doctor, Your Majesty.'

James's face lit up. 'Ah, good news. He is a charmingly moral gentleman, of original conversation and effervescent wit. And no doubt he is accompanied by his dutiful ward. Show him through.'

The Doctor entered. James was immediately struck by two things. Firstly, Victor was absent. Secondly, the old man was a positive picture of worry, his fingers flickering about like butterfly's wings. 'Ah, Your Majesty. I've been searching you out in the hope you might have encountered young Victor.'

'Would that were so,' said James. 'It has struck one. His fitting must surely be finished.'

'Yes, yes. I am sure.' He tutted. 'But boys will wander off, I suppose.'

Cecil rumbled, 'I would say there was a difference between idle wandering and the ignorance of a royal summons.'

James found himself agreeing. 'You speak truth, Cec. What say you, Doctor?'

The Doctor looked unconcerned. 'Victor has a conscientious character, Your Majesty, and would not contemplate disobedience. My feeling is that he has lost himself in these sprawling and most impressive passages.'

'Your feeling is wrong,' said Cecil. 'The palace is crowded, and anyone would stop to give directions. Your Victor must be in hiding.' James noted the antagonism crackling between the two men, and wondered if their hard treatment of one another concealed a secret dispute.

The Doctor's next words were spoken in honeyed tones. 'Thank you for your escort, by the way, but it was quite unnecessary.' He stroked his chin thoughtfully and said, more loudly, 'I wonder, Your Majesty, if perhaps Victor has somehow wandered accidentally out of the palace grounds?'

'Impossible,' Cecil snapped. 'All the approaches are monitored. He would have been turned back. More likely that if he is gone he had a will to leave.'

The Doctor ignored him. 'Maybe I could be given leave to seek him beyond the walls?'

James considered, and finally shook his head. 'Cecil is right, Doctor.' He tapped the arm of the throne in irritation. 'Wilfully or not, Victor has gone against me, and I do not like this. You shall remain within the walls until he is found or shows himself. Make this known, Cecil.'

'Gladly, Your Majesty,' said Cecil. He turned smartly and withdrew.

The Doctor's fingers described anxious patterns in front of his chest, as if they were searching for something that usually hung there. 'Very well,' he said. With a nod to the throne he flounced out as grandly as he had entered. His head was raised so high that he narrowly avoided a collision with the Chamberlain, who was on his way in.

'Watch where you're going, you blundering oaf,' the Doctor said.

'I could say the same of you,' said the Chamberlain. He waited until the Doctor had turned a corner and then entered, performed the necessary prostrations, and said breathlessly, 'A matter has raised itself, Your Majesty. It was not my doing, I protested that you were at work and should not be disturbed, but the Lord Mayor has been so insistent –'

James made another show of looking up from his speech. He growled. 'What now?'

The Chamberlain scurried forward. 'It's the Lord Mayor, Your Majesty, of London.'

'Well, what does he want?'

'Something peculiar,' said the Chamberlain. 'A wooden box, they say it's the size of a large, upright coffin, was found along the eastward approach to the city yesterday, and as it looked abandoned and none cared to claim it as theirs, it was carted off to be chopped for firewood.'

'What do I care for this box?' thundered James. 'I am King!'

The Chamberlain went nervously on. 'There is more to this. The box was taken to a yard and men set to with axes, but the wood was as hard as rock and could not be broken. Next they tried burning it, and the flames would not take hold, merely licked about it. Now, one of the masters of the yard is an alderman, and he passed message of this unholy box to the Mayor, who ordered it to be carted to the Guildhall that he might inspect it for himself. He found that it had writing on its sides, in code, and a lock that will admit no key. And now, baffled, he requests you examine it.'

James sighed and put a hand to his brow. He could feel the first faint beginnings of a headache. 'Blast this box!' he shouted, so loudly the Chamberlain almost fell over in fright. 'The prorogue is over, Parliament opens Tuesday night, and you would have me looking at wooden puzzle boxes!'

'Not me, Your Majesty, the Lord Mayor.' He lowered his voice. 'He fears – witchcraft.'

For a moment James's resolve faltered. He had an acute and enduring dread of witchcraft, a dread that had encouraged him to write a couple of lengthy treatises on the subject. The mere mention of the word sent a cold chill through his marrow. 'A magic box? And what would the Mayor have me do with it?'

The Chamberlain swallowed. 'As king, the people believe you can banish its spell and exorcize the demon within by the touch of your hand.'

'Ignorant clot-polls. My touch is not heavenly, it is for my aptitude and strong mentality that the Lord made me king.'

'Begging your pardon, Your Majesty, but that is not what the people believe.'

'Whaa-at?'

'I mean,' said the Chamberlain, 'that, although they have an abiding regard for your intelligence, they believe that the monarch's hand can rid a taint of disease or evil.'

James snorted. 'Then the people have pickle between their ears. Tell them to get a priest. I am too busy to be spared my duties.'

Sybil ran so fast under the archway leading into the shoemakers' yard that to Ian she appeared as a gingery blur. Her hair was disarrayed under her mop-cap and her pretty face red from exertion. Her appearance caused a sizeable stir among the men, many of whom cried coarse greetings as she tumbled past.

Firking raised a welcoming hand. 'Have at it, Syb!' He turned to Hodge and Ian and grinned broadly. 'But does she fly from Mother Bunch or some fellow that would have at her? Nah, in faith, it's more likely that the fellow would be fleeing, such are her wanton passions!'

Sybil crashed to a halt right in front of their small group in the corner. Her green eyes were alive with sparkles. 'Oh, truthful Firking, God make it so mundane!' she gasped. 'I'd stake my maidenhead, and that's much, for some shift and turnabout in the fortunes. But I have dashed here in the hope of finding this godly gent, and my heart leaps to speak what my mind knows.' She pointed to Ian and clapped her hand over her mouth, plainly filled with terror. 'I fear very much that they have done away with your wife!'

Ian forced down his reaction. 'Sybil,' he said urgently. 'Speak more slowly.' He had one remaining hope. She had said only that she feared for Barbara's life. 'What do you know?'

'Oh, Ian, my doubts for your wife's safety are strong. I met with her captor, Red Robert the cursed Taig, in the street, and he was powerfully laughing and cursing when I enquired of her.' She choked back her sobs. 'Ah, it is a fearful episode, all told!'

'You saw him? Where? When?'

'Not half an hour since, around the houses in Lark Street. I witnessed him loping about, his hair and apparel all in disorder, and I tracked him, keeping myself silent and to the dark places. But he found me out, and meant to strike at me, till I countered with my query on Barbara.' She paused to draw breath.

'And what next?' prompted Firking.

'He laughed and made jokes, called me a drab and a mutton-collar, and said if I told my tale I'd be chastened and laughed at.' She slumped. 'And, in the broad flow of it, I suppose he is right in those details.'

Ian felt both relief that Barbara might still be alive, and anger that Sybil had exaggerated her fears for dramatic effect. Keeping himself calm he asked, 'Did you see where he was going? Did you find out anything about him?'

Sybil nodded excitedly. 'Ah yes, Ian, I did so, for the foolish hound let his name slip.' She came closer and whispered, 'It is Robert Catesby, but will that help? It brings no dividend, I fear.'

At first Ian felt a spasm of fear, a swift jab between his shoulder-blades, but then, as his memory served up the facts to fit the name, he was overcome by the simple delight of being 'in' on history. 'Catesby,' he breathed. He looked around the yard, at Hodge's blank and uncomprehending brow and the plastic sandal on his workbench. 'Against the opening of Parliament . . .' The Gunpowder Plot was an event of which he did have a decent working knowledge. As part of his all-round teacher training he'd been required to brush up on it – on one occasion he'd had cause to surprise a class of Coal Hill third formers with his knowledge when standing in for Barbara on a sick day. The sudden flashback to Coal Hill almost sent him reeling. He snapped himself out of his musing and addressed them firmly, 'What's the date? I'm losing track of time.'

Firking answered. 'Third day in November.'

'And Parliament opens on the fifth,' Ian said wonderingly. He gently laid the back of his hand on his forehead as if to settle the thoughts whizzing around inside. He recalled the Doctor's behaviour of the previous morning and shook his head in grudging admiration. 'So that was his game.'

'What game is this?' asked Sybil. The bells of London began to peal and she was distracted. 'Ah, you see, I must not linger, I am late already, and Mother Bunch will have me peeled like a potato gone to jumbling!' She smiled up at Ian and wrinkled her little upturned slope of a nose. 'Wishing you the best of it in all ventures,' she said, already slipping away. 'Find that Catesby and stuff it to him, I say!' With a cheery wave she departed through the archway, starting to pick up speed through the scattered sawdust.

Ian squared himself. 'Thank you, Sybil,' he said quietly. 'I'll remember you.' Already a strategy was shaping itself in his mind. He only hoped that his training, and his memory, wouldn't let him down. He turned to Firking and stuck out his hand. 'And you too.'

Firking's brow furrowed. 'Are you off with only a name as your guide?'

Hodge put in, 'Who is this Catesby? Not known to me. You are much altered by the news, Ian, but your standing strong against the knave can't lead you to his door.'

Ian wondered how best to phrase his next words. 'I have an advantage. Some foreknowledge. I must leave, straight away. But I won't forget the shelter you gave me.'

Firking beamed. 'We were glad to give it.' He added significantly, 'In the hope of having some reward for our service.'

Ian smiled, fumbled in his purse, and handed over a couple of the larger gold coins. 'Reward enough?'

'Ah, a porpentine each.' Eagerly Firking passed one of the coins to Hodge. 'That'll keep us in pies for a six-month! A pie a day!'

'Yes, pies,' added Hodge. 'A 'prentice's wage our master pays us, the scurvy toad, even after five years' service, and though we have lodging and keep thrown in, a pie is a scarce treat in our humble lives.' He rubbed his hands. 'A pie a day, a pie a day, such reward.' He beamed at Ian. 'Visit us again, Chesterton, for we'll make you an honorary son of the gentle craft!'

'Thanks again,' said Ian, who was impatient to be off.

He gave a final nod of farewell and strode with renewed purpose through the archway and back into the London streets.

Vicki was going over her last moments of consciousness. Having given the matter some consideration she was fairly sure that she had kept the TARDIS key clenched in her fist right until the fall of the knock-out blow. Which meant that the assassin had either removed it, or it had fallen from her grip as she fell. The tunnel, she reminded herself, had been totally dark, and no light could have fallen on the metal of the key. Most probably it remained where it had fallen.

Suddenly, there were footsteps.

She backed away from the door as they came closer. She swallowed involuntarily, her mouth drying up, as they reached the other side of the door and there was a fumbling of keys, the sharp report of a bolt being drawn, the click of a latch, and the gruesome creak as the door swung inwards.

Vicki steeled herself. Please, she found herself thinking, let it be the Doctor, or Ian, or Barbara, one or all of whom could have ended this adventure, set things to rights and have come to pick me up on their way back to the Ship. They could be lurking behind the door, determined to string out my anticipation as a tease, a cruel joke.

Instead, two men appeared. Each man was broad and well-muscled. Their heads were shaven, and they wore identical white linen outfits. Their faces were totally expressionless. In a way it made them more frightening. They walked in and stood either side of the door, which creaked open a second time.

A shadow fell on the carpet, seeped around the door, brought with it a spectral figure: the cloaked assassin, his cowl thrown forward, the blade of the dagger he held in one of his long-fingered hands catching the candlelight.

Vicki stepped foward boldly. 'Who are you?' she demanded. Her voice quivered despite her resolution.

The assassin closed the door calmly, and slipped the key

into a concealed fold of his cloak. Vicki registered again the deformed shape beneath the robes. 'Who are you?' she repeated.

He raised his head, and although she was standing two feet away from him in reasonable light she could see nothing in the darkness behind the cowl apart from the hint of a hooked nose and curled lip. Without making a sound he walked towards her, the knife outstretched.

Vicki backed away. If, somehow, she could slip behind him, and overpower him . . . She reconsidered. He was a foot taller than her, and powerfully built. And there were his bald flunkeys. She had no chance.

'Please,' she begged. 'Please, listen to me, I don't mean any –'

She gasped as, still walking backwards, she tripped up and toppled back over on to the bed. She was spread-eagled, defenceless, unprotected.

The assassin reached up with his free hand and ripped back the cowl. He did so with a savage eagerness, combined with a slackening of the muscles, as though glad at being able to unburden his need for secrecy. The action sent a thrill of terror through Vicki's body; for if he was showing his face to her, didn't that mean he intended her never to tell the secret?

What he revealed was something far stranger than she had expected. His head was encased in a thick black stocking, with holes for his glittering green eyes, around which was fastened a string that held in place a false nose and lip, made of a shiny substance like china, over his own.

Vicki slid back, horrified. She watched as he reached for the back of the stocking and began to pull. The disguise, nose and lip and all, came away in his hand.

Underneath was the face of Hay.

'Well, my dear girl,' he said, in a voice very different to the one he used in the company of King James, 'I have delivered one of my secrets. I think it only fair that you should render me some of yours in return.'

8

Strange Allies

The Doctor strode along the passages of the palace, the corners of his mouth turned down gravely. He didn't realize he was talking aloud. 'Bad enough that Vicki has vanished,' he muttered. 'But the key, the key . . .' He stopped at a junction and leant against a pillar. 'Oh, it is a foolish thing I've done,' he said. 'But I couldn't control my own curiosity. I only hope Barbara and young Chester– Ian are safe.' He raked a hand through his long silver hair. 'But what about Vicki, eh? Where can she have got to?'

'Perhaps I can help you, Doctor,' a voice whispered over his shoulder.

The Doctor covered his surprise at this interruption, as he concealed everything that might be construed a failing, by pretending to be angry. 'And who might you be, sir?' He turned about and saw Cecil, who appeared more pensive than usual. 'Ah, it's only you, then. What do you want with this skulking?'

Cecil looked the Doctor up and down, his gaze lingering on his frock-coat and checked trousers. He spoke slowly and without insinuation. 'In my career I have seen service in all the countries of Europe, and your attire is unlike any worn there. And not at all in the native style, either. Yet you are clearly an Englishman.'

'Oh, am I? Am I?'

'You are no doctor. At first I had you marked for a Dutchman, trained to act in our ways.' He shook his head slightly. 'In my heart I knew you were not. I have men ringed in all sectors of the Dutch Provinces, and no plan made there is secret to me. There was no word of your coming. No, you are a menace more homegrown, from some . . .' He waved a hand distractedly. 'Some other England?'

The Doctor liked to be thought of as mysterious, and he pulled his most inscrutable face. 'Perhaps, perhaps.'

'You fought off the man I sent.'

'Ah! You admit it, then.'

'Yet you are old and seemingly feeble. And worst of all, you know what no man could know.'

'Eh, what's that? What do you mean?' The Doctor was thoroughly enjoying stringing his opponent along. 'Ah, yes, you mean the Gunpowder Plot?'

Cecil flushed and gripped him by the shoulders. 'For God's sake, man, be quiet! Make mention of it again and I'll be forced to cut out your tongue, here and now!'

The Doctor shook himself free. 'Rather,' he said sternly, 'than send another man to do your butchering, eh?' He stepped back and regarded Cecil. 'You loathe the Catholics, and you consider James to be too soft on them. Am I right?'

'When I arranged the succession I did not anticipate his stubbornness or his laxity. It is a simple thing when considered. He must be made to understand.'

'I see. By some, er . . . explosive gesture?'

Cecil checked that nobody was in earshot before bringing his head uncomfortably close to the Doctor's. 'How do you know this?' he whispered fiercely. 'Only the Spaniard could have told you.'

'The Spaniard? Now that would be that disagreeable hooded henchman of yours, yes? No, I'm afraid our acquaintance has been very brief. There was no time to talk, he was too busy trying to throttle me.'

'Then how? And who sent you here?'

The Doctor raised a finger. 'First, a question for you. Where is Victor?'

'Victor,' Cecil mused. He essayed a brief, tight smile. 'When the King finds out he has been deceived on that front he will be angry.'

'And if,' the Doctor said threateningly, 'he should find out that his closest adviser is planning to blow him and his parliament to the high heavens? I imagine he would be slightly peeved about that too. Except you aren't, are you? Because in one deal of the cards you can be rid of the hothead Catholics and the King's opposition to your political designs. Well, sir, I must credit you. It's very, very clever and very, very unscrupulous.'

'And how do you intend to stop it?'

The Doctor huffed. 'Really, my dear chap. Your connivings are of no concern to me.' He lowered his voice. 'This is my bargain. Return Victor – or rather, Vicki – to me, and we shall gladly take our leave of you.'

Cecil narrowed his eyes. 'What impious device is this? Your tongue makes strange turns, Doctor, and I am not cozened so quickly.'

'No trick is intended,' the Doctor said. He was taken aback by Cecil's manifest surprise. 'You mean – you really don't know where she is?'

'My assumption was that you had hidden her away. She cannot be in the palace, she would have been seen by now.'

The Doctor's face fell. 'Then . . . where is she? Where is she?'

Barbara woke. She was lying on a comfortable bed. She stretched out an arm and her fingers connected with something warm and hairy.

She leapt up. Fawkes lay beside her. To her great relief they were both fully clothed. In the lantern light his face was made golden and chiselled. She took one of his hands and held back a tear. Was there nothing she could do to prevent his death, to repay him? The plot would be discovered anyway, with or without Fawkes. If she advised him to flee abroad, what difference would it make? The Stuart line would continue, November the fifth would be commemorated by some other name.

In her mind she saw the Doctor looking on disapprovingly. She knew her duty to his precious web of time. Fulfilling it would now be even harder. It was an indication of the perspective she was gaining on her travels that she did not seriously contemplate an attempt to alter things. She had learnt before that her feelings were a tiny tragedy in the great scheme.

'If there was any other way . . .' she breathed, squeezing Fawkes's hand tightly.

He was roused by the sound. One of his big blue eyes flicked open and he smiled, devastatingly.

Barbara sat up. 'Guy, you must do what I said. Return to Catesby.'

He frowned. 'And be led on to what destiny holds. Is that your wish?'

'My wishes don't come into it. It's cruel, but destiny doesn't allow exceptions.' She smiled. 'I'll never forget you, or how you saved me.'

'Nor I you.' His deep masculine tones reverberated through his stocky frame. 'It is not a thing a man should usually speak of before a lady, but I have known many women. The battlefield makes a fellow thirst for love, and I have taken a full swig from Aphrodite's bottle. But none as fair as you.' He pulled away. 'My work waits. Goodbye, Barbara. The Lord preserve you.'

'And you,' she managed to say.

Then, her heart torn by almost physical pain, she closed her eyes and listened to the sounds of his departure. The door closed, he descended the stairs, his footsteps disappeared into the mass.

Firking poked his head around a street corner and hurriedly pulled it back. Ian had chosen the same moment to look back over his shoulder, perhaps aware that he was being followed. 'Hey, what's going on?' asked Hodge, jabbing Firking with his elbow. 'Let me have a glance.'

Firking put a finger to his lips. 'Cease your dribble and hold!' he whispered. 'Our Ian is questing about and about these darkened streets.'

'Then your cause of stealth's lost,' sighed Hodge. 'It could scarce have succeeded. With your swag-belly midriff and your nail boots you were hardly built for silent pursuance.'

Firking grimaced. 'Slim sceptic, return if you're not in for this game.' He rubbed his hands and stuck his head around the corner once more. Ian had walked on past the fire lit at the end of the street. 'He continues his trail west,' mused Firking. 'It's strange. He walks with the air of a man that both knows the streets yet doesn't.'

'He said he'd been away a long while.' Hodge tapped his mate on the shoulder. 'Are we going home, then?'

'Home? Why home?'

'Well, you've sated your nose and seen your share of Ian's business. He'll be away to his master the Doctor at the palace, that's all.' He pressed a finger to his cheek. 'And talking of palaces makes me think of that pair of boy's shoes I should be working at.'

'Ah, fine Ralph.' Firking turned to face him. 'Your brains reside in your hands. Can you not see? Ian walks to danger. He was startled by the name young Syb gave, Catesby, and became resolved to fight. He goes to confront the villain.'

'What, with not so much as a bird-spit in his holster?' Hodge shook his head. 'Against those Catholic varlets with swords and shields raised? He'd be a fool.'

Firking nodded excitedly. 'You see the point at last.' He laughed. 'Point, ah, 'tis a good pun in connection with swords, rare funny. Ah, I am a poetic knave.' He controlled himself with difficulty and went on, 'But serious, Ian is of the old-fashioned sort, and his unfamiliarity with new ways leads him to these risks. He is too much like a knight of old that would draw his weapon only at the last. The world has changed, though, and we should protect him.' He leant closer. 'And think on, Hodge, for the honour of the gentle craft. Give service in the King's name and we'll bring honour on our own heads. And where there's honour there's silver.' He licked his lips. 'Think of it. Silver.'

Hodge smiled. 'Yes . . . venison pasties, fritters, custard cakes . . . We'd eat like kings.'

Firking nudged him and winked. 'Ay, and drink and drink! Whippincrust'll flow like water!' He gathered his wits and pulled Hodge around the corner. 'But soft, for we must keep track of our quarry.' He slinked on along the street, heading for the turning Ian had taken.

Hodge trailed behind. 'Here, Firk,' he said after a moment's thought. 'We have no swords either.'

'I wondered when you'd notice,' Firking replied.

The Doctor had cautiously accepted an unusual and unexpected offer from Cecil to take some light refreshment in his rooms.

'Doctor,' said Cecil. 'You force me into alien territory.'

The Doctor nodded good-naturedly. 'You mean – powerlessness?'

'Blast your impudence. I will know how you came by your information.' His eyes flashed dangerously. 'Come. All cards on the table.'

'My dear fellow,' the Doctor began with his most patronizing inflection, 'your own machinations are far from clear. I am, frankly, amazed you have been able to manipulate your opponents so masterfully. Through this Spaniard chap, I presume? But who is he, tell me?'

'The issue is who you are.'

The Doctor smirked. 'I sense your unease. But if your lips are sealed, I will be forced to extrapolate from the known facts. And I warn you, the reasoning power of my brain is phenomenal, yes, quite phenomenal.' He pondered a few moments, allowing Cecil to stew, then said, 'Now, Catesby must believe himself to be the plot's originator. It would be impossible to plant such an idea in his mind, so let us conclude that he is. There is no possible way that a person as conscious of security as he would allow his group to be compromised by one of your agents. And none in his group would rebel, it would go against all the principles of their character. Therefore, news of his reckless intent was passed to you independently, by some third force.' He pointed at Cecil, whose eyes had fallen to an examination of the elaborately tiled floor. 'I see by your face I am right.'

Without looking up Cecil spoke. 'The Spaniard came

to me in private audience, one day in spring last year, at a function held in the King's honour. He was disguised as you saw him last night. At the time I had cause to wonder at his sudden appearance, because I had a list of the guests present and all were accounted for, and no other person could, I thought, have penetrated my security. I later learnt of the man's devilish ability to appear and disappear seemingly at will.'

The Doctor gulped. 'You don't mean that literally?'

'No,' said Cecil. 'I mean that he can absent himself from a place with a speed that's uncanny.'

'Thank goodness for that,' said the Doctor. 'For one moment there, I thought this episode — I mean to say this episode of my life — was going in a different direction. Please, forgive my interruption, do go on.'

'In his curious, halting heavily accented voice, he told me of Catesby's doings, of his insane scheme to destroy Parliament. I listened and found I needed no proof. Catesby has long been a thorn in this nation's side, and his handsome head would have been basketed years since, had Elizabeth not taken a liking to his pretty smile.' He winced. 'I pray for a monarch that can ignore the pulsings of their groin. Anyhow, my initial instinct was to close on Catesby and his band, as had long been my intent. Then an inner voice counselled me. Would it not be better to encourage the fools, lead them along on a string, using their friend the Spaniard as my roller? The Spaniard is a quick, clever, deadly man, but gold's his motivation, and I've more of it than Catesby. The tellers of the Exchequer know better than to question the openings of my purse. And Catesby, the crackpot, believes the hand of God protects him in his work, that it was God's purpose to have him spared after the Essex riot. He would swallow the most unlikely fortunes as evidence of Divine Providence.'

'For example,' said the Doctor, 'the house in the approach to Parliament coming free?'

Cecil nodded. 'It was simplicity itself to let Percy take up the rent. He is often about in the court, and it would not arouse suspicion for him to reside in the area. Many other Catholic noblemen do. With my authority, employed in secret, the Spaniard had some thirty barrels of gunpowder delivered to them. What we had not anticipated was the thickness of the dividing wall. When that was reported, I was forced to conjure up another, even more unlikely, freeholding. The chamber beneath the House of Lords. It seemed scarcely probable they would not question their luck, but they are desperate men. And when the barrels were settled there the success of the plot was assured.' He chuckled. 'My plot, not theirs.'

'Yes, I heard you prompting the Chamberlain,' said the Doctor. 'Very artful. Let him take the credit of the discovery and avert direct suspicion.'

Cecil gripped the arms of his chair. 'God's teeth, man, is there no cranny in this palace you do not inhabit? I saw no eavesdropper!'

The Doctor smiled mysteriously. 'I was lurking behind the arras.'

'You are no theatregoer,' said Cecil, 'or you would know that such lurkers bring only ill fortune on themselves.'

'My dear Cecil, we are not in the theatre.' The Doctor narrowed his eyes in concentration. 'Although I cannot suppress a suspicion that there is another hand at work in these dealings, an accomplished playwright of plots within plots.'

Cecil flinched. 'You are the only rogue element, as far as I can see.'

The Doctor regarded him levelly. 'You are a great man, and your achievements as a diplomat cannot be faulted. However, in this matter, I believe that you have acted with all the perspicacity of a dunderhead, in fact with a level of foolishness equal to the Catholics you so despise.' He punctuated his judgement with a haughty sniff. 'It is you, Cecil, who have been strung along.'

'You are free with your insults,' said Cecil, still unruffled. 'The plot is my creation.'

'You still can't see it. Probably because you don't want to. Self-deception is a dangerous quality, and I would advise ridding your personality of it, as I have done.' The Doctor pulled himself up. 'There is a question, central to these events, which has obviously not crossed your mind. And it is this: what's the difference between a powder plot and a powder plot?'

'I don't follow.' Cecil's tone remained light but he was leaning forward now, his facial muscles tightening.

'For goodness' sakes, man! This Spaniard, whoever he may be, has led both you and Catesby right into his trap. Catesby was the only man who would wish to blow up Parliament, you are the only man with the resources and the cunning to let him try. And this third force has brought the two of you together!' He stood, flinging his arms dramatically. 'Can't you see? He intends to ignite Parliament using Catesby as the tinder and you as the flint!'

'But, Doctor,' Cecil faltered, 'I shall have the plot discovered, as you saw, by the Chamberlain.'

'And what, sir,' the Doctor replied, 'if, by some accident, you don't? What then?'

Cecil covered his mouth with his hand. 'Oh my God. I must have the thing uncovered now, right away.' He stood and made as if to leave.

The Doctor halted him. 'No. Think. That is exactly what you must not do.'

Away from the King, and out of his disguise, Hay cut a markedly different figure from the fop seen in court. He removed his heavy cloak with masculine deliberation, and where before his movements had been fluid and youthful he was now solid and purposeful. He hung the cloak on a hook by the door and walked back over to where Vicki still lay across the bed.

'I don't understand,' she said. 'It can't be you.'

He lifted an eyebrow. 'And why not?'

Vicki thought for a moment, then clicked her fingers. 'For one thing, Hay is much shorter than you.' He pointed downwards. Vicki looked, and saw that his feet were balanced effortlessly on a pair of block-shaped wooden stilts. It explained away her second objection, the Spaniard's strange walk, so she decided to come straight to the point. 'Why did you try to kill the Doctor?' Her mind went back to the events of the previous night, and she recalled the meeting between the King and Hay she'd overheard while hiding in the darkness. Of course! After being disturbed, Hay, dressed as the Spaniard, had run away and then bumped into the King. He'd mentioned the intruder – himself, in fact – to check James hadn't seen him in that guise. Afterwards, he'd simply run back the other way around the gallery and attacked the Doctor.

Hay sat down on the bed beside her and smiled unkindly. 'Why has the Doctor come to the palace?' Although he was slight Vicki felt endangered in his presence. His knife was tucked into his belt, and she recognized the rectangle design in the hilt.

She countered with another question. 'Why have you brought me here?'

He frowned. 'We cannot sit here and quiz one another into the night. I fear our time will be spent less civilly. Because I am not going to answer any of your questions, and you are going to answer all of mine.' He gestured to the door. 'I have means, you understand.' He coughed loudly, and the two bald men stood forward. 'Eunuchs,' said Hay.

'And the same to you.' Vicki shuffled away from them, unnerved. 'What do they do?'

'Oh, you have led a sheltered life.' He clamped a hand on her upper arm and the grip was iron-strong. 'They obey me,' he said. 'That is what they do.'

Vicki tried to pull herself free. 'You can't make me do anything.'

'I can,' he said. He pulled a small paper packet from his belt. The eunuchs moved as one, and gripped her by the shoulders. They were so strong she couldn't even struggle. Hay brought the packet under her nose and broke the seal. A pink, sweet-smelling powder shot up her nostrils. 'I will start now.' His voice spun around her head and she felt a sudden need to relax. 'Who is the Doctor?'

Vicki felt resistance slipping away.

'The Doctor,' she heard herself say, 'can travel through space and time . . .'

The Chamberlain knocked as loudly as he dared on the door of the King's chambers. He was admitted by a guard who, as he ushered him in, shot him a suffering look. It was a long-established signal, dating back centuries, and the Chamberlain's heart sank. Monarch moody, proceed with care. 'Ah, Your Majesty,' he began, 'pardon this further intru– oh.' He was pulled up short by the sight of James, who lay sprawled in an extraordinary position in his ornate throne-like armchair, his legs dangling over one arm and his head thrown back over the other. A serving boy was pouring wine into his upturned mouth directly from the bottle, pausing every few seconds to mop up the spills, but this didn't seem to be making the King any happier. His speech lay unrolled on the floor at the base of the chair.

The King beckoned to the Chamberlain. 'What ails you?' he tried to say, sending wine spattering everywhere. He sat up slightly and pushed the page away, then said it again, more successfully.

'I – I am so full of apologies,' the Chamberlain stammered.

'You always are,' James growled. He fixed the Chamberlain with a beady stare. His speech was rather slurred. 'My hope is you are not come with more hopperarsed tales of devil's boxes. Trouble me not with these, for I am out of joint, my innards in a jitter.' He patted his bulging tummy. 'It is as if I am with child, until my eyes settle again on my precious peach.'

As further developments with the devil's box was the main part of the Chamberlain's business he bit his tongue, and enquired gently, 'You mean the lad Victor, Your Majesty?'

The King clapped his hands to his ears. 'Ah, that name, that name, I would not hear it, but I hear it everywhere! When you say "devil's box" I hear "Victor's Victor"! When Cecil says "Parliament's opening" I hear "Victor's Victor"! Ah, why doth he torment me with the turning of a thousand daggers?'

'He's only been gone a couple of hours, Your Majesty,' the Chamberlain pointed out respectfully.

'Hours that take on the seeming span of years!' the King cried. He propped himself up on his elbows and grabbed the bottle from the serving boy. 'I have cast aside the tedious learning of that speech, for politics is nothing in equation with love, and have set my mind to the devising of a good rhyme, a very flower of a rhyme, to act as a garland for my lost love's head. Very firm in bearing hangs the peach from the vine, In succulent roundness it has no equal –'

The Chamberlain decided he really had to intervene, for the sake of his own aesthetic sensitivities. 'Your Majesty, I have to tell you, the city aldermen who were gathered to inspect the box have fled the Guildhall.'

The King snorted. 'Those grave men in black gowns that shadow the Mayor's footsteps, running like wee lasses, no doubt bunching their petticoats over their ankles as they splash through puddles! What are these aldermen but whitepot churls, to flee a wooden box!'

'They have said,' the Chamberlain pointed out, 'that when the boldest of them laid a hand upon it that it was warm to the touch, and that it sighs all the while like a sleeping beast. They entreat you to come to it, knowing your holy presence will sanction a release of its evil forces.'

'They wish me to come now?'

'Yes, Your Majesty.'

James growled. 'It has struck nine of the night! What do they expect of their king, who if they knew it, is a man confounded in the maze of spurned love! Do they not know of my heavy burden, of the making of the speech, of the rehearsal of its delivery!' He hurriedly, and drunkenly, reached out for the scroll. 'The devil take the devil's box, says their king, and he can take them and all!' He got to his feet, and swayed. 'I am away to my empty bed. I will take a peek at it tomorrow, all right?' He staggered, and clicked his fingers at the serving boy. 'Support me!' he barked, and disappeared through the chamber doors with the boy attempting desperately to shore him up. It was a sad sight.

The Chamberlain sighed. 'And to think,' he said, 'my father used to complain about Henry the Eighth.'

Ian had several times caught a glimpse of his pursuers, who were so clumsy at concealing themselves he had a good idea of their identities. As he neared the parliament buildings, using the familiar frontage of Westminster Abbey for navigation, he slowed his pace deliberately and tucked himself into a shadowy corner, then waited for his followers to pass by. He was amused when Firking and Hodge stumbled into the fading light of the street torches and looked about like a pair of startled dogs.

'Where's dapper Ian got to?' grumbled Hodge. 'Ah, my feet are sore from tramping these long miles, with all the speed I have, and now he has upped and vanished. An evening wasted, and another man at my table, working on the King's boy's shoes! It is a merry mockery!'

'Hush, you knave,' said Firking. 'I had Ian's resolute stride in clear sight not a minute hence. I will scent him out.' He craned his neck, peering along the numerous turnings leading from the small square.

Ian realized he was quite glad of their company. He stepped from cover, tapped Firking hard on the shoulder, and barked, 'You there!'

Firking yelped and his terror-stricken expression as he turned was a picture that had both Ian and Hodge laughing. 'Ah, I thought perhaps you would be one of Catesby's arrant varlets,' he said, trying to save face, 'and was giving the appurtenances of fear in order to put you off guard and so let forth a blow.'

'Of course,' said Ian. 'Now why have you followed me?'

Hodge smiled. 'We were afraid for you, sirrah. You go unprotected on your mission, and Red Rob, from the evidence of what we've seen, is a violent man.'

Ian laid a hand on their shoulders. 'Perhaps you're right. I could certainly use some friends if I have to save Barbara.' He wondered how much he should reveal, and if the Doctor would be angry; then he remembered the Doctor's abandonment of himself and Barbara and said, 'The parliament buildings. I've a good idea Catesby will be in there.' He pointed to the large interconnecting stone structures of the parliament building, on the far side of Westminster Abbey. The moonlight picked out the multi-roofed outline in ghostly detail. To the left was a long, high-ceilinged hall, which led to the central block Ian recognized from school history lessons as the House of Commons. It was by far the most imposing section, a brownstone church-like building with four slender towers at the corners of its slanted roof. To the right was its companion, the smaller and less architecturally fussy House of Lords, sandwiched between two outer chambers. There was evidence of rebuilding work, and Ian thought some of the smaller connecting structures looked like the remnants of an older building. In the gaps between the yards and chambers he could see the passage of the Thames.

'Catesby, a parliamentarian?' Firking was sceptical. 'They have some papists in there, more's the pity, but surely not he?'

Ian smiled grimly. 'Oh, I don't think he's exactly a supporter of Parliament.' He pointed to the House of Lords. 'Now, we must get into the cellar that's below there.'

Hodge regarded him as if he was mad. 'The cellar? Are you unhinged? What do you want in a cellar? If it's coal you lack we'd have given you a sack if you had asked.'

Ian started walking towards the parliament buildings. 'Look, there's no time to explain. We have to find Barbara, and I've a feeling that's the best place to start looking.' He looked over his shoulder. 'So, are you with me or not?'

With the air of men who have committed themselves too far to turn back, Firking and Hodge fell in behind him. He led them across the small paved square that led to the parliament buildings, and then turned right, intending to follow the wide road that a wooden sign proclaimed was Parliament Place and then turn into the approach to the House of Lords.

Catesby sat hunched in the cellar's darkness, his still-throbbing head thrown forward on his knees. He had come here as if guided by instinct. The place of destiny.

The pain and the incessant ringing in his ears made it difficult to arrange his thoughts, but in a bizarre way he now felt composed and confident. It was all so inevitable. The English had turned their backs on God, and God had selected him to bring them back into line, giving him shelter, bringing him the necessary tools, providing the opportunity. Restored to Rome, England would become great again, the internal squabbles that had dogged it forgotten in the explosion. United, there was nothing the people of this blessed island could not achieve. And he was merely the instrument, the tool of the Lord. Evil, when it gathered above, would be wiped out from below.

He was the master puppeteer.

Ian crouched in the shade of one of the trees that lined the yard leading up to the House of Lords. There seemed to be little or no security in these parts of the complex; occasionally he caught a glimpse of a patrol on the prowl around the Commons, but the small wooden door let into the wall right in front of him – in the exact place his history lessons had said it was – was unprotected. He shook his head in bewilderment. 'I can't believe this place is so badly guarded.'

Firking, who was bent over immediately behind him, said, 'Not to fear, Ian. When the nobles return the place will be a-swarm with pikemen.'

'Still,' said Ian, 'we've not been so much as challenged.

It feels wrong.' He pointed to the door. It seemed so innocuous. 'Through there. It's locked, I'm sure, and we've nothing in the way of –'

'Ssh!' Hodge slapped a hand on his back and signalled for silence. 'Someone comes,' he whispered, pointing out a cloaked, hatted figure moving from the trees opposite. Obviously his approach had been as clandestine as theirs.

They watched as he strode from cover, his eyes watchful and intelligent, lantern swinging in his hand. Ian felt a cold chill of recognition as the man walked to the door, slid a key from a clanking set at his waist, and held it to the lock. The lantern's light shone up at his face for a second, revealing a suspicious, troubled expression beneath the gingery-blond beard. 'Good God,' Ian heard himself whisper. 'It's him . . .'

'True enough,' said Firking. 'The varmint that was at the inn with Catesby.'

Ian shook his head. 'No. I mean, yes, but . . . I didn't realize. I'd never have known. It's Guy Fawkes, going down to the cellar, the lantern in his hand.'

Hodge's brow furrowed. 'Why this babbling? See, the door is open. We should bring him down while it remains so, and thus gain entrance.'

'You're right. Come on.' Ian slid from cover and tripped swiftly across the yard.

Catesby heard movement, then the fall of steps descending the small steep staircase running down to the cellars. He recognized the careful, rhythmical tread. It was Fawkes. His mouth dried, and he stood, put his hand to his sword, squared his broad frame, and tried to look as resolute as possible. The effort made his head spin, and he was forced to clutch at the edge of one of the barrels that filled this small place of destiny. There was definitely only one pair of steps; Fawkes returning alone meant two things. First, he was still committed to the plot. Second, he had released the devil woman.

Fawkes's key grated in the lock, and a second later he was inside, his cloak pulled about him, his face wreathed in shadows, his lantern held before him. 'Rob,' he called. 'Rob, are you there? I have been to the house, and could not find you, and –'

Catesby lurched into the open. He realized he was dribbling with anger. 'Where is she?' he demanded. 'Where is the devil woman?'

Fawkes bristled. 'She intended no harm,' he said.

Catesby snarled, reached out and knocked him back with the flat of his hand. 'Can you in truth be so stupid? After the years, the wretched years I have spent on this work!' His voice cracked with the strain, became a strangulated gargle. 'Wretched years!'

'No harm is done,' Fawkes said in his infuriatingly amiable tone. 'She has fled with friends, and is already out of London. Our meeting with her was pure chance.'

Catesby struck him again, with greater force this time. 'No such thing, man! No such thing as chance! Only the contest between God and Satan, and you were conjured to the dark side!'

Fawkes advanced. 'Hush, Rob, or you'll have the whole house down on top of us.'

'I thought that was the idea!' Catesby laughed shrilly. His senses reeled, giving him a sensation of floating upwards, that his legs were getting longer and thinner and he was being elevated, lifted on high. 'Yes, yes,' he muttered, 'yes, the course is set, I see what I must do . . .' He lifted his sword.

'Are you sick?' Fawkes reached out and tried to guide him to sit on one of the barrels. 'Here, rest yourself, Rob, your face is pale and not good.' He raised his lantern, and although he was now standing over Catesby, Catesby saw him as if from the height of a cliff. The man was insignificant, useless, unreliable. 'That blow I dished you was a harder one than I'd thought. You sit here and I'll away to fetch water.'

'Traitor,' Catesby croaked. He shivered convulsively. 'Traitor!'

'Remain here,' Fawkes repeated, backing away.

* * *

Ian turned the corner of the narrow staircase, leading the shoemakers to a scene straight from a children's history picture book. All one might have expected was present. The barrels, covered by large greasy sheets; the heaps of faggots and stacks of lumber; the lantern bearing Fawkes's name. The ceiling was low, the sulphuric stench of the powder adding a further layer of oppression on the senses. And in the midst of it all were Guy Fawkes, who had turned his back and was heading back towards the stairs, and Catesby, who was white-faced and jibbering.

'You need good meat and good wine,' Fawkes was saying. He sounded mildly irritated, which Ian, from his lofty vantage point, could see was a suicidal error. He should have been more concerned, because Catesby had leapt up from his perch and was poised to strike, his sword raised. Fawkes went on, 'You have been so long bound up and up in the folds of your dealings that you cannot –'

He would never complete the sentence.

Catesby sprang. Ian, losing all sense of self-preservation and not having time to consider the implications, yelled, 'Look out!' Fawkes's head whirled up, but Ian's shout had left him doubly unprepared for the attack.

The sword, wielded with amazing strength by the drooling Catesby, entered his lower back with a horrendous crunching noise. Its tip emerged a second later, soaked in gore, from the centre of his chest. He had no time to scream.

Guy Fawkes, a startled look on his face, sank to his knees and died staring into the face of Ian Chesterton.

9

A Dead Man's Shoes

Ian saw the sight leave Fawkes's eyes. With a gurgle like a blockage being poked from a pipe, a torrent of blood burst from the dead man's mouth. It streamed over his face and formed a purple halo about his head, seeping into the sawdust strewn around the lumber room. The sword was pulled from him with a revolting plop, and Catesby staggered with the weight of it, tottering back against the far wall. He sagged against a buttress for support, his complexion the whitest Ian had ever seen on a living person, his beard flecked with droplets of vomit.

A thousand thoughts whizzed through Ian's mind. This was a major change to history's pattern, and an irreversible one, but his immediate concern was for Barbara. He strutted across the low-ceilinged room, taking care to step around the messy remains, and stepped into the light of the lantern that rested on one of the barrels. Catesby was hunched over, babbling incoherently. Although his eyes were wide open he seemed not to see Ian, who grabbed him by the shoulders and shook him. 'Where's Barbara?' he demanded. 'What have you done with her?'

The gory sword clattered from Catesby's hand. He muttered, 'I am Red Rob . . . and I have killed my best, my most loyal man . . .'

Ian shook him again. 'I said where is she? Answer me, damn you!'

At last Catesby seemed to register his presence. 'You. You are the one from the inn.'

'The woman who was with me,' Ian said urgently. Surprising himself with the force of his reaction, he took a firm hold of Catesby's baggy red overgarment, lifted him bodily and flung him against the wall. 'What have you done with her?'

All life seemed to have gone out of Catesby. Ian's blow had been hard, had banged his head against the side of the buttress, but his thin features and sunken eyes displayed no pain, and when he spoke it was in the same quivering monotone as before. 'The new era . . . it was to be ours . . .' His fingers scrabbled inside his tunic and Ian had a moment's illogical fear that he was reaching for a gun. But he pulled out a small wooden crucifix, stroked it lovingly, and began to pray in Latin.

'Catesby!' Ian knocked it away. 'Where is Barbara?'

For the first time Catesby focused his eyes on Ian. 'That woman. It is her doing. She drove the wedge between me and Fawkes, it is her fault.' He chuckled and his eyes glazed over. 'She lives.'

Ian quelled his urge to whoop for joy. 'But where?'

Now Catesby seemed to be staring absently into space, over Ian's shoulder. He slumped further into his alcove and his voice took on an eerie melancholy. 'Ask Fawkes. Ask Fawkes. He would know.' There was a taunt behind the words.

Ian was about to ask for clarification, but three things prevented this. Firstly he realized that what he had taken for a vacant stare into nothingness had in fact been a non-verbal signal to a person standing beside him. Secondly he heard an unfamiliar, unexpected noise, a dull jarring of metal brushing against leather. Thirdly, as he turned to investigate, a hand was clamped tightly around his throat.

Firking had watched as two new arrivals entered the lumber room. 'Oh, spit!' He rubbed his chin thoughtfully.

'Ian's done for,' breathed Hodge.

Firking's chest swelled with patriotic feeling. 'Oh no. You were right, Ralph. We must find swords.' He stood.

'We should fetch the watch,' Hodge protested vainly.

But Firking had already slipped away.

* * *

'Here, Doctor.' Cecil's finger indicated a spot between two of the towering oaks at the far end of the Privy Garden. 'It was always here.' In the light from his lantern his face seemed more long and more grave than usual. The recent revelation had shaken the guile and confidence out of him, and he looked like the short and unimpressive man he, in fact, was.

The Doctor shone his own light around over the bare, frosty soil, an action that succeeded only in startling a grey squirrel from cover. The little animal bolted out of its hiding place and flashed by with scarcely a rustle to indicate its passing. The Doctor was reminded of Cecil's description of the Spaniard's movements. 'Hmm. Appear and disappear,' he muttered. 'I do wish an answer to this conundrum would present itself.'

Cecil shivered against the biting November wind and looked back over his shoulder at the palace. 'We have our answer,' he said. 'If I go at once to the King and have the plot exposed —'

The Doctor silenced him by lifting a hand. 'No, no, no! As I have said, picture the consequences. You could not hope to emerge untainted by the affair, which would mean the executioner's block for you and a royal household blackened for ever in its subjects' eyes. The nation might never recover. No, Cecil, you have painted yourself into a corner, and you must end what you began.' His eyes swept keenly over the twigs and dry grass and up to the high brick wall, which was sturdy and its width of several feet too thick to conceal a hidden doorway. Then he stamped the hard ground methodically, section by section.

'What are you doing?'

The Doctor continued to stamp. 'I fancied an underground tunnel.'

'In the palace grounds? Who do you suppose could have dug it under our noses?'

'Someone with daring and intelligence,' the Doctor said acidly. 'Someone very like the Spaniard, in fact — ah!' He raised his foot and brought it up and down repeatedly over a small area of the ground around the base of one of the oaks. To any other observer the difference between that area and those surrounding it would not have been noticeable, but the Doctor's acute senses had picked up a slight echo that indicated a hollowed-out cavity. 'Yes, promising, but where could the entrance be? There's certainly no trap or any similar mechanism.' He knelt down and started to rap on the side of the tree with his knuckles. 'I'm convinced this is hollow.' Cecil came to stand above him. 'Don't just stand there, man. Lend a hand.'

'I am not used to grubbing about in the soil.'

'Don't worry,' the Doctor snapped. 'It's cleaner than politics. Now come along.' He beckoned Cecil to kneel and gestured to him to scrape at the tree's outspread roots. 'Try there, feel for a hinge or something.'

Cecil said, 'Your own motive remains unknown to me, Doctor.'

'It will stay so,' the Doctor replied. 'I don't respond to personal questions. Just be satisfied that I am here and willing to help you, that I have a special interest in –' He broke off as his fingertips connected with a raised vein on the tree trunk that was a fraction too thick and regular to be a natural bark formation. 'Here, I have it.' He stood, taking care to keep his hand perfectly still, and gently traced the outline of the cavity. The panel was rectangular and about four feet high; any person of reasonable height would have to squeeze to pass through.

Cecil brought his lantern to bear on the Doctor's discovery, and the hidden door was revealed. It was, the Doctor thought, rather like an image concealed in an optical illusion. Now it had been pointed out it was plainly visible, the design etched into the wood. He tapped around the outline in the search for an opening mechanism. 'Perhaps he uses a special key,' Cecil suggested.

'Unlikely,' said the Doctor. 'I have extensive experience of secret passages. A concealed spring triggered by a simple sequence of knocks is more probable.' As he spoke his knuckles detected a tougher nodule of wood on the left-hand side of the door, and he pressed it confidently. There was a splintering crack and the panelled area opened outwards. 'Shall we enter?'

Cecil prepared to squeeze in, his lantern clutched to his chest. 'We should take a sword. I have only a small dagger on my person.'

The Doctor waved his objection aside as he clambered in. 'I have many more effective weapons.' He held out his lantern. The vestibule, for want of a better word, of the tunnel was not much higher than the entrance panel, and he was forced to bend almost double. The walls were composed of big stone blocks running with ice-cold drips and covered in mossy green stains. A few feet ahead was a rough-hewn arch, and beyond that a narrow flight of descending steps. The Doctor put a finger to his lips. 'It's very dark and cramped in here, and sounds will travel. We shall have to whisper. And watch out for hidden traps, wires and the like. I should hate to end my days in this gloomy vault.'

Cecil crouched beside him. 'This is an unholy place. And situated directly beneath the King's palace. I would not have credited the Spaniard with this. Where does it lead?'

'Logic would say,' said the Doctor, unable to keep the excitement he felt from his voice, 'to his lair.' He extended his foot tentatively on to the first step and began the descent.

Barbara arranged her hair in the cracked mirror over the fireplace. Her make-up was smudged by her rough treatment over the last couple of days, and as there were no tissues or towels to hand she wiped it away as best she could with the corner of a sheet.

She was drawn by an inexplicable urge to the window. In the square below a bonfire had been lit, around which children played games of chase and sang simple rhyming songs. The chatter of the city folk below was oddly reassuring.

'. . . and they say it breathes with a life all of its own!' she heard someone say. The voice was round and fruity and so was its owner, a large woman in cap and shawl who stood, baby rocking at her breast, directly under the window talking to two others in similar attire. Her listeners' expressions were sceptical. She went on. 'My husband knows one of the fellows that dragged it there, and all. A great wooden box like a standing coffin, it's not right it is.'

One of her friends said, 'Ah, you have a fine tongue for the blabber, have you, Mrs Gurton.'

She bunched herself up defensively. 'I swear to you it's truth! On my husband's honour! It wouldn't be opened at the yard, where they had dragged it to be smashed for firewood, and so they bore it to the Guildhall. It sighs to itself, my Gurton says, and none of the aldermen nor none of the colonels of the King's companies will dare to lay a hand upon it.' She lowered her voice to a ghoulish whisper. 'And this being so close to Hallowe'en, who's to say it ain't the work of Old Nick himself, he says?'

The other women laughed. 'The work of your Gurton blowing up his tale in the telling, more like,' one said. 'Wood is wood, no matter the strength, and they should have at it with an axe, swing-ho!' She nodded to her friend and they started to saunter away. 'Trip by, Mrs Gurton, and when we next see you bring us a finer story.'

The woman snuggled her child closer to her chest and looked about for new prey. 'Here!' she called, signalling to another passer-by. 'Hear tell! My Gurton has been up to the Guildhall where they've unearthed a cabinet, like a big dresser, and it pours out flames and growls!'

Barbara stepped back from the window. The Guildhall, then. All she needed to do was get there and wait for the others.

After a last look around the small room she was on her way.

The cramped tunnel was thick with cobwebs and shadows, and the drip of water down its crumbling walls echoed incessantly. Cecil observed, 'This is no new construction. I would say it has been under here for decades.'

'Quite possibly centuries,' the Doctor replied. He was hunched with more difficulty than Cecil, and the strain of bending over had given him aches and pains that he remarked on with little sighs and mutters of irritation. 'There are no corners or twists, which suggests classical influences in the design, possibly Roman. The wooden struts have been replaced recently, and there are several sections of the wall that show signs of patching.' He splashed one of his shoes in the couple of inches of the stinking water through which they shuffled. 'This was caused by subsidence, a further pointer to great antiquity.'

'Surely not,' said Cecil. 'How could it have lain here undiscovered and unused for so long?'

'Undiscovered and unused by you,' the Doctor pointed out. 'You weren't looking for it, old fellow.'

Cecil swallowed, trying to take in the enormity of the revelation. 'I cannot credit this. Persons have been able to saunter in and out of Whitehall, undetected, for the length of its usage.'

The Doctor sniffed. 'And longer. This part of London has always been the administrative centre, and I dare say it will continue to serve as such for generations to come. A route like this is very handy indeed.' He stopped abruptly and lifted his lantern a little higher. 'Ah. I think we have reached a turning point in our journey.'

Cecil squeezed forward to see what he had found, thankful for once of his bony frame, which allowed him to share the narrow tunnel alongside the Doctor. Facing them was a junction. To the left and to the right were continuations of the tunnel, similarly draped with lichens and sloshing with water. Directly ahead the ceiling angled upwards sharply to a height of over eight feet. Beneath was a heavy door of dark wood, accessed by three stone steps that kept it above the level of the swirling water. It was featureless save for a large knocker. As the Doctor swept the beam of his lantern over it Cecil glimpsed the design lovingly hand-crafted on the boss: three geometric shapes, a large square containing a triangle and a rectangle. It was innocuous in itself but its unnatural precision, its foreign character and its lack of an instantly recognizable standard or symbol made his skin crawl. 'A strange significance,' he muttered. 'I have not seen its like.'

'Nor I,' said the Doctor. He stepped forward, unbending himself with evident relief, and reached out to examine the knocker. His finger traced the pattern slowly. 'Pythagorean principles. Hmm, mathematics, a discipline out of its time.'

Cecil straightened up and stared at him. 'What's this you say? Speak clearly, man, your language is laden with gibberish.'

The Doctor stepped back. 'Now how do you suppose I should gain entrance?'

'I suggest you knock,' Cecil said acidly. He snapped his fingers. 'Come, give me the weapon.' The Doctor looked at him blankly. 'The weapon you spoke of. I would have it when we confront the Spaniard. He is quick and ruthless, and an old man could not stand in opposition to him.'

The Doctor puffed himself up. 'You forget, sir, I already have. And the weapon I referred to cannot be handed over. It's up here.' He tapped his temple. 'The greatest weapon of all, intellect.' His hands moved over the door. 'Against which there can be no barrier.' He pondered a few moments. 'In this case, however, you may well be right. What are knockers for, eh?' He put his hand forward.

Cecil gripped his forearm. 'We are defenceless,' he said. 'I have only this.' He whipped out his dagger. 'I would return to the palace and rustle up a small squad of trusted men-at-arms.'

'Quite unnecessary.' The Doctor knocked three times, loudly. The sound reverberated off the cavern walls for what seemed to Cecil like an eternity.

And then, with a crunch that sounded almost organic, like a bone breaking up in flames, the door creaked open.

* * *

The face that confronted Ian was, if possible, even more crazed than Catesby's. But whereas Catesby had the look of a sane man who had lost all self-control the newcomer's curly fair hair and bulging green eyes made him look like a natural lunatic. His clothing was immaculate, a superior version of the garb worn by all the rich young gentlemen, and around his neck was a lightweight chain formed from linked bands of gold. His skin was soft and unlined for a man in his thirties, and when he spoke it was with odd emphasis. 'Hold him hard, Winter,' he instructed the big dirty man whose arm was clamped around Ian's throat. To Catesby he said, 'Who is this man? And what is the cause of this devilry?' He nodded to the body of Fawkes.

Catesby ignored the question. 'I was to see you at the house this night, Percy,' he babbled. 'We were to prepare our flight. Are the horses ready, and placed well? And the boat?'

'Ay, we looked in the house and found it empty.' The man called Percy cuffed him lightly under the collar. 'Damn the horses! What is the use of our plot with no Fawkes to light the touchwood? Has there been treachery?' He gave an ironic laugh. 'I think not, else we would not be standing here unaccosted. Tell me, what has happened?'

Catesby made a dreadful lowing noise and broke out of his niche in the wall. Ian watched as he crossed to Fawkes's body and started to thump his chest. 'My most loyal one, slain by my own hand.'

Percy clapped a hand on his shoulder. 'But why? All is well, why quarrel?'

'He crossed me,' said Catesby falteringly. 'He went against my orders. A witch came among us, I ordered her dead.' Ian held his breath. 'He would not do it, and struck me down in her place. He absconded with her, set her free.' Catesby shook with rage. 'He raised his fist to me. I, who have worked cogs within cogs, put my life into the balance that we might save this great nation from Scotch heretics and those who serve to appease them. Can any other man know what I know, that has not seen the building up of this plot? I have turned the screws of security so tight I started even to doubt my own power to stay quiet. I have made certain of all the materials and collated all the details. It has been my life's work to free the world, and yes –' he stopped to wipe a fleck of dribble from his beard '– yes, it has made me mad!' He clamped his hands to the sides of his face. 'It has made me explode inside! Won't somebody pour a lotion in to stop the frightful ringing in my ears!' He began to sob.

Percy regarded him with pity. 'It is terrible. The strain has broken his mind.'

Winter, the man holding Ian, said, 'But his task is complete, Tom. Fawkes is dead, but all we have is here and in readiness. Still nobody suspects.' He jerked Ian's head roughly to one side. 'Although I would still know what this one is about.'

Ian tried to speak. 'Let me explain,' he gasped. 'I was here to look for that woman he spoke of. She is no witch. Set me free and I'll go to her. I have no quarrel with you men.' Even as he spoke he knew the plea was hopeless.

He was right. Percy laughed in his face. 'No, my chum. It is a sorry thing that you have blundered in badly, and I do not understand half this recent business over the lady, but know this. You cannot be freed, you who have seen all this.' He gestured around at the barrels and heaps of kindling.

'Then take me along with you,' said Ian. 'When the deed is done you can release me.'

Percy shook his head calmly. Ian had a sudden flash of realization: the firebrand Catesby, master strategist and organizer, had been nothing but a foil for this urbane, calculating man. 'I shall have trouble enough,' he said, 'loading up my cripple-brained friend Rob on to a horse. And I have no care to waste on reckless strangers. No, I have a better idea.' He nodded to Winter. 'Tie him.'

Winter released his grip, but Ian was too woozy from lack of oxygen to put up a struggle, and his hands were pulled behind his back with embarrassing ease. He felt the bristled segments of a thick rope brush against his skin. 'What are you planning to do with me?' he asked boldly.

Percy smiled. 'When the time comes, tomorrow night, I shall light the touchwood and retire immediately. You will remain here.'

Ian blanched at the thought. He recalled the historical accounts of the night of November the fourth. The grim events were fitting into place despite the death of Fawkes. 'You mean, I will stay here, and . . .' His mouth dried. He began, rather late in the day, to struggle in his bonds.

'Yes,' said Percy. 'You will stay and die with your masters above.'

Part Four

Explaining the Plot

10

The Grand Behemoth

Beyond the door was a narrow hallway, about twelve feet long and three feet wide. Its wooden panelling was painted white. There were two items of furniture: a velvet-padded chair set in front of a marble-topped table upon which were a pot of ink, a quill, and a supply of writing paper and wax for the making of seals. Illumination was supplied by black candles that were hung high along the walls at regular intervals and cast an even, balanced glow. Noting this, and apparently confident he was alone, the Doctor shook out his own lantern and laid it down gently on the carpeted floor. Then he extended a hand back through the door and beckoned in Cecil.

Cecil's wonted acuity was muted by his first sight of the inner quarters. The Doctor scrutinized his reaction closely, and noted the traces of anger that passed across his face. How galling it must be, he thought, for a man who considered himself true protector of the realm to discover that he had been tricked so brazenly, for a man who believed he was the architect of all events to find he was merely a token in somebody else's games. The outward expression of this inner turmoil was a scowl. 'Such opulence.' He gestured to the table and chair. 'How were these conveyed here unscathed through that filthy tunnel? And who admitted us? Is there magic in this too?'

The Doctor put a finger to his lips urgently. 'For heaven's sake, man, keep quiet.' He pointed to where the hallway ended in a blank wall, and went on in a whisper, 'Successful magic is a simple matter of foxing the observer. The way through to the inner sanctum is probably worked the same way as the door we have just come through, I think, by a series of pulley mechanisms activated by knocking on it.'

Cecil considered this for a moment, then nodded. 'I admit that is possible.' His steely gaze swept around the room. 'So we are alone in this luxurious warren. We shall await the Spaniard's return, and then –' he produced the little dagger from his pocket and for the first time the Doctor noted the sharpness of the blade's point '– I shall hack at the guts of the crafty villain.'

The Doctor tsked. 'You shall do no such thing. My poor Vicki is down here somewhere, remember, and I will not have her harmed.' He moved to the writing table and picked up the top sheet from the pile of paper. It was yellowish and felt old, square in shape, and when he held it up to the light he saw that the watermark had all but faded away. 'Hmm, now I wonder what to make of this?'

Cecil stared over his shoulder. 'That design, I know it. It is an imprint used by the government of the Netherlands.'

The Doctor stiffened, trying to recall his history. 'Which is a Spanish dominion, am I correct?'

'Of course.' Cecil snatched the sheet from him. 'So it is from Holland my enemy is come.' He squinted and held the page up to the candlelight. 'I can see the markings of the nib from their impress on the sheet above. But it is too vague to make sense of.'

The Doctor took it back. Cecil was right. Although individual words and letters could be made out, the paper was too thick and coarse to have taken a full copy of the Spaniard's most recent penning. He thought for a moment and then began almost unconsciously to pat the pockets of his coat. 'Ah, now it is just possible that I still have them about me . . .'

'Have what about you?' asked Cecil.

'I'm sure I didn't leave them in the TARDIS after that last experiment with magnetos.' The pocket-patting continued. 'Or did I?'

'To what do you refer?' snapped Cecil, exasperated.

'My iron filings,' the Doctor retorted, as loud as he

dared. At the same moment he pulled a small stoppered glass tube from one of his inside pockets. It contained a glittering black substance. 'There we are. Now, let's see.'

Working industriously, the Doctor unstoppered the tube and tapped it, pouring the filings carefully on to the upturned sheet of paper, taking care to cover as much of the surface as he could. He gave them a moment to settle and then gently raised the sheet, jiggling it as he did, until most of the iron mixture had fallen in a fine shower on the carpet. He gave the sheet a final shake and then slipped on his spectacles to examine the findings.

Cecil fidgeted as he looked on. 'A clever trick of spies. I have heard it described but never seen it done. What is uncovered?'

The Doctor struggled to link the faintly outlined whorls and loops of the handwriting, and as he did his face grew graver. ' "My lord Monteagle," ' he began, ' "out of the love I bear to some of your friends I have a care of your preservation. Therefore I would advise you, if you value your life, to devise some excuse to shift of your attendance at this parliament. For God and Man hath concurred to punish the wickedness of this time . . ." ' He trailed off and fanned himself with the letter. 'Oh dear, dear. This makes it all much more confusing.'

'It is a warning to some Catholic lord,' said Cecil, the colour rising to his pallid cheeks. 'Then it is indeed a popish plot, born of Dutch hands.'

The Doctor heaved a sigh. 'Please try to think without prejudice. The Spaniard owes loyalty to neither side of this petty dispute. He intends the plot to succeed, remember, to cause maximum havoc in every quarter. After the explosion there will be mayhem, unparalleled acrimony and recrimination. The leveller heads will attempt to calm things down and re-establish order. What better way than this letter to see they don't succeed? The Spaniard will arrange for it to be discovered, and the desire for revenge will be so strong that blood will flow. I imagine he has similar tricks waiting to be played on all the factions. All it takes is to be utterly unscrupulous and to exploit the worst aspects of human nature. His ploy certainly worked on you.'

Cecil shook his head, not comprehending. The greyness had returned to his face. 'What you mean to say, for all of your cant, is that England shall be consumed by waves of blood? A commotion that will topple the nation and leave it ripe for invasion?'

'Invasion, eh? I wonder.' The Doctor made a gesture around the narrow hallway, as if pushing aside such a trifle. 'With their cunning, these people could have achieved that easily. I suspect their aim is something more magnificent.' He tucked his spectacles away and grunted. 'Their techniques are fiendish. The hand that wrote this is most peculiar. This is deliberate obfuscation, to set men against each other.'

The words had scarcely left his mouth than a section of the far wall facing the door cracked open in a sudden, violent movement, and two burly figures burst through. It seemed impossible that two sets of such broad shoulders could get into the hallway. The Doctor had no time to register anything but the size, strength and ugliness of the attackers before he was grabbed in a hammerlock hold about the neck, his legs were kicked away from behind at the vulnerable spot just above the calves, and he was forced to his knees. His senses reeled, his lungs heaved, his eyes watered. A couple of moments went by before he became aware that a similar fate had befallen Cecil. There was a bright ping of sound which he took to be the throwing of the dagger; it went wide of its target and embedded itself in the side of the writing table. The sounds of struggle were replaced by a heavy silence.

Then the Doctor's hair was gripped in one of the same fists that had chopped him down and his head was pulled up in a surprisingly gentle movement. Standing before him, framed in the inner doorway, was Vicki, dressed in a simple one-piece white smock. Her eyes were huge and unblinking. Instinctively he offered her a smile. It was not returned. Her expression remained alarmingly blank and her hands hung limp at her sides. The Doctor sniffed and detected a sweet fragrance clinging to her. He felt a pang of guilt. 'Oh, my poor child, what have they done to you?' There was no reaction.

She was pushed gently aside by another person. Revealed was a short, physically unprepossessing fellow with a liver-spotted face and a brutish expression. Such was the change in his demeanour since their last encounter it took the Doctor a moment to place him.

It was Cecil who gave the first choke of recognition. 'You,' he spluttered. 'No, it cannot be . . .'

In a heavily accented, faltering voice Hay said, 'I thought this moment would never come.' In his own voice he continued, 'Bring them through. There is much afoot.'

James had staggered up the steps of the Stone Gallery, supported on both sides by soldiers, and collapsed on his big old bed in a pleasant alcoholic fug. The rafters of his bedchamber cartwheeled above him assuringly. The two big important things in his life — the Victor thing and the parliament thing — had been magicked away by wine, his oldest and most dependable friend. How much? Ah, a few bottles. He remembered deciding to count how many, and then losing count and deciding he wouldn't bother.

As sleep loomed over him he found himself wishing that a potion could be mixed up that would whisk him two days ahead in time. Everything between now and then was so inevitable. Speeches, debates, ceremonials. That daft bloody crown pressing on his head like a diamond-encrusted chamber-pot. In two days, all done and dusted. He could get back to hunting and loggets and drinking and loving. The concentration and serious effort of the last few days had exhausted him. He snuggled beneath his sheets, soothed by the sound of his snores and the rise and fall of his big tummy. Thunder was grumbling over the Thames, an agreeable counterpoint to his big body's internal complaints.

Just as his mind was about to topple, feather-light, into a most agreeable dream, the unmistakable tepid knock of the Chamberlain sounded, hauling him back to disagreeable reality. 'Teeth!' he shouted. 'I will not have this! I will not have this! Away, away!'

'Please, please, Your Majesty,' the Chamberlain twittered. Even through the heavy wood of the door his voice sounded even higher and more vexed than usual. 'It isn't about the box. Something – oh, something *awful* has happened!'

'Ugh. How awful?'

'*Very* awful, Your Majesty.'

James remained to be convinced. 'On a rising scale, if one is a stolen pie from the kitchens and ten is revolution in the streets, how awful?'

The Chamberlain hesitated. 'Oh, *eight*, Your Majesty.'

'Oh, doom.' James shook his head to clear it and managed only to encourage the start of a clanging headache. He groaned and with a tremendous effort, his muscles screaming, pulled his top half upright. He barked, 'Enter! And your mission had better be of the gravest character!' As he rose he caught sight of himself in the large looking-glass across the room. He looked haggard and dishevelled and bloated, not the dashing young hunter as he was always portrayed. 'Heck, that's not right at all,' he said, and his reflection mouthed the observation back at him mockingly.

The Chamberlain bustled in. 'Oh, Your Majesty!' He was waving an important-looking piece of paper.

James had an instinctive mistrust of important-looking pieces of paper, so he ignored it. He pointed to the looking-glass. 'I want that taken away, it doesn't work as well as once it did. I say we should throw it away and get a new one.' Then he turned his most forbidding glare on the Chamberlain and said, 'Well?'

The Chamberlain fluttered the paper under his nose. James saw now that it was an unsealed letter. 'This is a terrible thing, Your Majesty. Please forgive me but I had to bring it right up to you. Cecil is missing, and I –'

James beamed broadly. 'Cecil missing?' He rubbed his hands together vigorously and reached for the wine bottle at his bedside. 'The best of news! I say we raise a toast to his continued absence!' This was what he intended to say. It came out more like 'Beshanew! Ishay raise a toshe, er . . .' He brought the bottle's rim to his lips. Somehow it failed to form a channel with them and the wine trickled down his beard, over his chin, and splashed against his front. He looked down, surprised, trying to figure out how that had happened, and registered many more similar splashes. How had they got there? Never mind, couldn't remember. Didn't matter. He threw the bottle away contemptuously and fell back on to his pillow. The dream loomed agreeably again, spiralling down through the whirling rafters. A green dream, an outdoor dream, a lovely dream . . .

'Your Majesty, this letter,' said the Chamberlain's voice.

James snorted. 'Who let you in?'

'You, Your Majesty.'

'When did I?'

'Just now, Your Majesty.'

'I don't recall. Go away.' He rolled over and nuzzled his nose in his pillow. The room and the bed faded out, and there was only the warm pillow and his lovely snores, and a nice rushing sound like the sea in his ears, and the dream taking him away to the green place, to a sunny hill and a strong steed, with deer in sight and Victor in the saddle before him, tugging on the reins. Hmm, wonderful lovely dream. Stringed instruments tinkled distantly, there was birdsong, it was springtime.

An irritating voice intruded. 'Please. I beg you. This is a grim portent.' Suddenly, in place of the deer, was the Chamberlain, waving an important-looking piece of paper. 'A warning of some terrible calamity for Parliament. It was delivered early this evening at the house of Lord Monteagle, who sent it straight here.' The letter quivered in his feeble grip.

James wondered why this awful little man, who was always pestering him about something, should turn up in his wonderful dream. Some hidden guilt on his own part? Unlikely; he didn't feel guilt, it was unnecessary in a king.

Perhaps his dreaming mind was offering him a chance to say in the night what he wanted to say during the day to this mincing busybody. Yes, that was probably it. That explained the change from deer to man. Aha, some sport! 'Silly arse!' he growled. 'You are naught but a wriggling worm! Won't you leave me alone for once!' In his dream the Chamberlain and his letter were suddenly transformed into a worm, and he roared with laughter.

The worm spoke in the Chamberlain's voice. 'Please, Your Majesty! With Cecil gone, and you in this, er – er, incapacitated – what am *I* to do?' It wriggled as it spoke, its pink body glistening with dew.

'Ah, worm. Worm, worm, worm,' James burbled. 'I sing the song of the worm, worm, worm . . .' And then, as if it was too wonderful for his mind to hold, the lovely dream folded itself away section by section, dispersing to the corners of his consciousness, and he slept.

'We are known by many names,' Hay said. 'I am known by many names.'

He was taking villainous relish in the capture of the Doctor and Cecil, who remained on their knees before him. Cecil knew that any act of physical rebellion against such prodigiously muscled captors was doomed to fail, and the thought further emphasized his dilemma. For the first time in his life he felt powerless and foolish. Why? Because he was and he had been. The sneer on Hay's face, a sneer he had longed to strike, was made even more maddening by the change in his character. The boy – Cecil corrected himself, for he could see now that Hay was in his late twenties at least – the man strutted around the room, his face contorted into an expression of total triumph. He continued his speech of introduction to his true self. 'I have worn so many faces in my young life. The hooded messenger and the King's boy are only two of them.'

Cecil shook with rage. 'I should have known it. The day you first came to me as the Spaniard, at the gala to celebrate the success of the Anglo-Scottish talks . . . it was the same day you approached the King, as Hay.' He gave a bitter smile. 'It was your plan from the beginning.'

Hay inclined his head in a gesture that was not quite a nod. 'I had the two of you dancing to my tune with even less effort than I had anticipated. Your thirst for revenge on Catesby's band blinded you to all else. I had worried that you might one day suspect, as you were reputedly a man of great intelligence and foresight. But those qualities deserted you in our dealings.' He tapped the purse attached to his waist. 'And the gold you paid the Spaniard was most helpful. Both you and your idiot king were eager to lavish riches upon me.' Briefly he assumed the swagger of his persona at court. 'There were times I thought I might sink into the floor under the weight of all the gold.'

To hear the King referred to in this way made Cecil snarl. 'Criticism of the King is a criminal offence.'

'That incurs a hefty fine,' Hay finished for him. 'As I am shortly about to blow up Parliament I find it difficult to care somehow.' He smirked. 'Poor James. In a way I'll be sorry to see him go. He picks his nose and drinks too much, and in that he is well qualified to claim domain over the English, I suppose.'

The Doctor had fallen into uncharacteristic silence since their capture, and his eyes darted regularly to where his companion, the drugged girl, stood at the foot of the bed. He spoke at last. 'You became the King's favourite. The best way to get close to him, manipulate him, encourage his indolence. So that the plot might never be uncovered.'

Hay nodded. 'You have it, Doctor. I became close to James in all things.'

'Hmm, yes,' said the Doctor, picking his words carefully. 'Pardon me for saying so, but that does seem to be going rather, ahem, a long way in the line of duty. You must be very devoted.'

'I am.' He indicated Cecil. 'The plot was proceeding to plan. Encouraged by me, this fellow's warnings went ignored.'

Cecil glowered up at him. 'I would have blown the thing open, fox. I shall still. The seeds of suspicion were planted.'

Hay took a few steps up and down. 'You were due to meet with a terrible accident tomorrow morning. Hemlock in your breakfast draught, added by myself. You would never have had the chance to expose the plot. That lashing tongue of yours would have turned purple and choked you. By coming here you have saved me that little effort.' He made a signal to the henchmen, who immediately took Cecil by the arms and lurched him upright, leaving the Doctor unattended. 'It upset me that although I would be witness to your demise I would not be able to express my delight publicly to an appreciative audience. Now I can.' He indicated the Doctor. 'I must thank your friend here for that.' He laid a twisted emphasis on the word 'friend'.

Cecil flinched as the henchmen took a firmer grip on his upper arms. One tug from their powerful frames would be enough to tear both his spindly limbs from their sockets. Desperately he looked towards the Doctor. The old man was standing up slowly. He licked his lips, as if trying to rack his brains for a solution to the situation. Oddly neither Hay nor the henchmen seemed to pay him the slightest attention.

Hay bore down on Cecil. 'Yes, the Doctor has done me good service. To think that I came close to killing a master of my own order.'

Cecil gulped and looked towards the Doctor. The old man looked as surprised as he was at this pronouncement. 'No, that can't be true,' Cecil babbled, as his arms were lifted up over his head and twisted at an obscene angle, the bones at his joints crunching, the pain spreading. 'No, not you . . .'

The Doctor coughed. 'Mr Hay, I fear you are under a misapprehension. I am not a member of any order, least of all your peculiar brotherhood.'

Hay's response was to throw back his head and cackle. 'How typical of a Grand Behemoth to deny his own wisdom.' He lowered the top half of his body in a reverential gesture that was not quite a conventional bow, and said exultantly, 'Kulkukula!'

The Doctor reacted with an uncertain nod.

Hay pointed to Vicki. 'Your apprentice has told me all, Doctor. You are a warlock of the highest order, a Grand Behemoth.' He bowed. 'And I am honoured to be graced by your presence on my humble mission.'

Drained of feeling, her awareness blotted out, Vicki was oblivious of the events unfolding in the underground room until a tingle of pins and needles, initially so distant and boxed-off it felt like a thing observed rather than experienced, ran along her arms and legs, and triggered curious questions in a recess of her mind. Drowsiness receded and the blur of sounds and colours that washed over her became gradually sharper-edged. She took a breath, and found the air tasted dull and musty. She craved the sweet odour from the golden thurible, and the pain of its absence acted as a jolt, bringing her rudely back to consciousness. She saw Cecil, down on the floor, his arms twisted back so far it seemed impossible they hadn't snapped in two like dry twigs. His stoic lordly face was contorted as he tried not to scream. Observing this were Hay, who appeared to be enjoying it, and the Doctor. Vicki's rush of joy at seeing him again was quelled by the disinterested sneer on his face. If she had never met him before she would have guessed him to be a tyrant, a person for whom cruelty was prosaic. His words, made sense of slowly by her still drowsy brain, would have confirmed it.

'A suitable end,' he was saying, 'for a man of this calibre. If the cleverest diplomat in all England is deceived with such ease, it is a nation that deserves what is to come.' A howl of pain burst from Cecil as if to punctuate the observation. 'Witness. A craven breed of mongrel ancestry.'

Hay nodded. Vicki noted the way he deferred to the Doctor as he said, 'I agree, master. My workings in the court fell out better than the most hopeful of the brethren could have devised.' He raised his hand and made a slow circling motion in the air with a finger. His henchmen responded by increasing their pressure on Cecil. Again the Doctor made no objection, merely observed the scene with the disinterest of an emperor at the arena. Hay went on, 'It was wise of you to test me, master. I should have known from your strength that you were more than any spy.'

The Doctor waved a dismissive hand. 'It is of no matter. You acted as I expected, confirmed my expectation of your abilities.' For a moment he assumed his normal manner, clutched his lapels and said chirpily, 'The old Doctor and his ward. A transparent device. I foresaw Cecil would come to you and that, fearing I was an impostor with some knowledge of your plan, you would attempt to kill me. This would reveal your identity and put us in contact.' He harrumphed. 'Unfortunately, young Vicki appeared in my room before I could state my intention. Then, as you know, I brought up my secondary plan and engineered Cecil to bring me to you.'

Hay shook his head slightly in admiration. 'You are the mightiest engineer, master. I thought I should never look upon the face of one of the Behemoths, one of the Supreme Order of the Rectangle.' He gestured to Vicki. 'Your wizardry borders on the marvellous.'

'Indeed,' the Doctor said loftily. 'What exactly did she tell you?'

'Enough to show that you are the greatest worker of spells. You have conjured her to hold that she is a child from the future, that she travels through the heavens. She believes it totally. You have supreme control of her mind. You could only be a Behemoth.' He paused and added, 'My hope is that you will find favour with my humble work.'

'You know it is unwise to ask for the opinions of a Behemoth,' the Doctor said grandly. 'Privately, I would say to you that I am well pleased. Now, go over the exact details that I might discern your, er, artistry.'

When Hay replied, Vicki once more got the impression that he was glad of a chance to unburden his secrets. 'I was entrusted by the Grand Council, as you know, to bring havoc to this country. The scheme was devised at Grammont by the councillors. But their faces were known in England, and with regard of my earlier triumphs they chose me to fulfil it.'

The Doctor nodded patiently, although Vicki could tell from his shining eyes that he was fervent with excitement inside. 'A single man to bring about all that has happened.' Catching Hay's quizzical reaction to his words, he added hastily, 'It is the way we have always worked. Go on.'

'I linked up first with Cecil, then Catesby, told each man what they wished to hear of the other. Their contempt for the Spanish was an excellent lever in my support, as they were eager to paint their mysterious contact as money-grabbing and self-seeking, which are the celebrated characteristics of that race, and not to question his motives further. I worked hard. Cecil arranged for the gunpowder to be brought right in under the Lords, and changed the security roster so that each group of guardsmen believed another had patrolled there. Catesby and Fawkes hovered around the city like expectant vultures, their fellow plotters scattered and ready to flee whenever necessary.' He smacked his lips together unpleasantly. 'Now, my three man's song, in which I took the lead part, is almost over. The letters have been dispatched. When parliament is a smoking wreck the wars will begin. This country will be torn apart by its hidden tensions.'

The Doctor threw back his head and flared his nostrils. He was, thought Vicki, doing a most convincing impersonation of a power-crazed lunatic. 'And then . . .' he said in stirring tones. She could see he was prompting Hay. But Hay seemed to be waiting for him to finish the sentence. 'And then . . .' he said again.

Hay realized that he was being cued. Still unsuspecting, he said, 'And then begins the reign of Darkness, for which we have so long prepared, master. The fall of England will crush the spirits of all Europe. France will fall, then Spain,

Germany . . .' His eyes glazed over. 'Everlasting Darkness!'

The Doctor was looking agitated. 'And then . . .' he re-prompted.

Hay frowned. 'Darkness ever more.'

'Of course, of course. Darkness ever more, quite, quite. Splendid.' The Doctor quickly scrabbled for his masterly air. 'Well, yes. You've done very well, I must say.'

'Your approval, Behemoth, is the best part of my reward,' said Hay. 'I beg the forgiveness of you and all your agents.'

'All my agents?' asked the Doctor suspiciously.

'I mean the man Ian and his wife Barbara.'

The Doctor's eyebrows shot up. 'Oh, those agents. Er, they tested you as well, did they?'

Hay grinned. 'Yes, Behemoth. They behaved most strangely, put themselves into the plot's workings. I encouraged and observed them to deduce their true purpose and became more and more confused. Now I understand all of it.'

'And you know where they are?' To Vicki's relief Hay nodded. 'Superb. Well, how about finding them and bringing them in here for me, eh?'

'I will grant any boon for you, master.'

For the first time since Vicki had surfaced from her trance, Cecil spoke. His voice was not much more than a strangulated gasp. 'You . . . cur . . .' he spat. 'Why do you . . . do this?'

Hay answered. 'To ask why is to question. There will be no questions when the old world is returned. Only darkness, and magic. Idiot, you thought you had true power.' He indicated the Doctor. 'Here is true power, the old knowledge of Kulkukula! You are privileged to look upon the face of a Behemoth, one of the highest circle of our order! He could make you into a toad or raise mighty Mephistopheles!'

Vicki hoped ardently that the Doctor would not be pressed to prove this. So, evidently, did he. He stepped forward and said to Hay, with a cursory glance at the agonized Cecil, 'Well, you seem to have it all wrapped up rather neatly. Vicki and I shall be on our way.' He beckoned to her. Feeling that she ought to keep up her pretence that she was still entranced she kept still. But the Doctor must have seen the sparkle in her eyes; he sighed and clicked his fingers under her nose, and she made a show of coming to life.

'It is a miracle,' said Hay.

The Doctor took her by the hand. 'There, there, my dear. We must be getting along.' He pulled her to his side and made for the door. Vicki couldn't believe that the Doctor would leave Cecil to die, even though he had been their enemy.

'Farewell, Behemoth,' said Hay.

'Farewell,' said the Doctor. He winked. 'If you keep up to this standard, young fellow, you never know, you might be a Behemoth yourself one day.' He turned to go and a thought seemed to strike him. He said casually, 'Oh, one thing. This chap.' He indicated Cecil. 'Would it not be wiser to lock him away rather than kill him?'

Hay slumped. 'Why do you say that?'

The Doctor smiled wisely. 'Because if he dies now you'll miss the opportunity to increase the mayhem after the explosion. Think of the furore if he suddenly appears, without a scratch, the only survivor?'

Hay's eyes shone. 'By God, yes. Passions would be inflamed. He would be set upon by the mob, torn to bloody pieces . . .'

'Exactly.' The Doctor gave a final wave goodbye and pushed Vicki ahead of him through the door and into the narrow hallway outside. She drew a breath to speak; he raised a finger urgently to his lips and shooed her through the far door and into the dripping tunnel beyond. He followed a moment later with lantern relit.

Vicki could not hold herself back another second. 'Doctor, that was brilliant. You're a genius.'

His chuckle echoed around the tunnel. 'Yes, I suppose I am, aren't I?' He ushered her onwards. 'Now, chop chop. We're not out of the woods yet.'

* * *

Haldann's eye seized on a thing so joyous, so beautiful, so ... *remarkably* inept that the years were lifted from his hunched shoulders, his lungs opened up, bellows-like, to their fullest extent and took a lusty draught of air, and he might have burst spontaneously into one of the young people's tiptoeing dances had his lower back not warned him, just in time, that it was probably not such a good idea. He slapped his finger down on the error to mark it and cried shrilly, 'Otley! Oh, Otley!'

His imperturbable foe's voice echoed from an annex. 'That tone signifies foolery.'

'Aha, yes, yes it does!' crowed Haldann. 'Foolery of an exalted magnitude! But on your part!'

Otley emerged into the main workroom, and the worry behind his smug mask was a delight to behold. 'Really, Henry, you are pathetic.'

'Oh no,' cried Haldann, waving the sheet triumphantly, 'it is *you* who are the pathetic one!' He shoved the paper under Otley's bulbous nose and jabbed theatrically at his discovery. 'There! "And Salome, before being instructed of her mother, said 'Give me here John Baptist's head in a *colander*!'"' He hooted. 'A colander. My treacle slip-up pales in comparison.'

'Give me that,' demanded Otley, at the same time grabbing the sheet. He scanned it, swallowed, and handed it back curtly. 'I think you will see, if you inspect the entire sheet with clearer eyes, that although the work on St Matthew is begun in my hand, it ends in yours.' He sniffed.

Haldann snorted. 'Dear, dear. Trying to shift blame.' He tapped the sheet two-thirds of the way down. 'I took over Matthew here' – then moved his finger up – 'and the colander sits here!'

'The dictionaries give several alternative definitions. After many hours' concentration the mind wanders.' Otley's attempts to brush away the accusation could not conceal his anxiety, and Haldann felt like breaking into song. 'One word can easily be remedied, a string of falsities takes hours to correct!'

Haldann wished for the long lost strength of his youth, recalled how once he had been able to raise a fist without a moment's preparation. He entertained a violent fantasy of boxing Otley's ears, and was pondering how best to make it a reality when there came an urgent thumping – almost a hammering – on the door. Instantly he and Otley assumed their indignant expressions. To show his own maturity in the face of their spat, Haldann made for the door. But Otley had had the same idea and with his seven-year advantage got to the knob first.

'And who,' he bellowed before the caller could be seen, 'threatens to tear our beloved door off its hinges? This is a holy –' He broke off as he saw the Chamberlain, whose face, for once, was white rather than pink. The man looked as if he had been punched in the middle.

Haldann guessed that the burdens of organization had at last exacted their toll. With a delicacy and kindness that surprised himself he took the Chamberlain gently by the hand and guided him across the threshold. The workroom's cool monastic ambience would likely soothe him. 'Chamberlain, what vexes you? Here, seat yourself on this trestle and unburden yourself.'

Otley sneered. 'We aren't running an almshouse,' he muttered.

The Chamberlain sat down and smiled weakly up at them. 'My dear fellows,' he said, 'I have hurried here in a perfect quandary. I have a terrible dilemma.'

Otley huffed again and looked pointedly up at the rafters. 'Then go seek a priest or one of the lords, as we don't do dilemmas.'

Haldann shushed him. 'Go on, Chamberlain.'

'You see,' the Chamberlain went on, 'I cannot tell a priest or a lord, for if the news I bear was imparted widely the court would be in uproar. And you two have always seemed to me like wise, good character'd men.'

'All right, then,' said Otley. Obviously he expected this new tizz of the Chamberlain's to be nothing out of the ordinary, and had failed to detect the signs – the strange pallor and unusual stillness – that indicated the opposite.

The Chamberlain produced an opened letter from his robes and handed it to Haldann. 'This was delivered late last night to the home of Lord Monteagle.'

Haldann scanned it quickly. He took childish pleasure, for which he reprimanded himself, in keeping the writing out of Otley's sight and assuming a grave countenance. This was not difficult; the implications were plain. 'Well,' he said. 'Well, well.'

Otley snatched it from him. 'Let me see that.'

'You discern my predicament, then,' the Chamberlain said, putting his hands on his head.

Haldann considered. 'Well, no, not really. Go and see the King.'

'The King is . . .' the Chamberlain began hotly, and checked himself just in time. 'Tired and emotional.'

'Ah, I see. Cecil, then.'

'Is nowhere to be found.' The Chamberlain wrung his hands and wiped beads of sweat from his brow. 'What to do? And another thing presses on my thoughts in this connection.' He bit his lip, as if unsure whether it was sensible to speak, and continued, 'With all the planning we've had lately it's slipped my mind, rather. But yesterday Cecil came to me about a discrepancy he'd noticed in some rental agreements.' He gulped. 'The lower lumber room beneath the House of Lords is being used to store fuel by Thomas Percy.'

'Percy, Percy.' Haldann thought hard. 'Ah yes, he would be that wild fellow about the court. Good-natured, if rather wild. Catholic, isn't he?' The implication of his last statement occurred to him. 'Oh, I see. You posit a Catholic powder plot in Parliament's very bowel?'

'Well, yes,' said the Chamberlain. 'The calamity referred to in the letter seems to bear it out.'

Otley laughed scornfully. 'Oh, brave! I think perhaps the King and Cecil make sport with you.'

'Unlikely,' said Haldann. 'The King, maybe, not Cecil. He is not renowned for his knavery.' He thought a moment longer. 'Chamberlain, you do well to worry, although this will probably come to naught. Cecil is most probably tied up with security affairs, and this Monteagle letter is likely a device to stir up enmity and interfere with the processes of government.'

The Chamberlain looked up pleadingly. 'Then what do your wise heads bid me do?'

Before Otley could speak Haldann clapped the Chamberlain on the shoulder and indicated the door. 'Hurry to the barrack room. Rouse that handsome young guard captain, what's-his-name, the fierce one.'

'Knyvett,' supplied Otley.

'That's the chap. Whisper your ideas in his ear and take him down quietly, but with all haste, to Percy's lumber room. You are within your rights to make an inspection, are you not?'

'Oh yes, yes,' said the Chamberlain. He gripped Haldann's bony hand and squeezed tightly. 'Awfully clever of you. As you have said my worry is most probably unfounded. If so, we'll keep this' – he held up the letter – 'secret, yes?'

Haldann nodded and showed him the door. 'As we are your friends. Now go.' He watched the Chamberlain's departure, noted that some of the bloom was returning to his cheeks and turned to Otley. 'I handled that rather splendidly, did I not?'

Otley waved a dismissive hand. 'Nothing to handle but the womanly ditherings of a clucking old hen.' He took this opportunity to dart back into one of the annexes, conveniently forgetting the earlier dispute.

Cecil watched as Hay posed in front of his large mirror. He took a compact from his pocket, pure gold and fashioned with a shell design inlaid with pearls, and dusted a little powder on his cheeks. He hummed a foreign-sounding tune as he squirted scent on to his wrists and rubbed them together. Cecil knew this display had been calculated to infuriate him and tried to soothe the savagery which threatened to overtake his puny body. He had been set down by the guards and was now convulsed by shooting pains along the length of his arms. Escape, if it had ever been viable, was now impossible. He doubted he could stand. And the two servants of Hay stood before their door, arms folded across their smooth, muscled chests, their faces as blank and expressionless as ever.

'I have calls to make in town this morning,' said Hay smartly. 'The Doctor's agents are to be collected. Will you, dear Sir Robert, excuse my lapse of manners in leaving you here?' Once more his voice was the voice of the King's favourite.

Cecil growled and tried to lift an arm to shake his fist. Even this simple action was too much for him and he fell back on the thick carpet. His eyes closed and he summoned all his will to resist the taunts that were to come.

'Treat this abode as if it were your own,' said Hay. 'In a way, of course, it is.'

'You are a slimy worm,' was the only riposte Cecil could manage.

He heard Hay move closer. When he opened his eyes, the villain was leaning over him with an almost pitying expression. 'You are your own victim, Cecil,' he said. 'Look to your own self to apportion blame.'

Cecil snarled. He put his discomfort aside for a moment and asked, 'This unholy brethren that counts you and the Doctor among its number. Whence came it?' He saw Hay's reluctance and added, 'If I am to die, why not reveal your secrets?'

His political acumen, his skill at deciphering the character of an opponent, had not deserted him. He had read Hay right: the man could not resist the chance to gloat in the face of a defeated enemy. 'Whence come we? From all sides, men of great character, exalted and magical. You have seen a Grand Behemoth in the shape of the Doctor. It is men of his breed that will dominate all nations in the new world, and the earth shall be cleansed by fire and returned to its rightful state. There will then be no talk of a share for all. Slaves shall be slaves, and masters masters, just as it was before the rise of hated Greece.

Practitioners of the forbidden knowledge shall outstretch their fingers, and pleasure will fall at the feet of only those who deserve it.'

'Men like the Doctor,' breathed Cecil. 'That odious, deceiving rat.'

Hay kicked him viciously. 'You speak of a Grand Behemoth. Have a care that I do not rip out your tongue before I throw you to the dogs.' He turned to go. He collected his bulging cloak from the hook as he went.

Cecil called weakly after him, 'You shall not rend this country. It is a tighter union than you think.' The strain overcame him at last. He felt a rush of nausea and the room whirled around and around into a blaze of coloured lights. Then nothingless.

Vicki was only an inch over five feet tall and even she had problems negotiating the tunnel. The hem of her white frock was now sopping with mud and she felt sure she had a cold coming on. Her resilient spirit, spurred on by the Doctor, who retained an amazing degree of strength for a sexagenarian, kept her going, and as her system cleared out what remained of Hay's drug from her mind a familiar impulse reasserted itself. Oh no. She was going to have to ask some more questions.

Trying to keep her voice as mature and sensible-sounding as possible she asked, 'Doctor, do you really know anything about Hay's brotherhood or whatever-it-is?'

He turned his head a fraction towards her, and in the lantern light his features were kindly and reassuring. He had two ways of responding to questions, she decided. If he was unsure or lacked information he snapped; if there was a chance to show off he was charming. 'Well, my dear,' he said, 'let us put the facts together for ourselves, eh? Consider what we know. Hay is definitely not English –'

'He said something about . . . Grammont, was it?'

'Yes, yes,' the Doctor said impatiently. Well, perhaps she wasn't going to get the chance to put any facts together for herself, then. 'Grammont Abbey in Northern

France, it's been abandoned and in ruins since the tenth century.'

'Don't tell me. You've been there.'

'Hmm, yes, but not for another couple of hundred years. It's always been a place with an evil reputation. The original monks of Grammont were a very unsavoury collection, got up to all sorts of cabbalistic rites. Until young Hugh Capet, the first French king, put an end to them. There are tales of grisly ceremonies and sacrifices.'

'Really?' Vicki liked a spot of colour in the Doctor's stories. 'What sort of grisly sacrifices?'

He tutted. 'Oh, the insensitivity of the young. The details aren't important. Anyway, they were broken up.'

'Except they weren't,' said Vicki.

'And what leads you to that conclusion, child?'

Vicki felt herself floundering. Oh, why did he have to be so patronizing! 'Well, all that Behemoth stuff. They must still be at it, in secret.'

The Doctor halted for a second and pinched the bridge of his nose. 'When you receive information, Vicki,' he said with surprising gentleness, 'always examine its source.' He smiled. 'Hay's brethren would very much like to convince themselves of that. But it's doubtful. Secret societies operate by giving themselves airs. In their case, this rectangle business. They may well have adopted Grammont as some sort of meeting place, but I don't think there can be a direct link.'

Vicki sighed. 'All right. But it doesn't alter the fact that Hay has a base right under the palace, and has the skill to bring England to its knees.' She looked around the damp, gloomy tunnel. 'How did he get all of that stuff down here?' She clicked her fingers. 'Perhaps there are other exits along this main passageway.'

'Well done,' said the Doctor. He started walking again. 'There, you see, if you put your mind to it you can be quite clever. Yes, I think this is more a network than a single tunnel. He can pop up wherever he wants within a certain radius. As to who built these tunnels in the first place ... well, they may have been down here for centuries, their existence known only to a handful. Hay seems very thorough. He must have scouted them out and done all his decoration well in advance of laying his big plan. What a cunning fellow.'

'Then it's a good job,' said Vicki, 'that he won't succeed.'

'You're very confident.'

'Well, of course. The gunpowder never went off, did it? There was no everlasting darkness.'

'Oh dear, dear, dear.' The Doctor shook his head. 'You still don't understand the nature of time, my dear.'

Vicki's spirits sank. 'Don't I?'

He laid a protective hand on her shoulder. 'We are right here in the thick of things. Our actions over the next few hours may have a vital bearing on ensuring the version of events you have just described.'

Vicki boggled. 'You mean we're a part of this history?'

'Yes. Which is why we're going straight to the King to warn him of the plot, so that he can uncover it just as the history books say. We'll warn him about Hay, too, clear the whole thing up.' He beamed. 'It's all turned out rather neatly.'

'Well done, Behemoth,' Vicki teased him. 'And then,' she added hopefully, 'back to the Ship?'

He nodded. 'Yes. With Hay's help we'll pick up Barbara and Chesterton – and heaven knows what they've been up to from the sound of things – and return.' He looked rather shamefaced, and Vicki realized it was the first time they had spoken of the broken promise since her attempted flight from the palace. He fumbled for where the key normally hung around his neck and then raised a finger in self-approbation. 'Ah. I was forgetting.' He held out his palm to her and wiggled his fingers. 'The key, please.'

Vicki closed her eyes, wishing herself somewhere, *anywhere* else. For a second she considered whether running back to Hay would not have been a more preferable option. 'I haven't got it,' she said.

There was a ghastly silence in which the tunnel echoed

to the sound of distant drips. Surely, Vicki thought, he wouldn't be so cruel as to bawl her out here and now. Perhaps he might surprise her, and react with concern and care.

It was not to be. 'You haven't got it?' he thundered.

Tears came to Vicki's eyes. 'I'm sorry,' she blurted. 'I'm sorry I took it from you, only you were so ... *horrible* about leaving Ian and Barbara behind, and I was in a panic. I know I shouldn't have, but –'

'Never mind the apologies,' the Doctor said harshly. 'Where is it now?'

She swallowed the hot ball of emotion rising in her throat. 'Well, I was knocked out by Hay or one of his chums, and when I woke up I was back in that room, wearing this dress, and the key had gone. I don't know if he took it or if it fell out.' She wanted to cry into his shoulder but his expression was murderous. 'I really am sorry, I didn't mean to spoil things.' The awful silence continued. Vicki couldn't bear to meet his accusing eyes. 'You do still like me, don't you?' She heard her own voice, pathetic and childish.

The Doctor seemed to snap out of his trance. 'Oh, yes, yes, of course, now there's a good girl, don't cry.' He enfolded her in his arms and dabbed his handkerchief over her eyes. 'Here, have a hanky. I'm sure we'll find it, won't we?'

She blew her nose and tried to calm her shuddering chest. 'Don't you have a spare?'

'No, that would be very foolish, wouldn't it?' he said, his tone still kindly. 'Anyone might find it. Now, we shall just have to proceed as planned and keep our wits about us, won't we? Chin up.' He walked on. Ahead of him Vicki saw the worn spiral steps that led to the tree.

She pulled herself together, coughed, and pushed the hanky up her sleeve.

Ian watched in silent horror, with Winter's knife tight against her throat, as Percy and Catesby between them unwound a length of thick rope from a supply beneath the sheets. His eyes kept flicking to the door at the top of the steps, wishing for Firking and Hodge to burst in. But they didn't, and he couldn't blame them. From their hiding-place in the line of trees in the yard they must have seen Percy and Winter's entry, and decided that it was pointless to attempt to overpower four armed, desperate men. He was on his own.

Winter held him as Catesby wound the rope about his waist and the wooden support pillar he was pressed against. 'Make them good knots, Rob,' Percy said.

Winter growled. 'I say we rip out his gizzard now.'

'And I say no,' said Percy. 'He goes when the House goes, so that he may have time to think as the touchwood burns, and time to recant. As our fathers had time when they were at the stake.' There was an insane gleam in his eye, the mark of the true fanatic. As if to confirm this, he brought his lips right up to Ian's ear and whispered, 'Except your death will be a sudden and merciful one. You shall not feel the prick of the rising flames. It shall be over in a flash for you. You will hear the fizzing of the wood for a quarter of an hour, and you will get the great rush of heat from the barrels as they go, and then you shall be in hell with your masters.'

Ian grimaced. 'I've told you. King James is not my master.'

Winter slapped him. 'Do not disgrace yourself further by disloyalty. Ah, you Protestants are the dregs. It is a cleansing fire we build. I —'

'Ssh!' It was Catesby who interrupted him. He raised a hand for silence, and pointed up the steps.

Ian turned his head as far as he could, which was only a matter of inches. He heard a clatter of booted feet, the jingle of a harness against leather.

Winter leapt up. 'We are discovered!'

He whipped out his knife and raised it to Ian's throat. The blade's edge nestled against his skin and a wave of horror rushed through him.

There was a knock on the door and a cry of 'Open up!'

11

Nudging History

The Chamberlain winced at the harshness of Knyvett's knock and intuitively crossed himself against whatever devilry was to be uncovered. Knyvett was a hulking wagon of a man in the regalia of a guardsman, and the sharp raps of his knuckles were like blasts from judgement's bugle. He was a surly, tight-lipped fellow who was at his best when he was killing somebody or attacking something, and pretty much useless all the rest of the time. In their previous intercourse the Chamberlain had taken to him because he followed orders unquestioningly and with a ruthlessness that had become legend about court. But it was unpleasant to be stood right beside him when he was about his business; it was like sitting on a powder keg. Ugh – powder keg! This connection gave the Chamberlain a further shudder and he looked askance at the unyielding wooden door. Please, he prayed, let this be a silly mistake on my part. If there really is a plot, think of the complications! Endless reports, any amount of rescheduling and alteration of rosters, insurrection, recrimination! For an illogical second he caught himself favouring the option of being blown to ashes.

'Open up I say!' Knyvett's meaty fist, packed tightly in a mail glove, banged on the door again. 'In the name of King James!' His other hand fell to the hilt of his sword and he squared his shoulders, preparing to charge like a bull and bring the door off its hinges.

A moment later bolts were drawn back carefully. The door swung open to reveal the handsome, agreeable face of Thomas Percy. The Chamberlain cringed. Here, in dawn's early light, that face shone with honesty and good intent. The nod of greeting he gave was even and full of the charitable character of the Percy family. How could perfidy have been imagined in these environs? All because of that stupid letter.

'Ah, good morrow, sirrah,' said Percy, and doffed his hat. The vivid green duck's feather in the brim quivered as if to emphasize his harmlessness. 'And how may I aid you?'

The Chamberlain, who felt foolish, blurted, 'Oh, an error, a foolish mistake on my part, I –' He swallowed under the steely gaze of Knyvett. The man had no facial expression at all, it had been trained out of him by years in royal service, but it was not hard to tell what he was thinking. 'Er, well, in actual fact, I wondered if I might be permitted – ah, that is to say, I would like to, er, inspect, your lumber room beyond.' He chuckled. 'Nothing personal, you understand, only "procedure".' He shrugged to give the last word a jaunty inflection.

Percy raised an eyebrow. 'Really? I did not realize. Oh well, by all means, come in, come in, inspect, inspect.' He stepped aside and waved them through the door. 'There's not much to see, I'm afraid to say.'

The Chamberlain stepped over the threshold, Knyvett at his heels, and into a scene that was entirely ordinary. This was indeed just a cellar-sized storage space with a low ceiling and a damp, musty smell. Heaped in one corner was a large pile of billets, laid one on top of another in an uneven rickety structure, which was surrounded by a circle of faggots. The Chamberlain's attention was more taken up by the three other men who stood in front of an object or collection of objects that was covered by a huge dirty sheet. The first man was tall and well built, and his face was vaguely familiar from some Catholic scandal in Elizabeth's time. In contrast to his lean, athletic body his face was pale and unhealthy-looking. The second was Winter, a friend of Percy's who was often entertained at court. The third fellow he had never seen before. He was youngish, with a balanced set of features and dark hair. While the others looked relaxed he seemed slightly aggrieved, and his posture was strangely rigid, as if Winter was holding something behind his back.

The Chamberlain waved nervously at them. 'Hello,' he said.

'Hello,' they returned casually.

Percy had descended the steps behind him. 'Lads, the Chamberlain just wants to give the place a look-over. I suppose with the opening tomorrow night you can't be too careful, can you?'

'Indeed not.' The Chamberlain waved Knyvett forward. 'But I can see it's all in order down here and I'm really terribly sorry to have bothered you.' He started to back out. He hated confrontation and was starting to feel short of breath. These chaps were all perfectly friendly. He should never have listened to Cecil or those translators. 'Well, bye-bye, gentle—'

'Hold one moment.' The interruption came from Knyvett. He pointed to the pile of billets. 'What is this?'

Percy came forward. 'It is only kindling for use in the coming winter. My rental agreement with the Crown confers on me the right to store such materials.'

'Of course it does,' said the Chamberlain. 'Sorry to have put you to any trouble.' He edged towards the stairs. 'Now, Knyvett, shall we —'

The guardsman would not be drawn away. 'And who are these?' he asked, pointing to Percy's friends, suspicion ingrained on his weathered face. The Chamberlain supposed he must have seen so much of life's darker side that scenting trouble was now an instinct. 'Why are you gathered here?'

Percy sidled close to the Chamberlain to give his answer. 'We are all married men, your grace. And though we love our wives, there are occasions when their nags and cares tire us, and so we slope down here to drink and play cards and smoke pipes of tobacco.' He pulled a pipe from his doublet and waved it about. 'You see?'

The Chamberlain nodded. 'Very well, yes. Correct in all details.' He nodded to Knyvett. 'Come, let us away.'

But Knyvett did not budge. 'One more thing,' he said. 'What lies under that sheet?' He pointed to the strangely shaped object in the centre of the room.

The Chamberlain could not help view the thing with a little fear, although he was certain of its innocence. Situated there it was directly beneath the very centre of the House of Lords. 'Yes, er, what is that?' he asked casually.

'That?' For a moment Percy's face was blank.

One of his friends, the man in the red suit, spoke up. 'It's a selection of wines,' he prompted. His voice, like his clothing, was ragged and defeated. 'Wines that improve when placed in a cool place and under cover.'

'Of course, yes,' said Percy. 'Our lovely wines, that we would venture to keep secret from our thirsty wives.' He laughed and clapped a hand on the Chamberlain's shoulder. 'Why don't you stay and drink with us to the King's health?'

The Chamberlain flinched. 'Normally, yes, I'd love to.' In fact he was desperate to get out of this uncomfortable cellar and away from the insinuation he had made. 'But with the opening tomorrow I've a hundred things to attend to.'

'Well, of course.' Percy waved him farewell and steered him gently to the steps. 'Feel free to drop back in any time you want.'

'Oh yes, do,' his friends chorused.

Knyvett ascended, apparently satisfied. The Chamberlain followed him, and turned for a last look round at the top of the steps. 'Sorry to put you to bother, good Percy,' he said.

'Oh, you didn't put me to any bother,' said Percy. But the Chamberlain could tell he was eager to be alone with his mates again and get back to all the back-slapping and heavy drinking that men did in such groups. So he nodded and made to withdraw.

As he turned he saw something that caused him to yelp in fear. 'Ah, what's that?' He pointed to a darkened corner of the cellar, over by the pile of kindling. In the light from one of the hanging lanterns he had caught a glimpse of the lower half of a body, a pair of legs parted at an odd angle. 'Over there, in the corner?' He gesticulated wildly. 'Is it a –' He swallowed. 'A body?'

There was another unpleasant silence. Then Winter replied with a nervous laugh. 'Ah, 'tis a body all right. The soused body of our mate, so full with drink he did topple over.' He laughed falteringly. The others, apart from the young dark-haired man, joined him.

The Chamberlain found himself laughing too. How could he ever have laid treason at the door of these charming fellows? 'Oh, silly of me to think otherwise.' He raised a cheery hand in farewell. 'Again, my apologies. I withdraw.'

He backed out of the door at last and back into the fresh, frosty air of the November morning. He took a moment to look up at the parliament buildings, and sighed. They had never been as secure; his jumping to conclusions was ridiculous.

He nodded to Knyvett. 'We shall return to Whitehall. All is well here.'

Knyvett looked as if he wanted to say something, but he was an obedient character who trusted in the wisdom of his betters, and so he simply nodded back and led the way across the yard to where their coach was waiting.

The Chamberlain noted an odd sticky sensation beneath his foot. He looked down and saw that his shoes were leaving a trail of some red deposit across the cobbles. For a second he felt a blast of fear. It couldn't be blood, could it? Then he looked more closely, and recalled Winter's words. Spilt wine, obviously.

He upbraided himself mentally for being such a nervous type, and followed Knyvett away from Parliament.

The King stepped from the royal carriage outside the Guildhall and gave his massed subjects a desultory wave. A path had been cleared from the carriage right up to where the strange box stood, over which a red carpet had been laid down, and he staggered along it, supported by a boy on either side, his head spinning from the excesses of the previous night. He longed to tell the wildly cheering crowd of stupid commoners to shut up. Ah, if only he'd lived in Imperial Rome. There was none of this tolerance for the ordinary man in those days. He could have ordered the whole lot slaughtered. The image of carnage this conjured up lifted his mood slightly.

He had been woken at the ungodly hour of half-past six by some quibbling underling, who had told him his coach was ready. 'But I haven't ordered a coach,' he'd slurred in reply. 'Oh,' the official had said. 'But it's waiting to take you to the Guildhall, as agreed. The people have turned out in droves to see you.' James had pulled himself out of bed, dimly aware that he ought to put in a showing. Never go back on a promise to your subjects, his poor father had said. Courtiers you can lie to, advisers and ministers you can fob off freely, but start letting the herd down and you'll have trouble. And after all, it wasn't the most challenging of tasks, to step out on to a balcony every now and then and wave a bit. As the coach made its way through the streets, James had reflected also that he was just a little interested in this devil's box.

Now, as he approached it, he felt disappointed. He'd expected fiery demons, unholy symbols, an object that resonated with evil. Instead it was solid and dependable-looking, and rather unmenacing. He waved a hand across its surface. The onlooking crowd gasped, expecting magic. He suppressed a desire to scream for them to shut up.

The Lord Mayor, a tall man with flecks of distinguished grey at his temples, bowed before him. 'You see, Your Majesty, it cannot be opened, and it breathes with a life all of its own. Most horrid.' He shuddered.

James remained suspicious. The sooner this was over the sooner he could get back to . . . the other things he'd been doing. He called over a guardsman, and pointed to the pike he carried. 'Let me have that.' The guard handed it over. James summoned all his strength, raised the pike over his arm to another irritating gasp from the crowd, and jabbed the sharp end into the door of the blue structure. On the evidence of his senses, which told him this was just a wooden container, he fully expected it to be marked at least.

The end of the pike skidded on the surface. There was no grip; the wood was diamond-hard. Astounded, he raised the pike again, and struck harder, with a grunt of effort. The result was the same.

He felt a rush of superstitious terror, backed from the box, and crossed himself. Straight away he realized that had been the wrong thing to do. His beloved subjects took this as a sign of his defeat, screamed, and stampeded away.

'Oh, for heaven's sake,' he sighed. He called after them, 'Come back, you daft Sassenachs! Ah, useless.' He shrugged to the Lord Mayor. 'You'd think they hadn't been educated.'

The Lord Mayor said, 'They haven't been educated, Your Majesty.'

'Ah yes, right you are.' James took another look at the box. 'Well, I don't like this. And I do scent devilry. It doesn't burn, you say?'

'No, Your Majesty, although we have tried several times.'

James rubbed his hands together. 'Nothing for it but exorcism, then.' He turned back towards his waiting coach and summoned his supporting boys. 'And I know just the fellow for the job.'

Vicki scrunched up her eyes against the morning light as she squeezed through the oak tree. Across the Privy Garden the palace's main buildings looked strong and tall and unruinable. In a daze she walked forward, a hand raised to her mouth, her heart full of wonder. 'One man,' she said, 'has the power to destroy all of this.'

The Doctor pulled himself out, and closed the hidden panel carefully. 'Well, not any more, my dear. The truth is, I have outfoxed him, haven't I?'

Vicki thought it was safe to risk a small barb. 'You were very lucky that he mistook you.'

'Luck?' The Doctor tugged absently at his cloak. 'It was hardly luck that got me into that tunnel, now was it? I should say it was intelligence and strength of character. Now come along, we have to warn the authorities.' He set off across the lawn.

Vicki followed. She was confused, and she felt a question coming. 'The thing is, history doesn't say anything about Hay's plot, does it?'

'What's the point you are making, child?' For once his tone was curious rather than patronizing.

'Guy Fawkes got the blame, just as Cecil wanted,' she went on. 'But if we go blundering in there now, the whole thing will be uncovered, and history will be changed.' She had the feeling she had said something incredibly dumb. 'Won't it?'

The Doctor gnawed on his knuckles. 'Goodness me, you're right,' he said at last, as if it was the most astonishing thing.

'Oh am I? Great.'

The Doctor's usual demeanour flooded back. 'No, as a matter of fact, it isn't great at all. Cecil's part in the scheme would be uncovered, and that could lead to turmoil.'

His pause was obviously designed to elucidate another question. Vicki didn't want to disappoint him. 'How do you mean?'

'The new alliance between England and Scotland is still in its early, delicate stages. Cecil's activity would besmirch James's name, exacerbating the tensions that will in thirty years' time lead to outright civil war. History would be altered irrevocably. With no Cromwell to express it, the reforming principle will likely be crushed. The United Kingdom will fall apart.'

'Well, if you will go mucking about in time,' Vicki grumbled.

'I have never mucked about,' snapped the Doctor. 'Now listen. We must tread very carefully, very carefully indeed. Fawkes is due to be discovered tonight, and not a moment before. We must make sure that happens without implicating Cecil.'

Vicki remained puzzled. 'But Cecil's still Hay's prisoner. He wasn't killed around now, was he?'

'No, he lives for many more years.' He put a hand to his temple. 'I think I have a headache. This is always the problem when one arrives in an era with which one is familiar. One has to be careful only to tread on the right pairs of toes. We must proceed with caution, whisper in the King's ear rather than storm in demanding action.'

Vicki lifted the muddy hem of her skirt in order to traverse the grass. 'The King?' She stopped. 'Doctor, look at me.'

His eyes swept up and down her. 'A spot of mud won't trouble him. This is urgent.'

'Not that. If I'm a boy, how do I explain what I'm wearing?' As if to punctuate her point the wind blew and the dress billowed around her.

'Ah.' The Doctor considered a moment, then waved her objection aside. 'It doesn't matter, does it? When weighed against the imminent destruction of Parliament?' He started walking again.

Vicki looked down at the dress and sighed. 'What if he decides to chop off my head?'

Dawn broke to reveal thick grey clouds lowering over London. The sun was concealed and the wind blew colder than before. To Barbara, threading her way carefully along the narrow streets towards the Guildhall at the heart of the city, the weather had never seemed so oppressive, and heavy with the weight of destiny. Bonfires were being lit on street corners, perilously near to the wooden eaves of houses, adding further irony to her bitter thoughts. Her heart remained heavy with sorrow and regret. Several times she had felt her eyes pricking with the beginning of tears and had held back the emotion. Thankfully, much of her concentration was taken up with navigating. It was unwise to stop and ask for directions, as it exposed one as an innocent, and so she walked confidently with the flow of the people, her ears pricked for any fragments of news in the conversations around her. From these she learnt that the TARDIS was still at the Guildhall, that a large crowd was gathering there, and that the King himself had given his assent to lay hands on it and cast out its spell.

By the time the city bells had chimed seven she was with the other early risers, by their garments mostly apprentices or beggars, who had nothing better to do than gawp outside the thick wrought-iron bars that sectioned off the Guildhall building. A number of stalls dispensing hot food and drinks were setting up, like flies around rubbish, and doing a brisk trade. Maintaining her air of casual interest, desperate not to draw attention (a task made easier by her newly dishevelled clothing), she joined the back of the ever-swelling crowd and craned her neck to examine the focus of their attention. It was a lofty construction, high and old and weathered grey, with large wooden double doors that stood guarded by a couple of nervous-looking pikemen who had, it appeared, long ago given up any attempts to disperse the onlookers. Its name came from the gilded fittings appended to its higher, unreachable ramparts. Through the windows, which were surprisingly clean, Barbara caught glimpses of ornate decoration and fastidious scrollwork through which strolled robed dignitaries, a telling contrast from the ragged architecture of the streets. Between the gates and the hall itself was a courtyard tiled in a red and white diagonal pattern, and sitting squarely in the exact centre of this was the dependable, bizarrely incongruous shape of a tall blue police telephone box, the focus of all eyes. Barbara caught a glimpse of its tiered roof and sighed longingly as if she had been reunited with a lover. Oddly, although perhaps this was just her own imagination, a tingle passed over her forehead and she experienced a little peak of pleasure. It made her think of her childhood, of her father's kiss as he left the breakfast table and went off to work. Could the TARDIS be glad to see her?

There was a slightly hysterical atmosphere around the place, and the tightly packed crowd were restless and goggle-eyed. Had they, Barbara wondered, stood out here all night in the hope of catching sight of the devil? Massed groupings of this sort had always made her feel uneasy, and she was not comforted by the realization that returning to the TARDIS would require getting through the heavy security cordon. Worse than that, she had no key. She would just have to hope that the Doctor or one of the others would hear of this discovery and hurry here as she had, with some devious plan to hand.

With these thoughts at the front of her mind, she stood on tiptoe and swept her gaze along the sea of heads – there were, she guessed, about four hundred spectators – checking for the most striking characteristics of her friends; the Doctor's flowing white hair, Vicki's cherubic cheeks or Ian's broad shoulders and redoubtably heroic expression. She matched none of them.

Disheartened, shoulders slumped, she started to elbow her way back out of the crowd. The odour was making her eyes water and she thumped her chest to clear the cough brewing there. As she did she felt another bony elbow jab into her side. Feeling irritable, she turned her head to deliver a rebuke and was brought up short by the face that greeted her. It took her a moment to place the perky smile and the freckled, upturned nose. When recognition came she clamped a hand on the serving girl's arm and pulled her free from the mob and on to a clear stretch of pavement.

'Oh, mercy!' the girl cried. She reached up and gave Barbara a tight squeeze. Barbara was prepared to overlook the excessive familiarity of the greeting in the circumstances. 'God save you, good mistress, and you in fine health!'

Barbara smiled back. 'Sybil, isn't it? From the tavern?'

'That's right.' The girl's lively blue eyes studied Barbara intently. 'Ah, your husband Ian was maddened with care for your safety. But I see you have taken your leave of those Catholic curs. There's one in the eye of their dark doings. Well done!' She clapped Barbara on the shoulder. 'But where is your sturdy, handsome young Ian?'

Barbara shrugged hopelessly. 'I hoped you might be able to tell me.'

'Oh, his whereabouts are a mystery to me,' Sybil replied, looking crestfallen. 'I haven't set eyes on him since just after your capture. He was distraught, by my troth, pacing about up and down, up and down, and white for fear. We could not help him, and he would not call the watch, so we let him go by.'

Barbara held back a curse. She thought quickly. A stout ally like this spirited young girl was what she needed. 'Sybil, do you know anything about this strange box?' She nodded to the enclosure.

Sybil shuddered. 'Oh, gross! Only what I hear tell, my lady. That it's a very devil's cabinet, that belongs to a wicked old magic-maker, that is the word among the mob.' She spat and crossed herself. 'The Lord protect us. It's a dark sign, I say, an ill omen for the city, and I would say Romish work. For is the Pope not the Antichrist hisself? Oh, it makes me shiver and quiver most like a ship tossed by storms. My skin creeps.'

Barbara seized on her words. 'An old magician, you say? Has he been – captured?'

'I warrant you, if he had been he'd have been ducked in the Thames by now.' Sybil looked around, making sure they could not be overheard, and whispered, 'By these bones, I have heard comment that the old wizard lies in the King's company. If any man can spike a confession of witchcraft it's our kind, God-fearing James, for has he not published widely on the subject of the damned arts?'

The Doctor, captured by the King's men and tortured to make a confession? Barbara shuddered. She could not believe that he, with all his guile and resourcefulness, could fall into such a fate. Trying to keep her manner as casual as possible she enquired, 'Where is he held? The Tower?' As she spoke, the idea of an unarmed solo raid on the Tower of London took shape in her mind. She almost laughed aloud at the idea.

But Sybil shook her head. 'I would not say so. The gossip abroad is that he languishes in the Palace of Whitehall, where he thinks himself the King's guest, unknowing that the trap is about to be sprung upon him and that his box of conjurations has been found out.'

That sounded a lot more likely. It would be typical of the Doctor to ingratiate himself with royalty. And he had warned her and Ian to stay out of things! 'Whitehall Palace,' she murmured. Her heart sank. It would be futile, surely, to try getting in there.

Sybil blithered on, 'I have business there myself this morning, for it's Monday and my day away from the scold Mother Bunch, when I earn an extra couple of angels for scrubbing pots.' She nodded brightly and made to move away. 'Good fortune, miss, for it is good to see you and I am sure you'll soon set to beside your man-love.'

Barbara grabbed her by the shoulder. 'Sybil. Please take me with you.'

'To the palace? Whatever for?' The girl's brow furrowed suspiciously. 'What do you want with the scrubbing of plates?'

Barbara improvised desperately. 'I think Ian might have gone there. To alert the King to my abduction.'

'Ah, good thinking, for it might be so.' Sybil took her arm. 'Well, then, come along with me, Barb. We shall go there and put the word out that you are free and would be united with your mate.' She tittered. 'I love to see love set right between man and wife.'

Barbara allowed herself to be led away from the Guildhall. She gave a final longing look at the TARDIS and then pulled herself together. The Doctor had saved her life on many occasions. Rescuing him would be a favour returned.

For once in his life the Chamberlain felt in control. Perversely the strange absence of Cecil had lent an air of uncommon calm to the court, and this was reflected in his measured, stately tread through the passages. The arrangements were in place, messages had confirmed the arrival of all the lords and parliamentarians from across the country, and the last distant worry of a Catholic plot had been banished from his mind by his meeting with those charming chaps in the cellar. The fretting of the last few days had fallen away and he felt marvellously refreshed. He was on his way down to the kitchens to check the menu for the banquet tonight that would welcome the most senior, most trusted men in the King's service. It was to be a magnificent occasion, particularly if Cecil's seat remained empty.

He turned a corner and bumped straight into the Doctor, who was walking at a frenetic pace for an old man. Each pulled himself up and gave a nod of apology.

'I'd almost forgotten you,' said the Chamberlain. He sighed. 'I suppose you'll be wanting to come tonight, won't you? Throwing my seating out again.' His eyes widened at the sight of the boy Victor, who was wearing a white surplice and was covered in mud. 'Heaven forfend!'

The Doctor said airily, 'He has just been out, er, rolling in dirt.'

'In a girl's attire?'

'It is an acolyte's robe.'

'Oh, I see.' He nodded to Victor. 'The King is furious with you both for ignoring his calls and disappearing as you did.'

The Doctor looked surprised. 'Disappeared? We've not left the palace grounds.'

The Chamberlain pursed his lips. 'Hmm. Well, nobody at the gate saw you go. Then, neither did they see Cecil, who has vanished also. Have you?'

'Have I what?'

'Seen Cecil.'

The Doctor blinked. 'Er, no. Ah, in fact, we were just on our way to the King.'

'Hmm.' The Chamberlain pursed his lips. 'He's only recently returned from a call in town. He was asked to look over a —'

'Never mind that,' said the Doctor. 'Come along, Victor.' He shooed the boy along the passage.

The Chamberlain, who was beginning to feel immune to rudeness, was about to continue his journey when the

Doctor, apparently as an afterthought, turned and beckoned to him. 'What is it now?'

'Everything is set for tomorrow night, then?' asked the Doctor brightly. He looked as if he was expecting something.

'Yes,' said the Chamberlain haughtily.

'Not anticipating any, er, trouble?'

'Not at all.'

'Ah.' The Doctor stepped closer. 'You've searched all the parliament buildings, I presume? Just in case?'

'In case of what?'

'Well, you know. Er, things.'

'Parliament is secure. Cecil sees to that.'

The Doctor lifted a finger. 'But Cecil is away, you said.'

The Chamberlain was beginning to feel very irritated. 'I am perfectly able to handle these matters.'

'So you've searched, then?' asked Victor.

'Yes, I have. One of the Catholic lords got some sort of a crank letter. Warning of a plot. Nothing in it.' The Chamberlain stared at them, daring them to ask another impertinent question. 'What is your interest in this?'

The Doctor looked surprised. 'You *have* searched? And found nothing?'

'Nothing I did not expect to find.'

Victor blurted, 'Not even below the House of Lords?' He added quickly, 'I mean, if that's where anybody was going to put anything — not that they have, or would — they'd put it there, wouldn't they?'

The Chamberlain flushed with anger. 'I haven't time to spare on such chatter. Directly beneath the House of Lords is a lumber room where a trusted friend to the throne keeps kindling and a store of wine. You two are as bad as Cecil with your shadowy fancies.'

He tutted and set off for the kitchens. Nobody else was going to disturb his day with their odd suspicions. Everything was going smoothly and it was not going to be spoilt.

* * *

Barbara was becoming suspicious. Sybil had led her west from the Guildhall and into the familiar streets around Mother Bunch's tavern. It could have been a lifetime since she and Ian had walked through the city gate and along this way, Barbara had thought, with a rueful glance at the alley that ran parallel to the length of Lark Street. Sybil was astonishingly lithe and walked with a man's loping strides, and Barbara had to lift up her skirts and canter to catch up.

They came eventually to a low stone passage that was situated at a strange angle between two houses. It seemed unnatural and out of place. As like as not, thought Barbara, it was a relic from a bygone architectural era that had been left untouched by the surge of new building that had consumed London during Elizabeth's reign. Certainly it led nowhere: it was narrow and tapered and led to the blank back wall of a newer structure. Sybil indicated for her to pass down, and explained, 'It's an old way to the palace not used by kings or queens, and is a bit smelly, but let that pass. Go down, I say, if you'd see your Ian again.' Barbara, not wanting to question her helpfulness, ducked her head under the rotting timber support of the passage and walked through. Sybil squeezed in beside her, and with a complex hand movement that was so quick it did not register as more than a blur opened a rectangular aperture of about five feet by three. She made a frantic shooing motion. 'In you go, quick now, Barb. If you tarry now you'll perhaps lose your husband, as he might go by again in his hunt for you. Go on, and you'll soon be held in his arms.'

'But how did this tunnel get here?' she asked. 'It seems remarkable.'

'Away with ifs and buts,' said Sybil, giving her a shove. 'Fear nothing and you shall be rewarded. The tunnel has stood here for years, it's all anyone knows. Now pass through, I say.'

Barbara conquered her hesitation and, by pulling in her shoulders, stepped through the rectangle and into an enclosed space that smelt of damp and dripped with foul, greenish water. Sybil followed, and having closed the panel behind her, ushered her forward into the darkness. She took a small candle from a bundle, lit it, and cast its glow over the rock walls, casting spectral shadows.

The quiet of the place made Barbara shiver and the journey was difficult and unpleasant. Several times she had to stop to free threads from her dress that got caught on sharp points of rock. Sybil went unusually quiet, as if she was brooding. Barbara guessed the ambience of this awful tunnel was not conducive to conversation.

Now they stood in a small space formed by a slab of rock, triangular in shape, that had fallen from the ceiling and formed an arch. Sybil swept her candle around, casting out the gloom, and sighed. 'Ah, it's a sorry turnout, and after all my haste, but I am lost. I am sure I've never been down this way before, and have taken a wrong turning.'

Barbara's spirits were crushed. 'You seemed to know the way.'

'So I do,' Sybil lamented, 'having walked it many times before.' She bit her lip, then seemed to reach a decision. 'Here. You remain and I'll go along and seek the right way. It cannot be far.' She turned to go.

Barbara caught her arm. 'Wait. You can't leave me here alone.'

Sybil's face took on a disapproving aspect. 'You noble ladies are of a piece. You see menace where there's none and would stay in all day with a ball of wool if you could. Don't take on. I won't be more than a minute.' With a resigned shrug she moved off along the tunnel, taking the candle with her.

The last thing Barbara noted before the light faded out and she was left in dripping darkness were Sybil's heavy boots making large splashes in the water.

James settled himself in a padded chair in one of the staterooms. He had an uncomfortable feeling events were creeping up on him. The opening was tomorrow night! He'd purposely travelled to London three days early in order to gather his wits and learn the speech. Where had all the time gone? There had been too many diversions. Victor, and now this odd box. He shuddered at the memory of it.

He snapped his fingers at one of the guards on the door. 'You. Fetch the old Doctor of Divinity.'

The guard looked unhappy with the order. 'The Chamberlain says the old man has vanished too, Your Majesty.'

James was not willing to be crossed. 'I said fetch him!'

The guard, terrified, turned and opened the stateroom door. Revealed on the other side was the Doctor, his cloak now besmirched and tattered, his fist raised to knock. 'Ah, there you are,' he said to James, and bustled in without further preamble. James's eyebrows shot up in indignation. 'Er, I mean to say, good morning, Your Majesty.' The bow that accompanied the greeting was delivered with an unpleasant hastiness. Dad had warned James to start worrying when people started bowing with bad grace.

The reprimand died on his lips at the sight of poor Victor, who trailed in after the Doctor, hair messed, bedraggled in a muddy robe. Oddly the dirt made him more beautiful than ever. 'Ah, at last my peach!' He gave a little wave, using only his fingertips. 'Where have you been hidden, eh?'

Victor smiled gamely. 'I don't know what all the fuss has been about,' he said in his delightfully boisterous way. 'I got lost in the grounds.'

James clapped his hands. 'That's what I thought. Now why don't you step up and rest here on my royal knee and tell me all about it?'

The Doctor coughed. 'Your Majesty, before any of us can rest, there is a matter of some urgency that we must attend to.'

James groaned. 'What now?'

'Yes, straight away.' The Doctor came forward. For a second James flinched from his deep brown stare. He had the conviction and sincerity of a holy man. Perhaps he'd like to be Archbishop of Canterbury? The present one was pretty useless. The Doctor went on, 'Sir Robert Cecil has left the court.'

'I know,' said James. 'I can't say I mourn his departure. He's a terrible sulker. He'll be back.'

The Doctor entwined his fingers in a steeple shape and knelt to address him. James liked that. 'Your Majesty, I fear that Cecil may have uncovered some plot.'

'Dear Doctor, is that all? He uncovers a plot every other day. Catholics, I suppose?'

Victor spoke up. 'Please, Your Majesty, give this your most serious consideration.'

James thought for a moment. 'If I do, will you sit on my knee then?'

His shoulders slumped. 'All right.'

The Doctor continued, 'I suggest merely that you might have some guards sent for a thorough examination of the parliament buildings.'

James considered. 'It isn't my job to arrange searches. I've got a speech to learn. I've no time to indulge Cecil and that spawny Chamberlain.' He licked his lips. Victor looked hesitant, so he waved a teasing finger and said lightly, 'You promised, you promised.'

Just as Victor was about to sit down, with a pained expression on his muddy face, the King had a brainwave. 'Oh, yes! I almost forgot.' He pointed to the Doctor. 'I wonder if you can do me a favour.'

The Doctor spread his hands. 'I will endeavour, as always, to serve you, Your Majesty.'

'Good. Well, the senior clergy of London are all tied up at present, and it's a pressing matter. Right up your street, I reckon.'

'Please, go on.'

'There's this strange box, you see,' said James. Before he got any further he noted the alarmed expressions that passed between the Doctor and Victor. 'Sorry, did I startle you?'

'Not at all.' The Doctor's face was suddenly alive with worry. 'A box, you say?'

'Hmm. A wooden one, blue with a funny lantern on top. It was found on one of the outer roads and dragged in to make firewood. But, and this is strange but I've seen it myself, it won't burn or be chopped or even scratched.'

Victor asked, 'Where is it now?'

'They've taken it to the Guildhall. Nobody will approach it, and there's a great gawping crowd looking on in case the Devil climbs out. I didn't like the look of it at all.' He looked at the Doctor. 'Could you possibly see your way to exorcising it?'

To James's confusion the Doctor gave a high, chirruping laugh. 'Oh, gladly, gladly. Yes, ah, I could do with the, er, exorcise. The Guildhall, you say?' He nodded to Victor. 'Less than an hour's ride from here. We'll get started right away, shall we?' He covered his odd enthusiasm with a sudden cry. 'Evil must be stamped out!'

James stood up. 'Steady on. Does Victor have to stamp on it too?' He looked down sadly at his vacant knee.

'I'm afraid he does,' said the Doctor. 'I'll need someone to hold my prayer book open, won't I?'

'I suppose.' James blew a kiss to the lad. 'Watch yourself and beware of spirits. And I won't forget that promise you made.'

Victor smiled back. 'Just see you don't forget that inspection. I can't sit on your knee if you've been blown to bits.' He bowed stiffly and followed the Doctor from the stateroom.

Alone and happy, James sighed. 'Ah. He cares.'

Vicki and the Doctor found a deserted spot in the corridor outside and embraced. The Doctor's smile seemed to lift decades from his face.

'Capital!' he said. 'Everything is falling into place. You see how the Chamberlain thought for himself after seeing the letter, without Cecil or James to advise him.'

'Not that it did any good,' said Vicki. 'He must be the most useless statesman of all time.'

'Oh, I don't know,' the Doctor mused. 'There was that fellow Howard . . .' He pulled himself up. 'Now, I must prepare myself for this ceremony. And you must go and collect the others.'

He spoke as if he was asking her to do the simplest thing. Vicki swallowed. 'What – go back down below?'

'Yes, yes. Don't worry, it's quite safe, isn't it? You can bring Ian and Barbara directly back here. And Cecil too, as a matter of fact. Contrive a reason for his release.'

She was so used to being decried for her uselessness by him that she felt strangely honoured. 'Oh. And is there anything else I can do in my spare time?'

'Yes,' he said tartly. 'Bring back the key!'

It was twenty minutes later. The tunnel was starting to feel familiar to Vicki. She had followed the Doctor's instructions on how to open up the tree, and now she was sloshing her way through the water back to Hay's underground rooms, filled with foreboding. Every few seconds a new objection to the Doctor's plan occurred to her. There were so many liabilities. If Hay twigged, if he couldn't find Ian and Barbara, if the TARDIS key was lost . . . She tried hard to push the worries to the back of her mind and concentrated instead on keeping her balance and holding back her bile. The smell of the place, she was sure, had got worse.

She hadn't travelled more than a hundred yards along the tunnel when she sensed a movement. Something slow, deliberate. For a second she had a definite feeling that there was a person standing right beside her in the darkness. Panicked, she whipped round, her heart thumping against her ribcage. 'Who – who's there?' It was a stupid thing to say, as usual. The meagre light from her lantern showed nothing but the slimy cavern walls. Vicki sighed, angry with herself. She stamped her foot, showering herself with the filthy water. 'Why am I so totally useless?' she asked bitterly, and went on.

She estimated it had taken herself and the Doctor twenty minutes or so to travel from Hay's secret room to the tree on the outward journey. The return trip seemed to be passing more quickly. Only a few minutes after her shock she was back at the junction and the imposing wooden door. She shuddered, tried to swallow her fear, and reached out to knock.

There was another deliberate noise. But this time it came from ahead, from the unexplored route of the tunnel that continued past the den towards London. And this time she had no doubt. It wasn't her imagination.

She listened hard, not daring to move a muscle. She heard splashes as the unseen person moved closer. The steps were diffident, uncertain. Not Hay, then, or one of his henchmen. She crept forward, held the lantern up above her head and cast its full beam on the mouth of the tunnel. A shadow was cast by the person approaching. A familiar shadow.

Vicki's heart leapt. 'Barbara!' she cried and ran forward.

The schoolteacher appeared at the mouth of the tunnel. Vicki cannoned into her with such force she was nearly knocked off her feet. They crashed together and Vicki felt an outpouring of emotion that brought her close to tears. 'Oh, Barbara, I'm so sorry, I didn't know the Doctor was lying, I promise, I would have stopped him –'

'Ssh, ssh.' Barbara proffered a shoulder for her to cry on. 'It doesn't matter, Vicki. Now where are the others?'

Vicki looked up and brushed the tears away with a cuff. She noticed for the first time that Barbara's hair and clothing were in as dishevelled a state as her own, and that she had a bruise and a small cut over her left eye. 'I've just come from the Doctor,' she burbled. 'He sent me down to fetch you.'

'From the palace?'

Vicki nodded. 'Yes. The tunnel leads there.' She peered around. 'Where's Hay?'

Barbara looked blank. 'I don't understand you.'

'Didn't he bring you here?' Vicki swung her lantern away from Barbara and illuminated the tunnel she had emerged from. 'And where's Ian?'

'I lost track of him a couple of days ago. Who's Hay?'

Vicki gestured impatiently. 'The man who brought you down here.'

Barbara retained her confused expression. 'I don't know what you mean, I was . . .' She trailed off. 'It isn't important. Is the Doctor safe? You know about the Ship?'

'Yes, we've got it all in hand. If it wasn't for Ian being missing. It's all a bit complicated. I'll try to explain as we go.' She pointed to the door of Hay's den. 'In there is the seventeenth-century equivalent of a villain's base.'

'This Hay?'

Vicki nodded. She started to lead Barbara back along the tunnel towards the palace. 'But the Doctor's got one over on him. He's convinced him – well, really, Hay convinced himself – that the Doctor's some sort of grand wizard and that we're his unsuspecting lackeys.'

Barbara managed a smile. 'Not so far from the truth.'

'He's fallen for it completely. Which is just as well, because now the Doctor's going to have the plot uncovered. The Gunpowder Plot, I mean.'

'That'll be uncovered anyway.'

'Don't you believe it,' said Vicki. 'The whole thing's more complex than you can imagine. But I think the Doctor's sorted it out. The truth's certainly not in the history books. You can ask him when we get back.'

Barbara held up a hand to indicate that she would. Vicki was on the verge of asking her about her adventures when she said, 'You didn't see anyone on your way from the palace, did you?'

Vicki shook her head. Then, with an abruptness that made her tense up again, someone stepped out in front of them. To her relief it wasn't Hay, but a young woman with curly red hair pushed under a cap.

'Oh, Barbara, there you are,' she cried. 'I have got us so fearfully mislaid. This isn't the way I come usually at all.' She looked fearfully at Vicki. 'Who's this?'

Barbara smiled wearily. 'A friend.' She made a gesture of introduction. 'Vicki, meet Sybil.'

Vicki took the girl's hand, which was smooth and unusually long-fingered. Her honest face was somehow familiar, but there was no time to spare for worrying about such things. 'What are you doing down here?' she asked.

'I was going in to the palace with Barb and lost all sense of direction,' she said, stepping closer. 'I use the tunnels every week and have never turned down these passages before.' She looked exhausted. Vicki found she didn't mind when Sybil leant an arm on her shoulder. 'The place is a warren, I've never seen such complication.' She pulled something from her rolled-up cuff. Vicki assumed it was a handkerchief.

'Where did you meet this one?' she whispered to Barbara over the girl's shoulder.

'She's been a great help,' Barbara replied. 'She brought me here to meet up with you and the Doctor.'

Something switched in Vicki's mind. A cold wave of fear settled upon her. Because she knew what Barbara was saying was impossible. Nobody, least of all a servant girl, could know of the secret passage. And nobody could have known to bring Barbara here except...

Except Hay. And if they were one and the same, then Hay had been lurking in the passage, and had overheard their conversation. Overheard her saying, 'The Doctor's fooled him completely.'

Before she could pull away Hay, his face contorted by a twisted smile, drew the knife out from the sleeve of his serving maid's dress. He pulled back his arm and aimed the blade upward, to find her heart.

12

Covering the Cracks

It seemed an age before Vicki moved. In fact it was a matter of seconds. She heard herself make a noise that was half a scream and half a call for help from Barbara; she twisted away from the blade in a snake-like movement; Hay's arm, the powerful muscles concealed beneath the sleeves of the maid's dress, jutted upwards. He realized his target had moved and swerved around to deliver a second blow, his features contorted in a devilish, confident smile. He moved so fast that the knife was reduced to a metallic blur. Vicki dodged him again. She backed away, consumed by unthinking terror, her feet scrabbling for a grip on the uneven ground of the tunnel. Hay lunged a second time, and converted the movement halfway through, twisted the blade so that instead of aiming for Vicki's heart he was slashing at her head. She survived this assault only because her foot had snagged on a spar of rock concealed beneath the swirling water and she fell backwards with a splash. There was a horrible, shuddering impact, and then she was kicking and screaming in the cold clammy water. Her eyes stung, a sour taste invaded her mouth. As if from a great distance she heard Hay manoeuvring himself into position over her flailing body, taking his time, choosing his moment. She was defenceless. Grimly she closed her eyes and prepared for death.

There was a sickening thump and a moment later something crashed into the water beside her.

Without stopping to think, Vicki scrabbled desperately for a grip on the tunnel floor, for anything to serve as a lever. Blinded by the spray she was starting to panic. Another wave of icy darkness washed over her and she battled to raise her head above the water.

A hand grasped hers. Barbara's hand, interweaving its fingers with hers, pulling her up. She staggered to her feet, burst from the water and shook her hair like a dog. She had never felt so soiled or so terrified. She blinked frantically to clear her vision. There were lumps of matter in her eyes and ears, and she felt an overwhelming desire to run.

Barbara's voice slowly became distinct. 'Vicki, it's all right. Everything's fine, you're safe.'

Vicki coughed and her ears popped. 'I'm sorry, Barbara. But that was horrible.' She cast around to see what had become of Hay. His body lay face down in the water at her feet. The dress billowed around it. 'What happened?'

'She took me by surprise,' said Barbara. 'I grabbed a piece of rock and bashed her over the head with it.'

'Not her,' said Vicki bitterly. 'Him. Another of Hay's clever disguises.'

Barbara was incredulous. 'Sybil is a man?'

Vicki nodded. 'It makes sense. He dressed up like that to lead you down here.'

'It makes sense, yes,' said Barbara. 'I'd already seen her, I mean him, as Sybil. If he'd appeared as himself I would never have trusted him.' She shook her head. 'But why do it?'

Vicki had regained enough composure to remove her hand from Barbara's. She regarded herself. She was dripping in dirt and slime. 'Must be something connected with the Gunpowder Plot,' she replied. 'It's all his doing, really.'

Barbara clicked her fingers. 'And did Hay disguise himself with a cloak and a hood thrown forward over his face?'

'That'll be the Spaniard,' said Vicki.

'But that's incredible,' said Barbara. 'He must have changed over in seconds.' She knelt down carefully and tugged at Hay's shoulders. Vicki took a sharp intake of breath. 'He'll be out cold for a couple of hours,' Barbara reassured her. 'I used rather a large rock.' She pulled the body over. To Vicki's relief there was a sizeable gash on the forehead. Barbara then pulled at the collar of Sybil's dress. It came away with surprising ease, and the fabric on the other side, now swollen and sodden, was heavy and black. 'The cloak. It was reversible.' She rubbed her chin and pondered. 'As Sybil, he must have listened in to the plotters after passing his instructions to them. To ensure they wouldn't go against him or make any alterations to his plan.'

'You're probably right,' said Vicki. 'But I think we'd better go. We've got to get back to –' A thought struck her. 'How stupid of me! I nearly forgot the key.' She stooped beside Barbara, her fear forgotten, and felt inside Hay's clothing. 'He must have it. The key to the TARDIS, I mean.'

Barbara frowned. 'And how on earth did he get that?'

Vicki smiled. Barbara had not quite left behind her schoolmistress's tone. 'Oh, that's a long story. Come on, help me find it.' She tore off the top half of Hay's disguise, revealing the tight-fitting doublet he wore at court beneath. His covering garment was ingeniously designed, the different facets of his three personas stitched brilliantly together. She took the knife from his hand and passed it to Barbara, who tucked it safely away into her belt. But there was no sign of the key.

Suddenly the door of Hay's den opened. Vicki leapt up and wiped some of the muck from her face. She positioned herself hurriedly before Hay's supine body and nudged Barbara with her shoe. 'Go along with me,' she whispered. Barbara nodded.

One of the henchmen – it was impossible to tell which – stood framed in the doorway. He pointed to Vicki and, frowning, said slowly, 'Where is Master Hay?'

Vicki swallowed. Summoning all her strength, aware that everything hinged on her handling of the situation, she said, 'The Grand Behemoth, the one known as the Doctor, has sent me here with orders.' She thought of the Doctor as she spoke, tried to invest her performance with his bluffer's confidence. 'You are to release Cecil to me.

The Grand Behemoth wishes to question him.'

The henchman glowered at her. 'Where is the Grand Behemoth?'

'That is not important,' said Vicki forcefully. Oh boy, she thought, here comes the real risk. 'If you do not hand over Cecil right away, the Grand Behemoth will cast a spell and turn you into a crawling spider.' She raised a hand dramatically and fluttered her fingers.

The effect on the henchman was dramatic. He bowed, and with a haste that was comic for a man of his build, retreated into the den.

Barbara whispered up, 'Well done.'

'Thanks. I wasn't overdoing it, was I?'

'Not at all. I suppose the Grand Behemoth is who I think he is?'

'Yep.'

'And by Cecil, you mean Sir Robert Cecil, Lord Salisbury?'

'That's the one.'

Barbara sighed. 'You have to hand it to the Doctor, I suppose.'

Vicki pulled a face. 'Oh, Cecil's not a friend, at least not really. He had a jolly good go at killing us a couple of nights ago. We're only helping him out to get history back on track.' She looked down at Barbara. 'I'm not confusing you, am I?'

Before Barbara could reply the door of the den was thrown open again. The henchman appeared, dragging Cecil's spindly and exhausted-looking body under one arm. 'The prisoner,' he announced. 'For the disposal of the Grand Behemoth.' With a contemptuous flick of his trunk-like arm he sent Cecil staggering towards them. Barbara, who was compassionate by instinct, reached out and grabbed him.

'The Behemoth thanks you,' said Vicki. 'And there is another matter. Bring me the key.'

The henchman grimaced. 'I know of no key.'

Vicki gave him her stormiest face. 'The key of power. Bring it to me.' She added, 'It was in my hand when

Master Hay took me captive.'

'Ah,' said the henchman. 'That key.' He bowed and retreated again.

'We'll be here all day at this rate,' said Barbara through gritted teeth. She turned to Cecil. 'Are you all right?'

Cecil looked at Vicki and said weakly, 'Your Doctor is a traitor.'

Vicki hissed at him, 'Shut up. We're getting you out of here. Look behind you.'

Cecil looked and saw Hay. He smiled savagely. 'Dead, I hope.'

'Not quite. Anyway, the Doctor was bluffing. We're actually on your side, in a funny sort of way.'

Cecil's head fell back. In spite of all he had been through there remained a glimmer of fire in his eyes. 'Ah,' he said. 'Who is to know truth from fiction in these days?'

The henchman returned. The key of the TARDIS hung on its ribbon in his hand. 'O servant of the Grand Behemoth, behold the key.'

Vicki gulped. The henchman showed no sign of coming closer. And if she or Barbara moved to collect the key they would expose Hay's body and blow their cover.

'The key,' the henchman repeated.

There was a heavy silence. Vicki wondered if she could grab the knife from Barbara's belt and make a rush for the key. Then she thought of the henchman's enormous strength, and his enormous mate.

The deadlock was broken by Cecil. He shook off Barbara's hands, stepped forward and slipped the key from the giant's fingers and into his own hand. Then he pocketed it.

The henchman looked puzzled. There was a second odd silence. Then Barbara spoke, addressing Cecil. 'Well done. You will obey all orders of the Grand Behemoth.'

Cecil nodded to her, acting cowed. The henchman, apparently satisfied, bowed to Vicki and closed the door of the den.

Vicki let out a huge sigh of relief. 'Thank heavens for

that.' She pointed back along the tunnel. 'Right, let's get back.'

Cecil frowned. 'What of this base crea—' He broke off. 'Where is he?'

Vicki stared at the space where Hay had been with blank incomprehension. He seemed to have melted away in seconds, without a sound. She looked up and down the tunnel. No sign of him. 'Oh no. And just when I thought I was improving.'

Hodge stared at his sword with considerable misgivings. It felt heavy and ungainly in hands that were more used to seaming and stitching with the most dainty and delicate of instruments. He looked across at Firking, who was crouched beside him in the shadow of the bushes by the lumber-room door. Nowhere on that rough face was doubt to be found. Indeed, Firking's whole body was rigid with delight, and his grip on his sword was steady and firm if not practised. His way of holding the weapon at an odd angle advertised his lack of acquaintance with it. Hodge was unversed in the arts of battle but he was sure of one thing. It couldn't be a good idea, could it, for a couple of shoemakers to rush in on an experienced cell of traitors with only good intentions and a couple of old swords to aid them?

He decided to vocalize his fears and tugged on his mate's sleeve. 'Here, Firking. I've got a horrible twinge about this enterprise.'

Firking make a shushing gesture. 'Keep that hunting horn voice of yours down, man. You'll have the watch upon us.'

'There is no watch here. And that makes me more nervous, 'cause how is that so?' He gestured with the tip of his sword around at the deserted courtyard. Evening was closing in. 'Night and day these quarters go empty and unguarded. The heart of the King's neighbourhood, with perfidy right in their centre, and only two poor cobblers to scent it out. Can it be right?'

'Hush,' said Firking. 'Things can turn out odd in life.

It's fallen to us to see off the menace.' He nudged Hodge in the ribs. 'And think of our reward then, eh? We'll be poor cobblers no longer. Lords, I should think, with manses down Kent way, and hot rum and water on tap, and girls to rub our toes, and –'

Hodge cut him off. 'And should we die?' He nodded to the door of the lumber room. 'A split corpse, undone in some underground cavity? That's not how I shall end my days.'

Firking sighed. 'Think of it in this way, Hodge. Tomorrow is November the fifth. When news of how you dealt here with the dastardly plotters gets about the same will be proclaimed "Ralph Hodge Night"!'

Hodge's knees quivered at the prospect. 'Ralph Hodge Night,' he whispered.

'Yes,' said Firking. 'And every Hodge Night, from the first, there'll be tables set up all along the roads from the Leadenhall, and they'll be piled high with nut brown beers and slabs of veal set in the shapes of shoes!'

'Ladies' shoes,' said Hodge unconsciously. Firking had a talent for sketching a scene. It was in his head, the image of Hodge Night. People might celebrate his finest hour for years to come, perhaps even decades. He tightened his grip on the sword as he had seen Richard Burbage do at the theatre. 'Then to damnation with these Catholic plotters,' he said bravely. 'Give the word, Firking, and we shall unstrap ourselves and chop them down, for Ian and St George!'

The Doctor was putting his exorcism kit together in a wooden box provided by the Chamberlain. 'Now, then,' he said. 'Bell, check. Book, check. Candle, check. Yes, yes, it all seems to be present and correct.'

James was looking on. He rubbed his chin gravely. 'You're sure this simple ritual will work, Doctor? Considering the weirdness of the problem?'

'Oh yes, absolutely.' The Doctor rattled the objects in the box. 'Now, there is the matter of my, er, mode of conveyance.'

'I beg your pardon?'

'Transport. To the Guildhall.'

James clicked his fingers. 'Ah, I see your meaning. Yes, I will have a carriage or something of that kind made ready.'

A guard entered the stateroom and whispered in James's ear. He nodded in reply, and a moment later, just as the Doctor was gathering his faculties and congratulating himself on his own cleverness, Haldann and Otley entered. They seemed to carry something of their library's atmosphere around with them. The Doctor's sensitive nose detected the aroma of dust and unopened pages.

Haldann bowed to James. 'Your Majesty. We are present as instructed.'

James indicated the Doctor. 'I thought you might like some conference with the Doctor. He is about to cast the evil from the terrible box at the Guildhall.'

Haldann sniffed. 'Ah. You did not think to consult us?'

'It has been some years since our last exorcism, yes,' said Otley. He was, the Doctor noted, taking pains not to criticize the King too openly. 'And though we have the bodies of weak and feeble men, our minds are alert enough to scare off any wizardry.'

'That's the spirit,' said James. 'I thought you'd like to come with us. We can all go down to the Guildhall together.'

The Doctor's ears pricked up and his new-found sense of security abandoned him. 'Us?'

'Why, yes,' said James. 'I like a good exorcism, and these two can pass on hints and tips if you have problems.'

'I assure you,' said the Doctor, waving a hand, 'I won't need any help, and I work better alone.'

James raised a reproving eyebrow. 'Don't strike a cheeky attitude now, my Doctor, just when I've begun to like you again. I can always have you thrown off the job and let my good translators have a crack.' At his words Haldann and Otley swelled importantly. 'And I don't think I've anything better to do this evening.'

The Doctor cursed inwardly. 'Your Majesty, I would

respectfully remind you of tomorrow's Opening of Parliament, and the learning of your –'

'Hush!' James sat up in his throne. 'You're beginning to sound the same as sulking Cecil, Doctor, and I am more than glad enough to be rid of him!'

These words were scarcely out of his lips when, with an impressive flourish, the doors of the stateroom were pushed open and a figure that was, at first, almost unrecognizable as Cecil burst in breathlessly. His previously immaculate black outfit was torn and spattered with droplets of caked mud, his beard was wild and tangled where it had been neat and pointed, and his posture was crooked as a broken doll's. The shock of his appearance silenced James from commenting on the unorthodox nature of his entrance. The first words he spoke were, 'Your Majesty. A plot.' He paused impressively, proof that he retained much of his political skill. 'A Catholic plot. Against you, and here is the proof of it.' He indicated the disarray of his clothing. 'They mean to destroy you by means of gunpowder.'

For the first time in their acquaintance the Doctor saw a ripple of genuine discomfort pass through James. He shuddered in his throne, and his guards huddled closer instinctively. Haldann and Otley made a show of throwing their hands up in shock. 'A plot? Gunpowder?' He put a hand to his head. 'This is not a stunt, Cecil?'

'I swear to you it is not, Your Majesty,' Cecil blurted. 'I have reason to believe that Catholics led by the hotheaded Catesby have readied powder below the House of Lords.'

Instantly James sank back. 'Oh, we've been through all this while you were absent, Cecil. Try to keep up, man. The Chamberlain has been down there and checked the place over, top to bottom. It's all a lot of . . .'

The Doctor's attention to this argument was distracted by a tap on the shoulder. He turned and came face to face with Barbara. She wore a weary smile, and looked bedraggled but unhurt. 'Having fun, Doctor?' she asked.

'Barbara, my dear!' He clasped her by the shoulders. 'Thank goodness you're well. Yes, we have been having some adventures. I trust you've seen enough theatre by now, eh?' He saw Vicki trailing along behind. She was covered in slime and looked as if she were going to drop any second. 'Heavens, what have you been doing, child?'

Barbara answered, covering a venomous glare from Vicki. 'She's been doing very well, actually, Doctor. And Ian and I never got to the theatre.'

Vicki whispered excitedly, 'They only went and bumped into Guy Fawkes.'

'Oh, for heaven's sake,' the Doctor grumbled. 'And I gave specific instructions for you not to interfere. Ah well, I expect it's all part of the web of time. Spice of life.' Barbara was staring at him as if she was annoyed, he noticed, so he carried on quickly. 'Where is young Chesterton, by the way?'

'I've absolutely no idea,' said Barbara in a violent whisper.

'Hay ran off before we could ask him,' put in Vicki.

Their conversation was interrupted by a shout from the King. 'Cecil, I am on the verge of ordering Parliament searched again, if only to ensure you are silenced once and for all on this subject!'

Cecil turned towards the Doctor pleadingly. 'But, Your Majesty –'

The Doctor decided it was time for more nudging. He stepped before the throne. 'Your Majesty, Sir Robert has a point. Is this Catesby fellow not dangerous? Is it not strange he should have rented the lumber room at that precise spot?'

'Catesby,' James said dismissively, 'is a zealous nincompoop but he is not stupid enough to try and blow me up, or clever enough to work such an implausible, audacious scheme. It is all hogwash, and I want to go to the exorcism; it'll be a sight more fun than listening to your rantings.' He looked past the Doctor and wiggled his fingers at Vicki. 'Aha, sweet one. You have been rolling about again, haven't you, Victor?' He slapped his thigh. 'We shall have to get you hosed down.' He peered at Barbara. 'And this?'

Barbara curtsied. Before she could speak the Doctor said, 'A nun, Your Majesty, of very pure heart.'

'Quite right. Just what you need for an exorcism, a good nun.' He stood up suddenly, clapped his hands, and pointed to the doors. 'Let us away to the Guildhall and the marvellous box.'

That said, he descended from the dais on which the throne rested and swept out of the stateroom. Haldann and Otley trailed behind him.

Cecil stalked over to the Doctor. 'I owe you my life,' he said simply. 'Although I will never understand you or how you came here, from your other England.' He took the TARDIS key from his pocket and handed it to the Doctor. 'This is important to you, I believe.'

The Doctor's heart beat a little faster as the key entered his hand. He felt a tingle in his wrist. 'Thank you.'

Cecil nodded graciously. 'The least I can do. I am . . .' He stumbled. Vicki hurried to support his weight. 'I am so tired, but there is still work to be done. I will send more guards to the lumber room, and then he will listen.' His face contorted in a strange smile. 'He is not a bad man, you know. In some ways he is easier to deal with and kinder in heart than Elizabeth. It was my hope he would reign for many years and bring a measure of order to this nation.'

Barbara spoke. 'He will –' She caught the Doctor's warning glance. 'I mean, he still can.'

'But is there any hope for us? I can have the plot uncovered, and Catesby strung up, but there is always this Hay to ruin me and bring all my achievements down. One man, and he will destroy all of that.'

The Doctor laid a hand gently on his shoulder. 'Not a bit of it. There is much to be striven for, and your plan isn't over yet. You have been foolish, yes, and too quick to trust, yes, but things will right themselves, yes, that I can promise you. Now, do what must be done. Summon your guards, accompany them to Parliament.' He pointed to the door significantly.

Cecil looked hard at him. 'I endeavoured to kill you.

You repaid me by saving my life. Why? Why lift a finger to help me?'

'Because, my good fellow, I'm not a politician,' the Doctor said curtly. 'Unlike you my concern is not winning. I just want the best possible result.'

Cecil lifted a hand in farewell and exited.

The Doctor chuckled. 'But winning has its pleasures too. Now, then, where were we?'

James's voice echoed from the hallway outside. 'Doctor! Hurry, or else I shall have you dragged out!'

The Doctor smiled at Barbara and Vicki and lifted up his box. 'To the TARDIS, then.'

He made to leave the stateroom. Barbara stopped him for a second. 'You do realize there's a massive crowd at the Guildhall. They'll be expecting something spectacular.'

'Then we shall have to supply it, shan't we?' he replied with a smile.

Ian watched as Catesby made a final circuit of the lumber room. His crazed blue eyes swept across the powder barrels, down the line of touchwood to the upturned box upon which Winter sat, the matches in his hand, Fawkes's lantern at his feet. With a decisive nod he turned to Percy. 'It is all in order, my friend. All as it was ordained.'

Percy gestured to Fawkes's body, then to Ian. 'Aside from these minor details.'

Catesby did a kind of pirouette across the room and clamped a hand on his shoulder. Ian noted with dread that much of his swagger had now returned. 'Minor indeed, when compared to the epoch that now begins.' He smirked at Ian. 'You will be the first to die. The fire will blast so quick you'll feel no pain. We are merciful.'

Ian felt he ought to supply a rejoinder. 'You'll have to be very careful, Catesby. There's still plenty could go wrong.'

Catesby shook his head dramatically. 'No. For we are under the wing of God.'

'You think the Chamberlain really fell for your story?'

'The Chamberlain? Ha! He and his guards are so weak to have virtually welcomed us here. It has all turned out as devised.' He tapped Ian hard on the head with two fingers, making him wince. 'Little man, you and the King's other agents have to be lucky all the time. We have only to be lucky the once.'

'We should be going,' said Percy. 'The horses will not wait for ever. Stratford beckons.' He climbed the steps and started sliding back the bolts on the door.

Catesby laid his hand on Winter's head and muttered a Latin prayer. 'We shall meet again soon. Conduct your work without qualm, for you have been chosen by God over Fawkes, who was too low and vile to serve as His messenger. You blow the bugle that will wake the world, yours are the hands that will call honest men to London, the flame you light shall –'

'We must go, Catesby,' Percy growled. He pulled open the door.

Winter raised a hand in farewell. 'God speed you to Stratford, fellows, and I will see you at Coronation Day –'

The sense of what he said next was obscured by the sounds of a scuffle at the door. It was thrown open wide and slammed into Percy. He was knocked off his feet and sent toppling backwards down the steps. Catesby and Winter leapt forward as one, drawing their swords. Ian craned his neck, desperate to see the identity of the newcomers. His mouth went dry and his heart hammered.

But it was Firking who tottered into the room, Hodge trailing a few feet behind, and glad as he was to see them, the sight they presented was more comical than fearsome. Their swords flopped up and down in their hands, and they peered short-sightedly into the gloom, their eyes unaccustomed to the dark. Ian realized that they had overpowered Percy by accident.

'Watch out!' he cried as Catesby, the slavering quality back on his features, ran for the steps, his sword slashing wildly ahead of him.

Firking did the best he could. He made a token gesture with the sword as he tumbled down the steps. The weapon went nowhere near Catesby, but such was the lack of skill in Firking's move that Catesby's blows, which had been made with the aim of second-guessing an intelligent opponent, went wild also. The two men merely brushed each other as they charged in opposite directions.

'Over here!' Ian called. 'Untie me, quickly!'

Firking caught sight of him in the glow from Winter's lamp. 'Ah, 'tis there you languish, Ian.' He bounded over and knelt to examine the knots. 'These are good-tied, I'll say.'

'Just set me free,' Ian said urgently. On the other side of the lumber room he saw Catesby recovering himself and Winter advancing on Hodge, who stood halfway down the steps looking more timid than ever.

He felt Firking's big clumsy fingers fiddling about his wrists. 'I've never been much good with knots, you know.'

'Use the sword, you —' Ian stopped himself just in time, feeling it would be rather ungrateful to insult his rescuer.

'Ah, yes, right you are.' Firking giggled. 'That's why you're the King's man and I'm a humble shoemaker, I suppose.'

As Firking sawed through his bonds Ian looked over at the extraordinary tableau presented on the far side of the room. Hodge had raised his sword and was waving the end through the air, dividing his attention between the two men advancing upon him up the steps. Even in this half-light long lines of sweat could be seen trickling down Hodge's thin face. The hilt of the sword was jiggling in the little man's hand. Ian felt a wave of anger mixed in with his gratitude. These two very ordinary men had risked their lives for him, and he was damned if they would suffer for it.

'You put those swords d-down,' said Hodge, 'varmints.'

Catesby gave a sharp, hateful laugh. 'This isn't the theatre, my friend. One man, and especially not a puny cobbler like you, can stand against giants.'

'I thought that was the Bible,' said Hodge.

Catesby nodded to Winter and both men hefted their

swords with the plain intention of running Hodge through. 'The Bible, as I have found out in the last two years,' said Catesby, 'is open to interpretation.'

Ian felt the ropes tying his wrists fall away. Instantly he leapt up and grabbed the sword from Firking. He tried to ignore the unsteadiness of his feet and the shooting pins and needles in his arms and legs as he strode forward. 'That's your style, isn't it, Catesby?' he said loudly. 'If you can't have your own way you resort to cowardice. You kill anybody that gets in the way of your crazy vision.'

Both Catesby and Winter forgot Hodge immediately, as Ian had hoped. They swung round. 'Who are you to say this?' growled Catesby. 'To call me a coward? You are a spy, and that is the most ignoble of all occupations. To creep and skulk is not the way of a man!'

Ian threw back his head and gave a mocking laugh. 'Creeping and skulking. It pretty well describes what you've been doing the last few years.' As Catesby advanced, the realization that one of them would have to die to resolve this conflict grew. And Ian was sure that Catesby had lived after the fifth of November, was sure he had been killed while fleeing London. 'You were persecuted, and that was a bad thing, but it doesn't give you the right to kill innocent people.' He tried to circle around the room, but Catesby and Winter anticipated his move and fanned out to block any possible route of escape.

Winter closed in. 'I was right. We should have killed you straight off. But as it stands there's no trouble. If these' – he indicated the shoemakers – 'are your best allies, our plan's in no danger.' He came in even closer, the tip of his sword brushing against Ian's.

Ian had decided long ago to follow the Doctor's maxim: only to kill if his own life was directly threatened. That moment was fast approaching. But even if he dealt with Winter, there was Catesby, and he had witnessed the latter's skill at the sudden strike. He was doomed. He glanced quickly back at Firking, who stood paralysed with fear and unarmed in a corner.

Salvation came from a totally unexpected quarter.

Hodge's voice came from behind Catesby, over by the barrels. 'I'll light your fire,' he called, his voice quavering but brave. 'I'll set your evil pyre going right now.' He had swiped up the matches from Fawkes's body, lit one, and was holding it directly above one of the barrels at the exact centre of the pile. He had wrenched open the top of the barrel, revealing the glistening grey powder within. 'Right now, you hear? And we shall all burn together!'

'Put it down, fool!' cried Catesby.

'Yeah, put it down!' Firking added. 'I thought you weren't of the heroic mould.'

The plotters had taken their attention away from Ian. He took his chance and swung into action. With all the strength he could muster he slammed himself sideways into Winter. As he had hoped his weight, coupled with the force of the attack, took his enemy by surprise. Winter's sword was knocked from his grip and fell to the floor with a metallic clatter. Winter himself was sent reeling into one of the lumber room's wooden supports. Ian grabbed his sword and threw it to Firking, then turned his attentions to Catesby.

'You heard my friend,' he said.

Catesby waited a moment, then shook his head cynically. 'He'd never do it. He's no faith, no strong belief. He's nothing to die for.'

In a cracked voice Hodge blurted out, 'I just want to go back home! I just want to do what I'm best at! I just want to make some shoes!' To Ian's astonishment he was starting to cry. 'I just want to make some ladies' shoes,' he added, in mournful tones. He lowered the flame perilously close to the powder. 'You lot clear off and leave me in peace. I've had enough of Catholics this and Protestants that. Shoes is all I care for. For it's my craft, and what the Lord has set me down on Earth to do. And I'll die for that, because that's my cause, you see. The cause of all the common people who just want to be left alone!'

Ian prodded Catesby with the tip of his sword. 'You heard him. Get out. Your dream's over.'

Firking, emboldened, did the same to Winter. 'You heard my man. Fly!'

Catesby's breathing was heavy as he sheathed his sword. 'Is this your test?' he asked Ian. 'It is hollow. You think I am a coward not to die for my beliefs. But I know that if I die I have betrayed them. This way, I can always come back and do the same again. And I will, make no mistake.' He nodded to Winter. 'We shall go now. And you shall not find us.'

They left the lumber room silently. As they ascended the steps, Winter bent down and swept up Percy in his mighty arms. The door slammed behind them and there was a silence in which Ian's mind raced. Was this all over? Were they free? Then what about the discovery of Fawkes? Hadn't the man been found down here with his taper lit after all?

He looked across at Hodge, who stood, transfixed still, his match over the barrel. 'Drop it!' he cried. 'No, I don't mean drop it, I mean put it out! Put it out now!'

Hodge let the match fall to the floor. He snapped out of his trance and ground it out with his heel. With a sigh he mopped his brow, staining his sleeve with perspiration. Slowly he sank down beside the barrels. 'Ah,' he said. 'I have decided power is a bad job all round. It made me feel most hot and discomforted.'

'Hold!' Firking said suddenly. His big nose twitched like a rat's. 'Ah, no!' He raced over to the barrels and let out a scream. 'Look, look!' He pointed to the open barrel.

Ian joined him. He felt a peculiar tugging sensation in his gut. A curl of sweet-and-sour-smelling smoke was rising up from the powder. He swore. 'It must have caught the heat from the match,' he breathed in horror. 'Quick, we've got to get out of here! The whole place will go up!'

Firking had already bounded up the steps. He wrenched at the door. It rattled in its frame but would not open. 'Treacherous papists!' he shouted as he pounded on the door with his fists. 'They have locked us in!'

* * *

Battered and bruised, his whole body a mass of aches and pains, his lungs half-choked by the black water, Hay stood before the parliament buildings. From the cover of the bushes in the courtyard adjacent to the lower storey, he watched as Catesby and two of his lesser associates emerged from the lumber room and locked the door behind them. They appeared oddly distracted and grave-faced, and they walked away with a feigned nonchalance. Hay reached instinctively for his dagger, then remembered that the Doctor's girl had taken it from him. It was a shame. He was an expert throw, and it would have been nice to see Catesby taken by surprise, to see the blade quiver between his shoulder-blades, to see him sink to cobblestones soaked with his own gore. It was not important. In the darkness to come he would find the man again, let him know how he had been manipulated. And then he would kill him, with exquisite slowness and delicacy.

Because his plot could still go ahead. The strange Doctor had not beaten him. The destruction of Parliament, even if nobody was in it, would send a signal for the disaffected majority of this nation to rebel. Blood would flow, darkness would descend.

He sauntered towards the door of the lumber room. In his hand he tossed a box of matches he had purchased from a street vendor. According to the plan, Fawkes was in there now, battened down, waiting for tomorrow night. Hay planned to enter, kill Fawkes, and light the touchwood. Cecil would arrive soon afterwards with his guards, ready to uncover the Catholic conspiracy.

By which time Hay would be settled a safe distance away, waiting for the glorious explosion.

A couple of days in the palace's stables had bucked Charger up considerably. Vicki stroked his mane gently as she rode him through the crowds outside the Guildhall. The Doctor sat behind her. He leant forward and pointed beyond the spiked railings to the courtyard. 'There it is. Just as Barbara described it.'

The Doctor's eyesight was rather better than a mere human's, and Vicki was forced to squint to see the blue police box, especially as night was closing in. The TARDIS stood, solid and incongruous as ever, in the middle of the courtyard, a circle of robed aldermen and other dignitaries grouped a few feet from it. The King and his small entourage, comprising his bodyguards, the Chamberlain, and Haldann and Otley, had gone on ahead, as dictated by procedure, and were already being greeted by the white-haired man she guessed was the Lord Mayor. The crowd went wild at the sight of James, a wildness he rewarded with a perfunctory wave of a handkerchief. They seemed to appreciate it all the same.

She turned to whisper to Barbara, who was riding another horse by their side. 'You wouldn't think a civil war was brewing, would you?'

'It's James's son Charles who causes the real problems,' she whispered back.

Presently they passed through the opened gates and into the courtyard, to puzzled stares from the crowd. Vicki had almost forgotten that she and Barbara were filthy dirty even for the standards of this period. But her attention was more caught up by the TARDIS. It was galling not to be able to run straight in. On their way here the Doctor had warned them against this, for two reasons. If they vanished inside and didn't come out, it was likely the TARDIS would be hurled from a height; it would be the only option left open to the confused populace. The Ship itself was able to withstand such falls, but it wouldn't do its passengers any good. And secondly, there was a chance, for a number of reasons, that only one or two of them might make it inside. The ones left behind would almost definitely be branded a witch, and the seventeenth century was not a good place to be one of those. No, they would wait for their moment, pop in, and then simply wait for Ian.

They approached to find Haldann and Otley fussing about the TARDIS. Haldann tapped it nervously with a long stick. 'There is no biblical precedent, I am sure,' he was saying.

Otley rolled his eyes. 'What about Ezekiel?'

'What about him?'

'False idols that will not burn,' Otley prompted.

Haldann tapped the side of the TARDIS again. 'Hardly a graven image. And if it is a temple, who can use it to worship? A cult of midgets?'

James held up a hand for silence. 'Battle not, sirs.' He looked to the Doctor, who was clambering off Charger with surprising agility, his exorcism kit tucked under one arm. 'Well, Doctor?'

The Doctor made a convincing show of looking the TARDIS over. 'Yes, it appears to be a most unpleasant, unholy object.' He delved into his kit. 'I suggest the sprinkling of holy water.'

'It's already been tried,' the Chamberlain pointed out with a pout. 'It seemed not to work.'

James nodded. 'The devilish lock is too great for water.'

'But,' said the Doctor, 'not too great for water combined with an incantation, eh?' He signalled to Barbara and Vicki. 'Come, my acolytes, stand with me. You shall proclaim the judgement of Almighty God while I do the sprinkling.'

Vicki hissed, 'Oh, you get the easy bit, of course. I don't know any Latin.'

'I know a bit, but not any prayers,' added Barbara.

The Doctor handed her the prayer book. 'Just find one and read it, for goodness' sakes,' he said pettishly. 'Latin is virtually a phonetic language. You're always telling us how clever you are. Now's your chance to prove it.' He handed Vicki a large bell. 'You have a good ring with this.'

Barbara flicked through the book. 'Doctor, there are two Latin scholars over there. They're going to see through this very quickly.'

The Doctor frowned. 'There'll be time enough for arguments later. Do as you are told. And make it last as long as you can, we have to time this just right and by my reckoning there's another hour to kill.'

'An hour to what?' asked Vicki.

'You'll see.' The Doctor made an impatient clucking noise. 'Well, get on with it.'

'Is there some problem, Doctor?' called James.

The Doctor waved back airily. 'None at all, Your Majesty. I was just, er, discussing the best way to conduct this exorcism with my assistants.' He took on a lordly air and nodded to the Mayor and the aldermen. 'This procedure must be followed accurately. I am sure you appreciate the dangers inherent in engaging with the elemental forces that dwell in this box. Unholy forces that must be stamped out thoroughly, and not suffered to transmit themselves by way of earth, air, fire, or water, beings that can take possession of . . .'

The Doctor droned on. Vicki caught Haldann and Otley exchanging a suspicious glance. And the King's eyes were glazing over. That was definitely bad news, as it sanctioned the Chamberlain to express his boredom with a yawn. 'Shall we start, Doctor?' she called.

'What? Oh, er, yes, no time to lose, of course.' The Doctor signalled to Barbara. 'Begin the incantation if you will, my dear.' To the King he said, 'I shall require absolute silence and concentration from all. So no talking or fidgeting, eating or smoking, thank you.'

Vicki lifted her arm and rang the bell. It made a disappointing sort of tinkle. The Doctor glared at her, so she started to move it around more slowly, creating a spookier sound, a continuous chime like the noise made by a wet finger run round the rim of a wineglass. At the same time Barbara began to read from the book in a low, chant-like register.

It was all Vicki could do to keep her face straight when the Doctor began to walk solemnly around the TARDIS flicking water at its sides. As he passed her on his first circuit he gave her a cheery wink.

When he came to reflect on this part of the adventure

later, Ian was glad that he'd had no time to panic. With a speed and presence of mind that he had never believed himself capable of he hoisted the smoking barrel from the top of the pile, tipped it over and shook the contents on to the floor with ferocious force. The glittering grey substance fell around his feet, still smouldering. Frantically he began stamping it out.

'You've thought cannily,' said Firking, coming up beside him with a big grin on his face.

'It was a miracle I thought at all,' said Ian. He examined the powder. It seemed to be dead again. It looked as harmless as soot. 'That could have been the end of us. And too much has been changed already without Parliament going up in smoke.' He shot Fawkes's body a rueful glance. How was he going to explain this one to the Doctor?

'What's changed?' asked Firking. He slapped his stomach. 'All that's altered is our fortunes. For averting the catastrophe me and Hodge'll likely pick up honours to befit a lord.'

'Never mind that.' Ian shook his boots to clear off the powder and pointed up the steps. 'We've got to get out of here. I –' He held up a hand. A key was turning in the lock.

'It's them, it's Red Rob,' cried Hodge. 'Come back with mates to kill us all!'

Ian shook his head. 'No, that's impossible.' He picked up his sword and climbed the steps carefully. The lock gave with a clunk, and the door opened slowly.

When it stood open fully Ian found himself face to face with an unprepossessing figure, a thin-lipped young man with liver spots dotted across his nose. His clothes were dripping with grime. There was something strangely familiar about his hazel eyes. His eyebrows shot up at the sight of Ian and the shoemakers. 'What the –' He attempted to cover his alarm. 'You. The third of the Doctor's party. Ian. Still you associate with these dolts from Mother Bunch's.' He sneered down at Firking and said in a high-pitched girl's voice, 'You never did lay hands on my charms, lusty Firk!'

Of the two shoemakers Hodge was first to react. 'Young Sybil! A fellow?'

Firking gulped. 'And she always looked so good in that bustle from behind.'

The stranger laughed. 'Padding has its uses. So where is Fawkes?'

As he seemed friendly enough, Ian pointed to where the body lay. 'Slain by Catesby.' He stepped closer, his curiosity overwhelming his manners. 'Who are you? And where's the Doctor?'

The stranger pushed past him as if he were unimportant and answered in a perfunctory manner, 'I am your true enemy,' he said. 'And you will find the Doctor at his box.' He stopped at the line of touchwood and smiled gravely. 'I should feel proud. I am one man, working alone, and all this was my design.'

Ian didn't understand him. 'The Doctor's at the TARDIS? You know about it?'

The stranger took a match from his pocket. 'A good opponent. A master of magic.' He struck it and held it above the tinder. The flatness of his delivery contrasted markedly with his actions. 'He deceived me, the genius of disguise, masterfully. You have seen to Catesby's flight and Fawkes's death, as the Doctor saw to the freeing of Cecil, but I have prepared too well.'

Ian advanced on him. 'Don't light that.'

The strange man turned his head slightly to face him. He said very softly, 'We of Grammont will triumph. History awaits us. Who are you to stop me? I shall drop this match and then I shall kill you.'

Ian prepared to spring. 'I don't know what you're talking about,' he said, using his words to step closer. 'But there are too many maniacs around here. We don't need another.'

'I plotted it all!' the stranger shouted. 'All my doing! I am the sanest person in this city! I shall –'

There was suddenly a sound of heavy footsteps, metal on metal, male shouts. The stranger's eyes flicked towards the door.

Ian chose his moment. He pounced, flung himself sideways at the stranger, knocked the match from his grip. In doing so he lost his own foothold and crashed down on top of his opponent. Distantly he was aware of Firking and Hodge's shouts, of the door bursting open, of a sudden influx of other people.

'A plot!' a voice shrieked triumphantly.

Ian picked himself up and saw that the speaker was a short, bearded man in a muddy black outfit. He descended the steps, a manic grin on his face, surrounded by guards in full uniform and with drawn swords. 'Leave these,' he cried with a sweep of the arm to Ian and the shoemakers. 'Take that one!' He pointed straight at the stranger, who was crawling away from him across the room towards the far wall, hatred glowing in his eyes. 'Yes, take him!'

The guards advanced on the young man, tramping past Ian without a second glance. He winced as he watched them drag the young man to his feet. The man with the beard stalked over to him. 'One of the ringleaders of the plot,' he said loudly. 'He was about to set the gunpowder alight!' There was a gasp of horror from the guards.

The young man spat into his face. 'Cecil, you are pathetic. One word from me to James and you are condemned.'

Cecil stood back a little and grinned. Then he turned to the leader of the guards. 'Knyvett, do you recognize this man?'

'No, sir,' the guard replied obediently.

'He does not put you in mind of any person from the court?'

'No, sir.'

Cecil reached out and squeezed the jaw of the helpless captive. 'No. Of course not. Because this fellow, my lads, is the mercenary and traitor Guy Fawkes.'

The young man struggled. 'No! You cannot do this! I will not –'

'I can do anything I like to you, traitor,' Cecil snarled. 'You may deny it now, but I have found you in the very heat of treachery, and these men are my witnesses. I will take you to the Tower, and there I shall extract a full, signed confession. By whatever means necessary.'

The young man's eyes widened in terror. Ian could barely bring himself to look upon them. 'The King will –'

'He won't want to see you,' said Cecil. 'He doesn't like to involve himself in security matters, you know.' He jerked his head to the door. 'Take him away.'

The young man was pulled, protesting every step of the way, past Ian and up the steps. As he neared the door, one of the soldiers punched him full in the face, smashing his nose with such force that bones cracked audibly and blood burst in a fountain from his nostrils.

Cecil barked out a series of orders to the milling guards. 'Have this place cleared out. Dispatch men to find Fawkes's associates, Catesby and his mates, they can't be far. Have the news of this discovery posted to all parts of the city. Evil has been vanquished.'

The guards hurried to obey. The man Knyvett nodded to Ian, Hodge and Firking. 'What of these, sir?' He pointed out Ian. 'This one was here earlier.'

Cecil nodded, strode over to Ian and took him by the hand. 'You, I trust, would know a white-haired colleague of mine.'

'The Doctor.' Ian grabbed his hand in excitement. 'Where is he?'

'The Guildhall. Where he and the others of your party await you.' He glared at Firking. 'These are your associates? You can vouch for their integrity?'

'Oh, we are most loyal and expedient servants of the Crown, your grace,' stammered Firking. 'We came here to bust up the plot and free Ian here.'

'And we did it well,' said Hodge happily.

Cecil regarded them almost with amusement. 'Then you may leave with Ian.'

Firking licked his lips and inclined his head. 'We was thinking, your grace, that there might be a reward in it.'

'Your reward,' said Cecil, 'is that I let you live. Now go, and speak not of this or I'll take back that gift I have bestowed.' He pointed up the steps. Firking and Hodge, terrified by his glare and their proximity to Knyvett's huge sword, scurried out.

Ian made to follow them, but Cecil stopped him. 'One moment of your time.'

'Go on.'

Cecil whispered, 'A message for the Doctor. Tell him first that I value his advice, and am grateful for his action in saving my life.'

'I will,' said Ian. He made to depart again.

Again Cecil stopped him. 'I haven't yet finished. Tell him secondly that I never want to see his disagreeable sour old face ever again, and that if I do I shall be compelled to have it cut off. The same goes for you and the two women.'

Ian wasn't sure how to react. 'Thank you,' he stammered, and hurried off into the night air.

The great bells of the city tolled midnight. James sighed pointedly. The witching hour, and the initial thrill of the exorcism was wearing off. No ghosts, no demons, not so much as a puff of smoke. Just that arthritic Doctor sprinkling water, the divine Victor ringing a bell, and their chum the nun declaiming Latin verse in an especially tedious and inaccurate way. For the first few minutes it had been quite spooky, in a hammy theatrical way, these three strange figures illuminated by torchlight, their shadows cast on the side of the box.

The sigh was taken up by the Chamberlain, then by Haldann and Otley. The Mayor and his aldermen cottoned on quick, and so then did the crowd. For a second it was as if the Guildhall was consumed by an enormous exhalation of air.

The Doctor and company did not seem to have noticed, so engrossed were they in their ritual. James had seen that ploy worked before. 'Doctor!' he called sternly. 'I would know what will be the final outcome of your sprinkling. I've tried to find it amusing but failed.'

Haldann shuffled forward. 'Indeed. I must presume to ask, sir, if you are at all familiar with the ceremony you purport to be performing.'

Otley joined him. 'It is a shoddy affair. A rough approximation. And throwing holy water everywhere about willy-nilly never got anybody anywhere.'

The Doctor motioned his companions to stop what they were doing, and stepped forward. He shook his fingers dry and then hooked them around his lapels in that irritating gesture of his. 'Your Majesty, I am glad these questions have been asked.'

There was a silence as everyone waited for him to continue. But he said nothing. There was an odd expectancy in the way he held his head slightly to one side, and his eyes flicked past the crowd and towards the city.

'Well?' fumed James.

'I am feeling fine, thank you, Your Majesty.' The Doctor bowed. His delivery of the words was unconscionably slow.

'Swounds! We await your explanation!' James tottered from his throne and wagged a stern finger. 'I could be back at the palace learning my speech instead of wasting time watching you prevaricate!'

The Doctor held up his hands. 'Prevarication is my least intention, Your Majesty.' He raised his voice, addressing the entire crowd. He enunciated each syllable distinctly. 'But in a case of demonic possession as advanced as this, preparation is essential. This process may appear unnecessarily laborious –'

'You don't say,' Haldann and Otley muttered.

'– but the spell around the box must be broken down, stripped away, piece by piece. To rush at casting off such an enchantment would be to invite disaster.'

James pointed to the blue box. 'Still, nothing appears to be occurring.'

Victor came forward. 'Your Majesty, I have seen the Doctor perform many such ceremonies, and each time he has driven out the spirit and set things to rights.'

At the sound of that voice James's impatience melted away. 'Oh, do my queries vex your loyalty to your mentor? If that is so, let my mouth be stitched right up.' He leant over and tinkled Victor's bell softly. 'Very well. The boy speaks clearer sense than any.' He waved the Doctor back. 'Carry on exorcizing.'

The Doctor nodded his gratitude, and signalled to the young nun to take up her Latin once again. Victor rang his bell with a smile to James, who sat back in his throne with a contented, drowsy smile on his face. Instinctively his hand curled down as if to stroke the hair of a person sat at his knee. He frowned. 'Chamberlain,' he whispered. 'Where's Bob Hay?'

The Chamberlain shrugged. 'He'd gone to his tailor the last I heard, Your Majesty.'

'Ah.' James played with his tongue, and thought. Bob was a pale shadow in comparison to Victor. Did he matter any more? Or would it just be a distraction, having him around? Was there any reason left to retain him? On the whole, no. One was tiring enough. No need for two. He told the Chamberlain, 'Cancel his access to the court. If he appears again, have him thrown out.'

'Very well, Your Majesty,' said the Chamberlain wearily.

'Do I scent a whiff of judgement behind your words?' snapped James.

'Oh no, no. I commend you, Your Majesty, on your discretion.'

The singing nun had barely reached her second verse of prayer when there came a sudden commotion from outside the courtyard. An agitated mutter started up among the commoners. In a couple of seconds it had become a wave of consternation that rippled forward like a small but very strong wave. James scented trouble. He sat bolt upright in his chair. At this cue, his entourage, including the exorcists, stopped what they were doing. He beckond his bodyguards closer. 'What's going on?' He waved the Chamberlain forward. 'Go on, dolt, discover!'

The Chamberlain had barely taken three of his nervous waddling steps towards the gates when a young man burst through the crowd and into the yard. He was unfamiliar to the King, although dressed in fine enough vestments, and his face was red from running. The guards around James raised their swords at his approach, but the first thing he did when he saw them was fall to his knees.

'Your Majesty,' he said, panting. 'I have come at the bidding of Cecil. I bring terrifying news.' He raised his head, and for a moment James thought he saw a strange look of acknowledgement pass between him and the young nun at the box.

But he was made too nervous by the words of the newcomer to take much notice. 'News? Oh dear, I don't care for news.'

'What has happened?' squeaked the Chamberlain.

'A plot, Your Majesty,' said Ian. There was a further gasp from the crowd. 'Cecil has uncovered a plot to blow up Parliament at the opening tomorrow. Gunpowder has been found in the cellars beneath the Lords and a man arrested.'

James's head reeled. So Cecil had been right all along! 'Oh my God,' he said quietly, feeling a sudden weakness in the bladder. 'It's Bannockburn all over again! How could they have got so close?' He dismissed the matter. It made his head hurt. The particulars could be discovered later. 'Oh, I feel faint. Have me borne away, quick.' He fell back in his throne and waited for the Chamberlain to attend to him. The world went spinning away, consumed in the shock.

How could anyone, he wondered as he fainted, want to blow up a king as charitable, wise and hard-working as himself?

'Now's our chance,' hissed the Doctor. He scrabbled for the key of the TARDIS and brought it up to the lock.

The Guildhall had become a scene of total confusion. The crowd were in uproar; King James had slumped into his throne and was being fussed over by the Chamberlain; the Mayor and the aldermen were standing around dazed, unsure what action to take. The exorcism, as the Doctor had planned, had been completely forgotten.

Ian crashed into Barbara's arms. She looked into his wounded brown eyes and felt like crying. 'Ian, Ian,' she sobbed. She pressed her head hard against his sturdy, masculine shoulder and pummelled his upper back with her fist. The relief she felt was intoxicating.

'Come along, you two,' the Doctor called. He had the door of the police box open and was ushering Vicki through. 'There's a time and a place, as they say on this planet.'

Barbara and Ian took a quick final look over their shoulders at London and then passed through the doors.

The Doctor made to follow. Just as he was putting a foot over the threshold, a voice cried, 'Wait! Look! What is he doing?'

He whipped round. Alone of the crowd Haldann and Otley had kept their attention fixed on the TARDIS. They advanced as one across the courtyard, their robes billowing behind them in the winter wind.

The Doctor could not resist making a parting barb. 'I am using my brain,' he called. 'And keeping intelligence active.' He chuckled. ' "How long halt ye between two opinions?", eh?'

Otley bore down on him. 'How dare you!' he cried.

Haldann gave a cry of outrage and leapt for the Doctor.

He slammed the door in their faces, still chuckling to himself.

'Hmm, a final miracle for them.'

The glass column at the centre of the TARDIS console slid smoothly up and down, the indicator lights inside, comprehensible only to the Doctor, flickering in complex patterns. Gradually the roaring of the Ship's engines receded, replaced by the soothing hum of the mechanisms that supported the vessel in its strange flight. The Doctor flicked down a line of switches with a satisfied grunt and raised himself from the controls. He became aware that three pairs of eyes were staring accusingly at the back of his neck. There was a silence heavy with implications. Finally, without turning round, he said, 'Well, that takes care of all that. Fascinating, yes, a quite fascinating period.' Still without catching their eyes he turned to the inner door. 'Now, then, I –'

Barbara moved forward furiously. 'I'm glad you're satisfied. Pleased with your experiment, are you?'

'Please don't take that tone with me,' said the Doctor. 'We are all here, and relatively unscathed.' He nodded to Ian. 'Congratulations on your timing, my boy. I was deliberately dragging the exorcism out as long as I could. I knew the news of the plot would break shortly after midnight, and Cecil's discovery of Fawkes, and that we could slip into the Ship in all the confusion. But I wasn't to know you'd bring the message yourself. Inspired, inspired.'

'Except,' said Ian gravely, 'he didn't discover Fawkes in the cellar.' He paused and looked between his friends. 'Fawkes was killed last night.'

Vicki's eyes widened. 'But that's impossible. Unless . . .' She caught the Doctor's sleeve. 'Unless history *has* been thrown off track by our presence.'

Barbara was the next to speak. She said earnestly to Ian, with a look that suggested more than casual concern, 'What happened to Fawkes? Tell us, from the beginning.'

Ian proceeded to relate his adventures in the lumber room, from Catesby's murder of Fawkes to the eventual arrest of Hay in his place. The others replied by filling him in on their own experiences, until a pattern began to form. The Doctor, his earlier sins now apparently forgiven, measured all the information supplied and, when the stories came to their end, cleared his throat importantly.

'Time has a way of taking care of these things,' he said. 'And we can, sometimes, be its unwitting agents. The pieces have fallen into place. Cecil's substitution of Hay for Fawkes is an inspired move, typical of the man's ruthlessness. He will take Fawkes's role in history. Torture, trial, and execution. All carried out very swiftly and arbitrarily by Cecil. Catesby, of course, never made it to the trial. Expired clutching a model of the Virgin Mary, so they say.'

Vicki was puzzled. 'Won't the King recognize Hay, though?'

'My dear, consider what we know of the man. It's unlikely he'll put in more than a token appearance at the plotters' trials. And Cecil, as we know, has the manipulative skills to cover up the entire affair and his part in it. Although the King will take all the credit. Monarchs always do.'

Barbara sighed wistfully. 'At least the real Fawkes died quickly. He was a good man, in a strange way.'

Ian frowned. 'He was a killer.'

'He had some honour,' she replied hotly.

The Doctor held up his hands for silence. 'Please. Fawkes could not escape his destiny. None of us can.' He went on, 'Hay went frighteningly far. If we had not appeared to confuse the situation I don't see how he could have been stopped. And that's what I meant earlier. It's our privilege to travel in time, but we carry a heavy responsibility.'

'Well, I don't see what's to stop Hay's lot having another go at the same thing,' Vicki pointed out.

The Doctor hesitated before replying. When he did, he spoke cautiously. 'I imagine the answer lies in Hay's character, my dear. His use of disguise was magnificent. As the Spaniard he ferried between Catesby and Cecil, as Hay he influenced the King, as the serving girl he could pass anywhere unquestioned and listen in whenever he liked. Think of how he reacted to our arrival, by using all three faces to sound us out and play us off against his other pawns. He was infinitely resourceful and cunning, with a level of daring I've rarely encountered in all my travels. Thank goodness he jumped to that conclusion about me being a Grand Behemoth. Although, of course, for a person with my natural dignity it's hardly surprising. No, I suspect nobody else in his brotherhood had the same abilities, and certainly there's no evidence of their existence in later centuries. But then,' he added, 'that's the trouble with secret societies.'

'What is?'

'They're secret.' He coughed as if the discussion were settled and rubbed his hands on his cloak. 'And I'm feeling rather sticky, I think I'll take a bath, if nobody else minds. I'll just put the, er, immersion on.' He flicked a button on the console.

Vicki coughed and pointed down at her muddy dress. 'What about me?'

'Yes, you're in a fine mess, aren't you?' he said. 'Right, well, I'll just find a clean towel –'

Ian interrupted him. 'Wait a second, Doctor. There's still one thing in this whole affair to be cleared up.'

'What now, Chesterton?'

Ian passed him a sheet of paper. 'This message. It was what got me and Barbara embroiled with the plotters in the first place. The Spaniard, this fellow Hay, was passing it to Catesby.'

The Doctor put his spectacles on and glanced at the note. 'Hmm, yes, this is in Cecil's hand.' He grinned. 'Poor fellow. The irony is that James never gave him what he wanted. There were many more laws to crack down on the Catholics, but in the end they were hardly necessary. The failure of Catesby's plot discouraged any further rebellion from them, and soon enough the nation was consumed by other conflicts.'

'That's as may be,' said Ian impatiently. 'What about the note?'

The Doctor took off his spectacles and handed it back. 'What about it?'

'What does it say?' asked Barbara.

'You mean you can't tell?' The Doctor blew out his cheeks in playful scorn and took Vicki under his arm. 'And to think, such people can become schoolteachers.'

Barbara was fuming. 'You understand the code? This pidgin French or whatever it is?'

'Of course,' he said dismissively. 'And really, it's hardly complex enough to be called a code. And as for it being French, oh no, no, no.'

Ian stood right in front of the Doctor and pointed to the exit doors. 'I really think I might have to grab you, turn you upside down and throw you into the space-time vortex if you don't tell us now, Doctor.'

He sighed. 'Oh, very well. This place is becoming more like a kindergarten with every passing day.' He pointed to the note. 'Read it again. Out loud this time.'

Ian obeyed. 'Scarlet. Orly Seine . . .' He stopped. 'It still doesn't make any – hold on.' He started again. 'Scarlet. All is in readiness. King suspects not. Remain watchful. Orange.'

'It's written phonetically,' said Barbara.

'Precisely,' said the Doctor. 'It hardly takes an Einstein, does it?' He turned to the inner door. 'Now, I'm sure I have a loofah somewhere about the place . . .'

He disappeared into the depths of the TARDIS, still muttering to himself, leaving his companions half in awe, half in exasperation.

As ever.

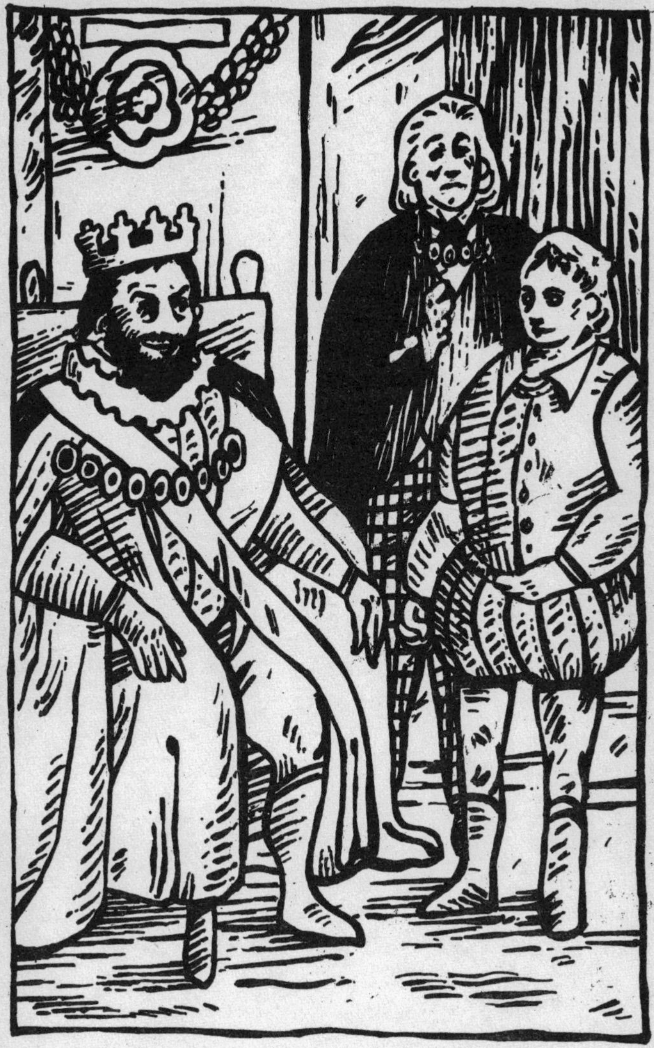

Available in the *Doctor Who – New Adventures* series:

TIMEWYRM: GENESYS by John Peel
TIMEWYRM: EXODUS by Terrance Dicks
TIMEWYRM: APOCALYPSE by Nigel Robinson
TIMEWYRM: REVELATION by Paul Cornell
CAT'S CRADLE: TIME'S CRUCIBLE by Marc Platt
CAT'S CRADLE: WARHEAD by Andrew Cartmel
CAT'S CRADLE: WITCH MARK by Andrew Hunt
NIGHTSHADE by Mark Gatiss
LOVE AND WAR by Paul Cornell
TRANSIT by Ben Aaronovitch
THE HIGHEST SCIENCE by Gareth Roberts
THE PIT by Neil Penswick
DECEIT by Peter Darvill-Evans
LUCIFER RISING by Jim Mortimore and Andy Lane
WHITE DARKNESS by David A. McIntee
SHADOWMIND by Christopher Bulis
BIRTHRIGHT by Nigel Robinson
ICEBERG by David Banks
BLOOD HEAT by Jim Mortimore
THE DIMENSION RIDERS by Daniel Blythe
THE LEFT-HANDED HUMMINGBIRD by Kate Orman
CONUNDRUM by Steve Lyons
NO FUTURE by Paul Cornell
TRAGEDY DAY by Gareth Roberts
LEGACY by Gary Russell
THEATRE OF WAR by Justin Richards
ALL-CONSUMING FIRE by Andy Lane
BLOOD HARVEST by Terrance Dicks
STRANGE ENGLAND by Simon Messingham
FIRST FRONTIER by David A. McIntee
ST ANTHONY'S FIRE by Mark Gatiss
FALLS THE SHADOW by Daniel O'Mahony
PARASITE by Jim Mortimore
WARLOCK by Andrew Cartmel
SET PIECE by Kate Orman
INFINITE REQUIEM by Daniel Blythe
SANCTUARY by David A. McIntee
HUMAN NATURE by Paul Cornell
ORIGINAL SIN by Andy Lane
SKY PIRATES! by Dave Stone
ZAMPER by Gareth Roberts
TOY SOLDIERS by Paul Leonard
HEAD GAMES by Steve Lyons
THE ALSO PEOPLE by Ben Aaronovitch
SHAKEDOWN by Terrance Dicks
JUST WAR by Lance Parkin
WARCHILD by Andrew Cartmel
SLEEPY by Kate Orman
DEATH AND DIPLOMACY by Dave Stone
HAPPY ENDINGS by Paul Cornell
GODENGINE by Craig Hinton
CHRISTMAS ON A RATIONAL PLANET by Lawrence Miles
RETURN OF THE LIVING DAD by Kate Orman
THE DEATH OF ART by Simon Bucher-Jones
DAMAGED GOODS by Russell T Davies
SO VILE A SIN by Ben Aaronovitch

The next Missing Adventure is *Cold Fusion* by Lance Parkin, featuring the fifth Doctor, Nyssa, Tegan and Adric.